ILLICIT ALLIANCE

Rukis

Illicit Alliance

Published by FurPlanet
Dallas, TX
http://www.FurPlanet.com

ISBN: 978-1-61450-576-1
First Printing, December 2022

Cover art by Rukis

Dedicated to my long suffering brother Reed. You can't escape the bonds of sisterly love, I will always be your 'Nestsky'.

ACT I - DOKURO

The island of Dokuro—a local tribal word for 'Murderous', apparently—was every bit the filthy, overcrowded, dangerous tropical hell-hole it was rumored to be. The streets, if you could really call them that, were shit-stained slop trails between ramshackle buildings mostly made of broken-down hulls, barrels, and coral walls. The humid air hung thick with a fog comprised only partially of water: mostly a mélange of disparate cooking steam, wood and charcoal smoke, and tobacco. An endless barrage of varied paw and hoof-prints stamped down the earth, palm fronds and overgrown vines bursting with torn, wide leaves barged into every available splatter of sunlight, and everything reeked of far too many furred bodies and musk, food, sewage, rotting vegetation, and the distinct sour notes of alcohol, both good and very, very bad.

In short, perfection. Exactly my kind of town.

My contact in this grotto seemed equally at home here, which, I have to admit, was somewhat surprising to me. I'd expected this unusual liaison would be as amusing as it was bound to be awkward, but I guess I'd underestimated the man I'd come here to meet. Or overestimated?

The point is, I'd thought this kind of culture, this kind of atmosphere, beneath a Crown Admiral of Amuresca. To be fair, I'd also imagined him different in every conceivable way.

The cattle dog, a full head shorter than me, walked at my hip without any airs or dismissive, disgusted looks towards his surroundings. He wore an outfit of humble clothing fatigued in all the right places to suggest he'd long owned them, not some temporary disguise meant to cover his true station. His fur was peppered not only with the spots one might expect from his breed, but black scarred divots in places, mostly clustered around his muzzle. Gunpowder burns, signs his nose had been broken more than once, minor scars from claws (probably from open fists). One of his ears had a temporary notch in it like he'd been injured recently. I got those all the time from scraps, myself. If they were anything like mine they'd heal up, but this one had certainly happened at least in the last week.

I had to admit a grudging respect. This wasn't some Pedigree swan.

Of course, I knew that. I'd dug up all I could on the fabled upstart 'Cerberus Admiral' before I'd arranged this meeting. There were certainly enough rumors swirling the seas about him by now since he'd taken to hunting the trade routes a few years back. He'd come the fuck out of nowhere with an old fleet trussed up in new sails, a totally new, terrifying style no one quite knew how to handle yet, and an inconvenient, never-fail ability to 'spook' his prey. By that I mean he seemed to know just how to sail up your tail out of nowhere, make it clear by means of a flank that he could send you to the rocky bottom if he so chose, and then give you the merciful but humiliating choice to run or stand and fight.

Thus far on the three occasions he'd caught me unawares, I had run. I'm not a stupid man.

It could be hard to separate the man from the myth (a fact I relied on quite heavily for my own reputation), but I knew a few things for certain. He was new money—not a son from some merchant dynasty, not a magnate, but a navy man who'd married up. Way up, based on what I'd heard. Probably blackmail or some kind of pregnancy involved. He'd inherited an already infamous, if dated, fleet, but if their recent performance was any indication, they'd modernized and slimmed down the Cerberus galleons. This Admiral preferred speed over firepower. Not that he lacked either.

He was a mongrel, a lesser breed, probably grew up poor. Which means he'd worked his way through the navy the old-fashioned way... and he knew his ships in a way a blueblood wouldn't, from the rigging up. Most of these curs didn't have a background with a shipwright family like I did. That was an edge I had on them.

I had more time in the game than he did, though. At least, when it came to managing being a Privateer in Amurescan waters. Denholme— that was his name, Luther Denholme—might have had me beat in time on the water owing to his joining the navy younger than I had taken to the seas, but he'd mostly served up north before his recent good fortune, apparently. With Richter... devil take that bastard's soul. He'd not been particularly merciful to my brothers, unlike his protégé.

Ha, protégé. If the rumors were to be believed, more than that.

I had a good contract coming up. A rare one, a year-long duration, for a particular Carvecian shipping fleet no one would miss. But they had connections in Amuresca, some kind of Pedigree magnate. It was threadbare but problematic enough that I knew I'd be risking technical piracy on Denholme's territory. And that bastard swung a wide leg. I didn't want to leave anything to chance. There'd be other hunters, there always were, but morale was particularly low amongst my boys whenever the subject of Luther Denholme came up. He'd put the fear of god in my men. Even the Atheists, which was hard.

I glanced down at the fairly unimpressive man. If they could see him now.

But, a big part of Piracy... pardon me... Privateering, was managing risk. And sometimes that wasn't as exciting as out-maneuvering an enemy fleet. Sometimes it meant sharing a drink with the sort of people who specialized in killing you, or otherwise fucking up your money-making ventures, and twisting their arm a little. Building bridges, you know.

8

Blackmail. Threats. Bribes. Whatever worked.

I didn't know what this man's plan here was, yet. But I had an inkling, and I was determined this negotiation was going to go my way.

We'd met near the docks, both came here on smaller vessels, as low key as we were able. In Denholme's case, he'd somehow hopped a small ship from I-know-not-where and disembarked like any other mutt in between jobs, blending in like a ghost. I'd come in yesterday and enjoyed the night-life until now, then set up my little trap. I wasn't really able to keep as low a profile as he was, but that was a given. I was known in most shithole ports like this, and I wasn't about to powder my gorgeous black fur, wear anything less than my usual dashing apparel (I only owned well-tailored double-breasted coats at this point anyway), cut my mane of dreads, or go without my gold and beads. Wolf's gotta have style.

I picked him out at the desired meeting spot, a busted figurehead they'd propped up in the 'square' as a sort of statue. Mostly by the smell of it, a place to piss. I'd greeted him warmly, he'd returned the greeting far more perfunctorily, and we'd made for the nearest dive I knew of that was any good. Or at least, that's what I'd told him. He didn't seem to care where we sat down to have a drink and speak, but I'd had a plan if he wanted to pick the place. A kid was keeping an eye out to tell my 'secret weapon' where to find us.

Still, this worked better. He'd be settled in and waiting.

We ducked (or rather I did, Denholme didn't need to) beneath the tilting awning over an open-air bar. This was where I'd passed out last night, a delightful little establishment serving up rum, hookah, and lasses plying their professional services. Some of them even did so around the back corner of the building nearby, which you could easily spy from here if you were of a mind. Not that I'd done so. Repeatedly. That would've been shameless.

No private rooms, no rooms of any kind really, but those were rare in a port like this anyway. Most men here slept on their ships, in and around the docks, slumped over a table or a crate. Or if they'd gotten particularly shitfaced and no one'd been looking out for them, in the sands to get bitten up by the rats and mosquitoes.

We moved past a rowdy dice game, and a marten I was dead certain was about to heave—on second thought, best to give him some space; that'd be distracting—around the back, then. An open table, if you could call it that, beckoned to me. Three crates. Just enough.

I plopped myself down, splaying one leg over my knee and smiling toothily at the man across from me as he took a seat. He didn't exactly move like a proper gentleman himself, but he seemed at least more reserved than I. Maybe wary. Watchful, at least. His gold eyes scanned the place briefly, but he must not have seen him yet, because he still seemed relaxed enough.

The woman working the bar knew not to bother asking. Just as Denholme had begun to open his mouth to say something, a heavy brown glass bottle clunked down between us, the busy otter sparing us barely a glance except to take a coin from my offered hand before heading off to another table.

"I'm assuming you carry your own measures cup," I said, fishing mine from beneath my coat and uncorking the bottle to pour for myself first. Only polite.

He watched me, gaze steady. But before I'd begun to drink, he took the bottle and poured some out for himself. "Unnecessary," he said calmly. "I don't care who drinks first. I'm certain if you wanted to kill me, you wouldn't have gone through the trouble of arranging this meeting."

"Maybe I wanted you alone." I couldn't help myself. Seriously, what the hell? My mouth.

He arched an eyebrow and finished downing his first cup before replying to me, "Why do you want to convince me you're planning to make a go at me?" He dismissed it outright, pouring himself more of the rum. "No. Your reckless reputation's hot air. You're careful, Reed."

I pounded a flat palm into my chest dramatically. "Sir, you wound me."

"You've run from me thrice." He pointed out. "Don't think I don't keep track. That Man-of-War of yours is hard to scrub from one's memory, no matter how much elbow you put into it." He got a vague smile that made my belly flip over for some reason. "Even if I only ever really see her from behind."

My eyebrow twitched. "You calling me a coward, Denholme?"

"Risk averse," he corrected me. "No insult meant. I'd count myself in that category. I breathe a sigh every time I force a retreat."

The admission warmed me to him some. Which was annoying. I was starting to like the cur.

"You have me squarely out-gunned," I said. "Easily best me in maneuvering capability. Where's the risk for you?"

"I'd consider losing even one of my beloved vessels to your behemoth a risk," he said, clapping his cup down on the table.

"Then maybe you ought to stop threatening me with them," I replied wryly.

"I believe that's why we're here, is it not?" he countered coolly.

"Yes, yes," I sighed, glancing once around the room. I caught sight of the gold-furred, large ears I was looking for, smiled briefly to myself, then back at him. "Look, I'm going to cut right to the chase. I'm not one to avoid foreplay usually, but you're not my type."

Finally, a reaction. Just a brief tensing, barely recognizable, in his shoulders. But it was there.

"You're not mine, either," he assured me. "So, spit it out. I know about the contract on the Lancaster fleet."

"Do you foresee getting involved?" I asked outright.

"The Magnate is a Pedigree," he said, rolling his eyes. "You know very well I'd have to, regardless how I feel on the matter. That's why we're here."

"And that isn't negotiable?"

He leaned back, the crate beneath him shifting. He was fidgeting. Good. I'd shaken him with the insincere flirtation. "What exactly do you want me to say?" he asked. "If we cross paths, it can't be helped. I won't be gunning for you specifically, if that's your worry. The Lancaster fleet's dirty. Everyone knows it. And I'm no friend of the Magnate."

"You said yourself you don't like the thought of engaging my Manoratha," I said. "I'm asking that you turn a blind eye. Neither of us want this, apparently. Seems there's an obvious conclusion to be drawn there. You scratch my back—"

"How exactly would you be 'scratching my back'?" he snuffed.

"By not gunning down one of your little vessels in an engagement neither of us want," I said, as though it were the most obvious thing in the world. It seemed pretty rational to me.

"We both get that," he reasoned, "but you'll also be pilfering spoils. What about me?"

I couldn't help it. A grin split my muzzle, realization dawning. "You want a cut of the take?"

Alright, then. Maybe this man could be reasoned with. No need for my 'asset' to put in work. This could go smoother than I'd ever hoped for.

"No cargo," he insisted. "Coin only."

"That has me putting in more legwork for a bribe than I'd like," I muttered. "What about something that can't spoil? Lancaster moves a lot of lamp oil, I hear."

"No cargo," he repeated. "Harder to explain away. My vessels are strictly military. Coin only." He snapped his golden-eyed gaze to mine. "Twenty percent."

I laughed out loud. Pretty sure I felt my teeth rattle. "Arrogant little mongrel," I said between huffs, "aren't you? I'd heard you were low-born, but you're as greedy as a Pedigree, alright."

He narrowed his eyes at me. I wasn't sure which part he'd taken offense to, but the calm demeanor had dropped. He had his game face on now. "It's an opening offer," he said. "Make me a counter."

"What could you need that much coin for?" I demanded. "You're not exactly scraping by."

"It's no concern of yours," he stated plainly.

I arched an eyebrow at him. Was his inheritance not all I'd heard? The Cerberus fleet was pretty small as far as fleets went, and it'd undergone massive repairs and re-fittings lately. Or maybe he wasn't financially endorsed by the Crown? That seemed unlikely, but it would have given him a lot more leeway to do as he pleased with his command.

That had to be it. He was starved for capital. He'd probably have to suck up to the throne to finance his fleet eventually or else let them go derelict. Or sell them off. And given what the Amurescan throne had been squandering their resources on of late, they wouldn't throw coin at an Admiral without tasking them to hold down one of their crumbling Colonies, or gunning down rebellious natives. You know, something awful like that.

"You're financing your independence," I said with certainty. If I was right, he didn't bother to confirm it. But he also didn't refute it, which I took as an affirmative. "Look, I feel for you, mate," I said honestly, "but I'm also starved for capital. We all are. So, you're going to have to come down. Way down."

"Fifteen percent."

"Five," I said, pouring myself another cup, "and count yourself lucky I'll give you that much."

"You're acting as if you have the advantage here," he said, splaying his hands before him. "This is a mutually-beneficial arrangement, like you said. Let's respect one another enough to meet somewhere in the middle."

"Five," I said again and lifted an arm to snap in the direction of someone over his shoulder. He must have assumed I was calling the bartender over, because he didn't bother to turn. "And I may not hold all the cards," I said before he could counter me again, "but I've got one in particular I think you might want to consider."

"Luther…" the voice broke through the din of the outdoor bar, piercing the moment like a blade. I smiled slowly as the cattle dog's seemingly unflappable confidence finally fell away, and he froze in place, ears tipping back rigidly. He turned slowly, looking up at the fennec standing nervously behind us.

I'm not into men, but I have to admit, Denholme had good taste. From the moment I found the lad, dug him out of the Huudari brothel in Aleshfaric, I'd had to appreciate the golden-furred fennec's soft beauty. It was troublesome really, keeping someone like him aboard the Manoratha. Like trying to keep a fresh cut chop safe from a swarm of sharks. Usually when I brought someone so well-groomed, so pretty and gentile, so obviously a prostitute aboard my vessel, they were on the menu for the boys. Respectful-like, of course, and well-paid. We didn't tolerate abuses of working pleasure folk on my ship.

Explaining repeatedly that yes—first off, the fennec was a man (he wasn't feminine exactly, but for a sailor into his cups…), and, no, he was not on-board for anything other than contract negotiations was a hard sell. There'd been talk, I'm sure. Already, some of my men were having a good laugh at my expense. But hell, let 'em. It's not as if I cared how men bunked up on my ship, so why should I care what they said about me? Anyone fool enough to underestimate me for it would probably find other reason to challenge me down the line, so if they showed their true stripes now, all the better. I'd deal with them.

At least if the men thought this was what I went in for, they'd think I only went in for the prettiest boys.

"Come on, now," I gestured between the two of them, "say hello. I brought that gorgeous lad a long way to meet you again. Don't insult me by pretending you don't know him, now."

Over the course of half a minute, the cattle dog's expression had gone from cold congeniality to white hot fury, burning in the pits of his eyes. It was honestly a little intimidating, although I couldn't let him see that. I could almost feel it radiating off of him, like killing intent made manifest. I glanced briefly around to be certain my men were present in case this became a fight after all.

I'd been expecting to catch him off-guard, but this was more of a reaction than I'd bargained for. Always a possibility with blackmail. Might've mis-calculated… what would I do if I actually had to kill him here? I started going over possibilities in my head.

Denholme turned slowly, a slight quake in his jaw as he finally spoke to the fennec. "Kafele," he said quietly, "are you in danger?"

The fennec quickly shook his head, earrings tinkling with the gesture. His arms shifted nervously, knuckles prominent as he gripped one wrist tightly with his other hand. "No, Kavish," I didn't miss the term of supplication he used, already begging forgiveness. "Admiral Reed has been kind to me."

Denholme's gaze flicked once back towards me, murderously. I only smiled innocently in return. "How is it you are here, then?" he asked carefully.

"Family debts," I filled in for him, wanting to get through this as quickly as possible and cool Denholme's anger. I felt like the reunited couple might go on for a while if I just let them talk it out, and I knew the fennec well enough by now to appreciate he wasn't the most socially confident person. He'd probably babble. "I don't know how much you inquired about his financial condition when you two were… acquainted," I said, putting up a hand as Denholme bared his fangs, and pressed on, "but Kafele here's got an uncle with a bad habit and a pack of siblings to feed. They're deep in the hole with the Beshlaika Clan. Bad enough they were considering an indenture contract to pay it down."

Denholme looked back to the fennec as though he'd been struck. If I didn't know any better, I'd think the hints of betrayal I saw there were because he was coming to grips with the fact that his whore had sold him out. But actually, I think it was something else.

"Why didn't you tell me?" he demanded in a harsh whisper. As if I couldn't hear them. Oh, this was getting good.

"This was long after your stay in port," Kafele insisted. "At least, the worst of it was. And in any case, I wouldn't have wanted to impose on you."

The first hint of hurt shown through. "You clearly didn't mind sharing your woes with him," Denholme barely avoided snapping.

"Now, to be fair," I cleared my throat, honestly not wanting to interrupt this little spat. It was getting pretty cute. "My lads didn't really give him much of a choice in the matter. Once we'd dug him up, we weren't about to let our efforts be in vain."

"So, he is here by force, then," the cattle dog's eyes narrowed, hand on the hilt of his saber.

"We ain't laid a hand on him," I insisted. "Just some heavy-handed 'convincing'. And in any case, it's not like you left the lad with a lifeline. He's not yours to save, Denholme," I shrugged as casually as I could. "Way I hear it, you were pretty firm on that when you left port."

Behind him, I saw the fennec's shoulders sag, something deep and raw in his eyes, like torn stitches opening afresh an old wound. It made me horribly uncomfortable, a sinking sensation in my gut, the kind I only get when I know I've overstepped into dangerous waters I have no right to be in. Like in this moment, I was the villain.

It'd pass. It always did, eventually.

Denholme's muzzle was set in a firm line, the edges of his eyes red. His whole aura was pressing down on me like deep, deep water, and for a few moments I earnestly did not know what he planned to do. The silence stretched on far too long.

"You don't intend to keep him, do you?" he asked at length, voice tight.

"I'm no slaver," I spat out irritably. "He's here to make a point. That's all. After this, he goes back to his family. That was the agreement, s'what we paid him for."

"What, precisely, was your 'point'?" the Admiral asked flatly.

Here, I paused. "Wh—" shit, don't stumble over your words. Feed it to him if he really has to hear it out loud. "Obviously," I strained, "that I can unearth your secrets. Those that'd sit poorly with your fleet. Your Captains. Your wife."

For some reason, he laughed at that. It was bitter, but undeniably, genuinely amused. He didn't betray why, but I could guess. They had some kind of arrangement?

"Is that all?" he asked after giving me another silent space to continue.

I looked past him to the crestfallen, beautiful fox whose heart he'd apparently broken. The man. Whose heart he'd broken.

"Isn't that enough?" I said disbelievingly.

He took another long moment, before replying coldly, in one word. "No."

"What do you mean 'no'?" I tried to force him to clarify.

"I mean you're not getting an agreement between us this way," he said, pocketing his cup and standing slowly. "You're not getting anything, actually. I'll see you on the water."

The warning, the promise, was exactly as chilling as he intended it to be. "You can't just say 'no' to this!" I exclaimed, standing and blocking his path before he could leave.

He assessed me, all that fury still there, but behind that irritating mask of cold indifference again. He turned to regard the fennec. "Kafele and I need to speak. Excuse us."

"You can't just leave with him—" I reached for the fennec's wrist as Denholme turned to usher him away, and that was the first of several major mistakes I'd make that night.

Normally, I'd say I was a pretty skilled swordsman. Maybe not the best (okay definitely not the best), and maybe I relied on my pistols more often than I should, but I shouldn't have been so easy to catch off-guard. Especially when I'd seen he was keeping a hand on his hilt before.

But damn if the man wasn't fast. He had his saber unsheathed, swung in an arc and pressed the collar of my coat into the thick fur of my throat, just like that. At once, my men sprung to their feet around us, weapons drawn in six different places, three pistols pointed his way and several more blades.

But the edge of his sword was already biting through my collar, and I could feel the strength in his arm and see the conviction in those predatory eyes of his. He was angry enough to do it.

I lifted my hands, palms uncurling. "It's alright, gents," I eased my men, lest one of them twitch and fire. "Let's all calm down. Denholme, I'm sure dying in a muddy pit like this isn't worth satisfying your temper, however righteously pissed you might feel towards me right now."

"You clearly don't know me at all," he growled, "if you think dying in obscurity is something I'm not prepared for."

I took in a shuddering breath, reaching over slowly with my free hand to grip the tip of his sword. "I believe you," I said, slowly tilting it away from my neck. "And you're right. I didn't gather enough intel on you. Clearly."

"Clearly," he repeated, voice like gravel. His sword fell from my neck, and I felt like I might be able to breathe again. At the last minute — almost as an afterthought — he withdrew it far too quickly, slicing along the finger and palm I'd risked pushing it away with. I yelped out and heard the click of several pistols, but held my other hand up once again to stay my men's trigger fingers.

It would be abominably stupid to kill a Crown Admiral over what amounted to a bad paper cut.

Dumbstruck, I stared down at my bleeding palm as he wiped his sword on his coat and re-sheathed it. By the time I looked up again, all I caught was his retreating figure, tailed by the fennec.

"Kafele!" I called out to him. "You know where we're moored. Return to us before tomorrow night if you want your trip home, as promised."

He stopped briefly to bow in our direction. "Thank you, Admiral Reed."

"I honor my contracts," I said, my voice gone bitter as I watched any hope for this alliance crumble away before my eyes.

Shit. Shit, shit, SHIT.

I found myself staring at my palm again, still processing what had just happened. Vaguely, I heard one of my boys sidle up to my left, asking quietly, "Admiral? What jus'happened?"

I dropped my hand and loosed a long sigh. "I fucked up," I said at last.

❧ ❧

Later that night, I tried to drink my troubles away. As one does.

I was midway through a pretty expensive bottle and deep down in the hole of aching worry and fear that I might've just doomed my fleet to be hunted to the ends of the earth by an angry cattle dog when I saw her.

She was a tigress with a light, sun-touched pelt. Curvaceous, built strong like tigers tended to be, with peach-soft, plush fur, like cinnamon drifting through fresh cream, with a dash of nutmeg stripes... damn, did I forget to eat dinner? Did I just... drink... for dinner?

Eh.

Lotus, that was her name. I'd seen, heard of her before, of course. There weren't many women with ships beneath their command, although it was certainly more common for Huudari women. But rarer still for a tigress. Usually if you ran across a lady Privateer, she'd be a hyena. Maybe a lioness. But I'd heard of her; she had two excellent little galleons beneath her flag, although I couldn't remember their names at the moment. She'd carved out a niche for herself taking smaller contracts and distinguished herself by preying primarily on other Privateers. It took stones to deliberately target armed vessels.

16

It had to be her. There couldn't be another tigress who happened to be in this part of the world, on these trade routes, wearing a pistol on each of her well-appointed hips, her fangs gleaming in the lantern-light as she laughed uproariously amongst a table of men, all decked out in red and maroon with gold bedazzling her ears and nose, and she was STUNNING. Just… a goddess. And while I knew some of that was the drink talking, not all of it was the drink talking.

This. This was exactly what I needed to recover from this disaster of a day.

Silently swearing my allegiance to any god or spirit that would have me, despite the hypocrisy of not believing in a one of them, I plucked up my bottle and crossed the bar towards her, hoping for luck this night.

Her eyes caught mine all but immediately, and the slow smile that split her large feline muzzle (those beautiful cheek ruffs, I wanted to feel them smiling into my palms) was very promising. Very, very promising.

"Grayson Reed," she purred my way. That wasn't the drink talking, I swear she literally purred.

"Lotus," I rumbled in return. "Fate conspires to brighten my evening."

"Indeed," she said, her voice sly and mirthful. "I'd been getting a bit bored, myself. But the way I hear it, when you're about, nothing stays boring for long."

"My reputation precedes me," I said wryly, pulling up a chair at her table. The men around her must have been her own sailors, because with a few dismissive flicks of one of her pink-padded hands, they began to disperse, only grumbling a bit. I put down the bottle I'd been drinking, and I saw her appraise it approvingly. "Although I do believe that's a kind way of saying I make trouble wherever I go."

"If I didn't like trouble," she said, reaching for the bottle and pouring some of it for herself, maintaining eye contact with me the whole while, "I wouldn't exactly be in my line of work, now would I?"

"Touche," I chuckled, shaking out my dreads and propping my muzzle up on my bandaged palm. She seemed to notice, almost appearing concerned. Likely because it still smelled like fresh blood. "Yeah," I grumbled, "I've had… a day."

"How bad of a day?" she asked curiously. I knew she was plumbing me for information, probably trying to decide if keeping company here with me right now would be worth it to her, but I didn't care.

"Nothing some fine company wouldn't smooth over," I assured her.

She smiled. "It's not often one gets the chance to sit down with the fabled Manoratha Admiral. You're welcome at my table." She sipped my good rum, smirking over her cup. "You could sit a little closer, even."

I grinned like a fool. Tonight was working out.

I-don't-know-how many hours and drinks later, I was unburdening myself to Lotus, and she was listening with her body pressed against mine, one arm snaking beneath my coat, wrapped around my back. That's as far as it had gone so far, but judging by the way her broad, soft palm was stroking through my belly fur and her eyes would take occasional journeys down my uncovered chest, I had this one in the bag. Big cats did this thing with their tails when they were eyeing prey. Twitching about, swiping back and forth, dancing just out of the field of my vision. She was either planning to eat me or fuck me, or both.

"I wasn'looking to piss him off like I did," I muttered. "No'that much, anyway. I mean what the hell? I've pulled this trick on five... six other Amur before, no problem. Dig up the mistress, y'know. Should be open an'shut. Man reacted like I'd set'is tail on fire. Uncalled-for." I took another swig from the bottle, realizing belatedly that we'd apparently drained it at some point during our conversation.

"But it's not the same," she said quietly.

I had to look down towards her, curious why her voice had gotten so much quieter. This was no soft-spoken demure thing. "What d'you mean?"

"It's not just some 'mistress,'" she said. "It's heavier than an affair. Darker secret. Heresy."

"It's a poorly-kept secret is what it is," I rolled my eyes. "Heard about it long before we dug the whore up. I'd wager to guess his countrymen have heard the stories, too."

"Right, but they can't confirm it," she said. "Can't prove it. You could have."

"That was the whole damned point, yeah," I said.

"You know what they do to Heretics in Amuresca, right?" she asked, again keeping her voice down.

I went silent. I was a shit liar when I was drunk, but beyond that, I didn't feel like I should deny it. Yes, I'd known the sword I'd be holding over his head. Again, that had been the whole point—

Oh.

"I think he was afraid," Lotus said, tipping her head back to brush her muzzle past my throat, "not just angry. You thrust his greatest fear in his face. That'll bring out the beast in most people."

"Huhh," I drawled quietly, bewitched by the low thrum emanating from her throat. She clearly wasn't judging me for what I'd done, which is saying something, because I was beginning to.

I put the bottle down. Hadn't the point of all of this been to forget the events of the day? And here I was talking about it, while a gorgeous woman was practically straddling me, giving me every indication that she wanted to bed me.

Not here, though. Someone like her deserved better than a public rut in a dirty bar.

"Do you want to go someplace?" I began to ask her.

"Yes," she all but cut me off, making my heart jump in my chest. I don't know what I'd done right tonight, but I wasn't about to question it.

So, without much further ado, we rose and headed off arm-in-arm. She was leaning heavily against me, either because she was drunker than she seemed or because she wanted more of an excuse to touch me. Regardless, I liked the way her heat bled into me, how the scent of her fur was all I could smell. Patchouli, rum, leather, and the distinct, thrilling aroma of genuine female arousal. I'd worried briefly before we'd really got to drinking that she seemed a bit too eager. Like maybe this was a power play, although I couldn't think what she'd have to gain other than my good graces. And that would've been fine, but honestly, I respected her a lot more as a woman chasing her passions.

We barely made it to her place—she had a place, apparently. I was surprised she wasn't just sleeping on her ship, but I knew a few sailors who liked to get solid ground beneath their feet whenever they could, so I tried not to judge. It was a nice little shack, a palace compared to most of the dwellings on this island, on a lot full of other white-washed shacks just like it. This one was lifted on stilts with a creaking plank floor, simple amenities consisting of a bucket wash basin, an uneven table, and an old four-poster bed someone had likely stripped from a scuttled ship.

Honestly, I barely had time to take in my surroundings before the fierce tigress had thrown me unceremoniously onto the bed, shoving me off my feet like it was nothing to her. The woman was nearly as tall as me and possessed the kind of coiled strength you'd expect from a big cat. As she shrugged the blood-red coat from her shoulders, her figure silhouetted and wrapped in silver from the moonlight piercing between the slats of the shack, I admired the powerful contours beneath. Her fur roiled like waves, soft velvet over a muscular core, folding around the fat of her curves. And I'd only just gotten a peek.

"Undress," she growled, unclasping her belt and hanging her pistols over a nearby chair.

I didn't need to be told twice. Unfortunately, my hands were refusing to work with me as dexterously as I'd hoped—shite, I was really drunk, wasn't I? No matter. I could tell by the discomfort growing in my britches that it wouldn't be a problem. I'd need to remember to drink a lot of water when this was over, that's all.

"Everything," she said when I'd gotten down to only my lower garments. "I want to see all of you, wolf. Let's see if the reality lives up to the legend."

"Generally," I spoke to ease the awkwardness of how long it was taking me to disarm and disrobe, "I'm not th'one putting on a show like this. So you'll have to forgive—" I stumbled as I got out of a spat, "—my... clumsiness."

She continued to watch, making no move to strip any of her own remaining garments. Her eyes roved me hungrily with that same dangerous glint that made my spine crawl in all the right ways. Her tail thrashed about lazily. "I refuse to believe you've never let a woman order you about. And if so, shame on you."

"Not many women are's comfortable as you seem to be giving orders," I huffed out, grinning.

She approached me, hips swaying with her steps, tail following suit in opposing directions behind her. "Does it displease you?" she asked quietly.

"No," the choked utterance came out more desperate than I'd wanted it to sound. God, I was hard. I'd heard tigers liked to play with their food, but...

She smiled knowingly and finally stood before me, her hands moving to inspect me, going right for the goods. I let out a short 'Ha' of a gasp as her large paw closed around my cock, her hand both calloused along the pads and soft where the fur fluffed up around them. The dual sensation as she stroked me, coaxing me embarrassingly easily the remaining way out of my sheath, was already setting my head spinning.

She seemed to be measuring me out, gauging whether I'd suit her or not. I should have said something, quipped at her, teased her, defended my honor somehow. She was treating me like a pig at a fair. Next, she'd be trussing me up like one.

Why did that thought shoot straight down to my groin?

"Hmmm," she purred thoughtfully, noting the bulge of my knot inside my sheath, her paw shamelessly gripping me there, next. That got a groan out of me, for sure. "Don't get ahead of me," she gave my cock a light slap, stepping around me, her tail curling over my hip as she made for the bed.

I'd finally managed to strip out of my britches at that, so I joined her, leaning my bulk down beside where she eventually sat. The old wood of the bed groaned beneath our combined body-weight, and I found it was just large enough that only my toes needed to hang off the end. Probably made for dogs, a little small for a wolf. Certainly too small for a wolf and a tiger, but I didn't exactly mind the thought of cuddling up to her all night.

She was still wearing a maroon-colored, light cotton shirt tucked into her just slightly too-tight leather britches, the excess of her fur and curves spilling over the hem. I could see the way she was packed into them from the moonlight glowing through the thin fabric of her shirt, although the swell of her ample bosom was somewhat more restrained, probably wrapped or bound by some kind of undergarment. Given how curvaceous she was, I could understand why. Wouldn't do to have those getting in the way in a fight, or... swaying into a lit candle, or something.

They could sway into me, though. That'd be fine.

I began to reach to tug free the hem of her shirt, but she slapped my hand away, one of her claws catching on the wrap around my injured palm. I glanced down, noting the amply-sized claw tugging at the bandage, then back up at her muzzle as it curled into a thirsty smirk.

"No touching," she commanded. "Not yet."

I'm sure I whined. She chuckled at me and shoved me down onto the bed, prowling atop me. Her weight felt... good, crushing me down into the old, worn blankets. Powerful thighs encased my hips, the heat between her legs teasing at my cock and making it jump against my belly. She finally set her hands to me again like she had been in the bar, sliding them up my torso, stroking and feeling the contours of my body. She bit at her lower muzzle, her claw-tips moving over the contours of my ribs as I took a deep breath in, strong fingers eventually finding and kneading at my nipples.

"Ahhh—" I huffed out in surprise at the sensation. "I-I'm not... a woman."

"Why it is men seem to think they're the only ones who like to play with chests is beyond me," she said with a glint of fang in her smile. She leaned down over me slowly, her broad, rough tongue lathing once at where she was squeezing. "Do you not like it?"

The fact was, I liked it more than I was comfortable with. I'd never known my chest was so sensitive. Well, you learn new things every day. "I swear to god, woman," I breathed out, "if you tickle me—"

Her laughter came freely and immediately. "Oh-ho!" She leaned on her elbows over me, tail thrashing. "Have I unearthed the great Manoratha Admiral's one weakness?"

"I will piss on your bed," I said flatly. "Don't try me."

She continued laughing, leaning over to one of the bedposts to grab for something. "Cross my heart," she promised.

When she came back into my field of vision, I saw what she was holding, and my heart skipped a beat. If anything, her grin grew, dangling the bundle of red rope before me.

"Is that... silk?" I asked warily. I knew to ask, at this point. I could handle a rough night, but my hand was already injured.

She began to twine and curl it around her hands, stretching it out. "'Tis," she purred. "Of course. I'm not cruel."

I let out a long, shuddering breath. "My reputation really does precede me."

"Denholme's not the only one whose bedroom habits have become fodder for the creativity of bored sailors." She clucked her tongue. "But it's alright. You're in good company."

"Obviously," I said, entranced by her hands as they wound the red rope about. "You came prepared."

"I have a favorite on my ship," she assured me. "But breaking in the Grayson Reed… far more exciting. Couldn't pass up the opportunity." And at that she'd gripped one of my wrists, yanking it up to the headboard. I watched her every motion as she expertly bound and knotted my wrists with the skill and precision of both a sailor and someone who favored knots for more pleasurable activities.

Honestly, I hadn't actually done this that many times before. Thrice with the same woman, but, although she'd been a professional, her heart hadn't really been in it, and that had soured the experience somewhat. Once with a Carvecian woman who hadn't known what she was doing. We'd used the wrong kind of rope; I'd had to explain away the raw patches on my wrists for weeks afterwards, but we'd both enjoyed ourselves despite all the fumbling, and I feel like if we'd had more time together, we might've gotten it right. I couldn't understand men who preferred inexperienced women. Territorial bastards.

Lotus seemed both well-versed and eager. The scent of her arousal had grown—you couldn't fake that. I flexed my legs against the bed, toes digging into the rough blankets. I could hardly stand it anymore.

I tried to lift my head to at least nuzzle against her cheek ruff while she leaned over me, but in response she only bit my ear. Hard.

"Not yet," she whispered.

"I think I might lit'rally die if I hafta wait much longer..."

"Impatient," she chided, sitting back to admire her work once I was well and truly bound. I tried testing the restraints and found the more I pulled, the tighter they cinched around my wrists. To a point.

"Perfect," she cooed. And then she hiked her hip over my body so that she was alongside me and slid off the bed.

Off. The bed.

I watched her, befuddled, as she fixed her shirt somewhat and sidled up to my right, her eyes still roaming me appraisingly. I felt a tickling at the back of my neck, like a flight response. A warning. The haze of alcohol and lust was clouding my senses, but some part of me still remembered this woman was a predator. Although, at this point, what good it might do me...

"He's bound, then?"

Oh fuck.

Oh. FUCK.

I struggled against the bindings the second I heard his voice, but of course it was no use. The bed shook as I craned my neck up as well as I could, the unmistakable silhouette standing just outside the slats of the shack on the beach outside. A head shorter than me, squared shoulders under a rough coat, triangular ears. That fucking Amurescan accent.

"What do you take me for?" Lotus replied, mock offended. "You think I don't know my knots? High insult."

"Fine. Not like I can't handle him, anyway." The door pushed open.

"He's hammered," she assured him, giving a sloppy smile of her own. "Good rum. He was half a bottle into it already when I found him."

Found me?

I gave a long groan, reality catching up with me all at once. Of course. Of course. My luck was never this good. Why the hell had I ever thought something might go right for me today? Any day?

Literally any day.

Luther fucking Denholme strode up beside the bed, golden eyes deliberately avoiding taking in my state of undress and moving straight to my face. Like he was some shy fucking maid. "How're you doing tonight, Reed?" he asked almost casually.

"You rotten, cock-sucking bastard," I slurred out viciously.

"You have me, utterly," he said, unblinking.

"Are you going to leave him intact, at least?" Lotus asked from somewhere behind me, past the point that I could crane my head back to see. "I might have use for him later, and you swore he'd come out of this alive. I'm holding you to that. His men are loyal. I don't have the energy to deal with some quest for vengeance."

Luther, whom I could see quite well because he was right fucking beside me now like we were casual bedfellows, waved a hand dismissively in her direction. "As agreed," he said. "You get your one-time pardon, whenever you need to cash that note."

"Sooner rather than later," she muttered, "given how often our territories overlap. Which irritates me, I have to tell you, because you're essentially poaching my prey."

"We protect our waters," he replied, smooth as silk. "You seize cargo, sink competitors, and bounty-hunt. Counter-piracy for profit hardly makes you a hero."

"I'm not pretending to be a hero," she snorted. Again, I couldn't see her, but I felt like she made a rude gesture. "Are you? You're the one who reached out to me, and all of this is pretty illicit, navy boy."

"I don't care what you consider me. I'm just fighting to keep the open ocean a place of freedom," he said, voice oddly quiet for a moment. "Not death."

Lotus guffawed at him, peeling off into full-blown, amused laughter. On another day I might've joined her. Denholme just looked so serious when he said that. I don't know if it was the booze or the fact that I was bound up and entirely helpless, but the moment earnestly shook me. Real, true-blue conviction wasn't something I encountered much in my line of work. In my life, really.

The Manoratha fleet—my fleet—had an unspoken code. We didn't sink civilian vessels. We tried not to kill unnecessarily. We press-ganged or otherwise re-located sailors and soldiers off commercial vessels if we possibly could once we'd taken whatever they were moving. Things didn't always hash out as neatly as I might've liked, but that was the game. In the heat of the take, men died. But executions after the fact were something I avoided as much as possible. You do that even once, and it sticks with you, rots away at you.

Besides, most any man you harbor in the belly of your ship in leg irons won't make trouble. They'll either beg you for a job or be quite content to get shoved off on dry land, wherever that might next be, rather than continue to fight against overwhelming odds.

Which, other than the fact that I didn't much like the idea of killing innocents, was another damn good reason not to do so. A merchant sailor might be loyal enough to their Captain or their company, but someone aboard a civilian vessel could have family they're protecting, and if you kill them? Your prisoners are going to be a lot less docile afterwards.

But the fact was that a lot of my fellows in this line of work weren't quite so discerning, and that's what men like Luther Denholme lived and breathed for. He wasn't even doing what he did for the Crown, or they'd be funding him and he wouldn't have to take bribes under the table. His Highness in the Amurescan Court was more worried about their crumbling Colonial Empire than protecting his own people on shipping and transport routes from...

...from men like me. And worse.

The Cerberus Fleet, as much as my men feared and loathed it, wasn't primarily interested in us. I ran afoul of them because of the line of work I was in, but I couldn't help but feel—now that I was really considering it—there might've been a reason the fucking cattle dog had let me run every time we'd nearly crossed swords. He'd made some excuse about not wanting to risk losing his smaller ships to my cannons, but I was certain that wasn't it. I wasn't his primary prey. His true wrath was reserved for the more vicious of my kin.

"Fuck," I vaguely heard the man in question curse. His rough, clawed fingers snapped in front of my face, forcing me to blink and refocus my eyes. "He's miles away. How much did he have to drink, you say?"

"I didn't," Lotus said. "And honestly I lost track, myself."

"Bloody fantastic," he grunted, leaning in and sitting on the edge of the bed, his weight causing my right side to dip. "If he's useless to me tonight—"

"I am rarely too drunk t'get hard, if that's your worry," I spoke up, bringing an instant frown to his face.

"He's not even flaccid right now," Lotus remarked with a slight whistle of appreciation. "I think he likes being at your mercy more'n he's letting on, Denholme."

That only got a deeper frown out of him, which almost hurt, really. Was I not handsome enough for him?

"It's all for you, lass," I assured Lotus. "Seems I'm apparently not choice enough meat for the great Admiral here t'sink 'is teeth into."

"Please. Stop," he ground out through a clenched jaw. "I don't appreciate the mockery over my proclivities. They are no mystery to anyone in this room, fine, but your attempted blackmail of my personal life is what got you in this mess to begin with, so—"

"I ain't mocking you," I insisted. Before he could interject, I said, "Yeah alright, I was earlier. And I did try'n blackmail you using what I knew. But it wasn't because I've got a problem with it, alright? S'because I know your kin do."

That quiet fury returned behind his eyes. "How is that any different?" he demanded. "Using my own countrymen's hatred against me yields the same result."

"Well, it's not great leverage if it wouldn't work," I reasoned. "But doesn'it matter tha'I don't personally hate you?"

"No," he replied near-instantly. "Because I don't really give a damn what you think of me, Reed."

"Harsh," I pouted. "You're not even going to ravish me, are you?"

The face he made at that was… indescribable and thoroughly worth whatever came of it. "No," he growled out, "this was simply a means to put you in your place and come out on top in our negotiations."

"That phrasing though," Lotus beat me to it, talking partially around her hand by the sound of it.

"For fuck's sake," the cattle dog rolled his eyes. "Grow up. The both of you!"

"Look, you interrupted us in the middle of somethin' here. It ain't my fault I've got sex on the mind," I pointed out, glancing down my body. Which led him to glance down my body, of course, out of instinct. And then I got the distinct pleasure of watching Admiral Luther Denholme's ears flush and his body actually fidget.

"Would you please stop that?" His eyebrow twitched, fingers sliding up between his ears to settle his choppy fur.

"What?" I asked as innocently as I could muster.

"Flirting!" he bit out.

"S'that what I'm doing?"

"Why are you letting him goad you?" Lotus said, finally sliding into view, her arms crossed over her ample bosom. "I got him disarmed, away from his men, tied up and everything for you. Why are you still pleading with him as if you don't have the upper hand here? Do I need to do everything?"

To his credit, Luther managed not to look cowed by her remarks. But he tucked back his ears and adopted a sterner expression, nonetheless. "Alright, Reed," he said, "here's how it's going to be—"

"You wanted fifteen percent, right?" I said, trying hard not to slur while we did business. I might have been hog-tied, naked, sloshed, and hard, but I wasn't going to let that get in the way of my professionalism.

He seemed taken aback at first, then countered, "I believe I started at twenty."

"Right, but tha'was your opening offer." I cleared my throat. "You were hoping for fifteen. You probably would've taken ten—"

"But then you insulted and blackmailed me," he snarled.

"—but then I insulted and blackmailed you," I confirmed. "So, fifteen's what's reasonable here, I'd say."

He was silent for a few moments, considering. "You're capitulating too quickly for my liking."

"Huh?" I blinked sleepily back at him.

"Amurescan is your first language," he said, visibly irritated.

"Not th'kind you speak," I muttered.

"Oh for — it isn't my job to expand your vocabulary." He pressed his fingers between his brows. "I thought you'd be more resistant, is my point."

"I mean, you bested me," I said, flexing one of my arms that was becoming a bit sore, pulled above my head as it was. "This is literally as bested as I can get, unless you were to… I don't know… torture or kill me. And my cock bein' exposed to all this salty air without a lick of relief in sight—"

"Nice," Lotus said from off to the side.

"—thank you, I try," I cleared my throat, "s'pretty well close to torture, anyway. By the way lass, are we still on, when this is all over? Or was all this just for the pardon? Because you seemed pretty into it before he showed up."

"Oh no," she clarified, "I am not letting that go to waste." I didn't need to be able to turn my head to know what she was referring to. "If you're still good to go despite all this, we can pick up right where we left off. No hard feelings?"

"None whatsoever," I shrugged. "S'business. And I got sloppy. Can't blame you for seizing the opportunity. 'Course you know this means I'll feel no remorse whatsoever in the future if you provide me th'chance to fuck you over."

"Of course." She smirked. "If I'm stupid enough to let you get the better of me, it'd be my fault anyway."

"If you breeders are quite done," Luther groused.

"Now he's just coming off sounding jealous," Lotus said down towards me, as if the cattle dog wasn't even in the room.

"Hey if I thought he was interested, I wouldn't mind sharin' you," I said. She hummed, glancing between us. "Even if I had to step aside for a bit, I'd watch you fuck him. Definitely."

"Excuse me?!" Luther again, of course. He was turning colors at this point. Honestly, I don't know what he'd expected. He'd put himself in this position, really.

I tipped my head up, the haze of alcohol making her proposition easier to picture without immediately recoiling from the thought. I really wasn't into men. I mean, I'm pretty sure I wasn't. I lived and worked around every flavor of man; they weren't shy about getting nude, and I'd never once thought of any of them that way. And I had a very active imagination. "I dunno," I said, "I guess, how do you really know until you've tried, right?"

"You can know before you have any experience," Luther muttered, sounding more tired than I think I'd ever heard him. "Trust me. And what the hell makes you think he'd be fucking me?! He's the one who's tied up!"

"That's what you're offended by?" she asked dryly.

"I mean I feel like if I'm going to go so far outside what I'm used to," I said, "I may as well switch roles entirely. Get the full experience, you know?"

"I have been berating, threatening, and humiliating you while you are bound and helpless," Luther sneered at me, "for half an hour now, and you're still somehow erect. You'd be my BITCH, wolf."

"The lack of tits wouldn't be as fun," I bemoaned.

"Oh!" Lotus said suddenly. "You know, we can do that. If you just want someone with tits to fuck you, I've got something I use on myself…"

"Damn," I would've slapped my thigh if I could, "why didn't I ever think of that before? See, if you keep at it, the perfect solution to most problems will come t'you."

"We'd have to go to my ship," she said.

"Well, I think we're just about done here," I looked back to Luther. "So, fifteen percent? And I thought I might throw something else in, just to make up for my…" I paused, trying to make sure my actual, real regret didn't tinge my words. Didn't need anyone knowing I felt such useless things. "…my mis-steps, earlier. I want everyone here leaving feeling kindly-disposed towards me. Seeing as you've both got a lot of firepower."

That seemed to pique his interest. "And what might that be?" he asked.

"Something I think might keep you busy enough to keep that fleet of yours out of our fur for a while," I said, glancing at Lotus, who also seemed interested now. "I know where Roccosal's fleet moors in between raids and what routes he's likely to take this season."

That bought me a moment of stunned silence from both of them. Lotus was the first to break it, sounding quietly wary. "You're willing to sell out Fathom Roccosal?"

"Yeah, I am," I said without missing a beat. I couldn't be sure if her tone was one of respect or if I was about to make an enemy of her. So, I asked. "If you've got a problem with that Lotus, that's fine. But it's not gonna change what I do here."

"Roccosal is far beyond my pay-grade," she said quietly, with a hint of fear in her voice. "I don't have the firepower to hunt him even if I wanted to—which I don't, for the record. I don't have a death wish. Have you ever seen his fleet?"

"Hard to forget," I muttered. "Dramatic bastard chains skulls to his figureheads."

"He's also got two bristling Man-of-Wars," Luther said, his voice sharp as a blade-edge now and his eyes gone vicious. He looked down on me more intently than he had this entire conversation. "And more carnage in his wake than most armies."

"He runs a flesh market for the Huudari off an island in the Shanivaar," I said, "one of the tinier ones that's not on any maps. Takes most of his catch that he bothers to bring in alive there. Gets a lot of them in the Kadrush, the way I hear it. Pretty snowcats for the brothels and wolves for the fields."

I noticed Lotus make a disgusted face at the mention of the slave market, and I was glad to see it. Not all people from Mataa—'Huudari' people, as they called themselves—were opposed to slavery. A lot of the species with power, like the lions and the hyenas, wanted to keep the practice ongoing through dubiously legal means, generally indentured servitude that was no better than out-and-out slavery in practice. I was glad to see Lotus disapproved of it. No Privateer or Pirate should approve of, let alone take part, in something that limited people's freedom. Press-ganging was one thing; they got paid, and they could leave any time we pulled into port. Owning someone like they were a mule? Couldn't abide by that.

"Roccosal's a real bastard, to be sure," Lotus said uncomfortably, "but you're selling out one of our fellows here, Reed—'"

"It ain't like we've got some code we all agreed on, Lotus," I said. "And you hunt your 'fellows' down for bounties all the time."

"He's not one of us," she said, gesturing at Luther. "If you were going to hunt Roccosal yourself, fine. But Denholme's—"

"You literally just sold me out to him," I snorted back a laugh. "I am only here having this conversation with the two of you, because you made a deal with him."

She paused, then crossed her arms over her chest, nodding slowly. "Alright, you've got me there."

"Where is the Dhole?" Luther demanded, his tone now pressing. "Fathom Roccosal. Where is he?"

I hesitated only a second more, remembering what had occupied my mind before. That assured my certainty. "The island is called the Mataa Chinaya a Shanivaar."

He squinted for a moment, clearly running that through his ears. "I didn't catch... is that... the 'graveyard of tears of Mataa'?"

"Shanivaar is the name for the chain of islands," Lotus supplied helpfully. "And yes, it does mean 'string of tears', you heard that right. Chinaya is 'graveyard', but that's hardly an official name. The island didn't have a name before he settled his fleet there, but once he did, the local people took to calling it that for... reasons."

"Unbelievable," Luther snuffed. "Does the entire Piracy world know where this mass murderer makes landfall? And no one's had the stones to do something about him?"

"On balance," I spoke up, "calling him a 'mass murderer' is sort of hypocritical. He's a pirate. He kills people. A lot of people, sure. Are you saying your war leaders and fellow Admirals are all 'mass murderers', too?"

"I would," Lotus stated from off to the side.

"Fathom brought a lot of disparate groups under one flag and eased a lot of tensions in the process," I said, "and his island's a haven for the kind of people the rest of the world generally tosses out. Some of which faced the same kinds of irrational exclusion and segregation you've likely contended with," I said pointedly at him. "He works with all species. He's even got women sailing in his fleet- sometimes in Command positions, I hear. A few of those lizardfolk too, if rumors are true."

"You're still telling me where to find him," he said, confused.

"...the slaving..." I sighed. "Everything else, I can overlook. Well, maybe not all the murder. Some of it really seems unnecessary, truth be told."

"He used to be less bloodthirsty," Lotus said weakly. "For what it's worth."

"I'll need actual coordinates," Luther insisted.

"Can we," I tugged at my bindings, "tomorrow? I mean this talk has effectively sheathed my sword for now, as it were." And it had. "But I'd like to get back to Lotus's ship with her, and unless you've changed your mind about joining us—"

"If you don't stop it with that shit," he warned, "I will take you seriously at some point and make you regret it."

෴ ෴

On the way back to Lotus's vessel, we hopped briefly aboard the ship I'd come here in, the Saber Rattle. She was a well-appointed, well-loved, and very well-cared-for 10 gun Sloop under the command of one Captain Lunden, a Carvecian otter around my age whom I'd found I got on with far too well for our own good. He had three such vessels and, on the surface at least, ran a legitimate cartography business. He used his fleet and his rather impressive navigation skills to map out little-explored islands and reef chains and plot routes for paying companies. Good work, when you could get it. I respected men in his profession.

That being said, he also seemed to have a bent for getting himself in trouble when opportunities arose. And a lot of those 'opportunities' had involved me. You might say I was a corrupting influence.

But who was I to deny someone a little adventure, now and again?

He'd been the perfect choice for this meeting. His ships were small enough to go beneath notice in most areas, but still well-armed for their size, fast as could be if I'd needed to beat a hasty retreat, and not out-of-place in a scummy port. Like I said, the man didn't mind slumming it now and again.

Perhaps most importantly, since I couldn't very well bring my behemoth around a place this small without attracting a lot of unnecessary attention, he'd been willing to play ferryman for this trip. I'd venture to say 'eager', even. Like he'd been hoping something might go tits-up and we'd have to fight our way out of here. Pity he was going to be disappointed.

I found him above-decks with some of his boys, watching a curvaceous vixen they must have paid to entertain them for the evening dance while one of his sailors played a lively melody on a flute. She was actually not a bad dancer, all in all. I mean, it helped that her top was off… but still.

He noticed my arrival after we'd made our way up the plank, and his gaze of course swept over Lotus before settling on me. I didn't blame him in the slightest.

The otter looked fairly sober, despite the fact that a few clay bottles of rum were making their way among his men. I'd rarely known him to drink to excess. He preferred to dress humbly and comfortably, as opposed to my flair for all things audacious and shiny. Tonight, he was dressed down even for him though, the thin cotton of his shirt settling over his sleek fur, just form-fitting enough to show off his tone to the women he was likely hoping to impress. He seemed to have Lotus's eye, at least.

"Just getting a few of my things," I assured him as I headed below-decks. "The lady and I won't be returning until morning."

"Afternoon," she corrected me, sighing. "Been a long night already. I'll be sleeping in for certain."

"How did it go?" he asked my retreating back, a smile already tugging at his whiskered mouth like he knew there was a story to be had.

"I'm sure Lotus will tell it better than I could."

I went to my quarters to grab a few things, just in case. I'd be wearing the same clothing tomorrow obviously, what was I, some missish Pedigree?

31

But I was out of rum, and I'd need it come the morning or I'd be sick as hell. And almost more importantly...

I grabbed my pistols. I hadn't brought all four of them with me when I'd gone to talk with Denholme earlier in the day (just the two and a long knife), and, given my luck of late, I felt like it couldn't hurt to be fully-armed. Especially considering where I was going and with whom.

I also rolled up a map I knew I'd need tomorrow to complete my end of the bargain with Denholme and a Chartruc silver coin to seal the deal. It was a dead currency, worth more if you melted it down at this point, but they were rare and unique; most people wouldn't throw one away, and I liked to give them to new allies to remind them to keep their word. The death's-head wolf skull on one side had inspired my flag.

By the time I made it back up to Lotus and Captain Lunden, she had him laughing uproariously. I had no doubt she had told him absolutely everything. Several of his other crew members were gathered around listening, too, so... this would become yet another infamous mis-adventure of Admiral Grayson Reed that was now certain to enter the public domain.

"If you're quite done humiliating me," I announced my presence, "can we get out of here?"

"No," she replied impishly. I wasn't sure what to say to that, then she corrected herself. "I mean, I'm not quite done humiliating you. We've got all night for that."

The various, scandalized 'ohhhhh's that went up amongst Lunden's men at her public promise to further debase me really should not... should not have made me hard again. But, here we were.

I glowered, stormed down the plank, and heard her call out a cheerful 'good night!' to the men aboard the ship. A chorus of laughter followed in our wake.

ᑎᐯ ᒍᑎ

Honestly, we barely made it into her cabin before we were tearing our clothing off again. I finally, finally got my paws up beneath that too-taut blouse of hers, filling my palms with the overflowing bounty of her breasts. And good god, it was everything I'd hoped and more. Soft, pillowy flesh and downy tufts of creamy-white fur I could run my claws through and over, grip and squeeze without fear it would hurt or even discomfort her. Tigers were literally thick-skinned. Tougher ladies you'd be hard-pressed to find anywhere. All she did when I kneaded her breasts was moan and encourage me with little kitten-licks along my muzzle.

She bore me down into her bed, and I was once again pinned under the weight and strength of her predatory body, which she clearly felt no need to hold back with. I relished it—wanted it, wanted more of it even. I wanted her to pin me down just as surely as the bindings had, even if my already-sore muscles protested and groaned from the strain. I wanted her to take me between those thick, striped thighs and ride me until my breath gave out. I wanted bruises that would last for days to remember her by.

Would she let me knot her? She could take me, I know she could. For most felines it might've been a struggle, but she was a big cat, all over. So maybe…

When her paws closed over my cock, both of them, stroking me slowly, languidly up and down, my thoughts just… stopped. And honestly, that was for the best. Fuck this day. I needed to relax.

"I need you so bad," I breathed out, my voice a rasp by then. "Lotus…"

She purred down at me, the deep noise reverberating through every part of her body in contact with mine. It made my spine quake and my body want to give way right there and then.

But no.

Of course not.

For I am, after all, Grayson Reed. And nothing ever EVER goes right for me, for very long.

The pounding at our door was explosive, sudden, and insistent. And joined not long after by a demanding, familiar voice, which I was certain would haunt my nightmares after this.

"REED! Where the HELL is Kafele?!"

Both Lotus and I shouted a chorus of expletives in at least three different languages. Once we'd gotten that out of our system, I demanded fiercely of her in a rough whisper, "How the hell did he get aboard your ship?!"

"I—uh," she blanched, "he's… staying here."

"You're the one who brought him to the island," I said, deadpan, the obviousness of it only hitting me now.

"We had an arrangement." She shrugged.

"I left him here in my cabin earlier today," Luther's voice from behind the door growled out. "He had nowhere else to be, Reed. He promised me he wouldn't leave the ship until tomorrow. Where is he?!"

Lotus glared down at me. "Alright, what did you do with his whore?"

"You've got be k—nothing!" I proclaimed. "I went straight from my meeting with him to you! And you know what happened after that."

"There were hours in between your meeting with him and meeting me," she pointed out. "And you have men here on the island. I know you do. If this is some kind of counter-scheme, I really do not have the patience for this bullshit—"

"All I did between meeting him and you was get drunk," I whined, flopping my head back down against the bed. "I swear to god, Lotus."

"You're an Atheist, Reed," she muttered. "Don't think I don't know that."

"I pray sometimes for the hell of it," I said petulantly. "Look, I didn't have any other plans for Kafele except to take him home!" I finally growled, letting my frustration show through. "Captain Lunden and I were headed back to Mataa after this, I swear to you, that is all we had planned for him."

"Is it possible he went back to Lunden's ship early?" she asked.

"We would have seen him between here and there, it's not that far," I said, closing my eyes slowly. "And he wasn't on the ship. I went below-decks, and he doesn't have a private cabin there. Fuck. Fuck."

"Something happened to Denholme's cute little fennec," Lotus murmured, her hands settling on her hips where they straddled me. "His ex-lover who he clearly has some unresolved shit with. The man you brought here, to a dangerous criminal-infested hell-hole, to blackmail him."

"Seems… that way," I moaned.

"You have to do something about this, Reed."

"I know."

"Or he is going to kill you."

"I know."

To say he looked absolutely furious when I opened the door would be a severe understatement. Livid is better, but still inadequate. Enraged might do it.

He was midway through storming the doorway when I cocked my pistol, keeping it level with his legs out of respect for our situation, but making it very clear I was holding it nonetheless. He didn't have to know it wasn't loaded.

"What the hell, Reed?!" he bellowed, stopping a mere foot or so away from me when he saw it. I could still practically feel his breath.

"You're a little… emotional right now," I said carefully, between my teeth. "And you casually split my palm earlier today, had me bound and held hostage—"

"Shall we assign blame where it's due?!" He literally stomped his foot.

"Yes, fine," I agreed, biting back the overwhelming desire to point out how his tantrum was robbing him of much of the dignity I'd mentally assumed of him earlier. This is why I didn't do relationships. They made you look and act foolish.

Also, it's not as though I'm a man possessing much dignity on the best of days, let alone after the night I'd had.

"But, look," I eased, putting my free hand, the one he'd injured, up in a placating gesture, "I need to get the facts from you calmly and collectedly here—"

"So, you point a pistol at me?"

"—without getting gutted in the process," I finished, sighing. I waved the pistol towards the room, beckoning him in. "Let's talk in private. Or, well, mostly. Lotus is here." I narrowed my eyes, flicking them between both parties. "But then you know that, since you two were apparently shipmates."

"Every moment we spend talking is wasting time," he argued, while still entering the room and slamming the door behind him. He refused to sit, of course, opting for leaning against the wall and crossing his arms over his chest. A gesture of defensiveness. Man really needed to learn more about body language if he wanted to be an effective Admiral. Spoke to his inexperience, really.

I fell back on my ass on the rumpled bed alongside Lotus, who hadn't bothered putting her tits away. Neither had I, to be fair. The cattle dog must really have only preferred the company of men after all, because I didn't see his gaze wander once. And if Lotus didn't do it for you...

"What the fuck did you do to my whore?" Luther demanded in a snarl. "Where did you hide him? Why? Is this another play? You are getting fuck-all , Reed. Just as soon as I get off this shithole island, I am going to wipe your sorry excuse for a fleet off the edge of the world!"

I blew a breath past my muzzle fur, muttering, "You lose a lot of that Amur decorum when you're angry, huh? I mean, it didn't really suit you—"

"I will shove my Amur decorum up your ass if you don't answer me RIGHT FUCKING NOW—"

"We didn't do anything with Kafele!" Lotus raised her voice over the both of us with ease. Big cats could always out-belt a canine if given the chance, and she didn't waste any of that impressive voice box. "Meshtah!" She swore in her native tongue, looking at me. "Are you just going to let him talk you down for no reason? I know you had nothing to do with this!"

I shrugged. "He seemed to need a good yell. I figured I'd just let him have at it."

Luther faltered with his mouth half-open. "Wait, you really don't—"

"Did it ever occur to you he might have just gone somewhere, mate?" I asked tiredly. "How long did you leave him here alone, anyway?"

"I told him I'd be back tonight," he insisted. "He promised me he wouldn't leave."

"Did he say he wouldn't briefly leave?" Lotus pointed out. "Like for dinner? Or a drink?"

"Why would he need to?" he persisted. "He could eat here—"

"No offense to our 'chef' Hasan," Lotus made a face. "But maybe he wanted something a bit… better? Hasan's been serving the same stew for the last three days, I'm pretty sure. We don't even keep him on for his cooking prowess in the first place, it's kind of a rotating position among the men."

"I'm aware," Luther said impatiently. "I took the shift before we made port."

"You cooked for Lotus's crew?" I chuckled despite myself. "Aw."

"Shut up," the cattle dog snapped, that golden-eyed glare falling on me again. "Kafele wouldn't be here in this dingy little port, getting himself into god-knows-what-kind-of-trouble right now, if not for you."

"We don't even know that," I rolled my eyes. "Lotus is right, he probably just stepped out for a drink or something. And yeah, he's pretty and clean and an obvious target for a fortune-hunter, but—" Lotus elbowed me at that, likely because the cattle dog's stare had suddenly grown more murderous. "But," I emphasized, standing slowly and putting my pistol away, "we don't know he's gotten himself into trouble. You know, the port I pulled him out of wasn't exactly a shining city of virtue. I'm betting the fennec is more street-savvy than you're giving him credit for."

"Not in a place like this," Luther said flatly. "Not Dokuro."

"I… have to agree with him on that one," Lotus said hesitantly. "We didn't get to know the kid well or anything—or, well, I suppose Denholme did. Inside'n'out."

He lifted his chin at her indignantly.

"Point is, he really shouldn't have stepped off the ship," she said, sounding increasingly worried herself. "We ought to at least find out how long he's been gone. And anyway, I don't think Denholme's going to agree to just sitting around."

"I still don't trust that this isn't some further plot of yours," he said to me.

"My plots aren't this complicated!" I sputtered. "How could I've known you'd hire a gorgeous Privateer to seduce me, kidnap me, and force my hand like you did?!"

The both of them stared at me in complete silence for… far too long.

"Oh, come on," I grumbled. "I'm not that easy a mark."

"You kind of—""

"—really are," they spoke nearly in unison with the overlapping statements.

It didn't take asking around the ship much to discover how long it had been since the striking fennec had last been seen. The answer? Too long.

It'd been folly to think any part of this trip was going to be easy, of course. Why had I gotten my hopes up? Honestly.

36

The cattle dog was practically vibrating with anger by the time we'd made our rounds through the limited crew. The absolute last anyone had seen of him had been, it seemed, shortly after Luther had left. Presumably to meet Lotus at the rendezvous spot, where I was soon to be delightfully accosted.

I was only now starting to fully sober up (much to my dismay), and at some point last night—because yes, it was nearing morning now—I'd thoroughly lost track of time. And so had Lotus, what with how much she'd similarly been drinking. But Luther hadn't, so we had his recollection to go off of. He'd left here around midnight, or thereabouts by his reckoning, long enough for Lotus to have lured me off. By the time we'd stumbled back here after our dealings, it had been at least three or four hours later. What with talking, untying me and all, meandering through the city, stopping by Lunden's ship… And now, it was showing the first signs of a blue dawn in the sky.

I was beginning to understand Luther's concern. Talking with the crew had confirmed that at the very least, Kafele's intentions upon leaving the ship were to get alcohol, not walk along the beach or stare longingly at the stars or some other tripe like that. He was dealing with what must have been a very awkward and uncomfortable conversation with an ex-lover the way a man ought to: booze. I don't know why the rum rations on Lotus's ship hadn't been good enough for him, but whatever. Difference of culture, I suppose.

The decision hadn't been a smart one. I didn't want to confirm out loud what Lotus had danced around, but I'd been traveling with the fennec for a month now, and I knew him well enough to know he was, in fact, in over his head in a port like Dokuro. He likely didn't realize that when he'd set out. The whole while I'd had him lying in wait to spring him on Denholme, I'd told the fennec to spend the day seemingly alone in one of the bars on the island. What he probably hadn't appreciated was that I'd had six of my boys on him at all times lest someone single out the obviously foreign, obviously beautiful high-class sex worker as a target of opportunity. No one on this island knew what he was here for, but that wouldn't have mattered. He was a ripe peach in a den of hungry ne'er-do-wells.

Now, I could very well claim at this point that this was no longer my problem, nor my responsibility. After all, for so long as he'd been in my care, he'd been safe. It was only once Luther had taken him away that he'd strayed into potential trouble. But firstly, I'd made a promise to Kafele and his large pack of rather adorable younger siblings that I'd get him home safe. I didn't make many promises that important, but when I did I sure as hell tried to keep them.

Secondly, and perhaps more importantly, everything with Denholme, everything we'd negotiated, would fall apart if I walked away now. And I believed him when he said he'd go out of his way to hunt me down if he left here angry. Before this meeting, I can't say I'd had as good a grasp on the nature of the Cerberus Admiral as I would have liked. I really only had rumors to follow and many of them were proving wildly inaccurate.

One thing was for certain though. Luther Denholme was a passionate man. He'd put up an air of cold indifference for all of... half an hour, really... until I'd brought out Kafele. But I'd seen now on several occasions over the last day how deeply he felt things, from the desperate sorrow in the brief conversation he'd had with Kafele to the inferno of anger he'd shown at having his taboo connection to this man used against him. There was just a lot there. And I had no doubt that he'd not only hold a grudge over this fiasco, but act upon it.

So, I had to fix this. I just hoped I wasn't too late.

After we'd spoken to the crew, I went back down to Lotus's quarters and suited up, donning my coat and pistols, even going so far as to borrow a saber from her just in case. Unlike Denholme, I didn't casually carry a long blade around. Generally, the firearms were enough. It was telling that he apparently prioritized the opposite. I was certain by now that he wasn't carrying a pistol. Usually that would've been an etiquette thing in Amur culture, dating back to their knightly traditions, I think. But he was common-born, so unless he really valued Pedigree rites of honor for some reason, I suspected it was more that he enjoyed a closer kill. I had men like that on my ship. Truthfully? That sort of attitude scared me. It was so devoid of common sense, so sadistic. Felt unnecessarily brutal.

I polished off what little was left in my flask just to keep myself sharp, then headed back above-decks. When I found the two of them again, Luther was staring out towards the city for some reason, leaning over the railing, and Lotus looked concerned. But then, that wasn't new.

There was a palpable air of unease amongst the few men on deck too, actually. One that hadn't been there before. They all looked like they'd seen a ghost.

"Tell me things haven't gotten worse while I was away," I muttered quietly to Lotus as I sidled up to her.

"What?" She blinked. "No. No... not exactly. We don't know any more than we did before. He wants to start canvasing the city."

"Obviously," I said. I began to open my mouth to say more, but at that point Denholme approached us.

"Are you ready?" he asked.

"I mean, I haven't slept," I growled irritably. "I've got balls bluer than the southern sea, and I'm staving off a hangover that'll probably kill me when all's said and done. But yeah, I suppose?"

"You are helping me locate him," he said icily. "You'll scour the whole of this island with me until we do. Am I clear?"

Something about his tone bothered me. Namely all of it, really. "You know," I snuffed, "you're acting awfully big and demanding for one lone Amur. I know you've sort of got immunity from Lotus and me, given that we can't afford to piss off your fleet by ending you or having you leave here swearing vengeance on us, but we could just tell you t'go fuck yourself and take our chances at sea—"

"He doesn't speak for me," Lotus said with a steely-eyed glare at me.

"Fine, then on my own behalf," I snorted. "This is bullshit. You lost him, not me. Which is riskin' me reneging on the word I gave his family, by the way. Real inconvenience to me and, worse, for my reputation. I don't have to take this kind of treatment from you."

"Oh?" he said with absolutely no mirth in his tone.

"Try being nicer, is all I'm saying," I reasoned. "I'm helping outta the goodness of my heart. And you're one man. I've got a crew here, remember. I know you two got a little quid pro quo going on here, but I doubt Lotus'll stand by you if you try anything out-and-out murder-y with me."

"I won't have to," he said with utter certainty.

"No, you won't," I spread my palms, "because we're gonna be more friendly with one another going forward, right?"

"No," he stated. "I won't have to do so myself, because my man will drop you where you stand if I give the word to do so."

"'Man'?" I laughed, showing my fangs. "Try again. I had my boys on you like fleas on a coyote from the time you showed at the figurehead. They would've seen…"

His expression hadn't changed. My grin slipped away slowly. Not because of him, but because I'd noticed a shift in Lotus's expression. And suddenly, her spike of worry made a lot more sense.

"There really is a 'man'?!" I asked her, because of course the cattle dog wasn't going to give me any more than he already had.

She averted her gaze. Not. A good. Sign. "He… didn't come aboard alone," she admitted at-length.

"How long has he been following you?" I asked him disbelievingly. And my men hadn't caught on? Shit, I was going to tear them a new asshole…

"I find the threat of the unknown a much more effective tool than blatant showmanship," he said cuttingly. "And, so does he."

"Where was he when Kafele slipped out?" I gestured wildly in the direction of the city.

That at least got a reaction from him. His ears drifted back marginally and something akin to guilt settled over his eyes. "With me," he admitted quietly. "Which I regret, but he was insistent. He seemed to think Lotus might have failed and that you'd have back-up, after all. In retrospect, I think we all overestimated you."

"Fuuuuck you," I drawled. Knowing someone else had apparently been witness—or at least nearby—to my earlier humiliation just added a new layer to this whole shit sandwich. I'd never live this down. Any of it. It takes a lot to make me feel real, palpable shame, but this escapade certainly qualified.

"He's out in the city looking for Kafele now," he confessed, glancing back out as another of the night lanterns were snuffed in the distance. "But I know him; he'll shadow close enough that we're never too far apart. So, don't try anything."

"I thought you were just a cocky sonofabitch," I muttered, bounding past him towards the ramp. "I was impressed by you and everything. Thinkin' you were confident enough to come out here on your own like we'd both said we would."

"You also brought back-up," he pointed out.

"Yeah but me cheating's to be expected," I said, as we all made our way down the pier. "I don't know why, but I bought into the stories; you being some poor-boy-done-good, righteous-hearted true-believer nonsense."

"Your mistake," he muttered.

"Guess so," I navigated us down towards the likeliest street the fennec had taken based on where we'd gone the day before. He didn't know the area; he probably wouldn't have strayed far from the few spots he recognized.

"By my country's standards," he said as we walked, "the only righteous thing I could have done with my life was accept the station I was born into. I only got where I am now through lies, manipulation, and a little luck. You're a man of the world Reed, you should know that."

"I should have," I agreed. "I'm getting an education here." I kept moving my eyes about as we walked, looking for anyone following us. It was frankly ridiculous where my imagination was taking me. I was even looking on rooftops, in the trees, in open barrels, like he'd just pop out of them or something. Who the hell was this ghost he had looking out for him? Had to be a lie.

But, no. Lotus had certainly looked spooked. And she must've had him on her ship for some time if they'd come together, which meant whoever it was, they unnerved her. Great.

At some point we passed Captain Lunden's ship, and I had a sudden thought. "Hey," I said aloud, stopping the two of them in their tracks, "let's get some help. More bodies are always a boon when you're lookin' for someone."

Lotus and Luther looked to one another. "He's not wrong." She shrugged.

"If this is just an excuse for you to cloak yourself in your bodyguards again," Luther warned, "I promise you, that won't matter."

"I believe you," I said wryly. "They apparently weren't of much help last time. But if it comforts you, I won't even gather my boys. I was just going to grab Lunden. He knows this port."

"The otter?" Lotus smiled a little. "I liked him. Sure."

Luther had no further objections, except that he wanted me to hurry, so I rushed aboard to get us some back-up. Truthfully, I actually did want to have more people on my side around me in case when we found Kafele, he was... worse for wear.

Captain Lunden was not hard to convince. It was a little disconcerting how excited he was that our trip here had in fact led to 'misadventure' (his words, not mine), and before I could so much as finish my tale of woe, he was strapping on his pistols and a long knife, and whistling for his boys. A large canine mutt of some kind and a spotted skunk joined us—two of his most reliable men, he assured me—and we were off. Only now, we had twice as many eyes to search with and twice as many mouths to ask around after the wayward fennec.

We were halfway down the pier heading towards the rum district (that's what they called the area of town where all the shanty bars were), when Lunden piped up with a question. "So, Admiral," he always addressed me that way, no matter how much I told him he could just use my name, "you two were out drinking the night before, right?"

"You're going to have to be more specific," I muttered dizzily. "It's hard for me to keep nights'n days straight at this point."

"I'm guessing that's a problem you contend with often," Luther said snidely. "One would think you'd be used to it by now."

"I am," I said without missing a beat, "but it's rare that my timeline matters this specifically, so it's not usually so much of an issue."

"So much boozing will make you fat," Luther muttered, without sounding like he actually cared for my welfare. More just grumbling for the sake of grumbling.

I actually laughed. "That's one I don't get often when people are chastising me for being a lush. Your concern for my figure is touching."

"You were fortunate in your birth," he said with a gesture of his palm, at... all of me. "Those of us with less height and more mundane features need to work at it," he straightened the collar of his duster pointedly. "I don't buy into the Pedigree bullshit, but there's no denying wolves have it

41

on most dogs in build and striking features. You should take care of your body."

He didn't know how wrong he was. My bloodline was anything but fortunate. How could he have known, though? I suppose it was at least good that the condition I'd been born with—the disease that would likely cut my life very short one day, and made me vulnerable at the worst of times—was largely unknown. It was the only secret I'd really managed to keep over the years. And it was the most important one, so… best it remain that way.

"Life's short, mate," I said instead, as casually as I could. "I don't intend to spend mine holding back from doing the things I love just because they might be bad for me. I'd think you'd understand."

He went silent at that.

"That being said, I'm flattered," I said, placing a palm over my chest and running it down through my belly fur. I hadn't bothered putting a shirt back on under my coat. "Good to know you've been enjoying my visage so much that you'd rather not see it tarnished by, god forbid, some excess belly fat."

"I've warned you about the flirting," he growled.

"For what it's worth, I'd love to see you with a bit of a belly," Lotus purred, raking her eyes over my figure with absolutely no shame.

"I'm young yet, give it a few years," I winked at her. "I'll see what I can do for you. I live to make the ladies happy, after all."

Smirking, she tugged a glass, rope-wrapped bottle off her hip and tossed it to me. It was one of those pretty rum bottles some people decorate up with complex knotwork and little charms. She'd probably made it herself. I admired it for a moment before realizing it actually had liquid inside and gasped as I uncorked it. "Oh, lady," I crooned, "you're an absolute angel."

As I drank, Lunden moved up beside me and asked again, "You went drinking with Kafele the night before all of this, right? Two nights ago?"

"You took him into the city the night before?" Luther asked, from somewhere further to my left.

I polished off what was in the bottle, wiping my muzzle and taking a moment to enjoy the burn as it seeped down my throat and the flavors of the rum that were so specific to Dokuro. The toasty afternotes of palm charcoal, coconut milk, a slight saltiness… it was the essence of this place and brought with it a powerful wave of associations and memories. Some of them recent, some of them from previous trips.

Rust-colored eyes… a messy mane of fur…

I blinked, shaking my head.

"I… yes," I said distractedly towards Lunden. He'd asked twice now; I was being rude by not answering him. He was being awful patient with me, considering. "Kafele came out with us the night before we were to meet Luther. Me and the boys. He wanted to see the port. Lad hasn't traveled much before. Was pretty trapped in his situation in Mataa, I think."

I awaited the scolding from Luther, but it never came. Instead, when I glanced his way, he only looked painfully guilty.

Lunden was speaking again. "So, if he'd wanted another drink, he'd probably go to the places you took him to, right?"

"Right," I agreed, "those'll be our first stops. Lotus," I looked to her, holding up the rum bottle. "What is this? It's local, right?"

"Yes," she said, "had it filled at a cask at one of the bars here. Don't remember which. But it was definitely made here. Dokuro's spirits have a distinctive—"

"—flavor," I finished for her, nodding. "Yeah. Something about it…"

"What?" she blinked curiously.

I shook my head. "Not sure. Just…something's…"

I didn't finish, because I honestly wasn't sure how to describe what I was feeling. I just felt like there was something I was… missing? In all of this. Something was bothering me. Something I couldn't recall.

Teeth flashing in a feral laugh. A glint of gold.

"What's going on with you?" Lotus asked me lowly.

"I, uh," I glanced down at the bottle. "I'm just… remembering things, I guess."

"Anything important?" Luther asked impatiently.

"I don't think so," I said uncertainly. "I mean, I don't see how it could be relevant to all this, anyway."

"Drinking flashbacks," Lotus said with complete understanding. Bless her. "Did you black out that night?"

"I mean, yeah," I shrugged haplessly. "But my boys were the ones looking out for Kafele. I had them bring him back to the ship once I knew I wasn't going to bother. I spent the night at one of the bars… somewhere. And as you all know he was fine the next day. Nothing happened to him."

"You're lucky nothing happened to you," Luther rolled his eyes. "Honestly."

"Most people in Dokuro know who I am and not to fuck with me," I said without any bravado. "I might be Admiral, but my fleet can function without me. You pick a fight with me, you pick a fight with the whole Manoratha crew."

"Still stupid," Luther asserted. "You could make a lot of mistakes that inebriated."

"And I'm sure I have," I chuckled. "But Lunden's right, let's start at the bars we drank at that night; those would've been the first places he would have gone, I'd guess. I even remember him saying something about enjoying the palm wine at one of the open-air establishments."

So that's what we did. But the whole time, as we moved from bar to bar, having to knock on doors in some cases because many of them hadn't opened yet, I just couldn't shake that lingering feeling that had begun when I'd finished off the local coconut rum. It was like a single fur pulled taut and snagged in a buckle, a constant reminder that something was wrong, something that was right there beneath the surface, if I could only reach out and pull forth the rest of it from my mind.

We exhausted the few places I could remember bringing Kafele rather quickly, even going so far as to check the brothels nearby in case for whatever reason the fennec did not share Luther's seemingly utter disinterest in women. The cattle dog was offended by the mere concept that he might have taken up with a woman for the night, which confused Lunden, given that he wasn't in on the whole plot (I hadn't thought it right to share the specifics of my scheme here, given the personal nature of them). Denholme was honestly, truly, really bad at keeping his 'dark secret'. How it wasn't known to everyone in his country at this point, I wasn't sure.

I could feel Luther growing more and more anxious as the hours went by. We strayed from the areas we'd thought he'd be in bit by bit, hoping we'd find him passed out under a table; maybe the wine had been too strong. Maybe he'd unintentionally imbibed too much. Maybe he'd taken up with another man, hell, I didn't know.

Once we'd exhausted most of the bars—which took a lot less time with twice as many people, as I'd said it would—at that point, the sinking sensation I'd been grappling with since I'd had the rum had grown to a nearly unbearable level. Moving through the shanty town, especially as it began to open back up and the streets filled with howling, hungover men and early-risers, merchants, and whoever else had business at first light, became a dizzying barrage of half-memories and that tugging feeling of dread. Like I was caught in a slowly-draining whirlpool, but it was coming on so gradually, I hadn't noticed it.

Something was about to hit, hard. I could feel it.

"Fuck, Lotus," I said rather out-of-nowhere as we waited near a hotcake stall. Lunden was getting some much needed breakfast for our group. Luther was off questioning a vendor with an all-night stall who sold Brukicker tonics, a mixture for folks with brutal hangovers that helped alleviate some of the worst symptoms. He was about to shutter for the day, but if the fennec had come by this area at any point last night, he would've seen him.

"What's wrong?" Lotus asked me, munching on a stack of… must've been five hot-cakes, mushed together with peanut butter. Damn. What a woman. "I mean, other than everything."

"I think I really fucked up," I said.

"Yeah, we've established that," she agreed.

"No, I mean…" I look around us, my eyes lingering on one of the bars we'd already visited. The woman tending bar wasn't the same one who'd been on last night, of course. That had been the case most everywhere we'd gone.

I swallowed. "I don't know. I just know I… I did something. I made some kind of horrible mistake that night."

She paused, swallowing a bite of her hotcakes and licking her muzzle. "You're alive, mostly unharmed. Kafele was unharmed, he clearly made it back to Lunden's ship that night, since you had him the next day. What do you mean?"

"I don't know," I emphasized, frustrated. "I can't entirely remember… I just know…"

She twisted her muzzle up for a moment, then grabbed me fiercely by the hand, tugging me towards the aforementioned bar. Stumbling, I followed her. "Easy!" I huffed. "What—"

"We're getting you a drink," she explained. "It'll help."

It took me a moment to understand what she meant, "Oh," I tripped to a stop beside her at the bar, where a squirrel was wiping down the counter. "I think I get what you're saying. Although Denholme is going to kill me if he thinks we're just drinking for the hell of it."

"You need to learn how to properly stand your ground against him," she said irritably after ordering some rum for me. I could smell it from here, the reserve they had in the casks at this bar was definitely of the local variety.

"We only just met," I insisted with an arched eyebrow, "and it's been a thoroughly humbling experience for me so far, to be fair."

"I don't mean you should make an enemy of him," she explained. "Mouthing off to him earlier wasn't smart. You need to handle Amur men with a more careful touch—"

"That only works for you because you're a woman," I pointed out.

She glared at me. "Not like that," she said. "Way to underplay my skills at dealing and diplomacy, by the way. And anyway, wouldn't you be the only one who could take advantage of that in this situation?"

I mused on that. "I guess you've got a point."

"He's an eccentric man," she said with the sort of understanding that only comes from sharing a small ship with someone for a few weeks, "but not… you know… like the rest of them. Not that he isn't painfully Amur—with all the buttoned-up aloofness and baggage that comes with anyone born into that country—what I mean is, he's not just an asshole once you get to know him. He's deeper than that, better than that, and also worse than that. You need to stop barbing him. Try playing nice every now and then; you do not want him as an enemy."

"I've gathered that much," I sighed, reaching out for the topped-off bottle of rum the bartender handed us, tossing her a whole crown for her trouble so early in the morning. She didn't question it, only snapped it up and tucked it into her cleavage before anyone else could notice.

I popped off the cork and brought the beverage to my muzzle, drinking slowly and letting it burn all the way down, trying to indulge in the sensations even more so than I usually did.

He wore more gold than anyone I'd ever seen. It was in his teeth, painted on his claws, dangling from his large ears, threaded through his dreads…

I swallowed, for the first time glancing around at where we were. I'd known this was one of the bars I'd visited that night with Kafele, but I hadn't really remembered when. This had been the last one I'd been at and the one we'd opted to make the meeting spot the next day. The one where I'd spoken to Luther. I'd been sitting over… in that corner…

A woman, her species was a blur, pushed against the wall panting, servicing one of the men—no, one of his men. I'd watched them go at it for a while, he'd asked if I wanted a go at her… I knew I was too drunk.

"Something coming back?" Lotus asked, pressing in against my side. Her fur was warm and smelled of the port and her quarters. Patchouli. She'd been burning it.

I inhaled sharply, another scent prickling my nose.

His fur had a distinctive, greasy scent to it. His musk, I suppose. Sharp and distinctive. He'd leaned in too, while we'd spoken. I'd thought at the time he was as drunk as I was, but I was no longer sure. He was asking a question…

He'd been on my mind since that night, lodged in the back of it. You don't meet a man like that, even plastered, without them making an impression. The fact that I'd met him—that we'd spoken—had stuck in some corner of my memories, waiting for the right moment to rise to the surface.

And then, when I'd been had, when I'd been tied down and laid vulnerable, looking for any bargaining chip I could grasp at, I'd thought of him. And what I knew.

"Oh, no," I said quietly.

Lotus still had her gaze locked on mine, so she saw the moment my memory came rushing back to me. And she saw, I'd imagine, my panic. "'Oh no' what?" she asked, glancing past me towards where I could hear and smell Luther was returning to our group.

I turned weakly towards him, deciding I'd have to meet the man head-on for this one. He deserved that.

"What the hell are you—" he began.

"Roccosal is here," I said quietly.

Both of them went rigid and tense at once. "Excuse me?" Luther was the first to demand.

"Fathom Roccosal," I said, "is here. In Dokuro. I spoke to him, here in this bar, two nights ago."

Luther's fur stood on end, anger rising in his eyes. "How... could you—you just tried to sell him out to me, last night! That isn't a coincidence!"

"No, it's not," I agreed. "Look, I don't know how to tell you this in a way that doesn't make me sound like shit, so let's just all accept at this point that I'm a pile of shit. That night out with Kafele, I got drunk, I sent the fennec back to the ship with my boys for his own good... and apparently at some point after that, I had a long conversation with Fathom Roccosal. Who is here. I'm absolutely certain of it. That must be why I thought of him when I was bargaining with you in the shack. I thought it was just a bolt of inspiration, but—"

"What. Did you. Tell him?!" Luther snarled.

"That part's less clear," I admitted, swallowing. "But I'm pretty certain he asked me about Kafele. Kid stands out."

"He has him," Lotus said with absolute certainty, and damn her, but she was right. She had to be. "He must've grabbed him as soon as he saw him out alone."

Luther sat down heavily on one of the stools beside us. He still looked angry, but now, more than anything, terrified. He didn't speak for fully a minute or more.

And why not? I'd accidentally handed over this trump card I thought I was using playfully—with no real intent to bring harm to anyone involved, just embarrass a man—to an honest-to-god, bloodthirsty predator. Denholme's heart and reputation might not have really been in danger before, since I kind of lacked the spine to ruin a man like that. But Luther had not really known that.

I'd effectively put him through this twice in two days.

And this time, I had no control over the situation.

Once we knew who we were looking for, who we were really looking for, it wasn't hard to find our way to him. And the object of our initial search, as it turned out.

Roccosal was a household name in nearly every port in… the world, really. But especially in ports thick with Pirates, Privateers, and mariners of all stripes. It was only because we'd been in such a hurry and so focused earlier that we'd managed to somehow miss that he was in town. If I'd had my wits about me, I might have picked up on the suffocating presence of so many boys clearly flying under one flag, even if I wouldn't have been able to pick out which one, exactly.

His men were a mixed lot, but they all had one thing in common — the black they tarred 'round their eyes. I wasn't actually sure what they used for it, likely a grease paint of some sort, but once you were looking for it, it was noticeable. Fathom Roccosal was a garish, tacky man, if a legitimately terrifying and competent one. He favored skulls for adornments on his flags, his figureheads, he even lashed them to some of his ships. Like I said, tacky.

I mean a flag? I get that. Nothing wrong with a skull on your flag. Sends a practical message. But there's such a thing as overdoing an aesthetic.

I guess the black eyeshadow was meant to give his men a 'skull-like' appearance. It wasn't anything regional I'd heard of before, and it seemed like an odd, overly-nitpicky detail to force on a disparate band of criminals. But credit where credit was due, he somehow got them all to do it. And that was certainly… something. Spoke to either the fear or respect he struck in the hearts of his men.

I said we found them, but in actuality, it was more like they found us. In that we found a large enough group of his boys who seemed to know what was what and amusedly told us their boss was waiting for me with his recent 'acquisition' and where to find him.

So, he'd already made the connection between Kafele and me. Guess it was too much to hope he'd seized the boy just because he was pretty.

As to how much he knew about why Kafele was here, I couldn't say. But I could tell it was all that was on Luther's mind as we made the walk through the bad part of town, into the worse part of town.

The cattle dog had barely said a word to me since my memories had returned and we'd figured out what was going on. I wasn't even getting anger out of him anymore, just cold condemnation. I could choose to take that as a good sign that he wouldn't murder me first chance he got, but his face looked pretty… murder-y. I was at least certain my mission here had failed utterly. When all of this was over, provided I survived it, he'd probably outright prioritize my fleet at sea from now on. Sail halfway across the world just to kick my ass, even when I wasn't in his backyard.

Y'know, I could be glib about it in my thoughts all I wanted, but the fact was I'd really failed my men here. And I couldn't take a whisker of joy in that. It was probably too late to make things right, but damned if I wasn't going to try, somehow.

We found ourselves 'escorted' by more and more men as we left the main districts of the shanty town and headed inland towards the less developed parts of the small island. The scenery here was limited—about what you'd expect for this area of the world. Overgrown and wet, but not many trees. This island like many others had been clear-cut at some point in the last few decades, likely by Luther's people themselves. The Amurescans loved to raid small island chains like this whether they belonged to them or not, cut down the palm for their oil and burn them for charcoal, then leave the place shelled-out for most anyone else who might have seen fit to settle it. Without the ancient palms, the monsoons washed away most of the good soil, and the place quickly became overgrown by whatever could thrive in the sand, which was usually red-tipped razor grass and inedible weeds. Not much good to people or feral animals any more.

Really, using a place up for all it was worth, then reducing its only living population to one species was... a metaphor for colonization if ever I'd considered one. It was almost impressive that they'd gotten so good at it; they could do it unintentionally now.

Now wasn't a time for politics. Denholme wasn't a colonizer, anyway. And I didn't believe in blaming a person for their country's evils, even if they did make a living defending said country's supply lines. Maybe if the cattle dog and I ever managed to be peaceable with one another, we could talk about that someday.

There were drier, raised sand trails through the nasty foliage and the occasional hovel even this far out of town. Some of the more permanent locals had their dens out here or were making a go at working the land or operating some form of business. I smelled rather than saw there was a tannery out here somewhere and the only real industry worth engaging in: fishing. We passed quite a few places fermenting sauce or oil in barrels and row after row of salted drying racks.

I was just thinking I might pinch a fish when Lotus jabbed me with her elbow. I quickly looked ahead of us and saw what she was indicating. A grove of young palm and dense palmettos ahead was looming, definitely a camp of some kind. Smoke trickled up into the sky from at least two bonfires, obscured by the many fronds. The smell of cooking food and freshly-uncorked booze, as well as less pleasant scents like stale booze, piss, and unwashed musk, confirmed that this was likely a large encampment. Large for this place, anyway. Nothing like the densely-packed warehouses and rooming houses my boys and I crammed into whenever we were in a major port, but then Roccosal couldn't have possibly brought one of his larger ships to an island this small without attracting far too much attention to himself. Also, just… in general. The reefs surrounding this chain were vast and went far out to sea.

Subtly moving my gaze about, I counted at least a dozen men so far that I could see, including the five escorting us. There would be at least as many in the camp, judging by the look of it. If I were in any other port, I'd have a few hundred of my boys. But owing to the 'secretive' nature of my meeting with Luther, I'd come here with only six guards, and none of them were with me now. It was just Lotus, the cattle dog, Captain Lunden and his two boys, and me. And I didn't much like the idea of getting Lunden or his guards killed, even if they'd volunteered to come along for this. They were probably regretting that now, speaking of…

I could have found my men in the city and gathered them up for this, but honestly, I didn't see the point. It was a given that we'd be outnumbered and outgunned here. And regardless, they had a hostage. We had to hope we could negotiate.

Glancing briefly at Luther, I wondered again how much—if anything—they'd gotten out of Kafele so far. I'm sure Admiral Denholme was wondering the same. I was fairly certain I hadn't said anything to Fathom about who Kafele was or why he was here with me, because I had been intent on using that information only against Luther himself. I wanted to trust myself enough to think I wouldn't have gone back on that promise, even drunk.

Was I completely certain of that, though? No. Unfortunately, no.

The camp was everything I expected it to be. And I'd been almost dead-on with the number of extra men. Somewhere between twenty-five and thirty counting the ones I'd seen already. No chance we were fighting our way out of here, no matter how much of a badass Luther thought he was. I, most certainly, was not that much of a badass. And I couldn't be sure if this ghost of his was still following us or how competent an assassin he—they, because who the hell knows—truly was. I think he'd called them a 'he'. But whomever they were, if they'd somehow been following us through the razor grass all this time without being noticed (which ouch), they'd still be at a marked disadvantage against so many men, even with the element of surprise.

And that was putting it mildly.

I tried to put on a confident face as we strode into camp, but inside, I was as uncertain as a baby bird fluttering in its first wind. How the hell was I going to get myself out of this one?

It was hard to miss the shock of rust-colored fur, even across a sand-swept, smoky campsite. The man in question was tall too, taller and broader than me, his mane only accentuating that further. It was currently cinched with a gold bangle, flaring out behind and over his shoulders. He wore the death-mask black around his eyes proudly, which really worked for him. I think it was probably tattooed on, based on the lack of smearing. It accentuated his rust-red eyes, and along with the sharp swipes of two other markings along his cheeks, the gold throughout his mane, pierced through his nose, ears and brow, made him look every bit the bedazzled death's head his 'brand' embodied.

He wore red and black, accented with gold buttons and thick bracelets along his wrists, and all of his weapons looked both expensive and deadly. Man had a fucking look, I'll give him that. And that's coming from me.

"Look who's up bright'n early," the Dhole crowed at me from across the camp, rising slowly from the barrel he'd been sitting on, sweeping his coat-tails aside, and taking several swaying, confident steps towards us. He had every right to be confident; he was flanked by four men larger than he was.

One of them—I noticed after a blink—had a fennec trailing behind him, half-obscured by his bulk. He looked bedraggled and tired, but not

hurt as far as I could tell. I knew the second Luther saw him, because his footsteps staggered.

"Look at you, assuming I slept," I countered, settling a hand on my hip. I did so intentionally, to make it clear I wanted him to see the weapons I had strapped beneath my coat. It wasn't meant as a threat, quite the opposite. It was only polite to show your hand in situations like this. Lay everything out in the open.

He knew he had me. It hardly mattered.

"Oiyahh," Fathom drawled in his mother tongue, reaching over to his left to grab at the shoulder of the fennec and yank him against his side. The fox gave a punched-out, soft 'oh' of breath as the dhole's thick, yellowed claws sunk visibly into the thin sleeve of his sherwani. I felt rather than saw Luther's shuddering breaths, his body tensing, his teeth grinding.

"Up all night again, Reed? Were you looking for this?" the dhole asked entirely too slowly. Gold glittered in his teeth — so I hadn't imagined that. I repressed the urge to roll my eyes. It's like I get it, you're rich. Bastard. I'd be more impressed if I didn't know for a fact that he'd made a considerable amount of that fortune selling people. Men (or women, couldn't forget about those rare pearls like Lotus) with real skill in our trade didn't partake in such low-hanging fruit.

Lotus was the gutsiest sailor here in fact, I'd wager. I couldn't discount Denholme, but I tended to give her the benefit of the doubt if we were gonna make that comparison. For all that he was powerful, Roccosal was a careful Pirate with several Man-Of-War to his name. It didn't take balls to build an empire the way he had, just smarts. I could be reckless, but as a Privateer, I mostly fed on contracts taken out by rich men wanting to fuck with other rich men and shielded myself from the legal consequences as well as one could in my trade. Denholme was a rogue compared to most of his people, but he was still a Navy lapdog if they called on him.

Lotus hunted people like us. With a couple of quick little frigates. That took nerve.

Glancing her way, I confirmed it for myself. She seemed entirely unshaken by the situation we were in. She had less to lose than us I suppose, at least professionally. But personally? She was still out here alone. None of her people to back her up.

Luther, on the other hand...

I willed him without words to stay calm. I doubt he heard my silent prayer, but maybe he sensed it, I don't know. Thus far, his temper hadn't fucked us. The fact was I didn't know the man all that well, so I wasn't sure if he could compose himself. But he'd been volatile in the two days I'd spent with him, on more than one occasion. And now would be an exceptionally bad time for him to lose his shit.

Fathom Roccosal wasn't even looking at him. I'd really hoped for this; he didn't know who the cattle dog was. I'm absolutely certain he knew who 'Luther Denholme' was, but that didn't mean he could put a face to a name. I hadn't known what to expect when I'd first met him, except that he'd be a dog, because he was an Amurescan in a position of power. I'd expected a Pedigree of some sort, and Fathom probably thought the same.

Luther had an intimidating air about him to be sure, and he certainly read as Amurescan, but currently he was dressed down, his looks were mundane at best, and he still carried himself like a commoner. He could've passed for any mariner or thug, and that's how we wanted it.

"Cut the bullshit, Roccosal," I sighed, trying to sound bored. "This is child's play. Honestly. Aren't we above this sort of thing?"

The dhole scratched his chin. "If I didn't know better, I'd think you were putting down my trade, Reed. To my face. But that wouldn't be particularly kind of you, now would it? Nor smart, given that you're here to ask something of me."

"This isn't about trade," I said indignantly. "It's about respect. Petty theft is what I'm speaking of. It ain't that you're buying and selling people in this port; that's none of my business. Now what is my business? Is you taking what's mine. We've got no disagreement currently, you and I. Let's not begin one."

"Now, it was my understanding…" The dhole visibly clenched his paw around the fennec's shoulder. The fox winced, and so did Luther. Only his wince was a lot more angry. "…that you didn't partake in my trade. In fact, I've heard that you and your Atheistic," he nearly spit the word, as though it offended him, "Anarchistic, rag-tag band of pond scum… seem to think it's somehow beneath you to do business in my ports or with my people."

I swallowed. Alright, shit. So, he knew I didn't think well of him. I doubted I'd said something insulting the night I'd gotten drunk or he would've knocked some of my teeth out then. This sounded more like something he'd been marinating in for a while. To be fair, I was known to run my mouth, and I'd been none too fond of the man or his methods since I'd come to know of him. I'd rejected, or rather just never responded to, his invitations to pull me into his little Empire. I found the whole of it pretty despicable, to tell the truth, and I… may have mentioned as much to a lot of people, over the years. I guess he was bound to hear how I felt about him sooner or later.

"Bit hypocritical for a man who don't believe in the Gods to get holier-than-thou with me, now isn't it?" he jeered.

"What's your point?" I growled out, allowing my irritation to show through. "I don't have to like you to respect you, Roccosal. We've never had troubles." I repeated my sentiment from earlier. "And I don't have to outnumber your fleet to be a real thorn in your side, when we're both back on the water. Doubt either of us wants it to come to that."

"Not at all," he confirmed. "But this isn't a fight," he spread his free palm out, "this is business. You seem to want to get your paws on my recent acquisition, here."

"I'm not buying back something you stole," I said. "Return him."

"You aren't a slaver," he emphasized, "which means the fox here wasn't yours to begin with. Just a free-floatin' citizen I picked up off the street. Fair play. Unless you're in the game, now?"

"Fucking hell. Semantics!" I belted out. "He's one of my men!"

"Oh, now I have a hard time believing that," the dhole clucked his tongue, reaching down and grabbing for one of the fennec's paws, tugging it up by the wrists and showing off his smooth, soft palm. "I don't know what he is t'you, Reed," his tone got far too sly for my liking at that, "but a sailor, he is not."

"Fine, let's say he's a slave," I fired back, out of patience for this game. "My slave. Every man here can guess what we keep him around for, so let's not mince words. The point is, he's my property, so respect the trade and give him back."

The dhole cackled, as did many of the men in camp. I was certain none of them had doubted what Kafele's profession or position on my ship was, but that was likely the whole point of that word game—just to get me to say it aloud. They could have it. I'd take admitting that I had a male pleasure slave... servant, whore, whatever each man here chose to call him... on the chin, if it meant getting us out of here. It meant little to me what damage it might do to my reputation, in comparison with what was at stake.

To Luther though, my declaration seemed to have been... earth-shattering. He was literally gaping at me open-mouthed, like I'd just lifted a frigate above my head single-handedly. It was helping our ruse of him being some third party, a hired thug or a man of mine, so I silently willed him to keep it up.

Roccosal's men continued to laugh at me, even as I rolled my eyes. Lotus was looking my way almost... sympathetically? I really would've preferred she not. I couldn't care less what a group of slavers or whatever contacts of theirs they'd doubtless tell this story to said about me. It wasn't worth her worrying her pretty feline head over it. I certainly wouldn't.

I was a little more concerned that people might think I'd started slaving, but... my stance on that was pretty well-known. Probably, most would just think he was a paid whore. Which was fair, because he... was.

When you've got a secret as actually dangerous as mine, you learn your priorities real fast. The world could think what they wanted about me; I knew what odds I was truly against every day. Each moment I drew breath,

I overcame. No matter how humbled, how humiliated, how thoroughly I was laid-low, I knew what I'd defied to live the life I had. No one could take that away from me.

"Is that all you wanted, then?" I demanded. "To drag out my secrets in front of your boys?"

"Well hold on now," he said between chortles. "How do I know we've got the right secret, here? Could be you're just telling me what I want to hear, because the truth of why you've got this," he glanced down at the nervous fennec, "admittedly pretty little thing, and I can see why if you're looking to bend someone and you're not feeling picky, you might mistake'im for a lass—"

Luther made a choked-off bark of noise I immediately raised my voice over, so he wouldn't blow his own cover, "Get to the bloody point!"

"Ohhhh, now that sounded concerned to me," he grinned, practically radiating mirth at this point. His maw opened wide in another gut laugh, and before I could blink, he'd put a foot on Kafele's back and kicked him down onto his knees, drawing the steel at his hip in the same motion. Roccosal's blade fell atop his neck where a collar might rest, right where his spine connected to his skull. Right where he'd cut to take his head...

The fennec cried out as he buckled on the ground, shaking and sobbing, begging in Huudari. His tears dripped down his nose, knuckles white as he clutched at the front of his clothes. It occurred to me then that even if they hadn't harmed him yet, they might have been terrorizing him all night, trying to get answers. Which he clearly hadn't given. He must've at least spent the whole of it incredibly frightened. Normally I'd wave that off, 'fear is part of living', something like that. But I'd brought the fox here, into this, everything that had happened to him was my fault. I was once again gripped with the certainty that no matter what, I had to make this right.

Roccosal grinned through his teeth and pressed the blade hard against Kafele's neck scruff. All of us—Lotus, Luther, and Captain Lunden and his boys—we all took an involuntary step forward, and I felt even my own hand go for my flintlock. Luther had drawn his blade fully. Roccosal's men closed in around us, stopping any further advance. My eyes swept the cluttered, tense crowd, lingering on the cattle dog's shuddering frame. He was a frayed rope pulled taut, one twitch away from snapping.

"What do you want?!" I cried out. "Was humiliating myself in front of your boys not enough for you?!"

"How could it be?" Roccosal sneered. "When you've been insulting me to half the world for years now? Did you really think there'd be no consequences for spitting on my name, Reed? And then you have the... absolute nerve... to cozy up to me when you're drunk, like we're friends?" He spit down in the fennec's direction. "You're a two-faced cur, wolf. You flaunt your presence in one of my ports—"

"Dokuro is no one's port," I couldn't help but interrupt. The gall of this man, calling a free port as 'his' turf.

"It's mine," he snarled out, drawing out the last word. "Everything in these seas is mine. The waters themselves are mine."

A sour look of revulsion passed over every single one of our faces. I didn't even need to look to confirm it. No free sailor—I don't care what origin, your wealth, your religion, your alliance—no one claimed the seas. It was antithetical. It was heresy. It was a betrayal of who we were. Only Kings and Tyrants claimed the water could be owned.

The dhole looked down at the huddled fox, his tone acidic and promising far worse to come. "Don't bring your treasures to me, leave them unaccompanied, and then bark angrily when I take them. This thing? Is mine now. It doesn't matter to me why he's valuable to you; I'm sure there's a filthy little story there, but I don't actually care about idle gossip. Especially not yours, Reed. It makes the rounds one way or another eventually anyway. Your shame is fodder for sea shanties across the world; it has no intrinsic value."

"Then what do you want?" I asked, trying to keep my voice level. "Coin? Some kind of arrangement?"

The dhole lifted his chin, grinding his teeth in a tight smile. "I'd take your head."

I guffawed, but he talked over me once more before I could speak.

"... but I actually suspect he's not worth that much," he waved his free hand. "I won't insult you. No. What I want... is proof that I had you and chose, in my mercy, to let you go. That you lowered yourself before me, that even the famed Grayson Reed is one of my conquests. I want the world to know, whenever you try to speak of yourself so highly above me again, that you were in fact my bitch. And then, any further shit talk from you, any defaming of my character, will be understood as what it is... the bitter talk of another bitch I cast aside."

"You are a very, very small man, Fathom," I muttered, almost so quiet that he wouldn't hear me. But with those ears, he absolutely did. He didn't seem deterred, only flicked his wrist so that his sword was blade instead of flat-down on Kafele's neck.

I bit the inside of my mouth, focusing on the pain so I could keep myself as calm as possible for whatever nonsense was about to come out of his mouth. "I don't know what the hell any of that means. Be clear. What's the price for the fox's freedom?"

He lifted his sword, which had us all breathing a bit easier, until he pointed it at me and opened his mouth again. "Your mane, wolf!"

My hand involuntarily went to one of the beads hanging from the longest dread, the one I always kept dangling over my shoulder so I could play with it. It had some of the turquoise from my family threaded through it.

"I want it, tacked up in my trophy room!" Roccosal crowed. "Another testament to my dominance."

"You're insane," I stammered. "Take my weapons. My... coat—"

"Easily replaced," he replied smugly. "Too easily replaced. No. I want a piece of your soul, Reed. I want to point at it and laugh. And I want my guests to laugh along with me as I tell the tale. There are no riches in this world as priceless as a good story. No satisfaction as sweet as knowing you've taken something that can't be returned. That's why we savor our virgins, our century-old wine."

Speak for yourself, I wanted to say. I preferred women with experience pleasuring men, and year-old rum got the job done just fine for me. I couldn't taste the difference between wines, and I was convinced that anyone who said they could was fooling themselves.

But none of that was the point, right now. Roccosal was still ranting and raving, but he'd named his price. He probably didn't even understand the cultural significance of what he'd asked. If I bothered explaining it to him, he would only take more pleasure in it. So, I didn't. I just gritted my teeth and stared down into the sand for a long time.

"To hell with him," Lotus said, keeping her voice low and reaching for my palm gently. "He's crazy. He'll probably just keep pushing for more even if you do it, don't give him the satisfaction—"

"What are our options here?" Luther whispered fiercely, his voice on the edge of desperation. It was odd to hear the man's confidence so shaken, but I couldn't blame him. Even with the blade off the fennec's neck, he was a miserable sight. I felt for him in my gut. I couldn't imagine what the cattle dog must be going through, whether he'd put the man in his past or not. They'd been close, once.

Lotus had an odd look on her face. "Do you think he realizes what he's asking? I doubt it. I think it really is just a grisly trophy, to him."

"Wait, is there a significance here I'm missing?" Luther asked, sharp as ever.

Lotus flicked her tail about nervously and lowered her voice even further, "In the Carvecian tribes—"

All of our eyes were focused on Roccosal and the way he was waving his sword about. On the men surrounding us. On Kafele. So, no one noticed I'd pulled a knife.

"Admiral..." Captain Lunden was the first to take stock of what I was doing. His voice trailed off, disbelievingly and almost reverently, laced with respect I knew I didn't deserve. Lotus and Luther noticed a few moments after he had, but by then it was too late.

Thankfully, I had a sharp knife. Otherwise, I might have lacked the certainty to saw through the thickest clump of my mane. I cut it right below my neck-line, where I had the bulk of it tied back. It shouldn't have hurt—couldn't hurt—as much as they mattered to me, it wasn't as though it was actually a living, bleeding part of my body. But when the weight of it gave way, I still felt an indescribable emptiness. A sense of loss that sunk in deep, as my head fell forward and the first sensation of wind brushed over the back of my neck.

The whole campsite had gone silent. Even Roccosal. I suppose he'd thought I wouldn't really do it. I don't know what he'd thought. I don't really care.

The grin that split his muzzle was like an open gash. Laughter erupted around us in camp, and I had to clench my teeth shut so hard my jaw hurt. My friends… and I suppose Luther, I wasn't sure how to describe his relationship to me… stared at me in slack-jawed horror.

Having trouble looking at the severed locks, I lifted them up in my paw nonetheless, so that I could unthread the beads and coins, before I handed Roccosal's 'prize' over to him.

"No, no," the dhole stopped me and slowly crossed the space between us, stepping apart from his other men to do so. He dragged Kafele along with him, which while obviously rough on the kid, was a good sign. It meant he intended to keep to his word.

I hadn't actually doubted that. Say what you would of the man; he was, at the end of the day, a businessman. If he got a reputation for not honoring his deals, it would affect his ability to make them in the future. When I'd asked him to name his price for the fox, we'd entered into a transaction. I knew he'd make good on it if I was willing to pay.

The ruddy-furred canine put out his scarred, rough palm. "All of it, as it is," he said flatly. "Don't remove a thing."

The very last of my connections to my heritage, to my family, to the past I still had so many complicated, conflicting feelings over, was threaded through those dreads. I didn't bother explaining that to him. He already knew, I'm sure.

That was the point.

But Lotus was right, he'd missed the deepest significance here. The one that concerned my future. And it was going to stay that way. He'd never have the pleasure of knowing that.

The locks slipped through my fingers as we made the trade, and I heard Lotus's angry snap from behind me, "This is some petty shit right here, Fathom."

"Leave it," I told her quietly. "It's just fur. It'll grow back."

The dhole finally shoved the fennec in my direction, and I caught him in my arms, squeezing his shoulders in my hands reassuringly before passing him to Luther, who'd moved up beside us like a good loyal thug would have. He mostly managed to keep the venom from his eyes as he backpedaled with Kafele looped protectively in his grip. The fennec let out a choked sob, all but throwing himself against the cattle dog's chest. I was a bit concerned at how that looked, but Denholme actually did manage to keep his wits about him and remain cold and professional in appearance. Just a subordinate doing his job.

"Now get the hell off my island," the dhole said almost good-naturedly. Like this had all been fair sport we'd been playing, and he expected us to be friendly rivals from this point forward. "Except you, lovely," he nodded in Lotus's direction. "You're always welcome in my waters."

"You have a death wish?" she asked boldly.

He 'hoho'd, sheathing his saber at his belt. "The oxen doesn't fear the eagle, lass. I'm too big to be prey to you."

"You say that about enough people, eventually you're bound to be wrong," she said, curling her muzzle.

He lost his grin, at that. And with good reason. The inference there was clear. His enemies were legion at this point. And if enough of us banded together...

He had to know that already, of course. For a single, tense moment, I worried that Lotus's words might have put us back in danger. But the tension passed, and he only snuffed at her.

"I thought you were smart, woman." He shook his head, clucking his tongue. "We might've had use for you. I might've had use for you. But now that you're closer... you've got his musk on you," he gestured at me, "so I'm not sure I would've wanted you, anyway." He looked back at me. "I hear you get sick from fooling with fox boys."

I was past worrying that Luther was going to lose his calm, especially now that he had Kafele back, but I was done listening to this cur. "Come on." I gestured at my group, turning my back on Roccosal. "We're done here."

We were clear of the camp, making our way back down the sandy path through the razor grass, when I heard the tell-tale, sharp whistle of a bolt, followed by a pained scream.

That had definitely been Fathom Roccosal screaming.

I whirled, just in time to see the man, still standing in the middle of the camp, apart from all of his boys, crumpling to one knee. The silver and black shaft of a crossbow bolt was protruding from his chest, dangerously close to his heart. But if it'd hit his heart, he wouldn't be howling like he was. The man's billowing coat and what looked to be a leather cuirass beneath it may have deflected the shot just high enough up that it'd missed his vitals. But regardless, it looked deep.

"Nice shot," I had to say aloud, before the expected cries of alarm and the cocking of rifles and pistols went up amongst the camp.

Followed shortly by Roccosal's strangled roar of, "KILL THEM!"

"Come on!" Luther grabbed for Kafele's hand and dashed into the tall grasses, the rest of us following suit. A few shots plunked down into the sand behind us, far too late and far too wide. And then we were surrounded by a forest of stinging, dense shrubbery, whipping and tearing at us as we fled.

Despite that, I couldn't help but laugh.

"Was that your man?!" I cackled in Denholme's direction. Or at least I think it was. It was a little hard to keep track of who was who in this invasive undergrowth.

"Of course it was," he answered between heavy pants. "He's going to be angry he missed the kill shot."

"Nice try, though," I shook my head. "That couldn't have been easy."

"I told you."

"Couldn't he have waited until we were clear?!" Lotus interrupted, sounding more irritated than angry.

"Probably thought it was the best chance he had," I shook my head. "Would've been worth it to take that bastard out if he'd managed it."

"You know this means war, right?" Lotus said. Again, she didn't sound angry. Just resigned.

"I'd say you already made that declaration yourself," Luther snorted.

"Ouuu, a Pirate War?" Lunden piped up, navigating the grasses with far more ease than the rest of us.

Otters.

"Don't sound so excited," Lotus muttered. A shot clipped by us in the grass, a little too close for comfort. Kafele was looking at all of us having this conversation while we ran for our lives like we were crazy people.

"Any war where sea charts are that important is good for business!" Lunden said excitedly.

"Hey, is your man going to be alright?" I asked Luther.

"He'll be fine." He seemed pretty certain of that. "Just upset he missed, I'm sure. Like I said."

We made it to a clearer patch sometime later, and we'd gotten far enough that I was pretty certain we were good to take a breather. Not for long, but Kafele in particular seemed to need the rest.

Slumping against a tree myself, I took a few moments to laboriously pull air in and out of my lungs and stare off across the horizon. I could smell smoke, see distant blocks of shapes that were probably buildings; we were coming up on the coast. Hardly surprising, it was nearly impossible to get lost on this island, it was incredibly tiny.

My thoughts went blank for a little while. I didn't even really process all of what had happened, I just... went peacefully numb and quiet inside. It took me a few moments before I began to realize it wasn't just my mind turning off for a bit.

And then I remembered I was, essentially, alone. Not in the physical sense, but no one here... no one here knew about my condition or what to do if this was going to be a bad one.

There was the fear. I'd only feel it for the briefest of moments, before I couldn't feel anything at all. As I always did, I wondered if I'd wake up from this one at all.

But thankfully... the tremors passed quickly. I felt myself slide down against the tree. My rear hit the sand, my legs splayed, my body tingled and nearly slumped, and then, it was over. I don't honestly think anyone noticed. Or if they did, they likely just thought I was exhausted.

Sometimes the seizures were like this. Small, inconsequential.

Sometimes I could hide them.

Luther and Lotus had been talking. Blinking, I looked their way and caught the tail end of what they'd been saying. "—never said what all of that was about," Luther said. "Some kind of cultural meaning, I'm guessing?"

"I..." Lotus hesitated, looking my way. "I highly doubt Roccosal knew about that tradition. He just likes collecting heads, scalps... man's fixated. I think it really was just a trophy to him."

Luther arched an eyebrow at her. "You know I'm just going to ask around and look it up when all of this is over if you don't tell me."

"It's a marriage offering," I spoke up, my tongue feeling clumsy in my mouth. "Tribespeople intended for one another, sometimes... not always, but sometimes, especially amongst the wolf tribes... they'll cut their manes for one another when they wed. It's meant to symbolize starting their lives over, making a change for someone else. We..." and at this I paused, "...we aren't supposed to cut them for any other reason, except for health."

Lotus got a subdued expression, her voice softer than usual. "I know you've left your tribe, Reed, but I'm sure even if they somehow knew about this, they wouldn't hold it against you—"

"I didn't cut it for Roccosal," I said, finally lifting my muzzle so I could look at my companions. I moved my gaze to Luther. "I did it for him."

The ragged-furred, exhausted cattle dog stared back at me. But he looked lost for words. "I..." he began.

"Don't," I shook my head, slowly pushing myself up, trying not to show how weak my legs were. "I don't want anything more from you, least of all

61

thanks, if that was your inclination. This... all of this... these two wretched days... happened because I tried to force something through leveraging your..."

I took too long deciding on my words, but all the same, he remained silent. Giving me all the time I needed to find them.

"I'm just really sorry," I finally supplied hoarsely. I opened my eyes slowly and inclined my head slightly in his direction. "For everything. I don't know if all of this was enough? But. I'm not going to ask you for another damned thing. Just take your fox and go."

"Uhhm," Lotus cleared her throat. "Not to break up your dramatic moment here, but we all need to go. Together. We need to leave this port, now, all of us. We need to sail together and get clear of these waters together, too. Roccosal's probably only got a few ships here, so we can count on his cowardice to keep us safe, at least until we can meet up with our respective fleets. But he'll pick us off if we separate."

"I hope you're ready to take that man on," Luther said, glancing sidelong at me with one predatory yellow eye.

I balked visibly. "Wh... you mean, with you?"

"You really do know where his cove is, right?" he asked.

I nodded, holding out a paw to him. All of the mess of the last two days aside, this sounded like a deal. And I wasn't so torn up over my mane, or hungover, or remorseful, to look a gift horse in the mouth. This was the whole reason I'd come here, after all.

In the end, if I got it... who cared how I'd gotten it?

"An Alliance," I offered, keeping my hand out. "Information, a temporary cease-fire, and a cut of the take from all his vessels?"

Hesitantly, he put his palm out as well. We clapped them together at last, and I swear to you, the relief that washed over me was damn near orgasmic. I hadn't... in fact... fucked this one up.

...not entirely, anyway.

"One thing I want one hundred percent of, though," I chuckled.

He tilted his head at me.

"My mane," I laughed. "I thought that'd be obvious."

"Oh," he rolled his eyes, then clenched his hand around mine. "Alright, yes. Agreed. And I'm taking Kafele. Obviously."

We released our hands, and I pulled him in by the shoulder, instead. He seemed still overall offended by my physical person, but went along with it. We were making progress.

"Although with you taking him off my hands, my crew's a man down," I said good-naturedly. "You ever considered taking up the Privateer life?"

He gave a mirthless laugh. "Hnfh. Don't tempt me. The general shame-lessness you so casually display is... a siren's call, to be sure."

I knew what he was referring to, obviously. Not wanting to re-hash my earlier embarrassment (the rumors that were sure to follow this would certainly do enough of that), I waved a hand, going to my usual place of respite. Humor.

"I'm serious! I'm down my 'male pleasure slave' if you're taking the pretty fox away-"

"A-huh?" Kafele only now just seemed to come to, realizing we'd been talking about him.

"Wolf, I have warned you about this," Luther growled out.

"Those are hard to come by," I continued, because I'm a fool and for some reason I couldn't stop myself.

"Reed," he snarled.

"So there's an opening—"

I had so little warning. I'd seen by now that the cattle dog was fast on the draw, but I hadn't expected he'd be so strong.

In retrospect, like all of the things that tend to happen to me, it was my fault for antagonizing him. Repeatedly. When he'd asked me again, and again, and again, not to.

His fist clenched in my coat, snagging in some of my chest fur in the process, and before I could process that I was being man-handled by someone a head shorter than me, my back was against a tree, my paws were losing traction in the sand, and his muzzle was crushing into mine.

I live large, I like aggressive, forward women, and I have been known on more than one occasion to piss my partners off intentionally, just for the sake of getting in one last hate fuck on their way out the door. So, when I tell you I have never been kissed breathless, I want you to understand the gravity of that statement.

It wasn't even a good kiss. It couldn't possibly have been, we'd connected too quickly, I'd been thoroughly unprepared, and he was way too strong. Our teeth clacked together, his muzzle was pressed to mine suffocatingly tightly, and when his tongue found mine—because yes it did, it absolutely did, because I'm a whore of a man and even under attack, I couldn't help but open my fucking mouth—we both tasted like booze, blood, and the kind of breath you only have after not sleeping for two days and only rinsing your mouth out with more booze.

And Lotus had the absolute nerve to whoop at us and laugh uproariously at my predicament. Even Kafele, who I'm fairly certain was still in a state of shock from the night he had, gave a quiet, 'Oh'. Lunden was snorting in laughter at me... and all the humiliation was starting to pool in a very inconvenient area of my body.

When Luther at last released his grip on my chest and pulled back, he looked hazy-eyed, dangerously relaxed, and far too smug.

"You really need to learn to stop digging yourself in deeper, Reed," he said, his voice like gravel.

I was finally able to breathe, but it still took me a few moments before I could speak again. "I really. Really do," I agreed.

❧ ❧

When we made it back to Lotus's ship, there was a distinctive silhouette waiting for us near the docks that I didn't recognize. That's not to say I would've recognized most people here. I was in a port of strangers. But this one, if they'd been a member of Lotus's crew anyway, I would have remembered.

He was really fucking tall.

My instant thought was that we'd been cut off—some of Roccosal's boys had beaten us here, and the tall dog was the negotiator, here to let us know what the terms of our deaths were going to be. Would've been right gentlemanly of them considering what had just happened.

Thankfully, we'd thought ahead, all of us seasoned in the arts of dealing with 'those that want to kill you'. Not a one of us in our mis-matched group (save perhaps Lunden) hadn't spent a portion of our lives on the run. So, I'd gone ahead, slipped up around each of the ramshackle buildings whenever we turned a corner in the city, and tried to make sure there wasn't an ambush somehow already waiting for us. We were ahead of our pursuers, one would think, but we'd stopped to catch our breath and for me to reap what I'd sown, so… who knew?

I was seconds away from giving the signal to run (our plan if we'd been caught up to was to try Lunden's ship next obviously, although Lotus was sour on the subject of abandoning her vessel) to my companions, when Luther jogged up to me and pushed me aside, squinting into the sun.

"Oh, thank God," he muttered, then much to my alarm, raised his voice. "Johannes!"

The tall canine turned our way, then began striding towards us. Even swaddled up though he was in a long gray cloak and hood, I could tell his ears were alert, his tail was rigid; he was as on-guard as the rest of us. And I couldn't help but notice something else as he drew closer. He was soaked from toe to mid-calf in mud, the edges of his cloak were similarly muddy and torn in places and there were shreds of razor-grass caught in his outfit. It was hard to see clearly what he was wearing beneath the cloak, but at least some of it looked like hardened leather, likely over a gambeson beneath.

It wasn't hard to put the pieces together. No one bothered armoring themselves any more save for adornment… or if you were a professional killer. My general rule of thumb was to not get into fights to the death in the first place. Even in my line of work, instances where I'd have to actually scrap with steel or risk being clipped by a round were rare. Most of the time, you want to rely on overwhelming odds or take your losses and run, like we'd done today.

Now, did I own some leathers? Absolutely. I just didn't wear them casually. The difference between a man who walks the streets in gear like that and a man who keeps them in reserve for a particularly bad day is like comparing someone who owns a ship like mine to a man with a leisure yacht.

"The infamous assassin makes his appearance, at last," I said with a broad grin, which was not returned by the man in question. If anything, his already dour expression soured further upon being greeted by me.

Rude.

"Why is he here?" was his first question, directed: at me of course, although it was clear he wasn't speaking to me. He had one of those really thick, odd Amurescan accents you could only pin down to a region if you were from the country.

"We've still got some details to go over," Luther said brusquely, putting a hand on the man's shoulder for a moment before walking past him. Even the slight touch spoke volumes, though. Amurescan men didn't touch one another on principle unless they were family or very, very close. And they clearly weren't family, at least not by blood; the tall fellow was a wolfhound of some sort.

"He can travel on the ship that brought him here," the wolfhound said tersely, still not breaking eye contact with me. He had the same aura of intimidation Luther had when we'd first met, with the caveat that I knew he'd literally just arrived here from trying to kill someone. Another man in my profession, even.

So obviously, it was time to antagonize him.

I had barely opened my mouth before Lotus shoved up beside me and bodily cut me off from whatever I was about to blurt out (couldn't tell you what it would have been, my thoughts go directly to my mouth sometimes, and even I don't know what they're going to be until they've already been said).

"You nearly got us all killed back there, you know," she said icily, crossing her arms over her bosom.

I probably would've said something similar, just more…fun.

He barely flicked a gaze her way. "It would have been worth it to behead that snake's empire."

"Awfully easy for you to say," she growled, "but it was our lives you gambled with. Including your Admiral's."

"He would have agreed with my choice," he said with dead certainty, turning and stepping back away from us. Notably, he didn't turn his back on us... simply stepped to the side so that we could walk past him.

She lifted her muzzle and strode past him, tail swishing—intentionally, I'm sure—around his ankles and past his groin as she did. He had exactly the reverse reaction to that I would have, curling his mustached lip and stepping back a further foot. His body language grew even tenser than it had started at, which was saying something. He'd been holding a collapsible crossbow, a nice model I'd never seen before, must've cost a fortune, pointed down and resting along his hip. His gloves were stretched taut over his knuckles where they were holding tight to it. The stark rigidity and discomfort he was clearly in made him... slightly less intimidating, if I'm being honest.

Lotus had clearly known she could get to him this way, too. She'd been sharing a ship with him for a time, now. Knew how to get under his skin and wanted to, for some reason. If I had to guess, he probably wasn't comfortable being on a ship captained by a woman. Might not be comfortable with women in general. There's an Amur for you.

"'Johannes,'" I parroted back the name I'd heard Luther use earlier, arching an eyebrow. "That's an Abbey name, isn't it? There's a collection o'names like that they usually assign to—"

"It is only by the grace of God that you are still breathing this morning," the wolfhound snapped out, quietly but firmly, turning his gray eyes on me. "You are absurdly fortunate that there happens to be another man of your profession here who is somehow more sinful, more murderous, and thus more deserving of my attention right now than you. If Admiral Denholme had heeded my advice? I would have spared the world the continued scourge of your existence the first day we made landfall here, while we had you separated from your fleet and easy picking. And I would have felt absolutely no shame in it. You deserve to hang and whatever judgment comes after."

"Fuck," I held up both of my palms. "Alright. I hear you. Although... if it were that simple man, why didn't you?"

"The Admiral was convinced you held some kind of ace, that you were acting too bold in inviting him here without some means to force his hand." He glared down at me.

I didn't say anything. I tried not to betray anything in my expression, either. I couldn't be sure if this man was in on the Admiral's secret or not, and I wasn't about to go ruining his reputation with a subordinate now that we were finally getting back on the right track.

So, instead I went with, "And?"

"And he was right," he said irritably, like it was obvious. "He tends to be."

I smirked. "You sound annoyed."

"A man's sins are his own to clean up, but anything that threatens the fleet becomes my concern." He gestured again towards the ship. "If you're coming aboard, do so now. Or go back to the vessel you sailed here in. I don't care. Whatever it is Luth—Admiral Denholme wants to discuss with you, we can do it at sea, if necessary."

"I agree that we should get moving," Lunden piped up from behind me, glancing worriedly back through the city. "If there's going to be trouble, I'd rather be aboard my vessel and on the water."

"I think we all would," I agreed, turning towards him first, then glancing out to sea. "Ahhh… alright. The bald cay, remember? The one you pointed out on the way here that washed out last storm season?"

Lunden nodded. "The reefs are broken up there, and it's mostly uncharted. Good place to meet. Sunset?"

I nodded back. "Make sure all my boys are aboard, please?"

He gave a lopsided smile. "You got it, Admiral."

We pulled out of port just in time to see some of those tar-eyed men sniffing their way around the docks. Of course, they didn't know which vessels we'd come here in, and it was a high traffic port. So, we had a good chance of getting away from this one clean. But I personally wouldn't feel safe until I'd made it back to my fleet. I'm sure Luther felt the same.

The skies were clear blue and endless, fading into the horizon. The delineation between the sea and the heavens was a hazy, eternal destination, marked only by waypoints, pinpricks of land in the vast expanse of churning brine that covered most of the world. It was simultaneously the most freeing and most terrifying sensation one could feel, being out on the water on a calm, clear day, seeing nothing but more and more blue in every direction. Sometimes I just wanted to sail, forgo navigation of any kind, just feel the gnawing unknown. You get used to climbing a mast, to being shot at or stabbed, you can get numb to most of the world's terrors. But the sea… it has never stopped frightening me. It has never failed to make me feel.

You can always tell the people who feel the same. Those that understand. That afternoon, as I stood leaning against the railing, watching Dokuro fall away from us so easily, disappearing behind the curve, I only had to look to my left and my right to know these two new acquaintances I'd made these past days, they were kindred souls. Lotus, I'd never have doubted. I would have put money on her being a real mariner, truly loving the sea, just based on her reputation. But Denholme…

There are many Amur men who take to a Navy life, who even command multiple vessels, who don't love what they do. But watching his eyes grow glassy in the salty spray, rough fur fluttering like leaves in the wind, all the tension bleeding out of his body as he soaked in the sun and stared like a man transfixed into that blue abyss… I saw all I needed to.

I was glad in that instant I hadn't made an enemy of this man. I was gladder still to see the fennec beside him, leaning just slightly against his arm on the railing. No one looking on would have batted an eye, the connection was subtle… and probably more complicated than I'd ever understand. We'd be dropping Kafele back home soon enough, and I had no doubt the two men would never see one another ever again. And it was probably best that way.

But, even if it had been for the wrong reasons, I was glad in that moment that I'd brought them back together for a short time. Maybe they'd mend some of what had been broken, whatever hurt they'd left one another with.

Maybe I was just trying to make myself feel better about this whole thing. I dunno.

Something brushed past my leg, and, unlike the puritanical wolfhound, I leaned into it. Lotus purred lowly as she moved past me, her hip scraping mine, her tail dancing across the back of my calves and curling around them for a moment before she sashayed off towards the Captain's quarters.

"Keep me appraised!" she called up to the lookout. A distant yell confirmed he'd heard her.

She glanced only once in my direction, but it was all I needed. Pushing myself back from the railing, I cut past several of her boys who were giving me knowing looks, then bounded down the stairs to the door she'd left open for me.

❧ ❧

The flood gates opened, the monsoon of pure, ravenous energy that was Lotus, the hull-cracker, the predator of predators, was unleashed.

The moment she got me inside her cabin, she wasted little time. We'd gone through every stage of this several times over now, and apparently she was no longer interested in drawing out the foreplay. She spun and pinned me against the door right off, slamming it with our combined weight and planting her big paws on either side of mine, her thighs pressing into my own a moment before the rest of her body did. She bucked her hips against mine to further secure me in place before her muzzle crashed into mine, tongue swiping past my canines before I'd so much as had time to take a breath.

I didn't care if I never breathed again. She was all I wanted in the world right now, and I mean that literally. Everything else, my entire fleet, would've been hers for the taking if she'd asked.

But the yearning was mutual, apparently. Anyone who says women don't desire physical affection—the indecent kind—is in the unenviable position of never being wanted by a woman. The fact is, when they've got a hunger for you, they can be as voracious as any man. And oh my stars, was I glad for it.

Our tongues explored one another's muzzles, sliding past canines and tasting one another for all we were worth. For better or worse really, neither of us had a chance to gargle with anything other than booze this morning. At least it was the same booze.

Her big, broad paws found their way up over my shoulder, the other beneath my coat and along my lower back, claws extending as they traced their way through my fur. She paused only when her touch found its way along my neck ruff, to the back of my head, where my mane had been chopped short.

She pulled away, licking at her muzzle and gasping out a sigh that I echoed. But her gaze turned softer, more concerned. I only shook my head. "It's fine," I assured her again. "Like I said before, I can grow them back."

"But your charms…"

I sighed out through my nose, stroking her cheek ruff. "They're just beads, coins, and shells. I'll get more."

"Some of them are irreplaceable, I'm sure." She was cupping my ear now, petting me comfortingly.

I couldn't help but tip my head into her ministrations. She'd clearly pet a canine before, and I wasn't about to let her skill go to waste. "Some of them," I relented. I couldn't deny it. I'd never be able to replace the turquoise beads from my tribe. I'd burnt that bridge long ago.

"I'll get them back for you," she promised, leaning in with one arm propped against the doorway, almost caging me in as she made the promise, so I couldn't look away.

I laughed despite myself. "You'll take on Fathom for me?"

"Not for you," she countered, brushing our muzzles together again. "But he's competition, I don't like his methods, and anyway… seems like we'll have help."

"You really want to engage in some kind of joint venture with the Cerberus fleet?" I asked skeptically.

"Why not?" She flashed her canines at me, nipping at my muzzle. "We can ride their wake. Let them do the heavy fighting, make opportunistic strikes where we can. Claim as much of his shit as possible in the process. And get what's rightfully yours back. We leave Denholme with the mess, and fuck all the way back to Dokuro." She paused. "Or whatever port we decide to offload our spoils."

I gave a long, shuddering sigh. "Goddamn, woman," I groaned. "You really are better at this game than I am."

"Intimidated?" she teased.

"Oh, absolutely," I nodded as I slid a paw around to grip her rear. "And I have never been so hard."

She gave a feral grin and slowly hooked a claw around my belt, stepping back into the room and tugging me along with her. Any other time, I might've taken in the sights, her room was lovely and eclectic and full of oddities she'd gathered in her travels, no doubt. I'd have to ask her about her décor later. For now...

I shed my coat and bandoliers as we made for her bed, a sizable four-poster that would easily support the both of us. Maybe it was a blessing in disguise it'd taken us so long to get to this point. At least we wouldn't break anything in here.

She similarly let her weapons and most of the possessions on her person drop carelessly to the floor, the both of us leaving a cluttered trail in our wake. What can I say? Some people prefer rose petals, but in our case it was long knives, flintlocks, and pewter cups.

She turned me when we made it to the bed, the back of my calves pressing into the mattress before she bore my top half down. She prowled over me before I could get my legs up on the bed, so half-hung over the edge they stayed, as she encased me between her thick thighs. She unlaced her top before finally, at long last, tugging it up over her head...

...only to reveal the wraps beneath. Of course. Someone as well-endowed as this woman wouldn't be able to go without. I think I'd noted that in the past, actually. Still, it was progress. She was on top of me, she'd removed her leather girdle, so I could finally see her soft, striped stomach. I chanced to press my palms up and over her hips, and she allowed me to stroke and squeeze her curves while her hands were busy behind her back. Undoing those wraps, I hoped.

"Pants. Off. Now," she commanded.

For a confusing moment I thought, for some reason, she was talking about herself... and then it clicked. "Oh," I said, before reaching down and unlacing my britches. I wasn't wearing a shirt, hadn't been all day, so this was really my last piece of clothing. Since I'd left polite society, I'd never bothered with smallclothes. And honestly, I'd never looked back. Useless. Just more steps.

She had to lift her hips up to allow me the chance to kick my britches and spats off. I was internally glad I preferred to wear them loose or that would've been an awkward chore. I was so distracted in completing the task for her, I didn't notice she'd reached down to grip my cock until she already had it in her palm.

"Fhhhh-ohhh," I hissed out as her rough paw pad stroked the length of me, squeezing the whole way up. A bead of precum gathered at my tip. Glancing down along my body, I could already see the bulge of my knot still in my sheath. That brought about an interesting question I'd mused on earlier, actually...

As if she was a bloody mind-reader, or perhaps because her eyes were following the path my own were making, she shifted her hand lower, gripping me by the fuzzy knot in my sheath. I nearly stopped breathing.

"Yes," she intoned. "All of you. I want everything you've got to give, wolf. And you'd better not half-ass this because you're tired. I think I've earned your full effort."

"Yes, ma'am." I swallowed, reaching up to grip and squeeze her hips, then her ass. I highly doubted she wanted me to be hesitant with her; she'd given just about the firmest consent I could imagine. And I would. After this, after we'd parted and gone off to whatever parts of the world we found ourselves in, I was certain I'd imagine this many, many times over.

She finally un-did her wraps, her breasts swaying free, her whole chest heaving with a relieved sigh I could feel in my bones. I wanted to give her that kind of relief myself, but it was gratifying seeing it all the same.

"I can't imagine," I chuckled, pressing my paws up along her ribs to cup and gently squeeze my fingers into the soft, warm fullness of her breasts. Her nipples were a soft pink, the same color as her nose, and quick to respond to my kneading touch. I kept my pressure soft and massaging for now, since they were likely tender from being wrapped up for... fuck. Almost two days now. Had we really been dealing with this issue that long? After this, I really needed to sleep.

"No, you can't," she agreed, popping the buttons on her own, far more tight-fitting trousers, before shucking out of them. She did so far more artfully and looked far more alluring than I had when I'd been wriggling clumsily beneath her. I was glad I couldn't see myself in these situations, honestly. I'm sure I looked much less appealing than I imagined.

Once we were both—at long last—nude, we got to the important business of touching one another absolutely everywhere. We were both exhausted and over-eager to find our pleasure in one another, so I doubted very highly that we'd go through the trouble and time of using the silk rope again. But we'd have a few days together at the very least, so I was in no rush on that accord. Right now, all I wanted was to grind my hips up against hers and rub my aching cock up into her soft, weeping mound. She seemed to concur.

I gave a guttural groan at the first feel of slickness. We'd found a good angle, or rather she had (credit where credit is due), and she was rubbing me into her crease, the molten heat and wetness there promising so much more. She was purring nonstop, the vibrations connecting with me through every part of her body in contact with mine. It was like an unending moan, a constant reminder to me how much she wanted me. I couldn't get enough.

I gasped out, somehow, "H-how... do you want me? Just... like this?"

"I'll ride you after a good rest," she whispered back into my ear, biting at it, tugging on my earring. She chuckled when I whined. "Right now I think I'd tire out before we got anywhere. You like playing with my tits?"

I guffawed. "Is that even a question?"

"Then on my back," she said, before finally rising up off of me and lying down beside me on the oversized bed. She looked utterly gorgeous, blinking hazily up at me. "Don't be gentle with my chest, either. I'm tough all-over. You ever been with a tigress?"

I shook my head as I moved up onto my knees, kneeling over her and gripping her thighs, my claws pressing into the downy white fur as I spread her out beneath me, drinking in the sight and committing it to memory as best as I was able.

"You'll know if you're going too hard, because I'll tell you," she reached up with one hand, cupping my cheek ruff before gripping my jaw and pulling me down for a long, smoldering kiss. "But on the whole, I trust you, Grayson. The rumors about you are all over the place, but... given what I've seen the last few days, you seem like a good man."

I kissed her again, gentler. "I'll give you all I've got, but I won't hurt you. I don't like hurting people."

"I believe you." She opened her muzzle and pressed back up into the kiss, and this time we didn't stop.

True to my word, I pushed into her, pausing only briefly on the first thrust to sink past that initial tensing, and then she released it in a long sigh, and I slid fully into her. I couldn't bottom out in most women, so it was incredibly satisfying.

I groaned into her muzzle, and she groaned back, and I braced my palms first against the blankets to begin rocking into her. But soon, I was content that I didn't need that leverage and moved to leaning on one elbow, so the other hand was free to go back to exploring her body. She was purring and moaning at the slow strokes, but those moans took on a different tempo when I began kneading and squeezing at her chest again. And even more so when I increased my pace.

I got up to a good rut fairly fast compared to how much time I usually preferred to take. She took it so well, wet and hot and deep, fully encasing me on each stroke. Her thighs were quivering where they clutched around me, body rolling back up into my motions, answering my verses like a shanty, her body calling back to mine. We fit so well together. When I felt my knot slip free of my sheath sometime into the act, I wasn't even worried.

If anything, it excited her. She began pressing her hips up more wantonly against my own, her moans into my mouth encouraging me, paws clinging at my shoulders and hips, claws a constant threat. She seemed to know just how much to extend them at all times, though, to avoid any real damage. I guess when you're a cat, it's something you do instinctively with enough practice.

Speaking of species differences…

"You ever," I panted out, my nose nuzzling its way down between her breasts now, "take a canine…fully…before?"

"I know," she huffed, one hand coming down to smack me encouragingly on the buttocks, "what t'expect. We've got nowhere to be."

I groaned at the implication and brought my hips down into hers just a little bit faster, a little bit harder, at that. I felt the first hints of her body trying to accept my knot, but one or two hard thrusts wouldn't do it. I'd have to really mean it.

My motivation wasn't far off. With her mouth free, her moans were more becoming wanton cries, which I was absolutely certain the people on the ship above and below us would hear. But if she didn't care, then I sure as hell didn't.

I could feel her tensing towards a crescendo, and it was a damn good thing, because I wasn't far off myself. I kept my pace up, lowered my muzzle to her chest and lathed her soft mounds with my tongue, even teasing with my teeth. And that did it.

She broke with a long, drawn-out roar and bucked her hips against mine. The intent was clear, so I braced myself and pounded into her with all the force I was willing to give it. The release of pressure as her body accepted my knot was an immense relief to me, but probably far more intense for her. Her moan cut off into a choking gasp, and I stilled inside her as her body slowly adjusted to mine. By then I was cumming, of course… burying myself fully in her had more than done the trick. But I was fully seated, so I had no issue whatsoever ceasing my motions, and just enjoying the feel of pouring myself down into her heat.

My whole body began to uncoil, my muscles wanting to give way and drop me like dead weight atop her. I held off, if barely. But I didn't resist dropping my head down against her chest and panting into her cleavage, getting some hardcore nuzzling in.

At length, she shakily began to pet my head, her body relaxing, as well. "I'm alright," she assured me before I could ask.

I snuffled out a non-response, barely able to form coherent thoughts at the moment, let alone words.

"Fuck," she breathed out. "It's about gods-damned time we knocked that out."

I started to laugh. It was all I could think to do at this point. Before long, she joined me.

We lay there, joined, somewhat hysterical in our relief. Somehow, we'd all gotten through this. It had gotten worse, and worse, and worse, until it finally got better.

And now?

Hard to say. But I'd made two new friends, one of which was willing to sleep with me. Maybe both of them could get lumped into that category, come to think of it?

All in all, a good deal.

ACT II — THE HUNT

Lightheaded. That's how I felt now; every waking moment that I took stock of myself, that I was self-aware enough to feel it. Which was more often than I would have wanted. The booze only helped so much.

I couldn't stop touching it, either. It was like having a bad tooth or a scab you couldn't stop picking. I'd reach my hand around my neck as was habit for me, instinctively thinking to push back my locks, to play with a bead or a dread, and it just... wasn't there. Not a one.

I'd had a short mane, and indeed no mane, at various points throughout my life. When I was young, when I'd first cut my ties with my family (or rather when they'd decided they were done with me), I'd cut it as short as a ponytail. Ultimately, perhaps out of vanity, perhaps out of nostalgia, I'd always re-embraced my cultural aesthetic, at least when it came to having a mane. It wasn't complicated. I liked the way it looked. And it was something that marked me as a Carvecian Tribesman—or at least a half-blood—that wasn't strictly tied to any of my tribe's religious beliefs.

While I found many of the stories and lore I'd been raised on entertaining, informative, oftentimes even deep... I wasn't a believer anymore. I was glad at least I'd never marked my fur. My tribe saw our ancestral scarification rituals as an impediment to 'globalization', to competing on the already brutal Capitalist stage populated by rival mercantile families who saw the Carvecian Tribes as degenerate savages, which ought to tell you all you needed to know about how deep my family's faith ran. I mean, if you were making sacrifices to impress people like that...

I didn't do shit as important as religion by half measure. At some point I'd realized I just didn't believe anymore, and while I couldn't say I knew the absolute truth of the world, I didn't want to make false oaths to spirits I no longer believed in. So, much of my heritage faded into the recesses of my new life and freedom on the open seas.

But, my mane. My mane was the last anchor I'd maintained, both as a reminder of where I came from, a proud proclamation that, yes, the Admiral Grayson Reed was born of a wolf tribe—and, perhaps most importantly, it was how people knew me by sight. Reputation, charisma, presence... all of these things were more than merely egotistical when you were in my line of work.

My men had barely recognized me when I'd rejoined them on Lunden's ship, and indeed I had trouble looking at myself in the mirror. This wasn't just petty vanity, this was an image problem. We hadn't made it back to the Manoratha and the bulk of my men yet, but already rumors of how Roccosal had essentially scalped me were making their way amongst the few boys I had with me. And rightly so; that's exactly what had happened.

Just because I'd wielded the knife myself didn't make a lick of difference. He'd bent me over, put me in a spot I had no escape from, and forced me to mutilate myself and my reputation in one fell swoop.

And he would pay for it. Oh, how he would pay.

I wasn't an angry man, generally. It's not that I couldn't get there, I was frightfully mortal and fallible and not at all immune to the whole range of emotions a man can feel. But generally, I found anger wasn't constructive. And I had limited time in this world, less than most would likely assume given my apparent health, so I didn't like to waste it spinning like a top. I preferred action over brooding.

This new... acquaintance of mine, that's what we'll call him for now I guess... the cattle dog, seemed overly fond of brooding. Even when he was spending what should have been downtime with his gorgeous little fox whom he'd just risked all to save and, rightfully, should be fucking nonstop belowdecks, he looked otherwise occupied with dark thoughts. I couldn't imagine an existence like that. I hadn't lived his life of course, so no judgment. But fucking hell. Buck up, mate. Focus on what you have in the present.

I had my own distraction going now too, with Lotus temporarily in my corner. Once we'd gotten to the bald cay , she'd occupied herself more with her men and taking stock of her ships, given that we could be running for our lives at any given moment. If I'd had my fleet here, I'd probably be doing the same. But she always made time for me at night, which was calming me down and helping keep my more aggressive impulses at bay.

Still. I was angry. This time, I was angry. Every now and then it crept in, most especially when I was reminded of what I'd lost. Which was more often than I would have liked.

It wasn't even that I'd been robbed. It was what I'd lost, and more importantly... that he had taken it. That he had it, would always have it, as some kind of trophy.

Now was one of those brooding moments for me. We'd been here three days, long enough that the fastest of Lunden's little ships ought to have made contact with the Manoratha by now, but not long enough that my fleet would have made it here yet. It was also still in that dangerous realm of wondering whether or not Fathom Roccosal had truly let us go or was still on the hunt. And we had no idea how close his larger ships had been, how many he had within range to call on, or what physical state he was in after that crossbow shot... there were so many variables.

I didn't know what Denholme's plans were, but that's what we'd gathered tonight to discuss. He got real hard at the thought of hunting down the Dhole, I'd seen that much for myself. But as to whether or not he was planning on taking the man down out here or somehow laying siege to his fortress of an island, I wasn't certain yet. Nor did I have any inclination of where his dreaded Cerberus fleet was. And that was a question I was prepared to leave unanswered, because no fucking way was he going to let me in on his fleet movements. Any information he gave me about where he preferred to moor or ride the currents while he was in between hunting was too valuable, and there was too much potential I'd put it to future use. We didn't trust each other that much.

I didn't trust him at all after that fucking kiss, let me tell you. It wasn't even that I'd minded it, I just hadn't seen it coming. He was bolder even than I'd given him credit for.

"Unlikely that we'll be lucky enough to catch him with his britches down out here, so far from his base of operations," Lotus mused, peeling an orange remarkably delicately with her big, soft hand-paws. Feline claws were no joke one of the most useful multi-tools out there.

She tossed a rind into the fire at about the same time Denholme spoke up, his voice low and a bit swallowed by the din of the ocean, but not so much that I couldn't pick up the pensive concern laced through it. "Do you think he knew who I was?"

"No," I said with absolute certainty. "He wouldn't have let you leave alive if he had."

"He's right," Lotus agreed. "He has no idea you're here. How would he?"

The cattle dog's ears tipped back marginally, and he gave the both of us a hard look, his predatory yellow eyes flicking between us.

"I take offense to that," I said to the unspoken implication. "I was serious about not sharing my reason for being here or any of the dirt I had on you."

"There's more?" he pressed.

I waved a hand. "Nothing near so damning as the existence of Kafele. Which I took the bullet for you on, I'll remind you. Sir-glaring-at-me."

"I'm sorry. I haven't forgotten," he assured me quietly. "But if you'll forgive me, you were able to forget Roccosal's existence due to your drunken fugue, and even you can't be sure what else you may have let slip. That night or any other."

"He's got you there," Lotus chuckled.

"...even if I was going to spit something that damning out while inebriated," I said, "it wouldn't be to him. There's no reasoning, sound or otherwise, to share information that valuable with a rival. And anyway, if I'd ever mentioned your name that night... not for nothing man, but... this secret of yours isn't much of a secret. You fancyin' boys is about the only trash-talk people spout 'bout you. There isn't much other material out there. Sure as fuck can't attack your prowess or the voracity of your fleet."

"Is it really that widely speculated on?" Luther asked, sounding vaguely worried.

I think I saw Lotus quietly, uncomfortably nod in the following silence, but I pressed on to move the conversation along. "Point is," I said, "if your name had somehow even come up and then the very next day he'd caught my boy whore, he would've put two and two together. Man's a coward, but he's not dense. It's the conclusion I would've drawn, and I'm hardly brilliant."

"We can assume he doesn't know you're here," Lotus said. "But that doesn't change the fact that he knows Reed and me, knows we've both got multiple ships, and, depending on the size of the fleet he has nearby, that puts us likely somewhere in the 'even odds' range. Roccosal doesn't travel without at least one of his Man-of-Wars, but the Manoratha's equal in size and equally bristling with guns. The Dhole likes to game his fights. No matter how angry he is, I don't think he'll risk it."

"How far are we from this island of his in Mataa?" Luther asked me.

I scratched the back of my neck again. "Lotus and I figured that out last night," I cleared my throat, glancing at her.

Nodding, she leaned to her side and reached into the haversack she'd brought with her to our nightly camp. The palm wood was crackling, the sky was brilliantly clear, the rum was good, and the company intriguing and diverse. Really hated how the prickle of anger lingering in the back of my throat was ruining all of this for me.

She carefully unrolled the weathered map we'd been consulting the night before—one of hers, since I had none of my own on hand—a good few feet away from the fire in the sand, where none of the popping sparks were likely to fall on it. Luther moved over at a kneel, heedless of the coarse palm bark splinters sticking out of the sand. His knees were bare, the Amur 'Lord' down to a worn pair of britches torn short at the thigh. If his countrymen could see him now, they'd certainly balk. But given his current company (Lotus was once again topless, which at this point I think she primarily did to keep the creepy wolfhound at a distance when we had these meetings) I suppose the cattle dog didn't really care. He was remarkably down-to-earth, when he stopped caring about putting up a front.

Or just hot, I suppose. The tropical nights had us all panting.

"Provided the wind favors him," she said, tracing a claw along the various routes we'd charted that we thought likely, "which... this time of year, he has the trade winds on his side... eleven days, ten nights? Conservatively, but I doubt it will be much more or less."

Luther blew out a breath through his nose, leaning back. "That isn't near enough time to hunt down a fleet we don't even bloody know the starting location of, let alone coordinate."

"Not to mention, neither of our fleets are reachable for at least..." I paused, "...I'm guessing, a day?"

"At least," he confirmed vaguely.

"He's going to outrun us," Lotus said, lifting her gaze to the both of us. "That's a given. If he's running."

"Which we can assume is also a given," Luther said grimly.

"If he were intent on hunting us down, he would have scouted this island out already," I hummed. "Lunden's more knowledgeable than most about these waters, and this little speck is largely uncharted, but it's close enough to Dokuro that he would've found it by now. The otter's been out there idly doing a circuit every day, and he hasn't even seen fishing boats out here. He ain't comin' for us."

"Maybe that wound of his is infected," Luther growled out. "Could be they're rushing him home."

"We can dream," I chuckled. "But my luck's never been that good."

"Nor mine," he agreed.

"At this point, we can rest easy he isn't coming for us I think," Lotus said, more than a little relieved-sounding. "And I'm personally glad for that. You gents might have your fleets out high-water, but everything I have in the world is here. And I wouldn't have liked my chances against him alone."

"The Manoratha will be here as soon as possible," I stroked a palm along her arm.

"That's no great comfort," Luther snorted. "That lumbering behemoth of yours isn't exactly famed for her speed."

"I don't open her up unless I have to," I snarled playfully at him. "You've never scared me enough to unfurl every sail. I could tell you were toothless the first time you let me run."

"But you did run," he arched an eyebrow.

"Boys, boys," Lotus gave an exasperated roll of her eyes. "Unless you're about to put on another show for me, keep it in your pants."

That got us both awkwardly mute. Apparently even the cattle dog himself was self-conscious about that 'moment' we shared. Unforgivable, really, since he was the perpetrator. He could at least own it.

But he didn't seem embarrassed or humiliated, really. Not even regretful. More… distant. Like he was reliving it.

I hoped at least I'd provided him with some wank material. I was worth that, I think.

"Still," Lotus continued, oblivious to whatever the hell was going on between the two of us. Or maybe she just didn't care. "If we wanted to catch up to him with any warships, mine would be the only option at this point."

"Right, but that's suicide," I said obviously.

Luther was leaning over the map again. I heard it crinkle as he tapped at it, the paw-pad of one of his fingers and one dark claw poking repeatedly at a spot you could've mistaken for a stain. But I knew better, because I'd plotted those possible routes. "Where is this?" he asked. "I don't recognize… is that an island?"

"It's not part of the Shanivaar chain," I said. "Before you ask. There are a lot of little isles out there, most of 'em too mountainous to settle well, other than by the locals. It's not a cay, though. It's sizable, bigger than Dokuro even."

"Every route you've plotted stops there," he said, gaze flicking back up to mine. "Why would he re-supply on such a short trip? It can't be more than three days out from his own island."

"He essentially owns it," Lotus explained. "It's part of his network. Technically Huudari territory, but the tiger clan there is in his pocket. He'll have a ship or two there that swears fealty to him, and at least a few Captains who'll fly under his banner if he calls them to task."

"We're fairly certain he'll stop there," I summarized. "Regardless which route he takes."

"How well-defended is this island?" he asked.

Lotus and I looked at one another. "What are you thinking?" I asked, crossing my arms over my chest. "It might be less defensible than his own island, certainly not the nexus of his fleet or his power, but if whatever fleet he's got out here with him is too much for Lotus's gunships—"

"And it is," she butted in.

"—and it is," I nodded, "then what's the difference if we happen to know a stop on his route? We'd still have to wait to coordinate our own fleets before we sail for there… that's at least a day or two, and we have no way to know how long he's going to dock there. Probably not long. It's unlikely we'd make it to that isle in time with our full power brought to bear, but even if we could, it's Huudari lands. Neutral waters. We can't just… I mean. That'd be war, man. That's why he's in bed with the tigers in the first place. The political connections serve him, not only because he can sell his 'stock' there, but so he's got a network of safe ports he can't be singled out in. They want him comin' in and out so long as he's bringing in the goods. That's how he built his empire in the first place."

"That's why his own island's location is so secretive," Lotus murmured. "He can't fly his own flag, rule his own little free state the way he prefers, if he's in bed with the Huudari there. Once he's home, he can't use them as a shield. No Huudari… no treaty. He's on his own. If your countrymen had the time or wherewithal to sniff out the heart of his piracy empire, he'd have no army to stand against your fury other than whatever he himself can supply. Which, to be fair, is formidable."

"Of course," I muttered, "that only matters in the case that the Amurescan or the Carvecian Navies care enough to find and pick a fight with him in his own waters rather than spending all their bloody time and resources on colony-building and turf wars with one another."

"I'm here, aren't I?" Luther demanded, a feral glint in his eyes.

I grinned. "That you are. You're the real deal, Denholme. Apex predator."

"Get to whatever your point was before," Lotus interjected. "You were going somewhere with all that. So what if we could catch him at this waypoint? Grayson's right, we can't pick a fight in Huudari waters. And really, we probably can't catch up to him there with anything other than my ships, since that's all we have on hand now."

"We don't need to fight him on the water," he said, "if we can catch him outside his fortress state. The Huudari are much more forgiving of assassination than open warfare."

Lotus gave a punched-out laugh. "Are you sure you're Amur?"

"I'm far more in my element on a ship than I am on land," I said uncomfortably. "And your man already made a damn good assassination attempt on Roccosal back on Dokuro. I don't think we'll ever have a chance that good again."

"He'll be hurt—"

"And paranoid because of that!" Lotus said. "No. No. I'm not in for this. I'm sorry. He'll be surrounded by his men wherever he goes. We couldn't handle him when it was just a few dozen in an open-air camp, let alone an unfamiliar island."

"I'm only throwing out ideas right now," he eased. "Thinking aloud. This is new information to me, remember. I need time to consider our options. The fact that we know where he will most certainly be for a few days' time is too tempting not to ruminate on."

They went back and forth like that for a little while, perhaps not noticing how quiet I'd gotten. I was chewing on a piece of hard tack the whole while, barely noticing when it broke and gave way at last. It was as tasteless as it was old, but the only other option tonight had been the stew that had caked itself like tar to the camp pot, and I wasn't that reckless with my health.

At length though, they seemed to take note of my pensive expression and lack of conversation. Luther was the first to snap me out of my trance, shoving at one of my shoulders to jostle me.

"Reed?" He quirked an ear.

Glancing up, I swallowed the hard lump of awful food and equally awful anxiety in my throat, before speaking.

"I… might… have an idea."

Two of the world's most skilled pirate hunters were suddenly staring me down. I should have been intimidated, having their full attention like that. But mostly it made me feel important, and I've gotta admit, I liked that.

"Alright," I cleared my throat, forcing down the stale remnants of hard tack that remained, "so… there's a window here. We could take advantage of it if we're very, very careful, and really fucking bold."

"I'm at least one of those things," Luther replied, lifting his chin and crossing his arms over his bare chest.

"I wish I could say I was the other," I muttered, "then we'd have all our bases covered."

"No, you two are both idiots," Lotus muttered dryly. "Wild, reckless idiots. When this is all over you need to get as far from one another as possible, to opposite ends of the earth, for both of your own good. You're bad for each other. And I'm fairly certain the two of you teaming up is bad for the world."

"Lucky you're not a lass, mate," I smirked at the cattle dog, who only regarded me with an arched eyebrow. "Or I of a different persuasion, I suppose. Usually when someone fires me up s'much as you've managed in so short a time—"

"I really shouldn't have to warn you about the flirtation again at this point." He glared, looking genuinely angry.

"I think this is just his resting state of being," Lotus swatted my shoulder, hard enough to actually hurt. I chuckled around an 'ow'. "I earnestly don't think he can help it. It's self-destructive as hell. But I do agree with him, for the record. If you two were compatible in bed, the seas wouldn't be safe for anyone. Small blessings."

"Kindred spirits," I grinned, showcasing a fang.

"We've hardly known one another long enough for that," he muttered. "Also, that's the most insulting thing anyone's ever said to me."

"Alright, enough," Lotus bit out. "Even I'm starting to think you should just fuck and get it out of your system already. Reed. Stop it. And what the hell was your point?"

"Trying for an assassination on the tigers' island is too risky," I said, hunkering over the map. "Like we've said, he's allied with them and they've invested a lot in keeping his Empire running. The last thing we need is to poke that hornet's nest and have the addition of a lot of angry tigers on our plate."

"Right," Luther agreed. "I've… known some tigers. In the Kadrush, so Amur tigers. But still, I'm guessing their southern counterparts are equally as tenacious."

"Tenacious, cunning, fierce," Lotus smirked, leaning back on her palms. "And let's not leave out 'gorgeous.'"

"—and trying to take him on in those waters is also not an option, because even if we were willing to tangle with the tigers, we can't get our fleets there in time," I continued. "If we were to leave now on Lotus's ships and use, say, Lunden to send word to our own fleets to meet us at a rendezvous spot, Roccosal would already have left that island well before we could blockade him. I'm certain he won't moor there for long. Just long enough to get reinforcements and, I suppose, medical treatment if he is indeed ailing from that wound."

"But, if he makes it to his own fortress of an island," Luther rumbled, speaking partially into his curled hand, "we'll be in for a tough siege. Even if you're dedicated to helping me, which I don't fully believe."

"Have a little faith in me, mate," I said, hurt. "We've been through so much."

"Again, I am not discounting what you sacrificed for me on Dokuro," he said, remarkably genuine-sounding. "But there's the issue of morale, even within your own ranks, I'm sure. My men are pirate hunters and on commission with the Navy besides. They will do their duty. To a point, obviously. Every force has its limits. But your men won't hold fast on this task for long. It has little chance of reward save infamy and whatever spoils they think they can weasel out from under my nose."

"I hate that expression," I muttered. "Very uncharitable to weasels. I employ weasels, you know."

He gave an exasperated sigh. "My... apologies? Look. The point is, a long siege of his island, while something I'd absolutely fall back on and pursue to its bitter end if need be, shouldn't be our first plan."

"It isn't," I shook my head. "What we need to do is catch him in between."

"That's impossible," Lotus said all but immediately. "The transit time between the two islands, disregarding a freak storm or accident, is too short a window for us to realistically catch up to him. Even if we use Lunden's vessels to coordinate, it'll be harder to find him out at sea than it would be to meet at a given point we know, like one of his islands. We'd have to get extremely lucky or he'd have to be delayed or slowed down considerably, somehow. While at sea, specifically... on land a delay wouldn't matter. Even if he's land-bound days longer than he should be and we've time to move your ships in, if either of your fleets are spotted by any of the flock of vessels likely to be on the lines out there this time of year, he'll just stay put if he knows we're out there. And neither of you can afford to wait him out indefinitely."

"Right," I nodded. "We'd need to delay him at sea. When he's straddling the tigers and the defenses of his own island."

"The weather is unlikely to cooperate with us there," Luther said. "Not this time of year."

"So, accident it is then."

That got me a silent, rapt stare from both of them. Luther was the one to break the dead air.

"You're talking sabotage," he said, realization dawning. And with it, the hint of that devil-may-care grin I knew he was capable of, but seemed to forcibly repress beneath the stuffy Amurescan mask that he wore like an ill-tailored coat. I saw right through it.

This one was a troublemaker, 'honorable' profession aside.

"Egch," Lotus made a noise that sounded at once uncomfortable and repulsed. "That's... heresy. Be-decked in skulls or not, his ships are master-fully-crafted, well-tended works of art. What kind of sailor are you, even proposing that?"

"He made me mutilate my mane," I snarled out.

"Shit, you really are angry," Luther said, awed and perhaps amused. The slur had also slipped out in a lower-class drawl I think was probably closer to what his natural speaking voice had been like before his elevation to the Pedigree way of life.

"You don't fuck with a man's ships," Lotus insisted, aghast. "We don't have many scruples, Reed... but that one..."

"Where's it written that I can blow him full of holes, but I can't cut him off at the knees so I can catch up to him to blow him full of holes?" I persisted, looking between the two of them. I spread my arms wide, palms out. "I'm an Anarchist, love! 'Scruples' ain't in my vocabulary!"

"Neither are words like 'aren't', apparently," Luther muttered.

"Weren't you peasant-born?" I let my hands drop noisily. "M'not meaning that as an insult, I just didn't expect you'd be so up my ass about propriety. Don't shame me for how I talk or for fighting dirty. We're outgunned here, we need to do what works or we'll be sunk."

"I'm not the one calling your idea 'heresy'," Luther pointed out, glancing at Lotus. "Also, that's a loaded word where I come from. Watch it."

"I know," Lotus growled. "Your wolfhound keeps muttering it under his breath at me."

"T'be fair," I sniffed, "you do keep flashing your tits at him."

"Have you seen how flustered he gets?" she snorted. "How can I not? Also, you walk around with your tits out every damn day, Reed. Why am I not permitted to? Gods-damned... man's world. I get hot too, you know. Why can't I air out?"

"You're preaching to the choir, lovely," I assured her. "I fully support your right to go topless as often as you like."

"And I just don't care," Luther stated, nonplussed.

"Honestly, I find that extremely refreshing," Lotus said to the cattle dog, sighing. "It's also not particularly liberating to be given permission to bare my body so I can be gawked at," she said while flicking her gaze to glare briefly at me, "and it's generally one of the two. Either my chest is a disgrace or a spectacle. To you, I suppose, it's just a chest. There's something oddly relaxing about knowing that when I'm around you." She considered that for a spell. "I think I need a man like you on my crew."

"You probably already have a man like me on your crew, and you're unaware of it," he said dryly.

"Wait, so," I was still on what she'd been talking about before, "does that mean to you," I poked Luther in one of his solid arms, "my chest is a spectacle?"

He said nothing. Only slapped a palm down onto his thigh, the irritation back in full force over his features, and began to get to his knees to move in on me.

I backpedaled into the sand, throwing out my palms defensively and blocking one of his hands grabbing at my shoulder, yelling out between laughter, "I yield! I yield! Please, have mercy!"

"Running again, are we Reed?" he said through a snarl as he tried to tackle me into the sand.

I kicked at his chest and thrashed against the palm shavings and sand, getting at least several pounds of it down my britches as we tussled. It was play-fighting at most, but the kind that would leave bruises, I'm sure. The fucking cattle dog was strong, holy shit!

Lotus watched us from the sidelines, casually eating her orange, utterly unimpressed by our antics. Despite that, there was a warm fondness in her eyes and the hint of a smile on her muzzle.

It was late, and we were circling round on ideas, waiting to hear back from our fleets. We didn't have to come to a decision tonight. I was content to let the conversation die there for now, especially since the impromptu rough-housing and Lotus's cute face were improving my spirits.

Dealing with the Dhole could at least wait until tomorrow.

Turns out I was no match for the Cerberus Admiral when it came to grappling. But then, I suppose he had a lot of experience at pinning other men. I... deliberately did not say that part out loud.

It was while crushed into the sand, spitting it out from between my teeth, with his knee between my shoulder blades and my arms yanked behind my back, that I spied a set of wide eyes in the dark. Given the enormous pair of half-moon ears that accompanied them, they could really only belong to one person who'd come to this cay with us.

"Your fennec," I wheezed out, "is watching us from that... clutch of palm over there."

He breathed out through his nose, slowly letting me up. He didn't sound surprised. "I know," he said.

I glanced up between us, at our position. He didn't seem worried, though. "He ain't gonna, like," I paused, "misunderstand—"

"Why would that matter even if he did?" he asked, looking down at me with knitted brows.

"I don't," I grunted as I pushed myself up, lowering my voice slightly, "know how it is between men, alright? But I just figure, you know… if it were me with one of my ladies, especially a past flame, there'd be about a fifty percent chance fur was about to fly if she caught me 'compromised' like that." I reached out and tried to give him a shoulder pat, but he recoiled away. "Just lookin' out for you is all," I explained, easing back from the gesture with my palms out. "You need me to explain things to him?"

"Oh, that I'd love to see. I can't begin to explain how or why you do the things you do," he guffawed. "Let alone how you keep dragging me into them."

"You were the aggressor this time! I was defending myself!"

"You're hardly an innocent victim."

"Lads, lads," Lotus rolled her eyes, "you're both terrible. Let's not point fingers."

"You know our past history," Luther said, indicating Kafele without looking in his direction. "Why do you assume there's something current between us?"

"Be…cause there… is?" I said hesitantly. Not because I was actually hesitant, but because the question was so asinine. "The little fox clearly still has feelings for you, you just saved his hide from certain enslavement, and he's gorgeous. Why are you even here?"

"We were speaking on something important," Lotus reminded us, although she sounded like she'd lost interest, too.

"You're also here," Luther pointed out, almost petulantly. "With your lady love. Talking strategy instead of… whatever." I swear he blushed in his ears when he said the last part, staring anywhere but at me. Adorable.

"Oh, I fully intend to have her paws-up later," I assured him.

"She is right there. Listening to us."

The tigress out-and-out laughed at him. "You think if talk like that phased me, I'd be able to run my own fleet? Or that I'd've agreed to seduce him for you, Denholme? He's in my bed because I want him there, and I'm hardly ashamed of that fact. Although if anyone's going to be 'paws up' tonight wolf, it's you. You'd best be able to saddle-up after all this time and energy you've wasted playing with the cattle dog."

Luther had gotten up at that point and put some distance between the two of us, as if all this talk was making him uncomfortable. An Amur at heart still then, despite his better nature.

I stayed reclining in the sand, watching him as he gathered his few things and dusted the sand off his knees, shaking it out of his tail. He had remarkably little sand in his fur compared to me. Bastard.

I could sense, rather than see, that Kafele had emerged from the palms and was standing in full view, now. Waiting. Likely for Luther to join him… if he even planned to. I don't think he'd intended to sneak up on us really, sneaking without meaning was just a natural tendency of foxes. And to be fair, we'd been making quite a ruckus. If you didn't know what was going on, you might think it was an actual fight.

"Things between Kafele and me," Luther paused, his voice quiet, eyes downcast, "are complicated," he said at last.

"Life's short, mate," I affirmed with perhaps more understanding of the concept than he'd give me credit for. "Not for nothing, and I'm not gonna take credit for it and claim it was intentional, but… you got a second chance, here. And whatever happened between you before, he never spoke of you angrily or even unfondly. Even during all the time he spent with my crew, before we got to Dokuro. Maybe if he's willin' to forgive for whatever transpired, you oughta—"

"You know nothing," he snapped, one hornet-yellow eye pinning me down where I lay.

I didn't respond. I couldn't. He had this way of putting emphasis into his words sometimes like a punch to the gut, with about the same effect. He didn't use it often, but that's what made it so effective when he did.

"My… relationship," he gritted out quietly, "with Kafele is, and was, never your business. You forget that you tried to use him against me, and that's the only reason he's here now, and subsequently the only reason I had to 'save' him in the first place."

I cast my gaze down, unwilling to quip at the man when he was so very, very right.

"And even then…" his voice trailed off, laced with regret and something worse, something wounded and old. I'd heard it, seen it, when he'd seen Kafele again for the first time on Dokuro. That very same venom of self-hatred curdled in my gut. The knowledge that I'd tread on something deeply personal and beyond my right to intrude upon.

"Even then, you were the one who saved him," he said, the emotion bleeding out of his tone until it went cold. "You sacrificed something for him. I… failed him."

He stepped away from the fire, beginning to make his way off across the sand. The last thing he left me with was the word, "… again."

12 YEARS EARLIER

Mischa's reception was every bit as overdone and over-served as her engagement party had been. Her father had rented out the largest hall in Olvaster—which I suppose wasn't saying much in a city this size—but it still managed somehow to be garish. New Amurescan Revalia-style architecture, a pale imitation of the ancient castles it pretended to be. Like most of the 'art' coming out of the Old Country these days, it was created to serve the Nationalist Revolution, the last dying gasps of the Pedigree Elite hanging on to the notion that they were still somehow the greatest nation on the globe.

Their crumbling Colonial Empire said otherwise, but what did I know? I was just the unfavorite son of the Reed Cartel, a marrying of Kadrush-Amurescan and Native Carvecian wolves. An unholy union that had dug in a place for ourselves at the time of founding of the now free nation of Carvecia. It had probably been hard for them… running gunpowder, salt, and food stores to the then-Rebels. It had all been an absurd gamble back then, with none of the fortune and security the family now enjoyed thanks to said gamble paying off. They'd risked their tails on a future contingent on taking on and besting the fiercest Navy in the world.

Sounded really fucking exciting, honestly.

The Reeds were pampered pets, these days. Me most especially. I'd been born useless, an unfortunate son from the time I'd first shown signs of the family curse… I'd been three then, I think. I didn't really remember my first seizures. My mother sure as hell did. She kept a book. Showed it to the Physician every month, even if she'd not had to update it. Every goddamn check-in.

I loved her, I mean, what kind of son doesn't love his mother? But her love was like a too-tight cravat sometimes. I needed to breathe.

It wouldn't have mattered if she eased up, because the entire family was aware of my condition and irritatingly concerned for me nearly at all times. Not always out of genuine empathy, either. There wasn't an event I attended where the subject didn't come up. It was like a morbid curiosity to all of them, like I was a house fire they could gawk at from their carriage. I was the first scion in two generations to manifest 'the curse', as it was whispered. I'm sure they'd hoped it'd been purged from the bloodline long ago, and in fact I'm fairly certain that'd been part of the reason for finally marrying outsiders.

Well, that hadn't lasted. Poor Mischa. Her new husband was a decent enough fellow, if you had insomnia and you wanted to be lulled off in conversation. He was a cotton man, one of those that got overly into his work in order to find some kind of purpose in life. Unfortunately, 'work' for a plantation owner mostly involved hybridizing seeds and literally talking for hours on end about the weather with like-minded peers... all of whom were also cotton men. Mischa's 'circles', if you could call them that, were about to get mind-numbingly boring.

And unlike me, she'd actually led an interesting life until now. She'd traveled, seen much of the civilized world, gone to Court in Amuresca, in frozen Kadrush ports, and all over Carvecia. Her father, my Uncle Luka, allowed her to travel with him from the time she was six, after her mother died. And while that had certainly been tragic, it had allowed her a kind of freedom that most women—even wealthy women—and unfortunately I, could only dream of.

Her new husband, much like myself, had never left Carvecian soil. I think he'd traveled even less than I and by choice. Very grounded, steady fellow. You know, dull. And I wasn't speaking out of turn. I knew him pretty well.

We were cousins, after all.

Second cousins. Which made him Mischa's second cousin as well, being as she was my first. I suppose given how close Mischa and I were whenever we had a chance to be in the same city together, I should've counted my blessings that the family hadn't arranged the two of us.

But then, there were other reasons for that...

That was the one freedom I had. No one in my family had ever pressed me to marry, nor gotten in the way of my less serious amorous pursuits. Even when I dipped below my class or outside my species, as was my preference. To put it simply, no one cared where a disinherited son spread his seed. Any bastards I produced (not that I intended to) would have no claim to the family fortune regardless. And I didn't resent any of that. Once I'd been old enough to understand the options before me, I'd embraced it outright. I'd thought then—when I signed my importance away—that cutting those strings would afford me more liberties. A life all my own. Finally.

But the reality was hardly that simple. While nothing was technically caging me in the suffocating embrace of my family, there were still those practical considerations, like what the hell I'd do to support myself if I went against my parents' wishes. I'd entertained many an idea and ultimately abandoned them all when pursuing the first steps into each proved more difficult and tedious than I'd imagined. Being a tradesman was a lot of work.

The only line of work I knew well enough to do professionally in any way was, of course, the trade my family had prepared and schooled me for. And I'll be damned if I was going to spend my life staring at log books in my family's Cartel Offices.

And the only thing I knew for certain I wanted to do was travel. Not just the roads of Carvecia or even the North Country. No.

I had the best education money could buy, tutors and masters since I was five years old, specialized in Maritime Trade, Nautical Archaeology and Engineering, Economics, and more. I spoke three languages, could calculate in half a dozen currencies, prattle off every Capital and major port in the known world, all this—

And I'd never been to sea.

Oh, I'd set foot on a ship. Many of them, in fact. At port. At various ports. In Carvecia, where I'd been born. Where I'd be buried. Because I was trapped here.

Going to sea with my condition was expressly forbidden by everyone who loved me. And several Physicians besides. High, slippery decks, tossing waves and unforgiving waters did not mix well with seizures. For the first ten years of my life my mother hadn't even wanted me to walk on docks, let alone ships.

I was an over-educated, over-privileged lay-about until I could find some measure of purpose for the life I'd been handed. I felt simultaneously frustrated by my condition at all times and also expressly aware that I was utterly safe and provided for, that I didn't need to do anything of use with my life. I could simply be taken care of, and no one would resent me for it. Because my limitations were not my fault and I'd been fortunate enough to be born into a family that was able to provide a wonderful, pampered existence for me, regardless how useless I was.

I didn't have to travel through the slums of Arbordale to know how good I had it. But sometimes when I was angry with my condition, I did. To remind myself to count my blessings, go home, buck up. I'd see the people just barely scraping by, or not. And that's when I'd begun to think— you know what?

Maybe Cartels were a really bad idea.

The problem with having a good education, you see, is you start to learn why things work the way they do. Like the delicate balancing game of managing exploitative labor conditions without rebellion or worker organizing, and which countries employ it most brutally to provide us with the best margins, or how we track market trends across borders and monopolize goods at peak times… how we make all of this work to maximize the Cartel's earnings and minimize expenses. How we stay rich and get richer every generation.

Except I was disinherited. So now I'd kind of lost that selfish haze you get when you're staring at a situation that benefits you.

I may have been a naïve young man in many regards, but I at least mostly understood how people's morals work. If I was actively invested in growing the Cartel, like say my younger brother or my father, I might be able to make all kinds of justifications in my head for why things work the way they do. Why we continue to ensure they work the way they do.

But more and more of late, I was finding I couldn't do that.

So what's a listless, jobless, worthless young man with far too much time on his hands, nowhere to go, and no vices to occupy him to do?

Well. There were these people who got together in Debriss sometimes. I met a few of them through one of my Economics tutors, a few years back. Once I started questioning it all, he... opened up a bit. And it took some convincing, but he eventually trusted me enough to take me to this bar. That's where it all started.

It'd been a few months now since I'd started considering myself an Anarchist.

"Gray!" my cousin's voice broke through the din. My ears tipped, trying to pick her out amongst the cacophony of clacking plates and silverware, drunken laughter, and conversation.

I smiled as I turned to regard her. Today might've been a shitty day—like watching an elegant bird of prey have its wings clipped—but it was her shitty day, and I wasn't going to make it worse for her in public. Besides, she looked genuinely happy right at that moment, although I couldn't imagine why. I think she just got off the dance floor. She'd always liked dancing.

Her blue eyes were bright against a mask of silver and gray fur bunched into white lace and silks that didn't suit her. I always thought of her in dark blue, her favorite color.

She looked beautiful, though.

"You look beautiful," I told her, because she did.

"Stop," she snorted, shoving at the shoulder of my waistcoat. "I'm not one of your felines, you don't have to flatter me."

"That's how you know I mean it," I smirked over the edge of my glass, draining what remained in one gulp.

She wrinkled her nose. "More of your cold tea? I don't know how you drink that shite."

"Keeps me sharp," I chuckled.

"You could stand to dull your blade some," she said wryly.

"They made me check my saber at the door, actually," I said irritably, because I'd meant to complain about it sooner.

"It's a wedding reception, Gray!" she laughed. "Who are you going to need to stab?"

"I've never actually stabbed anyone, Mischa," I muttered. "But I won that one at my last—"

"Oh, right, the fencing competition!" she beamed. "I heard! It's good your mother's letting you compete in those now."

"With a Physician on standby," I rolled my eyes.

"Still." She looped her arm through mine, taking a turn with me through the hall. "I'm happy for you. I heard you did well."

"Third," I growled. "Hardly what I was hoping for. I'm behind the curve for my age group."

"You'll catch up," she assured me. "You can do anything, Gray. I've seen what you're capable of when you put your mind to it."

I gave a half-hearted smile, but kept my muzzle shut. Now was not the time.

We stopped briefly by a vixen serving merlot, and Mischa paused just long enough to give me a look as she reached for a second glass. I didn't even need to shake my head, she knew.

That prompted a sigh from her, though. She took only the one goblet for herself, sipping from it for a moment before saying, "One glass isn't going to kill you."

"The Physician disagrees," I smiled ruefully. "And mother would smell it on me. Remember when we were eleven?"

"I didn't see you for a year after that," she recalled with a frown. "But Gray, you're a grown man now. She doesn't—shouldn't have so much say over your life any more. If you want to drink, drink. You're not a monk."

"Is this how you plan to get through your marriage?" I asked her, only half-joking.

"That's not funny," she admonished me. She also sounded like she was only half-joking.

"I don't feel like I'm missing out on much," I assured her. "At least... in that area, anyway."

"Well far be it from me to force drink on a man." She shook her head. "Good on you, chap. Someday when you marry one of those cats of yours, you'll be a sober and proper husband."

I laughed out loud. "'One of those cats'?" I quoted back at her.

"It's a lioness currently, right?"

"Was a lioness," I cleared my throat. "She went back to Mataa."

"Oh, I'm sorry"—

"Don't be," I waved a paw. "Just meant I was free to pursue this lynx I fancied..."

"You're a cad," she snorted, "but I'm glad there's something I can admonish you for. It's not healthy for a young wolf to be as clean-cut as you are." She sipped her drink, speaking after a swallow. "Makes the rest of us look bad."

I followed her into a parlor, a small private sitting room that was thankfully vacant when we arrived. I'd been wanting a few moments alone with her since the reception had begun some hours ago. Now was my chance.

"Mischa," I turned, releasing her arm then gripping her by both of her elbows once the door had closed behind me. She was barely shorter than me, so it was easy to look her in the eyes once I had her facing me. She seemed to realize the mood had shifted, her expression falling from one of contentment to concern, very quickly.

"Are yo—"" she paused, her eyes widening. "Do you need to sit down?"

"No," I said, masking that ever-present defensiveness that rose up in me whenever people assumed my condition was rearing its head because of any minor thing I did. "Mischa, no." I said more calmly, wanting to assure her. "I'm fine."

"You got very serious-looking all of a sudden..." she said with a nervous smile.

"Do you want to leave here?"

The smile fell away from her face completely. When she spoke again, she sounded more than worried. She gave the briefest of trembles. "What do you mean?"

"I mean, this," I gestured to the door and what lay beyond it.

"The reception?" she queried. "We're only halfway through the evening—"

"This," I said pointedly. "Everything. This... marriage. This life they're forcing on you. All of it. I know it's not what you want."

"Grayson." She began shaking her head, slowly. "I don't... what are you talking about? Are you certain you're feeling alright?"

"I'm fine," I growled out, and that sent her ears back. I felt bad, I didn't mean to intimidate her. I sighed, releasing her arms gently and running a hand back through my bound mane. "I've never felt better, honestly. After tonight, I'll be free. And you can be free with me. You don't need to go through with this."

She stared at me, taking a ginger step back, putting a foot or two of distance between us. "I don't... understand. You're not making any sense, Gray."

"I have a ship," I said softly, keeping my voice low despite the fact that I was utterly certain no one in the party would hear us in here.

"What—" She blinked. "How... can you have a ship? What are you talking about?"

"I can explain it all to you on the way," I assured her. "All you need to know is, I have a ship. She's ready to sail, she's fully-crewed... or well, mostly—"

"Where did you get a ship?!" She demanded, more loudly than I would have liked.

I winced, glancing past her to the door. But of course, no one had heard.

Looking back at her, I found myself smiling despite an anxious laugh bubbling out of me. "Actually," I huffed, "I mean… I suppose? I'm stealing it."

I expected another outburst, a scandalized proclamation of my name, or something of the like. I was ready for it. Instead, all I got was dumb silence. She stared at me, the white sclera of her eyes visible in her shock, muzzle opening and closing once. I looked to her imploringly, finally deciding to fill the silence myself.

"I'll explain," I began.

"You'd better," she said, voice almost at a whisper. "Gray, I don't understand… any of this. Where did all of this come from, all of a sudden? Are you sure you're feeling well?"

"Stop. Asking. That." I annunciated, being sure to temper my voice and not show the intense irritation that would doubtless upset her again. I let my breath out in a shaking sigh, gingerly moving my hands to clasp hers, squeezing them in a way I meant to be reassuring. "I am so tired of everyone walking on eggshells around me. Like I'm porcelain. My condition…"

Was hard to talk about. But here it went.

"… my condition," I wet my tongue, "is outside my control, and, no matter how much they'd like to insist otherwise, outside my parents' control, as well. The Physicians have no means to cure it, at least none that have worked, and I am tired of living my life around the idea that I have limitations—"

"But, Gray—"

"—which I myself know I do not have," I finished firmly. "Like… mother's superstitions of what brings on the attacks or father's need to keep me land-bound and under watch at all times. It's imagined safety, for one. The seizures could take my life in my sleep, that has always been the case. Cutting that life down to fit within the bounds they think will better my odds is just robbing me of my freedom to suit their own conscience." I squared my shoulders, narrowing my eyes. "So why can't I rob them in return? They can spare it, anyway."

"Wait— excuse me?" she coughed. "You're stealing… from your parents?"

"Is it really stealing if they're scuttling it?" I countered. "Sinking an incredible piece of functional art to the bottom of the gulf? I'd call it reclamation. Or… adopting, if we're being charitable."

"Oh, God," she said with a look of dawning realization. "You don't mean that behemoth in the bay?"

"She's called the Manoratha," I affirmed. "After that sea dragon from folklore, the one that ate an entire island? I'm glad I won't have to re-name her. It's quite befitting such an intimidating vessel."

"It's a wreck!" she exclaimed, looking mildly horrified. "Even I know that! Uncle Cullen's been bemoaning the purchase of that gold-sink since he got it three years ago. From what I hear, they'll barely need to punch many more holes into its hull to scuttle it than it already has. Are you mad? I thought you might be taking a... a schooner or something. What in the hells are you going to do with a ship that size?" Her worry, quite suddenly, turned accusatory. "Gray. Gray, what... where is all of this leading...?"

I closed my mouth for a few moments, uncertainty creeping into me like icy fingers were closing around my heart. I'd thought talking to Mischa would be safe. A sure thing. I'd pictured myself the hero in this scenario, whisking her away from a loveless marriage and off to a life of freedom. Something she could never have entrapped in her web of obligations here. The same as me.

But I guess there'd always been a part of me that had been planning for failure. I was taking an enormous risk telling her any of this... a risk I'd been expressly warned not to take by some. If they knew I was telling anyone else of our plans, they'd sure have something to say about it.

I wanted to think there was still a chance I could talk her into leaving. I was certain I was saving her from unhappiness. I only had to convince her of that.

I'd just have to be careful.

"I... I can't tell you what our end goals are just yet—"

"'Our'?"

"—or where we're sailing for," I pressed on, ignoring her questions for now, "but I can promise you this much: you won't need to marry a man you don't love, who will bore you for the rest of your existence, if you come with me. You'll be your own woman, answering to no one, with the world spread before you. We can travel together. You can show me all the places you've told me about, all of those ports you described to me while we poured over maps as children. Except this time, you won't have to answer to your father. Or any man."

She blinked slowly up at me in silence for a time. Long enough that I thought, briefly, that she might actually be considering it.

But then she said, "Gray," and squeezed my hand. "What security is there in that kind of life?"

I was stunned. Of everything I'd expected her to say, that hadn't...

"What good is 'security' if you're trapped?" I asked hoarsely.

"You couldn't understand."

A spike of not anger, but certainly frustration- came over me. "Are you kidding me?" I gave a mirthless chuckle. "Security without freedom has been my entire fucking life, Mischa. All of us are dying a little bit more every day anyway, the only difference is that I have to watch those days tick by from a gilded cage! To hell with 'security'!"

"You are a man!" she bit out, showing her teeth for a moment. "You can fantasize about embarking on a grand adventure across the world, unrestrained by your family and the protections they offer, because you don't have the same fears or worries that I have. You want me to treat you like any other man? You want me to ignore your illness? Fine. Leave the embrace of your family, never tell a soul what afflicts you, and pretend to be normal. That will hold out until it doesn't. But you'll have a grand ol' time until then."

She leaned away from me, separating our hands slowly, the ire dropping from her until her words returned, strained. More worried than angry. "Your illness is invisible, Gray. You can hide it. You can entertain this wild streak of yours, break away from your fortune and your family—who truly do love you by the way, even if you don't like how they show it—and run away to experience the world if that's what you really want. But the ramifications for whatever you do out there, your illness aside, will always be less than those I'd suffer if I shared in your mistakes. Because you're a man. A canine man, at that."

She worried at the hem of one of her lace-hemmed sleeves with her claws. All the finery still looked so wrong on her, to me. All of this felt wrong.

"What happens if you lose your ship somewhere?" she asked quietly. "What if you're marooned in a distant land with no coin? No connections? What if whomever you've gotten as crew turn on you? Decide they're better off ransoming you than... whatever it is you have planned? I don't know what's in your mind, and honestly, at this point I'm not sure I want to. I know you well enough to know you've got some kind of scheme going here."

I swallowed. "I wish I could tell you the specifics, but—"

She shook her head. "It wouldn't matter, Gray. I still wouldn't go with you. No matter how well you think you've thought this through, I've actually seen what it's like out there. There are times where... if I hadn't been with my father and his crew..."

"You'd be with me," I tried to insist.

Her eyes quivered as she looked at me. I could tell whatever it was she was hesitating to say, it was going to cut deep.

I wasn't wrong.

"Grayson," she gave a pained smile. "I wouldn't feel safe enough with just you. You couldn't protect me if the worst happened. You can't even protect yourself from what's inside you."

The party was a blur around me as I stalked my way hurriedly back through the main hall, Mischa's words ringing in my ears like cannon fire. I could hear little else. I tried to no avail to keep focused on the task ahead; I'd need to, if I wanted to be successful tonight. And a lot of other people were counting on me.

The disappointment and hurt I felt over the reality that I would not, in fact, be embarking on this next stage of my life with any family at my side—anyone I knew remotely well, really—was immeasurable. I was numb in the wake of it. I'd known for months (when I'd first begun hatching this plan) that following through with it would pit me expressly against the people I loved and potentially sever those connections for the rest of my life. And I didn't... want that.

I did actually love my parents. I didn't want to lose them. But I also couldn't continue living the way I was under their rules and restrictions. It was the conundrum of my life and one I'd spent no small amount of time agonizing over. I'd come to a tipping point in the last year for many reasons. But I think one of the things that had made the decision easier had been the idea that I'd be taking at least one of them, probably my best friend in the world and a connection to my kin, along for this journey. And helping her in the process. It had all seemed so perfect.

Logically, I'd known there was a chance she'd turn me down. But I hadn't listened to that thought. I was very good at drowning out doubts when I needed to. And now I was paying the price for that.

But the die had been cast. The truth of it was, much of this was already far beyond my control. I'd done my part in organizing and preparing for tonight and gathered the final pieces of our plan, the assets without which this whole endeavor might fall apart. But even if I thought my associates would let me back out now (which they wouldn't, they had made that abundantly clear), too much was already in motion to put a stop to what was to come. I could tuck my tail and drown in doubt all I liked... this was happening.

"Lad!" a voice boomed across the din of the room, begging my attention. I could pretend I hadn't heard it. It was plausibly deniable, with how loud it was in here—

"LAD!"

I stopped, the timbre of his voice resonating inside me in some deep recess that was still a young wolf, still somehow instinctively bidden to come when called by my father.

Shit. Not now, not now...

A heavy paw settled on my shoulder, the distinctive cedar cologne oil he preferred to rub into his fur hitting my nose like a nostalgic tide. There was no helping it any longer, so I turned to face him.

Deep blue eyes and a weathered, silver-creased face smiled back at me over the rim of a brandy snifter. I had my father's eyes, blue like the depths of the Kadrush Sea, my relatives said. My black fur was from my mother's side. My father, Cullen, was steel blue gray like a storm cloud and could be equally as tempestuous when his moods took him. Thankfully tonight he seemed to be in high spirits.

I knew full well that wouldn't last.

My father and I were the same height now. Had been for about a year, and I still wasn't over that. He'd been a mountain to me, growing up. Always this powerful, booming presence in my life whenever he was around. Which was fairly often—at least half the year. An impressive feat when you owned and took a heavy hand in operating a Cartel. My brother would take over for him soon, and I was glad of it, considering my own plans. Also, my father's health was waning as he spanned his fiftieth year, and he'd always thrown himself into his conquests with little regard for the toll it was taking on him.

I wanted him to settle down. Mom wanted him to settle down. I'd outlive him at this rate, and while that might sound natural for most sons, I was not expected to live a long life.

"I won't tell your mother if you want to have at the brandy tonight," he said, winking subtly at me. "You're with family. We'll keep an eye out. Have you seen Mischa? The Aunt Pack was asking after her."

I barely resisted rolling my eyes at his nod to his sisters. He had five of them, and they were fabled fierce women, especially if there was gossip to be hunted down. They were particularly voracious at family functions and events like weddings and funerals. To be honest I'd never had much in common with my aunts or much to discuss with them. They were all close to my father's age; half of them were widows by now and all had extended families and children. I suppose I should have been glad for such a large, close family, but it all went down a bit sour when you were the subject of incessant pity and constantly reminded that taking part in the expanding the bloodline as they were all doing would be irresponsible and selfish.

"That's alright," I said with a hand up, doing my best to force a slight smile. "And no, I… haven't seen her. Not for a little while, anyway. She was dancing, wasn't she? Maybe she went out for air."

I'd locked her in that drawing room. She was safe, of course, but she'd be found before long, and I needed to not be here when that happened. I wasn't even certain she would tell my father what I had planned, but regardless of that, I was honestly worried she'd try to stop me herself. She was certainly bold enough to take action on her own.

I felt a pang of shame lance through me—the first of many tonight, I was sure. I was ruining her wedding, at least for her. And even though I knew this wasn't a marriage she was entering into with high hopes, she'd seemed happy tonight before I sprung my ill-fated escape plan on her.

I was about to let so many people down. Literally every person who loved me, every person who called me kin. The most important people in the world to me. What the hell was I doing?

"Son," that voice again, deep but quieter, softened by alcohol and a trace of concern. I'd looked away from him. I forced myself to make eye contact again, praying to a god I didn't believe in that he couldn't see the war inside me.

He held my gaze firmly for a terrifying moment, the chandelier light reflecting off the diamond cuffs in his ears and the bits of emerald and gold in his mane. Our ancestors had worn their valuables on their person out of necessity, the Amur incursions and the constant shifting of the frozen wastes forcing us into a nomadic lifestyle. We'd never really settled in one place, even after we'd prospered. We were all wanderers.

All except me.

"Why are you having trouble looking me in the eyes?" he demanded coolly, but intensely.

I set my muzzle in a firm line. I'd said my good-byes to this man in my mind last night. Over a family meal I'd fully intended to be my last with them, at least until I'd proven I could handle freedom. I hadn't counted on having to see him on my way out the door, and it was freezing me up.

But when Cullen Reed asked you a question, you answered.

"You don't have to sink her," I said quietly, but audible enough that he'd hear me over the din of conversation in the room and the string quartet playing for the dance hall a room away.

He gave a frustrated huff and leaned back away from me. "This again," he growled as he finished his snifter, setting it down on the tray of a server walking past us. "I've indulged you too much in this. You've had your say—more than once, I'll add—and I think I've entertained your arguments more than I should have, already. I understand this is something you feel strongly about, for whatever reason."

"She's a work of art, dad," I balled my fists at my side, going on, "a true rarity, in this century. There's no other like her."

"That ship," he spoke with obviously fraying patience, "is an antique... from a grandiose age in which men lacked all sense and reason, and the Amurescan Empire was at its most arrogant peak. And just like their Empire, she is a crumbling wreck. She is a testament to reckless indulgence... not art."

"You're the one who purchased her," I reminded him.

He sighed. "A sin I have long since regretted. It just seemed such a pity to see her rotting in dry-dock for so long—"

"So you'd rather she rot at the bottom of the sea?!"

"—and I thought, at the time, that she'd make a useful if cumbersome cornerstone for the Southern Belt fleet," he continued. "A deterrent to anyone fool enough to prey on our lumber ships. But the Hammerhead has filled that role more efficiently and with half the repair costs and one third the men. The Manoratha is defunct, Grayson. Outdated, over-gunned, and too expensive to crew."

"Those men were on contract for a full three years," I said, trying not to say the words through my teeth. "There aren't enough ships hiring on in this port to take them all. Half of them are Huudari and barely speak the language here. You could at least sail them home."

"I can't sink her in the hyenas' waters without paying them for the privilege or ceding the vessel to them." He waved a hand. "You know this, we've had this talk before. We're going around in circles."

"Then let the hyenas have her!" I lost my battle to frustration for a moment, my voice exceeding a respectable threshold. A few people looked at us, but tried to make it seem as though they weren't snooping. I didn't care.

My father just laughed at me, full-on, showing off his fangs. "Well now you're just sounding like a child," he chided. "Son. I am not... handing over... a one-hundred-and-twenty-four gun first rate battleship of the line... to a rival nation full of pirates and privateers. I should not need to explain to you why. Do you understand the damage a vessel like that could wreak upon the shipping lanes if it fell into the wrong hands?" Before I could answer, he shook his head. "Of course you don't. Honestly, I don't know why I'm wasting my breath here. I tire of circling around back to this every other week. You do not understand the business as your brother and I do. You just think the damned boat is pretty."

I felt my ears curl back against my mane, my tongue tickling my teeth as I spoke. "I understand the Cartel far better than you give me credit for, father."

He sighed, long and through his nose like my mother always told him to do when he was losing his temper. "You've never even been to sea, Grayson. Your fixation on this ship is... unnatural. It's become an obsession. I regret bringing that wreck into our lives more than you can know. I don't understand why, but just knowing it exists has... changed you, somehow."

"I was already changing," I assured him.

"As well you should, and then some," he snorted. "You're growing up. How about a little maturity to go along with those brass balls of yours?"

"Don't sink her," I begged, one more time. I tried to put everything I had into the request, every ounce of humility I could muster.

Still, he was unmoved.

"She is obsolete, boy," he bit out. "How many more times must I say this? Ships like that have a very limited lifespan until their inherent failures compound and it is not worth anyone's time, money, or effort to keep them anymore. She leaks like a sieve, we can't berth her in half the ports in the known world because her keel runs too deep, there's structural issues across the entire hull because of how the length of her twists in the waves..."

He shook his head. "It's a deficient vessel, lad. It should have been left in dry-dock or destroyed. It's too dangerous to sell it."

"Then she's clearly of use to someone. Isn't she?" I demanded.

"No one who should have her," he said, his voice deadly serious. I felt his paw on my arm suddenly, his fingers sinking into my sleeve. "Son," he said, "if you wanted a more active role in the Cartel, I've been trying to offer that to you for years. I'm not trying to keep you out of the family business. Your mother and I want you to find your way, regardless of your... limitations. We want you to be happy and fulfilled. There was and still is a path for you. I know and respect your mind and how diligent you've been in your studies. You could do a lot of good for our family in an administrative position."

"I don't belong in your offices, tallying ledgers all day," I said sharply.

"Then," he gave me a long-suffering look, his eyes weary, "where exactly is it you think you belong, Grayson?"

My contact with the Dockworkers' Union was exactly where he'd said he'd be, at exactly the right time. The stout badger exchanged nary a word with me at the carriage house, merely brushed past me rough enough that I'd notice and dropped a creased, weathered old messenger bag on my table before giving me a meaningful look and moving back into the bustle of the evening drinking crowd.

I dragged the bag by its strap to the edge of the table and peered briefly inside to confirm it was what I knew it to be. Ledgers, the correct ones accounting for the cargo that had somehow fallen through the cracks in our Cartel's most recent imports. With such enormous volume, the margins were flexible enough to allow for quite a bit of embezzling, if you knew how to keep each time you skimmed just below the mark where someone would notice.

I'd facilitated this sort of thing for the Dockworkers' Union for years now without even the necessity of taking up an official position in the Cartel. All I'd ever needed was access to the Records Office and a bit of ink and a quill. As long as I got at a ledger before the bookkeepers there had and had one of the Union boys back up the shipment numbers were correct (which they always did because they were the ones profiting off the scheme), the various bookkeepers never apparently thought to question each other's work.

Ironically, my father was right. If I'd had any interest in this as a vocation, I could have quickly become indispensable to the Reed Cartel. If I could rob them without being noticed for years, I could sure as hell catch others doing the same.

But of course, I didn't want to. My focus was dispensation, not further hoarding. It had started as a pursuit borne out of bitterness, I'll attest. Once I'd come to terms with just why it was I'd felt uneasy with the truths my education was yielding, it hadn't taken long for my petty, self-indulgent issues with my family to manifest into something altogether more rebellious. In short, if they wouldn't pay the people who were the cogs in the machine of our Cartel better, I would.

Honestly, it was telling that they hadn't caught me. It went to show just how much they could spare before it was even of notice to them or the company.

This ledger—scrawled in messy ink by a barely literate man by the look of it—was the Union's farewell gift to me. I regretted leaving them without their inside man, but they assured me they had a handle on how I'd managed the grift for so long now, and one of the other bookkeepers was in their pocket. They'd get by without me.

No one other than the Dockworkers' Union could have re-supplied a ship intended to be scuttled in one night. They'd done it the night before in secrecy; I probably didn't want to know how they'd managed that, honestly. Hopefully it had involved greasing palms and not… violence.

I gripped the hilt of my trophy saber nervously. This part was over. The ship was supplied and seaworthy enough to make it to our first port of call. The local marine guard would not think twice about a vessel leaving berth at this time of night; it was a full moon, and many canine and feline crews sailed by the light of the moon. In her belly was a skeleton crew of men who knew her, many of them the sailors whose contracts we'd cut off without warning.

Organizing a crew for this had proven to be the most challenging part for me, because it was the end of the business I had no experience in. You could study maritime engineering, sailing, and navigation your whole life out of books—and it's not that I had no practical experience; I'd grown up around these ships and had spent as much time on them at port as possible over the last few years—but I was no fool. I knew all of that would mean next to nothing when we were out on the water. That's why I needed a Captain.

The actual Captain of the Manoratha was an ancient Amur ex-pat, an angry little cur by the name of Matthew Lawffrey. He'd been all too happy to retire and was a good friend of my father, so I'd instantly written him off. He'd want no part in any of this.

His First Mate, however, was more amenable. A coydog named Thaddeus Buckner. He'd caught wind of the plot at some point through his connections with the crew and hadn't immediately ratted us out. Although he'd been aggressive about muscling his way into the hierarchy ever since the first meeting he'd attended down by the pier and his penchant for intimidation and threats didn't seem to be winning him many supporters within the ranks of the already volatile crew we'd managed to gather up, he was no doubt experienced and willing to go along with our plan for the promise of a helm at his command.

A full third of my skeleton crew wasn't even comprised of seamen; they were Anarchists and Socialists and… persuasions somewhere between the two… from the collectives and groups I'd found myself a part of in the midnight meetings I'd attended over the last few years. It turns out embezzling and smuggling from one of the largest Cartels makes you some interesting friends.

They ran the range from political dissidents to actual criminals to… well, academics. Like myself. But what none of them was… was a Captain.

We needed a man with practical experience running a crew and a ship, and while I could probably take my pick from a wide swath of crewmen who thought they were qualified for it, Thaddeus was proven to be so. And right now, we needed 'proven'. We were taking so many risks as it was. I had to go for the sure thing when it came to something so critical.

I'd plotted our route and was hoping to fall into a Navigation role more easily than some of the more hands-on jobs on the ship. But it seemed folly to plan for my future aboard the vessel before we'd even gotten away with this yet. Primarily what I brought to the table in all of this was stowed in my travel bag, and it was truly irreplaceable. I would work out the kinks of what kind of sailor I would be once we got out there.

Gathering up my things, I finished my beer (in pubs like this they were practically water, so I allowed myself one every now and then) and stood, politely pushing my way through the crowd towards the back alleyway door. A rat came through it with a swinging clatter and a belch, still smelling like piss, likely what the patrons here used the alley for more than anything else.

Stepping outside confirmed that. I curled my nose at the sheer reek of it, my eyes watering almost immediately. Pressing my finger-pads to my closed lids for a moment, I took in a shuddering breath and tried to calm myself. My regrets, my anxieties, my fears… all of them were bubbling up like a broth threatening to push off the lid. I was an hour away from going to sea for the first time in my life. Giving it all up now would be the most profoundly cowardly thing I had ever done. And stupid, too, because I'd suffer the consequences of what I'd done so far either way. So, I may as well go through with it.

"Wetting yourself yet?" an only vaguely familiar voice called from the street entranceway to the alley.

I spun on my heel, my heart thudding in my chest for a moment before I recognized the coydog. His fur was a patchy mix of dull charcoal black with rusty brown legs and arms, so he blended into the dinge of the alley all too well. If you weren't an Amurescan who was up on their breeding you could easily mistake him for a dog, which is probably how he'd made his way up through the Cartel. He dressed like one, too… clothing too fine and tailored to fit in well with the rest of the eclectic crew and indeed most of the citizens in this district of the city. He wore navy blues and blacks, with meticulously-polished brass buttons and white spats, pretending towards a Pedigree standard there. Most men couldn't keep any part of their outfit that close to the ground so clean. Not even me.

He was also wearing an obviously-new greatcoat. Dressing for the job he wanted. I couldn't blame him. He'd probably been waiting for a Command position his entire life.

I started towards him, loosing a long breath. "You scared the hell out of me," I admitted. "I was worried I'd been followed."

"Do you have the maps?" he demanded in a voice that set me on edge with its aggressive intensity. He'd always been like this, though. Many Captains and First Mates, and sailors in general, were. My interactions other than at the docks, organizing crew members in secret, had mostly been limited to parties and meetings in our financial offices, but even then, many of the Captains I'd known had been very assertive and domineering.

"I do," I assured him, patting my travel bag. I was actually traveling very light, most of the weight in my bag was not my possessions. It was the key to all of this. The lynchpin in my plan and the promise for the Manoratha and her crew's future.

The Reed Cartel's shipping lanes.

This ship and the cargo in her belly, mostly dry goods and rations, would be the last things I'd ever steal from my family. While I hated the Cartel's practices, I couldn't bear the thought of using the Manoratha against one of my family's own ships. Destroying a Captain or a family member's future, reputation... and... if they chose to fight back... potentially having to take their lives...

But the Reed Cartel had information on various other fleets' manifests, planned routes, transfer locations, and Crew, including who was at the helm of each vessel. And that last one could be all-important. Because I knew which men were cowards and which might put up a struggle.

Which was sort of important because... one-hundred and twenty-four guns aside... we had no powder.

My father had obviously seen to it that the Manoratha had no powder or loaded guns when he was setting her up to be scuttled. And black powder was not something our Cartel shipped or traded in these days. That was its own business and was more often than not a federally-protected and monitored trade. It was next to impossible for me to get my hands on it through any means I'd been using so far.

Our guns were useless. But no one had to know that.

To really get up and running as a Privateer vessel, we obviously needed powder. I didn't have the kinds of connections men in that trade generally used—at least not yet—so we were going to have a rocky start to things if we couldn't get our hands on some. We didn't have enough pilfered cargo to trade for it on the black market without exhausting the ship. Which left... stealing it, obviously.

"Have you got our mark?" Thaddeus asked, cocking his hip and taking his time crossing the suspicious puddles between the cracks in the cobblestones as he approached me.

"I have a vessel picked out," I nodded, "a point on its route where it'll be isolated and too far from military aid for flares to be spotted, and a Captain

I happen to know from reliable sources would sooner swim than risk an open-water gunfight. And he's been across the ocean for the better half of the year, so he doesn't know the Manoratha's been stripped and decommissioned. It's the perfect get."

"Perfect," he repeated for some reason. He smiled just enough to show his teeth and reached out, settling a hand on my shoulder. "Y'did good for a soft-pawed rich brat. That the bag?"

"The other's the ledgers from the Dockworkers' Union," I said, glancing at the other bag slung over my opposite shoulder. "How are the crew doing?"

"Itching to leave," he said, glancing sidelong over his shoulder for a moment back down the alleyway. "We aren't letting anyone vacate the ship now that everything's sprung. If they want t'bail at this point they'll need to do so at our first port o'call."

"Right," I agreed, readjusting the strap of my main bag. "Alright, let's go."

"The bag," he said, holding out a hand. His other was still on his hip. I didn't miss it.

Nor the blade he was wearing there.

"I'll carry it," I said, trying to put the same kind of authority into my voice that my father always managed so effortlessly. It came out sounding like a pale mockery, and he was no more impressed than I was.

"Let's not do this." He 'tch'd between his teeth, clutching with his hand to indicate it was still empty. "You wanted to help the crew; you did that. I'm sure you had a good time slummin' it for a while and showing what-for to your old man, but it's time to go home."

"I can't go home!" I snarled. "What the hell are you talking about? I'm part of this now. I'll be arrested if I go home."

"Did you tell anyone outside the plot what you were planning?" His features tipped into something altogether colder. And now he wasn't just being aggressive, he was demanding.

I hesitated just enough that I think he caught it was a lie. "No," I said too quickly after the moment's pause. "Of course not."

"You stupid shit," he growled, pulling the long knife from his side. Its length flashed in the moonlight, but not nearly as luminous as the perfect sheen on my own saber. His weapon was peppered and worn.

Well-used.

I stepped back a pace, and he followed. My own hand went to my hip, closing around the hilt of my saber.

He barked a laugh at me. "Please," was all he said in response.

"Why are you doing this?" I asked, trying not to make it sound like a plea.

"I gave you the chance to go home," he curled his lip. "At this point you're just wasting my time, and we ain't got much of that. Did you honestly think I was going to let a ponce like you usurp my ship out from under me?"

"I'm not vying for Captain!" I got my saber out of its sheath since he was allowing me to for the moment. For all his bluster, he did honestly seem hesitant about murdering me right here in public. We may have been in an alleyway, but the street was visible from here, and I had to figure he'd rather scare me into leaving than actually run me through to get the bag.

I had to figure that, because the alternative was that I was going to die here, in a piss-stained alleyway, an hour after betraying everything and everyone I'd ever loved. I was barely a district away from the safety of my family. The safety I'd run from, because I found their overprotectiveness too confining.

They'd find my body, and they'd know everything I'd done because the ship would be gone, the crew would be gone, my murderer would be gone, and Mischa, my closest confidante and as close to a sister as I'd ever had, knew what I'd planned and would most certainly tell my parents when they were bereft, looking for answers.

My hand shook where it was fisted around my blade's grip. The tournament saber was unfamiliar to me, and the cording was rough. I wished I had my foil, but... I'd taken the saber because it was, despite its ornamentation, a real blade. And some part of me, naïve though I was, had entertained the possibility that I might need it.

I wasn't as good with a saber as I was with a foil. But that wasn't even what worried me the most.

I'd never been in a real fight, where my life was truly on the line before.

"Did you really think we'd let the son of the man who laid us off lead us out of here?!" He pressed in closer, giving me no space. I recognized what he was doing in some part of my mind that remembered my short arms training. He was giving me less room to maneuver with my longer blade.

"I don't want to lead; I just want to be part of the crew," I said, letting him back me up with a cross-step to my left, so that I could slowly turn us in the opposite direction. As expected, he went into the circle, keeping his blade trained on my right. Before long, my back was to the street, rather than the dead-end of the alleyway. Maybe someone would notice us...

"And in any case," I pressed, "I didn't meet much push-back from the men I pulled out of the dregs on the piers. They didn't care who I was, they just wanted their contract back or something like it."

"You didn't build back that crew, your money did that," he snuffed.

"You can't even speak Huudari," I said flatly. "Eighty percent of the men we got back are from Mataa. You at least need me as a translator."

"I've got the sand dogs for that," he said, using the derogatory term for jackals. They were frequently in-betweens for Amurescan and Carvecian canines and Huudari people. A lot of canines preferred to limit their circles to only other canines. It was disappointing to know the man I'd hoped would lead us was as specist as a Pedigree, but also not terribly surprising.

"Last chance!" he snapped. "THE BAG. NOW."

"If I give it to you, you'll kill me," I said, now certain of that fact. I tipped my ears back to listen for anyone crossing nearby on the street.

No one was coming.

"I didn't count on starting off making my name as a Scion-killer," he growled, his body weight shifting back a hair's breadth, "but it'll sure make an impression coming back to that wreck reeking of blood."

I don't think he expected me to catch his first swing. And I only barely managed it, his blade shrieking down the pristine edge of my saber and jamming against my basket hilt, locking us close enough that when he twisted free of me, he caught the front of my shirt and sliced upwards, the blade popping free of the fabric and nicking me under the chin.

Or at least, it had felt like a nick at first. The stench of blood soon joined the other unpleasant odors in the alley, and my throat grew warm and wet. He backed away, his blade-tip red a good inch down.

It was surreal. I'd been shoved, grappled, and battered about by my instructors, but I'd never been cut. I couldn't even feel the pain yet, his long knife was too sharp.

Would I even feel it if he killed me? Or would it just be... over?

"How can you call her a wreck?" I asked hoarsely, the words just bubbling up out of me, nothing going through my head or coming out of it making any sense right now. I was laid bare, moving and speaking at my most honest. All reaction, no thought.

"I loathe that boat," he said, taunting me with the bloody tip of his blade. "Everyone who's been aboard her does. You're a spoiled prat. You don't understand what it's like to be trapped in a broken, piece of shit vessel that could fail on you at any goddamn moment!"

Swallowing, I readied for his next swing. "Yes, I do," I said.

But he wasn't listening any more.

I saw my opening and didn't really think about it, my body just... moved. My problem on the tournament circuit had always been overthinking. Overplanning. While I was calculating, the more reactive opponents would get points in on me. My instructors had me practice drills, repetition builds muscle memory, my least favorite tutor had said on more than one occasion. I'd end the sessions exhausted, frustrated, and feeling as though I'd done little more than swing my arm like a pinwheel for two hours. I'd ache and curse their names for days. And then in the competitions, it would never matter, anyway.

This time, it mattered.

I don't know if it was the threat of death or the fact that I was using an unfamiliar weapon that had me move on instinct rather than plot and consider what I was going to do. But when he came in with a cut and thrust for my kidneys, I battered his blade away, shouldered into him until he lost his footing and spun, and suddenly his back was to me. And I just...

I stuck him right up beneath his ribs. It wasn't a run-through, not even close. But it was the most I'd ever sunk a blade into... anything. Let alone anyone.

My saber came out with much more than an inch of red, a full third of the blade. The stain began to spread from the slim puncture mark in his blue coat, soaking like ink through a tablecloth.

He stumbled and tried to turn around, staying standing and holding fast to his blade. I thought for a moment that he'd keep fighting. Or run. Maybe both of us could leave this encounter alive.

It seemed to hit him at a delay. He said nothing, only swayed on his feet and stared ahead, swallowing a few times before gurgling up blood and choking around an unnatural sound that had probably been meant to be words.

I backed away from him, and felt the first tremors shiver their way up my body, collecting in my limbs. For one terrifying moment, I thought I was going to seize. But it wasn't my curse causing the shaking. It was deep, primordial horror over what I had just done.

Thaddeus fell to the ground, pink foam bubbling out from between his teeth. I'd punctured a lung and likely worse. He looked like he was in pain—a lot of pain—blinking through tears, still trying to push himself up on his knees, grabbing at the slick cobblestones as if there were something there that would avail him.

I didn't stay to watch him die.

I ran... and ran... and ran... until my lungs were afire and screaming at me to stop, and I'd terrified every poor soul who had the misfortune to be out wandering the market district at this time of night. I ran until my legs gave out, catching myself against a signpost on a cracking, narrow street hedged in by shuttered homes at the top of a hill.

And that's when I saw her.

This was one of the few harbors that could accommodate her so close to shore, thanks to the depth of the bay. She was magnificent in relief, silhouetted save for the few lanterns lit on her decks, floating in the sparkling, moonlit water like the beast of legend she was named for. A true monster of the sea, real unlike her namesake.

And thanks to me, she had no Captain.

Aboard her were men of every stripe whom I'd promised work, fortune, and freedom. I'd been either too blind or too idealistic to see what Thaddeus had planned for me, and the way he'd spoken about it, he wasn't alone. He'd used me to get what he wanted, and he'd very nearly gotten it. There were others on that ship—I could only guess at how many—who would do the same if they thought they could.

But there were also people I'd known from the city. From school, from the parlors where we'd talked philosophy and economics, men from the Dockworkers' Union whom I'd known for years who'd decided to join us in this venture, and a lot of laid-off sailors that I'd talked to personally, listened to, and tried to get to know. They couldn't all think so little of me as Thaddeus had... they couldn't all be as vicious as he had...

But some of them would be. I wasn't completely inexperienced with the world. I knew some of the people I was getting into bed with to do something like this were dangerous.

My hands were still shaking. My legs were still shaking. Glancing down, I realized with a start that I was still holding my sword. My bloody sword.

It's no wonder that old beggar woman on the last corner had run from me.

I had no choice any more. Truth be told, I'd not had a choice since I'd started stealing from my family. It was always going to come to this point, one way or another. I was a criminal, now. I'd been a criminal for a long time.

I didn't feel wrong for stealing, not when I knew how my family made that money and how many people had been hurt, overworked, or cheated in the process. Cartel work was dirty work, and I was born into it. Whether or not I'd realized it or played an active part in it, I'd been profiting off of hurting others since I came into this world. Coming to that understanding is what had changed my entire outlook on life. Privateering wasn't a worse path... it was just a different one.

But killing...

I looked out again over the bay, and the beautiful monster my father wanted to destroy. She, and everyone aboard her, were relying on me. I could moralize and torture myself over my decisions and the look on that man's face as he died, crying, in a piss-stained alleyway... another night.

I had no other path but the one before me, not any more.

☙ ❧

The Isle of Sharhassal was an intimidating place to sail into when you were aboard one small schooner with minimal firepower and a crew of barely fifteen men and women. While it might be a weakness to admit this,

111

I had grown accustomed over the years to the might and the reputation that my own ship carried with it wherever we sailed. But the Manoratha was nowhere near as fast as Lunden's small charting vessel, and, more importantly, his ship was nowhere near as conspicuous.

We couldn't even sail into this port aboard Lotus's small warship. Her floral signet was emblazoned on the very sails, its tigress maidenhead and red adornments as eye-catching as anything on my own ship. We had a similar style. Get noticed, carry your reputation with you like a badge of honor, and intimidate your way through encounters rather than duke it out, whenever you could.

Which meant we were ill-suited for a covert plan like this. And if Luther's Cerberus fleet was anywhere nearby (they were, I was certain of it, not that he'd tell me where), they'd raise every eyebrow in port mooring here. The Amurescan Navy only ever came into these waters for diplomatic missions or as an escort. They weren't exactly trade vessels.

Which left Lunden's ships to get us here in the right time frame and beneath notice. While Roccosal's men might have seen the otter's vessels on Dokuro and may have even picked out by now that he was working with us, they hardly stood out. Unless we got unlucky enough that one of the very men who we'd run afoul of in our flight had somehow made it to port in time to see which ship we'd boarded—and remembered the nondescript features of it well enough to pick it out now—we were probably safe. And honestly, I can't think why any of them would assume we would have followed Roccosal all the way here. The last time we'd tangled, we'd been running away.

He didn't know the cattle dog I'd had at my side, who had said nothing throughout the whole encounter and was not widely known by appearance, was the fabled Luther Denholme, pirate hunter. Or that he'd chosen Roccosal as his next quarry. If he knew, he still probably wouldn't have assumed we'd chase him here in a tiny ship with next to no guns.

Because to be fair... that would be crazy.

I had to admit that Lotus was right on one point. I'd never known Denholme outside of his reputation until last week, but now that I was spending time with the cattle dog and experiencing what it was like to have another madman as a sounding board and an eager participant to play my ideas off of... the world would never be safe again. And honestly for all that Lotus tried to be the voice of reason, she wasn't much better. It had taken all of one night for us to land on the fact that it was either the sabotage plan or a months-long ordeal battling Roccosal on his fortress-island, and none of us had the stomach for that. Denholme was willing, but even so, he reckoned the morale of his crew might not endure for as long as it would take to crack that nut.

Lotus was the hold-out until the end, but in her case, it wasn't even because the plan was dangerous. She just hated the idea of despoiling Roccosal's beautiful ship. We'd settled on waylaying, nothing that might risk sinking the Man of War. We spent half the voyage here coming up with various methods, but we hadn't firmly settled on any yet. Our plan was coming together in pieces, haphazardly.

The only thing we knew for certain was that Lotus was going to be our coordinator. She couldn't possibly stow aboard one of Roccosal's vessels, since there was just absolutely no way to cover up the fact that she was female. She'd travel with us on Sharhassal while we might need the backup, be part of the planning process, and then head back to Lunden to reconnoiter with the Manoratha, her own fleet, and the Cerberus fleet once they phantom-appeared from whatever alternate world Luther had hidden them in.

Honestly, the man was spooky. I would kill to know how he planned his ambushes and always seemed to be able to sail in and out of hotspots and high traffic lanes without being seen. He'd alluded to the fact that he had a very small, unmarked vessel in his fleet that nearly no one ever saw (his fleet was the Cerberus fleet after all, I think most would assume he only had three vessels, and that was clearly intentional) running recon for the larger ships so they could float in and out of areas with no need to scout ahead themselves, and that he ran his ships very light and high in the water. But still.

"Without you there, aren't you worried?" I asked him as we waited, leaning against the railing and just now beginning to pick out the individual figures of people along the docks. This was a bustling trade hub like many other Huudari islands, the flags being flown aboard the dozens of vessels in the bay as diverse as the people here. I'd been to many ports like this, but rarely with such interesting company.

"What exactly do you mean?" he asked, not looking my way. He was taking in the sights, as well.

"I mean, I know you sent the wolfhound back," I cleared my throat. Good riddance to that one; the man made me uncomfortable. "Is he your First Mate? Will he be making most of the tactical decisions in your absence?"

"Johannes is the Captain of my flagship," he said. "My First Mate is a man named Fitzer. Unofficially. He's a rat, so he isn't legally allowed to be appointed to the position, but I've refused to appoint anyone else. He's good at crew management."

"Wait…" I blinked, "…so you aren't—"

"I'm the Admiral of the fleet," he assured me. "But Johannes is its Steward. He was appointed in charge of protecting my father-in-law's investment, and I prefer to keep him on as Captain. It's unconventional, but it works for us. Especially in situations like this."

"'Unconventional' seems to be your thing," I chuckled.

"Indeed," he agreed. "In any case, Johannes won't be directing the fleet, only his own ship. One of my Captains is appointed Tactical Coordinator in my absence. He's got a sharp mind… I wouldn't keep him around if he didn't. Disagreeable man in all other ways."

"Is he the Captain of your scouting vessel?" I guessed, pressing.

"No," he said, finally turning to look at me. "Have you plumbed the well enough yet? You're really pushing it."

"You're being all chatty," I waved a hand flippantly at him. "Not my fault I'm easy to talk to."

"Pester me for information all you like, Reed," he said, turning his attention back to the docks as we pulled in closer. "It won't help you escape or best me the next time I'm on your tail. My fleet is good at what it does because I have smart, skilled Captains, a fierce crew, and my ships are some of the most efficient predators that sail the seas right now. We're like a fine-tuned mechanism, and you won't figure us out by looking at the pieces individually."

"Spoilsport."

He only smiled, vaguely. But at that point, the bell went up that we were lowering anchor, and it would soon be time to disembark.

"Here we go," I exhaled.

We were off to a bad start.

Despite having pulled the remaining nub of my mane into a ponytail and stuffing it under a poncho hood, dressing down in second-hand clothes from one of Lunden's boys and removing all of my jewelry, we were barely in the pier district an hour before someone recognized me. Or Lotus. It was hard to say.

It at least confirmed that we'd been right. Roccosal was here. We hadn't seen his ships coming into port, but this island was long, and it was a well-known fact that the tiger clans had a private port for their own dealings on the eastern half of the isle. Going there without express permission, even coming as near as the passage through the reefs, was considered an act of trespass, so we'd not so much as tried. We assumed he'd be there regardless, so it almost wasn't worth confirming.

I didn't recognize the man, nor pick him out as in any way important, but Lotus had sharper eyes and a better memory. We were getting the lay of the land in the vendor square near the wet market and picking up some food that wasn't Lunden's pickled rations and day-old stew, when I felt her big paw close around my forearm and squeeze.

"Stoat," she said, "brown… one bad eye. Off to your right, near the fish vendor with the shark carcass hanging out front."

I tried to glance in the direction she was indicating without being obvious. I felt Luther shift from beside me, doing the same. I hadn't even caught sight of him yet, or if I had I couldn't pick him out, when her hand on me tightened and she cursed.

"Shit," she growled, "he's bolting!"

"You're certain he—" Luther began.

"Yes!" She peeled back her muzzle to flash her oversized canines. "He was on Dokuro, he's one of his boys. Come on!"

She bulled through the crowd in line beside us without nary a care, paving the way for Luther and me. I nearly tripped over my poncho in my hurry to get off the crate I'd been sitting on where we'd been having a drink, emptying my mug onto the ground and hurriedly clapping it back on my belt.

Denholme, though… he was like a feral dyre on a hunt. He sprung to a full-tilt run, weaving his way through the crowd with the kind of agility that only spry dogs and some types of cats can manage. It certainly helped as well that the man was ninety percent corded muscle. Lotus and I quickly fell behind.

Frantic, well-armed people shoving and ducking their way through an afternoon crowd must have been a common occurrence in this port, because people got out of the way fast, even going so far as to dive towards and plaster themselves on nearby shacks and ramshackle buildings to clear a path. A few people cursed us in Huudari, but no one tried to stop us.

Still, the bobbing, dark triangles of Denholme's ears moved ahead of us and more and more of the mass of fur and bodies began to grow between us. For a harried moment, I was worried we'd lost him, and then Lotus tugged at my sleeve. "There!" She pointed towards an alleyway behind a tannery.

"Fuck, I hate that smell," I curled my nose, feeling the start of my eyes watering as we peeled off down the narrow space between the two clay brick structures.

Denholme was already on the man—and I mean on the ground— wheeling back what looked to be a second punch, his other hand pinning the stoat to the dirt by his throat. His body weight was all that was keeping the thrashing creature from escaping for now, and while he was strong, he looked to be outweighed.

"Help him, I'll keep watch," Lotus said, backing off to move towards the entrance to the alleyway, where her bulk would hopefully keep prying eyes from bearing witness to whatever happened here.

I closed in on the two struggling men, realizing when I got there why it seemed like the stoat was so close to bucking Denholme off. The cattle dog had shifted first one of his thighs, then the other, to press down on the stoat's arms in an attempt to keep him from the knife on his belt. He had to keep his free hand on the man's throat, because the stoat was trying viciously to bite at his arm. It looked like he already had, tearing a good chunk of fur and leaving a bloody gash near his wrist. It was probably not as bad as it looked… but wrist wounds bled like a motherfucker.

Most obviously, I grabbed first for the man's knife, freeing it easily and tossing it back down the alley. Luther began trying to say something between grit teeth, but I only nodded and said, "I've got it, I've got it."

I fell to my knees on the other side of the struggling stoat and wrenched his arms over his head as Luther settled back to sitting on his legs. I pulled them together and knelt my weight down into them, pinning the man from the front while Luther had him pinned at the waist and legs.

He seemed to finally realize he was incapacitated and all at once went limp. The only sign he hadn't lost consciousness were his wide-open, yellow eyes and the persistent growling hiss rumbling through his teeth.

"You're dead men walking," he rasped.

Luther lifted his injured arm up and gave it an impassive look, before licking the blood from it as well as he could and frowning down at the man, the red still staining his muzzle. "Where is your Admiral?"

The stoat only laughed, spit bubbling in his mouth. "Get fucked," he snarled.

"What condition is he in?" Luther continued to press. "Is his wound infected? Did he even survive having it removed?"

"Oh, he's alive," the stoat said, the charcoal black painted into his fur around his eyes making their sulfur yellow color all the more venomous-looking. "N'you I don't know, Amur… but you…" the black pinpricks at the center of those yellow pits moved up towards me. "…you…he'n the boys are gonna have a good time takin' apart, piece by piece when they find out you're here. He was plannin' on hunting you down, anyway. He wants you for his collection. All of you, this time."

"How long since you arrived?" Luther demanded. "If he's tarrying here, he's being treated. How sick is h—"

"I said I DON'T KNOW YOU, CUR!" the stoat spat back at Luther, literally spitting in his eyes, although the cattle dog leaned away with a curl of his muzzle and most of it landed on his cheek.

The pinned man gave an uproarious laugh at that and, with little else he could do to retaliate, snorted back through his muzzle to spit at him again.

He never got the chance. Luther deftly pulled his boot knife and — as casually as one might gut a fish — rammed it down through the man's throat, his last-ditch attempt at defiance dying with him in a messy gurgle.

He leaned back on his haunches as the stoat's body went slack again, pulling the knife free with a pop. I slowly swayed back myself, forcing my

legs to put in the effort to get me upright before I lost the ability and made a fool of myself. They felt like jelly, but they obeyed.

I'd seen a lot of men die over the last twelve years. I'd seen every range of emotion on a man's face as he lost his life and just as diverse a range of reactions from the men who'd killed them.

Luther had called his fleet 'efficient predators'. I'd never heard a man describe their ships that way, not even vicious men. And I knew a lot of vicious men. But watching him dispatch the stoat, I suddenly understood what he'd meant. It was like watching a master craftsman. It wasn't just fast, it wasn't just practiced, it was… minimal effort on his part. No wasted energy, no wasted time, and no unnecessary suffering on the part of his victim.

It wasn't impressive. It was chilling.

"Who was your first?"

"Excuse me?" The cattle dog tipped his ears back and arched his shoulders aggressively, while cleaning his blade with something he'd taken off the man.

I ignored his bristling reaction. "Kill, asshole. Not everything I ask you's an invasive question about your sex life." I reached beneath my coat, masking the slightest quiver in my hand before I got my flask to my muzzle to still the rest. The first tang of copper hitting my nose still... fuck. The smell of urine from the nearby tannery wasn't helping, either. You'd think by now...

He just looked puzzled, as he sheathed his knife. "Odd question regardless. Why do you care?"

"Bit of a milestone, is all," I said.

"If you say so," he muttered, turning and tossing the rag he'd cleaned his blade with over the fallen man. "I don't think about it much."

"So?"

The cattle dog was canny. Too canny, it turned out.

Wheeling on me, he suddenly strode in my direction with enough verve that his very presence forced me back a step, my shoulder bumping the crumbling wall behind me. I opened my mouth to say something—anything, you fool—before his hand closed around my wrist like an iron vice grip, forcing my arm up past the comfortable, concealing folds of my coat, revealing the flask I was holding like I was some child caught pilfering sweets.

Except that I was a grown fucking man, and I was allowed to casually drink, damnit. What the hell was he getting at, here?

Grayson Reed, Privateer Admiral, was drinking again. Truly, the revelation of the century.

It certainly seemed to mean something to him, though. Right away. His muzzle ticked upwards a degree, and he got this... almost delighted look about him, but still with that sly edge his smiles always seemed to have. It made my fur stand on end. I wasn't sure if that smirk made me feel good or bad yet, but it certainly made me feel some kind of way.

"It still bothers you. Doesn't it?" he asked imperiously. He finally dropped my hand. My wrist stung from every inch of his skin that had been in contact with mine. He hadn't even been squeezing it hard enough to hurt, just something about it seared at my flesh like an accusation.

"Wha— murder?!" I nearly coughed on the words. "Bloody hell, man. Yes?"

He had no response to that, at least nothing in words. Only a mild chuckle. And then he turned and strode off, stepping over the fallen man in his path back down the alleyway.

We rejoined Lotus, keeping her post outside the alleyway. She gave Denholme a brief sniff, but said nothing of the air of blood wafting off of him. It had been a clean kill. I couldn't help but notice he'd neatly avoided getting any on his clothes, so the scent would soon get lost in the reek of the market.

We all moved back down the less busy street towards the wet market again, not walking hurriedly so as to avoid getting any more eyes on us than we already had in our mad dash here. This struck me as the sort of place where people didn't ask many questions and the city guard— wherever they were—didn't bother with the lower rungs going at it. They were probably mostly in the upper districts, protecting the Clan holdings.

It was unlikely his body would be found by anyone other than the tannery workers, and even if it was, he wasn't a local, so they'd probably just dump him somewhere. Still… not a good start to what was supposed to be a covert task.

Lotus moved alongside me at a comfortable pace, while Denholme walked ahead of us. We were mostly just putting distance between ourselves and the body for now, and none of us knew the city, so he seemed to just be heading north, away from the pier. I was content to follow for now, while I gathered my wits in the wake of what had just happened.

I felt Lotus at my hip, and then suddenly her velvety voice was in my ear. "This is why I told you not to get on his shitlist. He's a hunter," she said, just above a whisper, so that amidst the din of the crowded street, only I'd hear. She looked ahead of us at his triangular ears as they distantly bobbed through the crowd. "A predator, by his own words," she added, even lower. It was startling how we were both apparently thinking about the same thing. "And we're his prey. Never forget that, no matter how chummy you try to get with him… he will take you down, bring you in, and hang you if he gets the chance at it."

I wanted to tell her she was wrong. That, clearly, we'd bonded through all of this. I would stop short of saying the man might consider me a friend… although to be earnest, I think I might have liked that, if we'd met under different circumstances.

But.

Hang me? Would we really be enemies again, when all was said and done here? After all of this? We may have been in contrary lines of work, sure…

"Don't be charmed by him," Lotus's real, spoken words cut through my thoughts like a knife. Her voice begged my eyes to hers and once she had me, she locked me with her gaze. "Listen to me," she snapped. "I'm your only friend, here."

"You worked with him," I pointed out, "in that ploy of yours, to literally apprehend me and force a deal out of me."

"I'm a Pirate Hunter, too," she reminded me. "But that was then and this is now. And now that I've gotten to know you... I like you. You're a genuine soul, Reed. More than I gave you credit for. You're one of the good ones. When I tell you I'll never hunt you again, never hurt you again, because I've come to know you now and I like the man I've come to know, you can believe me."

I couldn't help the foolish smile that inched at my muzzle. She sounded genuine. And, yes, it was easier to believe those words coming from the soft mouth of a pretty woman. And maybe she knew that and was playing me. But I don't know. It sounded like she meant them.

"But Denholme?" Her eyes flicked back through the crowd towards the man in question. "He is not your friend. He will never be your friend. Hunting people like us is a sport to him. Even worse, he seems to be a true believer that what he does makes the world a better place, somehow. He's a zealot. He will never see you as anything other than an agent of chaos, a plague to be cleansed, and once this sojourn of ours is over he will use everything he's learned about you here against you."

She sighed, backing off on her ferocity a little and reaching down to curl her warm, soft fingers through my own colder, still somewhat trembling ones. I was mortified to find my hand was still shaking a bit. I hadn't had enough to drink yet, I suppose.

"Stop giving him ammunition," she said gently, squeezing my paw in her own.

❧

We had a limited amount of time on the island to accomplish our task: precisely as long as it took for Roccosal to decide it was time to move on, and who knew how the fuck long that would be. At the very least, our encounter with the stoat had gotten us some hard-won information.

One, Roccosal was alive. The stoat could have been full of shit, of course, but we'd all spoken since as we wandered the market and settled at least on that; he'd sounded dreadfully sincere on that point. Like he'd known he was about to die, but that we'd soon be dead, as well. So, that brought us to the second fact.

Two, the dhole had it out for us. I mean, fair play. We'd walked away from what could have otherwise been a bloodless, if humiliating (on my part) trade, then taken a cheap shot at him on our way out. Roccosal had been playing dirty, and we had the moral high-ground, etcetera, but no one really cared about all of that in the end. We could've ended this thing right there and then, if not for the third fact.

Roccosal was wounded. Probably badly so. Also not surprising, given how close that crossbow bolt had come to hitting its mark. I wished, in retrospect, Denholme's man had aimed for the guts. You could do all kinds of damage down there and sentence a man to a miserable death by sepsis, even if you missed whatever you were specifically aiming for. But the wolfhound had aimed for the heart, and when you miss the heart, at best you hit a lung. More often, you strike the ribs or the collarbone, and the shot had seemed high to me, not low.

Still, there was always infection. We could hope for that.

Roccosal was a tough bastard who'd lived and prospered for nearly two decades now as a Huudari Pirate. That was not a racket for the weak, and, big well-armed ships aside, he wasn't known for being afraid of getting his hands dirty. He liked to scrap, was known for it in fact. He'd sunk ships that would've been more valuable to take, just to make a point. He was notoriously petty, proud, and easily aggrieved, slaughtering entire crews he could have press-ganged or leaving them stranded at sea on compromised ships or boarding boats that had no chance of making landfall, fodder for sharks and storms.

The point is, he was a ruthless beast of a man, and while I was not much for religion or superstition, I did believe in strength of spirit, and he had that in abundance. He wouldn't let a passing infection or a flesh wound take him down. If he was suffering now, he would remember all of that suffering and use it as fuel to fire his hatred for me, the man he assumed responsible for this slight.

We still had no reason whatsoever to believe they knew or suspected Denholme was involved in any of this. Even though I'd taken my time and done some research on the cattle dog before this misadventure, all I'd gleaned about him physically was that he was a fairly average-looking Blue Heeler, sturdily-built, and generally wore his red coat at sea like most Amurescan Admirals. And without that there was really nothing distinctive about him. I hadn't even gotten an eye color, which now that I knew the man surprised me. I found his gold eyes very striking, even if no one else did. But I guess details like that just aren't the sort of thing that make their way into public knowledge.

He'd really dodged a bullet here, since Roccosal would never think to pin the assassination attempt on him or his fleet. That being said... I mean... I don't think he actually would have minded being the subject of the dhole's ire. The feeling was clearly mutual. But it gave him an advantage for now in that Roccosal didn't know he was involved. And he'd been so careful not to let on the location of his fleet—even to me. That secret was going to stay kept until it mattered.

If we failed here, but somehow survived failing, Luther could walk away from this. I on the other hand would be dogged across the seas by the dhole's bloody fleet until he'd avenged himself on me. And honestly, given all of that, the fact that Luther still wanted to do this spoke more of his character than anything else I'd learned about him so far.

Lotus could have her opinions on the man. I understood where they came from, and I wasn't dismissing them outright, but for now, I was inclined to trust at least that we were working towards the same ends for the same reason. Ironically, given who we all were, this was a matter of honor at this point. I guess in my case you could also say it was survival; this was, after all, the best chance I'd have at the man before he was hunting me. If it came to that, I stood no chance against his overwhelming numbers if I had to deal with him alone. So, having Lotus and Luther helping me was a good deal. But it was more than that.

We were all in this because we despised the man and each, for our own reasons, thought the seas would be a better place without him. Mutual hatred suited me fine as a motivator. It was easy to understand, predictable, and not likely to change.

Which brought us to four. I had a limited amount of time I could likely rely on these two, and I had to manage my expectations with them. We'd all somehow come to a consensus that sabotaging Roccosal's fleet while he was at sea, between the two ports, was the best option. It was nothing short of a miracle that we'd all agreed on a tactic so controversial. Pulling it off would be another matter.

The fact was we still didn't exactly have a plan on how we were going to do it. We'd agreed Lotus would be our coordinator. Once we had a plan in place and knew a general time-table for when Roccosal would be leaving (hopefully with us aboard), she would join Lunden again and use his speedy little ship to make contact with the fleets... which were hopefully convening as we spoke. I knew at least that the Manoratha and Lotus's vessels would do so. The Cerberus fleet I was less certain on, Amurescan lords were not known for working willingly with Privateers. But hopefully given the inducement of the target, the wolfhound would be able to keep them on task.

We'd had some amount of conjecture over the potential of sabotaging the capstan, since that wouldn't cripple the ship or endanger our lives aboard it, but would certainly slow the vessel down. But that was a highly technical idea, and a few nights spent in conversation with a bottle of rum between us had unearthed one very terrifying fact—I seemed to know more about marine engineering here than anyone else. Which means it'd be on me to implement whatever plan we landed on.

I also was the only one amongst the three of us who was familiar with the size of ship we were going to be fucking with. The Manoratha was, after all, a Man of War. Put simply, bigger ships required bigger, often more complex, engineering.

There was a lot to think over and plan for and very little time to do it. But right now, we hadn't even accomplished the first most necessary step: finding the damn ships to begin with. We knew where they were, even if we hadn't technically confirmed it yet. Still. It would behoove us to, y'know, be certain of that before we snuck, bribed, or broke our way onto that half of the island.

Thankfully, Lotus had been here in this particular port before, and she knew the local terrain. Rather... well, actually. Which suggested it was a regular haunt for her. Hardly strange given the local Lords were tigers. Suspicious, though. Made me wonder...

I knew next to nothing about her origins. And tigers came from all over this half of the world, so the odds she was somehow from this island were slim. Still, though. She clearly at least had connections here and that made me want to ask more when we had some time to ourselves.

Finding one of said connections was our first priority after dealing with the stoat. But even though she knew the man—she vaguely called him a 'procurer'—she didn't know exactly where to find him. In a place like this, very few institutions were permanent. Least of all a black market 'procurer', whatever that meant. When I'd asked what exactly he could 'procure' for us, she'd simply answered—

"Everything," with a long-fanged grin, before chomping down on some fried octopus.

I had a stick of my own, the battered tentacles dripping with oil and dried chili flakes. I don't know how she was eating hers yet, I'd tried and burnt my tongue immediately. Luther was staring at the two of us like we revolted him.

"What kind of mariner doesn't eat octopus?" I said after blowing on my stick a few more times and taking a crunchy bite. "C'mon mate, I know they're a little creepy, but—"

"It's not the meat that disgusts me," he assured us. "It's the fried batter."

"S'the best part!"

He only shook his head. "Bad for the belly."

"You're more hung up on that shit than most girdle-wearin' Carvecian women," I rolled my eyes. "Little bulk might do you some good, you're too lean. That stoat had you outweighed, y'know. Could save your life someday."

"I prefer agility to power," he muttered, then cocked his head in Lotus's direction. "Think this is the one, then?"

"Has to be." She blew out a breath, tossing her stick in a refuse pile as we walked. "I don't know many other lurks he'd be keeping to these days. If he's not here, he's dead."

"And what if he is?" he asked.

"We're going to have a hard time finding anyone else, least anyone else I know, on this island as capable of getting us everything, everyone, and every piece of information we might need," she said.

"'Everyone'?" I asked, making what I'm sure was a confused face.

"You think we'll be able to do this alone?" she countered. "We need someone who's been hired on by his fleet before, at least a dockworker if not a crew member. Someone who's not too loyal, someone on a temporary contract who'll do what we need for an immediate payout. I hope you're good on being the purse, Denholme."

"If it means netting the dhole, you can count on me there," he assured her.

"Good," she said as she walked ahead of us, shoving open a nearly wedged-shut, sandblasted wooden door into a patchwork building I might've mistaken for being abandoned, if not for the sudden influx of scents and sounds that came when she opened it. She looked back at the two of us. "Because none of this is gonna come cheap. Chester included. But if your coin's right, he can find just about anything you need."

"I've known middle-men before," Luther assured her. "You don't need to explain the concept to me."

"I wouldn't figure you for making purchases for your fleet on dark markets," I chuckled. "Learning more every day."

He gave me a sidelong glance. "I don't... really... not for—"

"Oh for goddess's sake," Lotus laughed at me. "Don't make him spit it out; the man might choke on his own shame. He buys prostitutes, Reed. You know that. Knowing that is what got you into this whole mess, remember?"

Luther only straightened his collar and avoided eye contact with us. Which was probably a step in the right direction. I feel like in the past, he would have glared daggers at her for speaking the obvious aloud.

I only shrugged. "I guess I just figured no one needs a middle-man for that."

"Try finding male consorts in Amuresca some time," he grumbled.

"Well now I'm going to, just for the challenge," I said with a shit-eating grin. "Should I send them your way?"

His only answer was to shove me roughly inside, which I acquiesced to, laughing all the while.

The cantina within the walls of the dilapidated building was an unexpected pearl in an otherwise decaying neighborhood. While the city itself was a bustling hive of activity and culture, the section of the settlement this particular establishment was in was run-down and neglected, its 'streets' little more than muddy paths in between tent cities and older, obviously previously-abandoned buildings. Based on the general lack of flora and the few cocked-over trees with their once-massive root systems exposed, it wasn't hard to deduce what had happened to this burb. The monsoon seasons in this part of the world were rough and frequently flooded entire sections of a settlement just like this, leaving little but a few mud-swallowed buildings and the remnants of whatever was once growing there capsized and collected in drifts. Whatever had wiped this area out had probably happened years ago, based on how the locals had cut their way back in and tried to establish themselves anew. But it was no longer prime real estate and had devolved into more of a slum.

Honestly, we'd just come from Dokuro, and it wasn't far off from that, nor most ports I hung my hat in. Besides, I'd felt more at home in the slums than I did in well-planned cities for a while now. Places like this, it was easy to go unnoticed and hard not to have a good time if you knew where to look. There were a lot of people suffering here, sure. But that just made it a good place to throw money around, get drunk and drum up business, and stimulate the local economy while you were at it. And very few people had the stones to shake down a man with a blade and three pistols on his person.

'Cept that one time. But I'd been really drunk—like sick drunk—and if I'm being honest, I'd probably deserved that one. Stupid.

That whole mess with the stoat in the alleyway had really sent me spinning, but walking into the little bubble of life and color that was this thriving, ramshackle cantina picked me right up. The place was a world unto itself, the double-thick door keeping the cacophony of music, voices, and smells inside right up until you stepped on through. I was immediately assaulted by the pungent scent of curry and tandoor-cooked flatbread, grain alcohol and fruit, old wood, and the unmistakable edge of brine. The entryway opened to an uneven, tilting staircase, suffocatingly-tight quarters for someone my size until you emerged into the warm light past the tattered sunburst curtain.

Given that the establishment itself must have been built in what was once the cobblestone basement of this old home, it was shocking how bright it was when we stepped inside. I had to blink back, my eyes having adjusted to the dimly-lit staircase, before I realized why. The whole left quarter of the building above us had crumbled at some point and sunlight was streaming down into the place through layers of cloth strung up over the hole, casting the hollow in an almost cathedral-like range of color. It was amazing we hadn't heard all the noise outside given the literal skylight, but the staircase and the remnants of the building above served to keep it mostly muffled.

They were using the skylight to vent chimneys out as well, likely for the cooking fires. How those cloth covers didn't get filthy when it rained was a mystery to me. Maybe they took them down, maybe they just… did get filthy, and they replaced them whenever they needed to. The place was a marvel of adaptation. Everything here was clearly scavenged, none of the chairs matched, some were just barrels or crates, the bar was made from old driftwood and pieces of what must have been ships at some point. Given all the tar that must have remained on them and the cloth strung everywhere (plus the cooking fires), this place was a matchbox, but I doubt the proprietors gave two shits about that. Flirting with disaster. But then, this kind of living always was.

And it was hopping. Not just with patrons, but with entertainment, swindlers, and vendors. It was a veritable market down here, every other table boasting a dice game, junk merchants or small-time craftsmen and women with trinkets, necessities and food alike. Everything from leather belts to onions to paw-jobs were for sale here, the latter plying their offerings near a few curtained off areas in the back. The bar and the 'kitchen' area seemed primarily there to serve those who came to browse, partake, or listen near the 'stage', a raised platform that had probably been a tabletop at some point.

A topless cloud rat bedazzled in cheap, but still very eye-catching belly jewelry and a loose sarong danced beside another very similar-looking young rat (brother or son? Your guess was as good as mine) who was playing a bansuri. Rather well, for someone his age. They were close to the entrance by design I'm sure, so I tossed a coin into her pot as we passed. She took note of the silver color, giving me a bright smile and reaching out in my direction with a crook of her finger, her hips bouncing as if beckoning me closer in.

Never one to resist bait, I stopped in my tracks and made to turn… but then Denholme bumped into me from behind and two annoyingly-strong hands grabbed me by the shoulders and righted me back in Lotus's direction.

"Stay on task," he growled irritably.

I gave a huff through my nose. "I wouldn't have stopped you if it was a pretty boy rat."

"Man," he corrected me, keeping in step behind me in the crowded space like the goddamn cattle dog he was, herding me in the direction he wanted me to go.

"I think the one playing the bansuri was rather young, actually."

126

"I mean I'm only interested in men," he said surprisingly out-loud. I'd never heard him admit to his predilection in a public place before. But to be fair, this was Mataa. Male on male relations were hardly unusual here. Maybe he knew that and felt more comfortable admitting it here.

Or maybe it's because it was so fucking loud in here.

"Well, I would hope so," I scoffed. "But it's not as though I don't call women 'girls' sometimes."

"I find the distinction matters, because so many male consorts try to look young," he clarified. "I'm not attracted to that. I prefer they look and act closer to my own age."

"Hmmhh," I hummed thoughtfully, throwing an arm around one of his shoulders. He, of course, immediately shoved it off. "Sharing our tastes in bed partners now, are we? Time-honored pastime of naval men. I like cats, by the way. The more they challenge me the better. Y'know, you're thorny and all and I get that's your thing, but I'm feeling a connection being built here mate, I really am."

"Just dispelling whatever myths you may have of me in your head," he muttered. "Or... men like me, in general. We aren't degenerates, we don't want to fuck every man we see, we aren't what they say we are. Alright?"

"I have literally never thought that," I assured him quietly and seriously, when it became clear to me what bone he was picking at. "I can't imagine it's much different than it is for a man like me. You've got your types, your varying levels of emotional investment, hell you're a navy man and you clearly like to hit 'em and quit port, but I'm sure there're sorts like you who want all the domestic shit, too."

"It is very different," he cut me off sternly, "for me... than it is for you. I would think given how we met, you'd know that."

"...yeah. Alright," I agreed, tucking my ears back. "Point made."

He was silent another beat, and I thought the conversation might be over. But then he added, quietly, so in the busy den I had to strain to hear him, "And don't assume I wouldn't prefer something more... 'domestic'. It just isn't possible."

There it was again. That raw nerve. If I was a much, much worse man than I already was, I could dig into that. He'd betrayed it multiple times now. He'd certainly given me enough to work with that I could unearth more, find out exactly what this man's damage was. Something in his past, I'm certain. Something beyond awful. It was right there under the surface, it clearly played a role in why he was unwilling to get involved with Kafele again, and I was clever enough that I was certain I could exploit it somehow if I got the whole story. Hell, he might have been hesitant to admit it, but he was beginning to trust me more. And he seemed more willing to share the more we talked… like he wanted someone to talk to about whatever was eating him alive. A willing ear.

I might have been the last person in the world you'd think a man like that would trust. But I was likable. I was the kind of fellow people opened up to. I could get him eventually, if I wore him down.

I felt like shit even considering it. But Lotus's words were still ringing in my ears. On Dokuro I'd cursed myself for what I'd nearly done to him and what I'd actually done to Kafele. But having leverage wasn't exactly the same as pulling the trigger and blackmailing someone. Was it… wrong… to have insurance on someone? I mean, just in case she was right and he turned on me, eventually. That was just protecting myself. Wasn't it?

Wasn't it?

"Chester Quincy Frink!" Lotus's voice broke through the din ahead of us. I turned in time to see the man in question—a long-tailed weasel with a fairly standard brown and tan pelt, in what may have been fine clothes at some point before they'd been patched ten times over—nearly bolt off his stool like someone had fired a pistol near his head. He looked about ready to split the place entirely before he caught sight of Lotus's cinnamon stripes through the crowd, and his shoulders sagged in relief.

"Hells, lady!" He took his lopsided hat in hand, pressing it to his chest dramatically. "You could scare a lad half outta his pelt with a pow'rful voice like that."

She laughed as she approached the weasel's part of the den, a table tucked back against one of the crumbling stone walls farther away from the sunlight. He had an oil lantern on his table to compensate, illuminating what I could only imagine were his 'wares'. They resembled many of the other tables here. A few obviously second or third-hand coats strung up behind him on the wall, belts, bags, and other leather goods on the table, all peppered and cracked with use, and a plethora of other junk ranging from flasks to small knives. All things useful to the folks in this port no doubt, but not a one of them of any real value.

Despite that, Lotus still seemed very glad to see him, so this had to be our guy.

"I'm sorry, we've just been looking for you for hours," she said, settling her big hand paws down on the table, one of them lifting and inspecting a knife, flipping it over a few times in her grip. "I'd begun to worry you'd crossed over."

"I'm touched, Lady Lotus," the weasel chuckled, showing off one of the gaps in his sharp teeth when he smiled. "But it'll take more than the rapscallions this port's got to offer to shove me off."

Lotus pushed aside some of his wares and pulled up a stool to sit at his table. Shrugging, I did the same, sitting beside her. Which left only the space right beside Chester for Luther to sit, and he did not seem fond of the idea.

To be fair, all weasels had a certain... odor about them that could border on offensive to canines. I'd certainly smelled worse, but it was clear the gentleman before us hadn't had a proper bath in a while. Luther eventually sucked it up though, perhaps realizing discretion was more important right now than his delicate sensibilities.

"So," he said as he slid his own stool over with a squawk of wood on the uneven stone floor, "Lotus tells us you can procure just about anything on this island."

"Just about," Chester confirmed, waving a hand wobbly-like in the air. "I don't deal in flesh, if that's your game. Too risky."

"What's with all the junk on the table, then?" I asked curiously. "If you're a legit middle-man... what is all this, some kinda code? A façade?"

"A-what-now?" he blinked, scoffing. "And don't call my wares 'junk', if y'please. This is my bread and butter. You may not think much of it, but to a man without one, a good warm coat is... well, a good warm coat."

"Amen," Luther said for some reason.

"You're Carvecian," I said aloud, curiously. "And far from home."

"Aye," he nodded. "And so are you."

"Are you running from something?" I asked, before I could stop myself.

"Are you?" he asked, arching a bushy eyebrow.

I opened my mouth to make some kind of pithy retort, but I had none. It wasn't exactly that he'd outsmarted me, I'd just been poking around and asking stupid questions of a stranger. What was with me lately?

"Lotus vets you," Luther said, breaking up the moment. "So, I'm willing to take it on faith that you are what you say you are. And in any case, time will prove that out. You said you don't deal in flesh—"

"Non-negotiable," the weasel insisted, putting his paws out.

Luther eased him with a hand of his own out. "I'm not asking you to violate your principles. Or... whatever it is that stays your hand there. But... what about mercenaries? Reliable. Preferably a local with a history working at sea."

Chester smiled slowly. "Well now, we're talking."

❦

When it rained in Huudari waters, it rained. And that night, it began to rain. And it never. Stopped. For the rest of the time we spent on that accursed isle, it never fucking stopped for longer than a few moments. It wasn't even monsoon season.

We'd hoped for bad weather to slow down Roccosal's fleet, and we got it. It was unseasonably bad in fact, so we'd gotten... lucky? Problem is, we also had to exist and travel in it, and it was misery.

Chester parted ways with us that afternoon with a promise to meet again the following morning on the eastern-most edge of the city limits at another run-down cantina that Lotus also mysteriously seemed to know the location of. We decided we'd wait out the night there or, more particularly, at a rooming house nearby that she knew of.

We were cold-soaked through and through by the time we got there, fur matted to our bodies and stuck into the seams inside our clothes. The city itself had canopies and awnings a-plenty in the market district, but most of those closed up shop and were torn down in a hurry when the rains moved in with almost military efficiency. The people here knew better than to bother being out in this weather. We, unfortunately, had no choice. We'd already told Chester we'd meet him at this cantina first thing in the morning, so we had to cross the entire city just around the time the storm moved in.

Thankfully, as aforementioned, Lotus knew the way and was able to get us there on what felt like a mostly direct route. She was far more familiar with this island than she'd initially let on when we planned this caper. Which... I mean, I liked to keep at least a few things close to my chest as well; it's not as though she had to lay out every detail of her past and previous escapades.

Still. I felt like she was keeping a lot from me—much of it unnecessarily, it seemed—and I suppose I thought I was entitled to know more about her, considering the promises she'd made earlier that I could trust her.

I guess I felt slighted. Which was a truly alien feeling to me. I wasn't really, nor had I ever been, a petty or jealous man when it came to women. I didn't like the feeling. It was irritating like a sore throat or a thought I couldn't put to words. I couldn't even really think of a way to broach the subject with her. Every sentence I ran over in my mind never quite made it to my maw, because they all felt embarrassingly shallow and childish. What exactly did I want from her?

Tell me more about yourself.

I know we've only known one another for a few weeks now, but tell me your life story.

You seem to know this place so well, and you've never explained why. Aren't I entitled to know why, given we're risking our lives here?

I just want to know you better. Please.

Nothing seemed adequate. The woman had said she was fond of me, and I earnestly did believe her. And normally, speaking to women came so easily to me. Why was this tripping me up so much?

I had an inkling. And it concerned the cattle dog.

The seed of distrust she'd sewn earlier, specifically as it related to Denholme, had begun to take root in my heart. It was disquieting, and I hated that she'd put it there, but the fact that it couldn't be so easily dismissed was because she had a point. And it's not as though she'd been cagey or sneaky about it. She was blatantly placing herself between the two of us, not driving a wedge exactly, but it certainly felt like she was trying to protect me from him. As if I needed to wise up. As if she knew better than I and was trying to look out for me.

I was, in fact, acutely aware of the remaining wisps of my naivete, owing to my sheltered upbringing. But I was wiser, more hardened now. The bright-eyed, utterly stupid young wolf who'd stolen a Man-of-War, allied himself with Anarchists, disgruntled seamen and dockworkers, strangers of all ilks, and somehow expected all of that to go off without a hitch? He was buried under a decade of mistakes, misadventures, and some very real pain and hard learning experiences, as well as a sobering view of the true depravity and amoral nature of the world and many of its worst inhabitants. I wasn't the lad I'd been then. Not even close.

I might still gag at the reek of blood and piss—a combination all too common when death-dealing became a part of your trade—but it didn't mean my claws hesitated on the trigger any more. It just meant I drank it off later, dousing my misgivings and avoiding the tumultuous tumble of the 'what have I become?' thought spiral before it dragged me below its depths.

I didn't treat men, money, or even women the way I'd always promised myself I would, growing up. I'd done some things that would haunt me to my grave. But I still had a code. A bottom. And despite what the wanted posters might say, I was hardly ruthless. I could see that bottom, feel the shame of scraping up against it. I was trying, desperately, to live this life without giving in to it.

Moreover, I had maintained my guiding philosophy. The reason I'd gotten into all of this. It wasn't just about freedom for myself. It was about freedom for the world. Freedom from government, from social mores, from specism, and all other arbitrary bias and hate, from every unjust hierarchy, and more than anything… from coin. The fact that the world's rules were written arbitrarily by a small group of men who happened to have the largest pile of shiny bits of metal stored uselessly in their coffers. People deserved to be liberated from them. Full stop. And while I wasn't quite grandiose enough to think I'd be the one man to do it—a whelp born into one of said families, raised with that very privilege—it felt like I had a duty to try.

Maybe I just told myself all of this as an excuse to live free and unbound from the restrictions my family had placed on me. I mean, it's not as if I was some revolutionary. I enjoyed the spoils of my labors, as did the men who served in my fleet... some might say overly much. Maybe I was full of shit with all this grander purpose stuff. I don't really know. The name I'd leave scrawled in my wake in the history books would be a mess for cleverer men and women to sort out.

But one thing I was generally fairly confident about (perhaps more so than I should have been) was that I could find like-minded folk who believed in... whatever the fuck you'd call my core philosophy and make allies of them. I had a lot of comrades and friends all over the world. I trusted them all to varying degrees. And many of our relationships had started out much the same as things had with Denholme. Not... exactly the same, mind you. But similarly hostile.

Not all of my friends and allies liked one another, either. I'd go so far as to say some of them were outright enemies. But Lotus wasn't even outwardly hostile with Denholme. Hell, she'd worked with him against me not a few weeks ago. It didn't surprise me that that was more of a temporary working relationship and that she was keeping it arms-length. Especially given the opposing careers we had.

No, the more I thought about it, the more sensible her warning seemed. She was just being careful and reminding me to do the same. It wasn't hypocritical that she still preferred to keep some of her own secrets from me, as well. Those two situations could exist side by side very logically.

So, why did I feel like I was being asked to choose?

The most obvious answer was that I was a Privateer... and she was not. Lotus poached other Pirates. What she did was closer to what Luther did than what I did, honestly, but she did not do so under the commission of a government or crown of any kind. She was a true Pirate, hunting the most dangerous game: others of her own kind. Despite my stated hatred of organized government, I still worked under contract for many. Including Amuresca at times, Luther's homeland.

I saw what we did as getting the better of them, dismantling their financial security, scaring Cartels, and we made sure not to favor any nation for our contracts. Which meant we weren't at the behest of any one nation for long. We were free agents, constantly slipping the noose and walking on eggshells between ports and international waters, never knowing when someone would decide to act on an old grievance or attempt an arrest despite a current legal contract. The Manoratha was a wild card, and I liked it that way. The day anyone could deduce what we'd do next or let down their hackles when they knew we were in their waters, we'd have failed our objective, and I might as well lay down command to someone more deserving. I couldn't abide knowing the men who ruled the world ever felt safe or secure in their power so long as I drew breath.

But I suppose, if you didn't know me particularly well, you might worry that a Privateer getting chummy with a Crown Admiral could lead to the taming and subsequent militarization of our fleet. And if that was indeed her fear, I understood it. The last thing the seas needed was a Privateer-turned lapdog to the Amurescan Colonial Empire.

I'll admit I liked Luther quite a lot. More than I'd ever thought I would. I'd expected him to be a stuffy if serious... and seriously skilled Amur Navyman. And I'd not been wrong on any of that. What I hadn't expected was the manic, zealous glint in his eyes when he stared at the sea and talked about freedom. I hadn't expected the occasional glimpse into that explosively-passionate personality he kept shoved down under all the Amur decorum. I hadn't expected I'd meet someone so fascinating, with so much potential.

There was a rebel in there, a man after my own heart. And I wanted so badly to meet him. But I knew prying him out of that hull would take time. More than we would have on this caper. More than we might ever have as two ships passing in the night over the course of a lifetime.

I really, truly felt that if he let me in, there was a deep bond to be forged there. Something rare. Something special.

Something we couldn't form at arms-length.

Lotus was probably right to tell me to keep my distance. A woman operating her own fleet, hunting the most dangerous waters with relatively little firepower and having the success she'd had? Building the name she'd made for herself? That was a woman who knew how to protect herself and her interests. She couldn't have afforded to fail as many times as I had in the past. She wouldn't have survived the mistakes I'd made, strictly because she had less of a cushion to fall back on. I could probably learn a lot from her.

I could probably learn a whole lot more from her if she'd be willing to trust me more. I understood keeping a wary eye on Denholme. Maybe. But me?

Petulant though it was, this was the thought process going through my head while we walked the darkening streets that night. The rain had come in with miserably cold winds, which often accompanied the nights here. This area of the world rarely experienced what most would call a 'winter', but the evening hours on some of these small islands—especially when the weather was poor—would give bleak Amurescan winters a run for their money.

We were chilled to the bone when Lotus at last announced she saw the rooming house. It looked to me more like a... regular house. That's mostly what was out here on the fringes, tucked into the terraced countryside of the wild island. The locals cut into the mountains, both for growing rice and carp trenches (basically watering ditches that doubled as long ponds to grow out fish in), but nestled in between the steps of land were the occasional house. They were your average construction for this area, stone or clay brick with no glass windows or 'new world' architecture in sight. Normally, I found Huudari cities a welcome change from the rigid, regimented world the Amur had built in their homeland and various colonies, but right now I was mostly hoping that wherever we ended up, it was dry.

The road leading there across the rice patties was flooding and muddy, its banks overflowing onto the raised, narrow strip of earth that crossed the field. It's not that it wasn't well-fortified earth; it's just that we were on the side of a bloody mountain and right now the rain was all running downhill, sluicing over field and walkway alike. I had to step around a few rebellious carp, jumping their breeding grounds into the world beneath. Likely just the lower neighbor's carp ponds, but hey, if they kept it up, maybe the river that cut through the island.

"Fare thee well, travelers," I said as we walked. Aloud, for some reason.

For a yet even more unknown reason, Luther stopped walking ahead of me at that. Which, of course, prevented me from moving forward, either. There was no stepping around him on the narrow walkway.

He turned to regard one of the struggling, unremarkable fish as it floundered its way through less than a claw's worth of water, gasping and forcing itself along on its belly and side.

I stood there and watched him watch the damn fish. The black skies continued to pour down on us relentlessly, and we both watched that little creature flop around until it had made it fully across the walking path and disappeared down the hillside into the muddy darkness.

"He has no idea where he's fleeing to," Luther said, his eyes unnaturally yellow in the dark. "He just knows it's got to be better than here."

"How do you know?" I asked, perplexed.

He stared down the mountain, eyes unfocused, distant. "He's trapped. They're eventually going to kill him here, and he'll never know anything outside this puddle. That's no kind of life."

"No. I mean, how do you know it's a 'him'?" I asked cheekily.

"I thought," he gestured at nothing, looking both irritated with and tired of me, "we were on the same page—I was obviously not just talking about the fish…"

He must have noticed at that point that I was grinning and silently laughing, because he batted at me with a palm, growling, "Oh, goddamnit. I thought we were having a moment. My fault for assuming you'd be serious about anything."

"We can have a moment!" I insisted. "Sorry. You were looking dismal, for some reason. I just wanted to snap you out of it. Let's pick up with the… carp metaphor. You were saying—"

"What the fuck is wrong with you two?!" Lotus called out to us distantly from the end of the walkway, hunkering in the pelting wind and rain. "Can we please get out of the rain?!"

We both ran to catch up with her with our tails between our legs. I mean, mine certainly was. Luther's may have been too, or it might've just been tucked to avoid the rain. Either way, by the time we made it to the main wooden door of the large building, molten light was pooling out in a scattered strip. Someone had opened it from the inside, I realized. And whoever it was, they were already involved in what sounded to be an argument with Lotus.

"Are we at the wrong place?" Luther asked in a low voice, his shoulder bumping mine as he leaned in. The house at least had a stone courtyard area with a sloping roof, so we were able to wait out of the rain. The... rain that wasn't blowing in sideways, anyway. So, like half of it.

The man—or woman, I couldn't tell—behind the door looked to be a loris, based on the eyes. They were an often-reclusive people I didn't have much experience with, but I knew enough about them by rumor to wonder at one running a rooming house. They were from all accounts not renowned hosts or much for society at large; they mostly kept to their own.

But then, to hell with rumor and conjecture. I was going to get to meet one and get to know them myself, hopefully. If Lotus could negotiate whatever seemed to be the issue with this one.

I listened in and felt rather than saw Luther trying to do the same. He was shorter than me and leaning close to me, and I could feel the minute twitches of his oversized ears.

"Are they full-up or something?" he asked. A shudder visibly worked its way through him, between what was probably near-constant shivering. I was cold too, and his fur seemed to wick water away better than most, but the man had next to no body fat and was only wearing a cotton shirt. He'd be the luckier of us tomorrow though, since I knew he had his coat packed away in his rucksack and it'd be dry, while mine would likely still be damp.

I glanced briefly back at him, but kept my ears on the conversation between the tigress and the loris. "You don't speak Huudari?" I asked incredulously. "What kind of sailor are you?"

He snuffed out through his nose. "Never been good with languages. I know bits and pieces. So many dialects. Most everyone speaks Amur these days anyway."

"That is the most Amurescan thing you've ever said," I laughed at him.

He grumbled. "So what's the hold-up?"

He shoved my coat aside for some reason, and for a moment I didn't quite know what to make of the sudden breach of my personal space, until he thumbed my flask off my belt and took it. I'd actually offered both he and Lotus free access to my spirits awhile back, but he'd yet to take me up on it. She certainly had.

While he guzzled a few gulps of the—I think it was spiced rum at this point, I'd lost track—I responded to his question. "They're talking fast, and you're right, the local dialect's a little strange, but mostly... I'm getting that Lotus wasn't expected, that they weren't told she was coming."

"Hmm," he hummed, swallowing another long drink of the liquor.

"You can handle your spirits," I noted, impressed. "In the time I've known you I haven't seen you drink much."

"Don't mistake my wanting to keep a clear head for having a weak constitution," he muttered.

"I know better than to accuse you of having a weak anything," I said dryly, then sighed, continuing to listen in. "They clearly know one another or have mutual friends. Someone named... 'Ahsan'. His name keeps coming up."

Luther scoffed. "That's like the 'Robert' of Huudari names. I've known probably a dozen 'Ahsan's."

"I think I have a dozen on my crew," I said with a nod.

"A lot of your crew is Huudari?"

"Over half, last I checked," I confirmed.

"So." There was a pause. And then he dropped his voice. "Do you think it's code of some sort?"

"This isn't a normal rooming house," I murmured. I'd figured that out as soon as we'd gotten close, to be fair. There were no signs, not even any lanterns. This was not a place open to travelers. Generally.

Of course, they could be old friends of some sort, but... if that was the case, they didn't seem kindly-disposed towards Lotus right now. I wouldn't call the conversation aggressive, but certainly harried. Imposed-upon. They were deliberately keeping their voices low though, so it wasn't just the language barrier that was making it hard to make sense of.

But then, the door creaked open fully, and the loris stepped back, gesturing to all of us to enter. So apparently, they'd reached some kind of mutual understanding.

Luther and I glanced at one another. Lotus impatiently waved a hand at us and said, "Come on. It's fine now."

Luther handed my flask back to me, and we shuffled forward towards the undersized door. Lotus had to duck and squeeze inside, and so did I, my saber catching on the edge of the small frame. This place was not built for people of our stature on the outside... but thankfully the inside was more roomy.

The home was fashioned in the style of many farm homes on Mataa, with a large central living area built around a clay oven and cookfire, sprawling and open around a small hole in the top of the vaulted ceiling.

The rain mostly avoided it thanks to the sloping roof and likely some kind of lifted stone cover over top of it, allowing the smoke to vent while keeping the place relatively safe from the elements. It was actually remarkably warm and dry inside. It might not have sufficed as well in the harsher northern climates, but the Huudari knew how to build for their own land with minimal use of unnecessary resources.

Even here, on this remote island, we'd seen the first signs of Amur construction being adopted. Likely by canine-run traders and businesses, or expats. I hated how conscious I was of what something like this brought, but I couldn't help it. Once you knew, you knew.

The Huudari used primarily clay and straw for walls and insulation. I didn't know the specifics that went into the construction, but it seemed to work and had been working for them for centuries. But Amur construction required bricks and lumber, and that necessitated clear-cutting islands like Dokuro, and worse yet... brick-making. Which was probably one of the most abusive trades in Mataa, outside of Divine fields. It was low-cost, low-yield, and necessitated heavy manual labor, which means it was more often than not a trade rife with indentured labor and outright slavery. And there'd only be more and more need for it, the more Amur construction was adopted here.

I tipped my flask up to my muzzle, draining the last of it as we stepped into the warm, lantern-lit living area. I could tell when I was depressive versus just tired. I'd spent more days on end lately getting too little sleep and drinking most of my meals. We'd just had to kill someone. I was separated from my men and the security of my ship and dealing with a lot of anger and frustration right now thanks to what Roccosal had done to me. So, I was spiraling. I needed some rest, decent food, and recuperation. And hopefully more booze.

Despite our concerns about the place being full-up, it seemed pretty... empty. I vaguely caught the light reflecting in three sets of oversized, round eyes staring down at us from a lofted area. The loft was on the opposite end of the house from the ceiling vent and only had twisting, dried driftwood lashed from ceiling to floor as a means to reach it. Likely the living space for the loris's family. Climbing up there would have been a real trick for a canine.

One of them peered over the edge, looking at us inquisitively. Again, hard to determine gender with these folk, but definitely a child. Likely all three of them were. I smiled and wiggled my fingers in a wave playfully at them before they ducked back out of sight and whispered between giggles in Huudari.

Yeah, I'm sure we must have been a sight, drenched as we were.

"You stay here," the loris directed us in broken Amurescan, their voice sounding decidedly more feminine now that I was closer to them. They were wearing a multicolored, layered sherwani, but they were short and petite, and Huudari clothing was often unisex, so I still didn't want to assume their gender.

They stepped out from the main tiled entryway into the commons room, again directing us with one long, lean arm towards the sitting area around the main fire. There were many pillows, sitting cushions and well-worn blankets about that looked comfortable enough. The whole place smelled of loris, of course, but also… others. I was distinctly picking up something feline, rodent, and… was that a fox? Maybe an odd kind of canine. Hard to say. But, with that kind of variety, it actually was possible this was a rooming house or travel stop. Just not a frequently-used kind of place. More for folk who were in the know.

My curiosity over Lotus's conversation with the patron persisted though, even as we set our things down and began removing our wet garments. The loris was busying themself in what looked to be a pantry area just off the main room with no door but through a small archway. They returned before long with an intricately-painted, well-worn teapot they placed carefully on top of the clay cooking stove, which looked to have been used recently. I could still smell the spice in the air from whatever they'd made. My stomach growled.

The loris looked at us and gave the briefest of smiles, if a tired one. "Travel long? Ah-! No! Wet! Wet clothes, off."

The bark of a statement had been at Luther, who had mistakenly tried to sit on one of the sitting cushions near the fire. He had no coat to remove like Lotus and I did, but the rest of him was just as soaked. There was a series of pole racks that looked specifically like they were for hanging garments on the edge of the sitting area, which is where I'd put my own coat. He'd bypassed them entirely for the fire, likely wanting to warm up as soon as possible.

"They've got you there, mate," I said. "You soak that, it's your bed. You'll have to sleep in it."

"You've got to be accustomed to that by now, Reed," Lotus smirked over at me as she tugged her usually billowy undershirt up over her head and hung it over the rack alongside her coat. Her breasts were wrapped, alas. At least I got to see some more of her beautiful stripes.

"Least I can do when I'm the one who's made the mess," I said, tossing my own balled-up shirt at her.

She flapped it out and hung it over the rack as well. "Wolf, if you're doing your job right, it's not all you."

"Why do male-female couples think it's alright to just… talk about these things aloud?" Luther wondered vocally, making a disgruntled face.

138

"Oh, you have to be quite a 'liberated woman' to keep up with Reed over there without being branded a whore," Lotus snickered. "At least publicly. Privately, I'm pretty sure most of the men in my trade call me that regardless."

"That's alright," I snorted. "I've been called a whore both privately and publicly. You're in good company."

"I'm pretty sure I saw children up there," Luther pointed out, glancing upwards. "Maybe watch your tongue more while we're here."

"They see and hear much worse," the loris said as they reappeared, tossing a small bundle of fresh wood into the brick oven. The pot they'd put on the heated top of the oven was starting to steam already. They gestured to it. "Tea. No milk… tomorrow, milk. Goat. Akson tareem," they made a gesture with their hands as if to denote something flat, "bread," they pointed in the direction of the pantry area, where there was also a low table. "Eat. All you want."

I didn't need to be told twice. After quickly shimmying out of my britches and hanging them over the poles as well, I headed in the direction of the pantry room and found the flatbread she'd been talking about, sitting stacked on the table, wrapped in a thin cloth. It smelled like garlic and oil and was still vaguely warm. I crammed half of one into my mouth before I'd even made it back out to the others, if nothing else to put some of the drool filling my maw to use. Damn, we really hadn't eaten enough lately… I think the fried octopus was all I'd had all day other than rum.

I wasn't entirely prepared for the sight that greeted me when I made it back out into the common room. Lotus was stripped down to her wraps and looked strikingly beautiful as ever, stretched out near the fire warming and drying herself. But the cattle dog…

He'd removed his shirt and britches as well, and it didn't surprise me he was doing so a bit more hesitantly, given the public setting. Sailors generally didn't give a damn about propriety when they were at sea, but this was a strange place with potentially more than one woman about, and Amurescans were militantly modest about their bodies, especially around the fairer sex.

He was as annoyingly chiseled as I'd expected, but though I could appreciate the tone in a male body for its aesthetic appeal if not in the carnal way I might a woman; that wasn't what caught my eye. His fur was choppy and short normally, flat to his figure in a way my own coat would never be, but plastered back with water, it hid even less than it normally did.

And I knew lash marks when I saw them.

They were old. Hard to say how old, but I had men on my crew who'd been disciplined in the Navy or otherwise, in work camps, by particularly cruel masters on plantations… you name it. They were years old at least, obviously from a time before he'd been a Crown Admiral. The patterns were different lengths and directions, some looking more long-healed than others, denoting whatever he'd received them for, it had happened... more than once.

He caught me staring, his ears twisting before his neck did. He looked back at me over his shoulder, his gaze unavoidable. I blinked, attempting to salvage the moment by holding out the wrapped satchel of flatbread to him.

"You should eat," I said.

His gaze was cold. He knew I'd seen. But he chose not to say anything more about it, instead reaching for and taking two of the pieces of flatbread and moving off to choose a place to sleep as far across the sitting area from Lotus and me as he could.

I sighed, sitting down next to her. Her nose twitched, and her whiskers shivered when she noticed the flatbread, her thick paw immediately going to the pile, taking a good half of them for herself.

"Are you going to explain exactly what this place is?" I asked her quietly, while we tucked into our 'meal'. I really needed more meat than I'd had lately.

She gave me a long look. What precisely lay behind it was hard to decipher, but at length she swallowed the food she'd been chewing and just gave an easy smile. "We're safe here, don't worry." She leaned in, nuzzling my nose.

I kept my eyes on hers, not letting the placating gesture go to my head, like I'm sure she wanted. I kept looking at her expectantly, making it clear I wasn't letting this go.

"I'll explain more tomorrow," she promised, sighing softly and rolling to her side, tail curling and uncurling. "Right now, I'm exhausted, and I know you are, too."

"Mnnhh," I agreed.

She wrapped an arm around me, giving my middle a light squeeze. "Get us some tea? We need to get up early to meet Chester again, something warm would go a long way right now to getting a full night's sleep."

She was right. The tea was good, even without milk or sugar. They mixed their leaves with dried fruit in this region, as well as herbs that aided in sleep. I barely finished a cup before I started drifting off, and with the tigress curled around me next to that warm brick oven, it was just about the most comfortable I'd been since I left my ship.

❧ ☙

The pressing need to urinate woke me from a dead slumber some hours later. Hard to say how late, but it was still entirely dark out.

I disentangled myself from Lotus easily enough, trying to be as quiet as possible as I picked my way through the unfamiliar space. The loris hadn't really shown us 'around' the place earlier, only to tell us where we'd be staying and where to find the leftover bread. But I knew Huudari dwellings well enough to know I'd have to relieve myself outside.

The privy house, as it turned out, wasn't far from the main home. It was easy enough to find it by smell, and thankfully the rain was taking a brief reprieve for the short trek. I only had my smallclothes on, but without the cold rain and with my fur now dry, the temperature was tolerable.

I stumbled sleepily back towards the main house afterwards, intent on diving right back into that warm pile of blankets and tigress, when a sudden strong scent and sound caught my attention. It might not have except that it was very strong, not a lingering scent of old musk or fur like I'd smelled inside; this was a person who was very acutely here right now. And they weren't a loris, a dog, or a tigress.

The other thing is, I'd heard them. Someone had given a slight squeak of surprise and stumbled through wet brush, somewhere near the entryway to the home. Pausing, I reached for my pistol or my blade on instinct and, of course, found nothing. I was basically nude.

I could hear their breathing. Raspy, quickened heartbeat... scared.

Slowly, I stepped around the edge of the building, hoping not to spook them. They were clear to see there even without the moonlight, standing on the opposite end of the front of the house, peering around the wrong side. Towards the road. That didn't last long though; their ears swiveled, and they turned to face me, wide eyes blinking in the dark.

They were foxes. That much was immediately apparent. Looked like a mother and child. The child was very young, maybe two or three at most. Hard to say what kind of foxes exactly, a variety from this end of the world I wasn't overly familiar with: sand-colored with thick faces.

The mother asked me in a hurried whisper who I was. In Huudari.

"I..." I paused, hardly knowing what to say. I couldn't admit to who I was here, even to a presumably innocent mother and child. Why were they here? Who were they? Why hadn't we seen them earlier? They'd clearly come from inside the house.

What the hell was going on here?

Blessedly, the door opened, interrupting the moment. Lotus leaned out, almost casually. She assessed the three of us, then looked to the little fox... then to me. "Had to piss?" she asked in Huudari, presumably to keep the foxes in the loop.

"Yes," both the little fox and I said in unison.

She nodded, then sighed. "There's a chamber pot in the root cellar. But it's dark down there, I'm sorry. They should have told you. You can take him down the way there... you see?"

The mother fox nodded, hurrying her child past me, looking me up and down once and presumably taking in my undressed state. But mostly, she looked worried. That whiff of fear was still there, too.

As they walked past me, I took note of what they were both wearing. Everything started falling into place. Lotus gave me a long... long look. Then she closed the door behind her quietly, shutting us outside and crossing her arms over her chest.

"You're lucky Denholme is still asleep," she said softly. "Those herbs really knocked him the fuck out. Are you steady on your feet?"

"Mostly," I muttered. "Higher tolerance, I guess. Are they—"

"You saw nothing, you understand me?" she said, her eyes glinting fiercely in the dim light. "We're going to leave here tomorrow, and so are they, and no one needs to know either of us came through this place and spent a peaceful night here. No one."

"The collars..." I said quietly. "So... they're..."

"No one," she said through her teeth. "Because you never saw them. Remember?"

I swallowed, blinking drowsily. "Lotus. Were...you..."

"What did you see here tonight, Reed?" she pressed, reaching forward and grabbing my chin. "Tell me what you saw here."

I took a moment, then replied quietly, "Nothing."

ACT III- TRUST

I'm not sure if it was nerves or the fact that I'd slept like the dead after being... somewhat non-consensually drugged, but I woke early. I'd known the tea would aid in sleep; they'd been upfront about that. But I'm pretty sure there was more than chamomile in that shit. Lotus and the loris innkeeper—if that's what she really was—had better have hoped Denholme didn't realize it, too. I suspected he wouldn't take kindly to the knowledge.

Lying there, still groggy but too anxious to fall back asleep, I had some time to myself to consider my situation. And my companions. Luther looked a lot less intimidating asleep with one of his ears twitching and the occasional weak thump of his tail where it hung off the edge of his sleeping cushion. But he wasn't the main focus of my attention.

I couldn't move an inch without potentially waking Lotus. She was sleeping beside me, warm, soft-furred, and gorgeous. One of her arms, one ample expanse of her thigh, and her tail were curled around me. And generally speaking, I would have been utterly content to wake to a powerful woman spooning me like an overgrown kitten. It had been one of the few silver linings of this trip.

But here, now, it served a more strategic purpose for her, and I knew it. She didn't want to risk me getting up again in the night without rousing her.

In many ways, it was too late. In the time it had taken me to fall back asleep last night and the hour or so I'd spent lying there in the dim morning light coming back to myself, I'd been putting together the puzzle I was now a part of. Despite rumors to the contrary, I was not in fact a stupid man. And I had enough information in bits and pieces at this point to guess what I'd stepped in.

Lotus was known for her fearsome reputation and somewhat remarkable gender, a rarity in our occupation in any kind of command role. But aside from that, I knew very little about her small ships, how she hunted... or why. Except that she strictly hunted other smugglers and pirates, she apparently hated Roccosal (she'd admitted that much to me herself) and for whatever reason she'd found herself briefly in the service of a Crown Admiral.

Notably, she had an unusually high success rate given the size of her vessels and limited firepower. That suggested she'd either had help all these years, which I didn't want to assume because I didn't want to discount her skill or... she had very precise information on her targets.

The island we were on now was the refuge of a clan of tigers who did business with Roccosal. Roccosal was a slaver, which meant it was very likely they moved contraband slaves and indentured peoples through this island, like traders would any other kind of merchandise. And Lotus seemed to know this place extraordinarily well. She had contacts here. She knew the lay of the land. She even knew the location of a safehouse.

Apparently a safehouse that ferried along indentured peoples. Those collars, metal and sealed with no hinge, could only have been affixed to those people by the Hyena clans of Mataa. I'd seen many like them before. People who beat the odds and managed to escape their contracts wore them for life, because only the hyenas knew how to get them off. I think there was an extremely expensive and risky means that had been devised somewhere in Carvecia, but it wasn't available to most. I had three men on my crew who still wore theirs. For some it was even a badge of honor. Proof of their liberation from a system of bondage that few ever escaped.

I had no doubt which side of the divide Lotus fell on. Her loathing for Roccosal was real, and if she knew of an underground network for moving indentured people to presumably freedom in a country where that trade was legal, that could only mean one thing.

She was an emancipator.

I knew my share of true revolutionaries and would-be freedom fighters. The seas were a refuge for those seeking freedom from borders, the law, and the shackles of every flavor of bondage. Anything from out-and-out slaves to people fleeing marriages, or trying to just live in a way that society at large considered taboo. You saw everything in my line of work.

But emancipation was a particularly contentious topic, because of its roots in the Great War. The Huudari and the Amurescan peoples had come to blows many times over the centuries, but their last conflict—nearly a century ago now but fresh enough in the minds of many to hold up their tenuous truce—had come about because of the two cultures' paradoxical relationship with the institution of slavery.

Put as simply as possible, it had been legal in Mataa, the Huudari Clans' nation, but illegal in Amuresca. The latter country having outlawed the institution after a particularly bloody and country-wide civil war led their Church to forcibly reform and declare the practice heretical by doctrine. Based on my study of history in my college days, there really and truly had been a movement within the Amurescan Faith amongst their Clergy to push for total emancipation of all enslaved peoples. But it had mostly been a concession by the Pedigree, the upper class, that was necessary to maintain their power over an angry and increasingly fed-up population. You can only oppress and brutalize a full half of your people for so long until they realize they outnumber you, and then you've got a real problem on your hands.

While the Amurescan people may have outlawed slavery for less-than-charitable reasons on the whole, it would be unfair to say there hadn't been some earnest empathy for their fellow man there. Like all things in Amuresca, it came wrapped in a cloak of holier-than-thou, patronizing scripture and a belief that they were the stewards of the world, But... in the end... they were staunchly opposed to the idea of owning people. And they'd stuck to it.

Organizing society so that most of the wealth flowed upwards and towards canines didn't count, obviously. Very fair.

As part of the final truce that had ended the Great War, they had imposed this belief upon Mataa as well. Slavery in all forms was technically illegal in Mataa now, under penalty of breaking the truce. Which no one wanted. The countries were both so inter-dependent on trade now, it would disrupt the whole damn world if they were at war again. The Huudari nation was still incredibly reliant on free labor for their agriculture and many other industries, though. And it'd be a lie to say that hadn't been a huge part of the reason Amuresca wanted it dismantled. It leveled the playing field.

But the Huudari had found a way around it: indentured labor, a practice that, honestly, employed the same kind of class stratification and inescapable poverty you'd find in most every nation world-wide, but was far more nakedly obvious for what it was. What with the collars and all.

So, emancipation in this day and age went by two different definitions, depending on which culture you believed was in the right. To the Amurescans, it was freedom fighting. To the Huudari... it was theft, and intimidation by a foreign power. Thus the contention.

It was a known fact that the Amurescan Crown and the Carvecian Congress put dark money into the pockets of Pirates and Privateers who disrupted the shipping or sale of indentured peoples. Anyone willing to poach Huudari vessels with live, thinking cargo aboard. Doing so weakened Mataa's economy, and made it more and more expensive and risky to continue exploiting their people for free labor. It was in national self-interest as well as a moral and religious imperative, and many emancipators were secretly and... not-so-secretly lauded as heroes in Amurescan and Carvecian folklore, songs, and art. Hell, my own father drank brandy and smoked with a few men I knew were engaged in the practice. It's why the Reed Cartel had so many Huudari sailors... and consequently why I now did as well.

You'd think it would be right up my alley. But here's the thing.

Emancipators were the bane of the Huudari Clans, and they didn't tend to live long because of it. You'd hear tell of fleets or rogue Captains who fit the bill now and again, and a year later they'd just up and disappear, sunk somewhere, publicly tortured and slain, or worse. Mataa had its own share of pirates and privateers, and they knew their seas better than any. They were brutal in defending their trade.

Roccosal was a prime example.

It made a little more sense that Lotus was as gutsy as she was, being a Huudari native. She at least knew the territory. But still. She was in a dangerous racket, if I was right.

She probably moved in Amurescan circles from time to time for information and leads. Maybe even funding. I don't think Denholme knew—no. He'd have said something by now. He was pretty staunch and unapologetic in his beliefs. And I'd never heard tell of his fleet being involved in something like that or anything remotely close. He stuck to defense and pirate-hunting.

Lotus stirred. Our embrace worked both ways. I was staring her in the eyes when she woke up.

She blinked blearily for a moment, an errant flicker of red morning light catching in her emerald and gold eyes, and fuck was she heart-stoppingly beautiful. I had to swallow back my admiration and stay focused. But it was hard. Lord, it was hard.

She released a long sigh through her soft pink nose, blinking at me a few times before murmuring in a sleep-roughened voice. "You want to have a word, I take it?"

"Several," I replied evenly.

Ten minutes and some fresh non-drugged tea later, we were standing outside beneath the awning, watching the sun come up over the island. Wherever you could see it between the clouds, anyway. You really couldn't beat the view from the terraced hills.

"So, here's my guess," I said, "and you can tell me where I get it wrong. You meet Denholme through whoever your contact in Amuresca is."

"Jumping to conclusions assuming it's not just him," she said as she sipped her tea.

"He's not politically-inclined," I muttered, "and he'd want nothing to do with all of this. He seems like a decent fellow—wait, no. That's being too charitable. What I mean to say is, he seems disgusted by the flesh trade at the bare minimum and certainly not fond of men like Roccosal. But he's focused on what he does, something like this gets messy and would take too much time away from hunting said men, which he's very, very good at and seems to feel passionately about."

"It's a pity," she said bitterly. "He's got the right kind of spirit for it. If he truly cared about the seas being free, he'd want that freedom for everyone—"

"—anyway, he's not your Pedigree patron. You don't have to tell me who is," I continued. "But whoever it is introduced you two at some point. And he reached out to you to help him tackle his problem with me. Probably—and I'm sorry, this isn't meant to cause offense—but probably because

146

you're a woman. It's not as if you and I knew one another well before this, so he must've chosen you for your more obvious assets."

"Offense taken." She rolled her eyes. "But fine. Get on with it."

"Trust me, it offends me too," I snorted. "It was base, assuming all he'd have to do was involve a member of the opposite sex and I'd completely drop my guard. But I can't very well deny it worked. I guess I was an easy mark."

She gave a rueful smile, but said nothing. Only sipped her tea.

"In my defense," I said petulantly, "you're very pretty and exactly my type, personality-wise as well. He couldn't have known that. He got lucky."

"Also, I'm a Captain in my own right with my own personal vessel," she emphasized, whipping my heels with the end of her tail. "I like how you keep leaving that bit out. He couldn't very well come to meet you on Dokuro on one of his own ships. Not many of his contacts would've fit the bill."

"I'm sure it helped you knew the area, as well," I sighed. "Worked out dandy. For you two."

"Oh, please." She gave me a slim-eyed smile. "This was always going to end badly for you. It was poorly-conceived, the absolute most wrong way to barter with a man like that, and morally defunct besides. If you even care about that."

"Honey, when my crews' lives are on the line, my moral compass is a lot more flexible," I assured her, swallowing my last gulp of tea. "We've all got something we'll go low-down for. The Cerberus fleet scared the ever-living daylights outta me, I'm not too ashamed to admit it. I genuinely thought this'd be a bloodless way to work something out with the man. I just didn't bother to consider how much more was at stake over a dalliance with a male floozy. That's where I fucked up."

"If you were Huudari I'd buy that." She shook her head. "But really? You were raised around their Faith. You really didn't know what you were threatening him with?"

"I..." I paused. I honestly didn't want to lie about this. To myself or anyone else. "...it was careless," I said at length. "I guess some part of me realized it was... different? But I didn't reflect on it enough." I waved one paw in the air. "I mean, I was more focused on the fact he was married than who he was fucking messing around with specifically. I've got boys a-plenty on my crew who bunk up. I've pledged a few of 'em to one another. I just didn't think enough on it. I feel like shite about it, now. I messed up bad this time."

She was silent for a bit. I'd expected some kind of quip about my not thinking about anything terribly hard, but instead she was just looking at me sort of softly. Like something I'd said was making her see me—fuck, I don't know, what the hell?

"You're looking at me strange," I said, glancing down at myself. "What?"

"Nothing," she said quickly, "just...."

Again, she was silent for a little while.

"I knew you were fun," she said finally, smiling a little. "Entertaining. Competent. A little dangerous, even. All qualities I enjoy in a man."

"... thanks," I said uncertainly.

"But humble? Very few men in my circles ever confess they were wrong," she said quietly. "Even to their peers, let alone to me."

"Haven't I done that a number'a times already since this all began?"

"Yes, under duress," she crossed her arms over her chest, "and mostly to Denholme. Just... let me be impressed, alright? I like you, Reed." She chewed on her lower jaw with one of her oversized canines. "There's a genuinely good man underneath all the chaos and murder you're known for. Somehow."

"I certainly hope so," I murmured, staring out across the dawn.

"That's got to be awful for you," she added barely above her breath.

Now it was my turn to respond with silence. God damnit, I wanted something stronger than tea.

"I mean, men like him," she jerked a thumb back inside. "I don't know when exactly he stopped caring, sometimes they're just born with their blood gone cold. It's an asset, honestly. And they're right to see it as such. They hesitate less. Sometimes that's all it takes."

I knew what she meant. I'd seen a lot of people die because they had slightly more compassion than the hollowed-out soul on the opposite end of a blade or a flintlock. Honestly, that could've been me more than once. I'd just gotten lucky so far.

"What's your point?" I sighed. "And what does this have to do with your... I'm not sure what you'd call it. Mission? Revolution?"

"Nothing so grand," she assured me. "It's honestly more of a grudge."

I arched an eyebrow at her, turning to regard her. "Lotus," I said, "would you please answer the question I tried to ask you last night?"

"Which was?" she asked, even though I'm certain she knew.

"Were you ever... you know." I toyed with the chopped-off locks where my mane had once been. "Enslaved. Indentured. Is that what this is about?"

"Not me," she answered, "no."

And for some reason a weight lifted off my chest. If this had been personal for her, if she'd been subjected to that kind of life at any point, it brought it just that much closer to me, and I'd have a much harder time keeping clear of—

"I have a sister."

Oh.

Her eyes found mine, irises shrunken to pinpricks in the warm peel of light peeking under the awning. We were experiencing a rare moment of sun between clouds that surely threatened another incoming storm. The shadows were purple with the promise they imposed.

It wasn't lost on me, the parallels between the natural world and my own small existence. This was a rare moment of calm in one of the most tumultuous weeks of my life, and it was about to slip away again.

I couldn't know then how long this particular storm would engulf me. But this was the start of it.

"You... have a sister," I repeated her words.

She nodded, finally looking away. Her jaw was tense, her arms crossed over her chest rigidly, defensively. Like she was protecting herself. But not from me. From something else that frightened her.

"At least," she said shakily, "I did. Over a decade ago. I... do. Somewhere. I have no reason to believe she's not alive."

It was just the act of speaking those words aloud. That's what she was bracing herself against.

"She was sold," she said just above a whisper. "When we were young. I was twelve years old, she was... just a bit older. Our parents died when we were just cubs in a flood. Esha and I made it to higher ground, we'd been out playing, and..."

I stayed silent, letting her speak.

She shook her head. "Well, we lived," she continued, "but we had no one to care for us, and we... tried to survive on our own, but the land was ruined. Our house was ruined. We were starving, so a friend of my mother's took us in. Another family in the village. They had their own children, and... over time, it became clear we were a burden to the family. It was decided," she paused, then closed her eyes, "that one of us would have to find work and... send money home."

I'd heard of arrangements like this. I knew what came next.

"They found a contract for her," she said. "They said she could learn the trade, pay off what she and I had cost the family, and then come back for me once she was free of her debt. She was the older of the two of us and my foster father thought I would have a better chance at marriage, because my pelt was lighter than hers. Everyone, even Esha herself, said it was what was best."

"You were a child," I insisted softly. "You couldn't have known."

"Our foster family knew the likelihood of her ever escaping that contract," she said bitterly. "I'm certain of that. But they kept up their end of the bargain. They cared for me until a marriage offer came my way, and I ran from that village and never looked back. They would have indebted me for the dowry, too. And they would have felt entitled to it."

I opened my muzzle, then shut it. What could I possibly say?

"The day she left with the Madame who was supposed to train her for the trade was the last day I ever saw her," she said. "I have tried... in vain... since then to follow what little information I could find to track down where she was sent. But they move girls like her around. They transfer," here she paused, swallowing heavily, "ownership... frequently. I was too young when she left, too much time had passed. I've never found any kind of paper trail, only word of mouth that's run me all over the country. I think she was moved towards the coast, but that only opens up every possibility imaginable. She may not even be on the mainland anymore."

She tipped her head back, closing her eyes, the dawn light turning the fur along her throat a halo so bright white it was hard to look at. "The world is too big, Reed. I keep hoping I'll find her, but...."

I wanted to hold her, but her body language told me any attempt to touch her right now would be unwelcome. She was thorny about having to tell me all of this, that much was clear. I never would have infringed on her private life or business if our acquaintance had remained casual, but that certainly wasn't the case anymore. And not because we were sleeping together. This quest of ours on this island had become entangled with the web of contacts and knowledge she had wrapped up in this whole emancipation business. Luther and I certainly wouldn't have gotten this far, this quickly, without her help. So I was grateful, obviously.

But it began to make a lot more sense. Her initial hesitance to do all of this with us. At the time I'd thought she was afraid of Roccosal, and I wouldn't have faulted her for that. But it wasn't that.

She had the resources to help us bring him down. Or at the very least, put us in a position where we'd have a chance. But doing so risked her other operations in this area of the world.

"Why didn't you explain all of this to me before we came here?" I blurted out, before I could really think about the question.

"This is a secret network for a reason, Reed," she answered irritably, as if that should have been obvious to me. It was, my mouth had just shot ahead of where my mind was at. Again. "Involving you, let alone him?" She glanced back at the closed door into the rooming house. "Do you have any idea how much of a risk I've taken even being here, helping you with this, without clearing it with my contacts and the information network first? We're supposed to verify every movement we make in advance, lest any one leg gets tripped up. All it takes is for them to kill—or gods forbid—capture someone who knows enough names, enough safehouses, and," she snapped her clawed fingers, "they come down on us like a hammer on an anvil. It's happened before. We pick up the pieces, find whoever's left alive and willing to aid us, and begin again. The Clans have managed to stomp out the fire we're lighting countless times, this time we've got a real movement going. Even tapping into fringe contacts, I'm risking disrupting things and getting in hot water with the…"

She intentionally stopped herself there, shutting her jaw forcefully.

"Let me guess," I cleared my throat. "This 'Ahsan' fellow one of the higher-ups?"

"Do not," she hissed, stomping up in front of me and grabbing me forcefully by the jaw, "say… that name… in any relation to this movement or to me. Do you understand me?"

"It's a code name anyway," I stammered, "isn't it?"

She released my jaw and stepped back, ears flattened, hackles raised. I'd seen her frustrated and fed up with me enough times since we'd met one another, but never angry. It was unsettling.

"I'm sorry," I said, keeping my voice down. I probably had been talking a bit loudly given the subject we were discussing, now that I thought about it. I wasn't about to tell her that Luther already knew the name. It would mean nothing to him anyway, and it was just guaranteed to get her more upset with me at this point.

"But," I sputtered, "you've talked about wanting us to trust one another. You didn't have to tell me specifics, but I would have liked to know some of this before, is all. Aren't I warranted to know if I'm getting—if you're getting us involved in a network like this? Even tangentially."

"I wasn't planning on that," she murmured, "but after the man in the city spotted us and that all happened, I realized… I was worried, rather, that something like that might happen again. And what you and Denholme are planning to do is unspeakably dangerous. I know you realize that, but this is the only leg of this journey until we reconnoiter with our ships where I can… help you. Help keep you safe. In any meaningful way. I thought about it a lot, trust me. I just wanted you to be able to rest somewhere secure, before you infiltrate that hornet's nest. I worried you'd be found and attacked wherever you stayed. This… seemed an obvious solution." She sighed. "Maybe I made a mistake. I don't know."

"We're safe," I said, my own hackles settling. "So, I'd say it was a good choice, personally. I just wish you'd trusted me enough to tell me… the broad strokes, I suppose."

"We aren't supposed to bring anyone into the network unless they're willing to become a part of it," she said, finally returning her eyes to mine again. "Both for our own good and for theirs. I do trust you, Reed. I was being earnest when I said I think you're a good man at your core. But are you really telling me you'd want to become a part of this? Because we could sure as hell use a heavy hitter like you—"

151

She must've seen the way my shoulders fell back and my tail stiffened, because she anticipated me before I could say anything other than an awkward, "Ahhh—"

"I didn't think so," she said, managing to mostly keep the disappointment out of her tone.

"I'm sorry," I said helplessly. "I have a crew of hundreds to think about. This is the sort of business that makes you the enemy of literally an entire nation of people very motivated to see you and everyone you know strung up and left to hang in the public square."

"I'm aware," she said darkly.

I swallowed. Fuck. This was just going to be an entire month of me finding newer and worse reasons to feel like a bucket of shit, wasn't it?

"You know," she spoke up, her voice small. I hadn't thought she was going to have a chaser for that. "The Amur and the Carvecians have bounties on your head, as well. You ply your trade to both in alternating years, and even if you've got legal contracts with one rich man or another, or one government or another, there are plenty of people in both countries who'd love to see you hanged if they got the chance at it."

"Nature of the game," I said, shrugging weakly. "They'd have to catch me first."

"The same can be said for what I do," she pointed out. "It's really not much different."

"The survival rate seems to be," I said flatly. "Not many Privateers get hunted down or arrested specifically, unless they get sloppy. Or taken down at sea. Which again… s'the nature of the game. There are acceptable risks when you do what I do, and then there's the sort of risks that mess with morale. You know that as well as I do; it's a balancing act."

"You were worried enough about Denholme that all of this happened," she retorted. "You obviously didn't think running across him was an 'acceptable risk.'"

"The Cerberus Fleet's a special case," I agreed.

"Is it the risk that really concerns you?" she asked, her gaze cold in that moment. "Or the reward?"

"I…."

"Not much coin or spoils to be had in freeing enslaved peoples," she pushed. "Is there?"

I sighed raggedly. "What do you want from me, Lotus? I have a fleet to run. Men to feed. A ship that needs constant repair. Even you've got some kind of Pedigree donor. You understand the economics of what we do."

"That's always what it comes down to, isn't it?" she muttered. "Gold."

"I take on and shelter my share of discarded people, Lotus," I said, standing my ground a bit if gently. "The price for your kind of work—both

152

in coin and lives—is just too high to pay. And I'd rather not be sponsored by some shadow patron. We value our independence."

"It never seems worth the effort or cost until they take something… or someone… priceless from you," she said, her tone judgmental.

I chose not to take offense. She was hurting.

"I'm sorry," I said again, instead. "I'm… sorry if I'm not actually the kind of man you thought I was."

She sighed, her posture deflating. "No, I… don't take back my words. I still think you're a decent sort of man, Reed. And hell, it might be over a personal trifle, but if you can follow through on this plan of ours and cut off the head of that serpent, of Roccosal's empire, that's a heavy blow to the flesh market in this region. It'll make a difference."

"Good," I said, nodding tightly. "Because I do want you thinking well of me, Lotus. Even after all of this is over, maybe we could—"

The door groaned and slowly swung open, two dark, triangular ears twitching upright as the cattle dog half-stumbled his way into the sunlight. Waning sunlight… I could hear thunder. The skies were about to open up.

"God-damn," he muttered, his voice a low growl when he was half-asleep that would've had most women weak in the knees, I'm sure, if they weren't utterly wasted on him.

He blinked blearily at the two of us, running his claws through the unruly scruff at the back of his neck. "I slept like the dead, can't speak for you two."

I drew in a tense breath, but he said no more on the topic. Only waited there swaying for a moment for us to respond. Still a bit out of it. And none the wiser.

Good.

The shame of it was, I couldn't taunt him for his tolerance being lower than mine. Missed opportunity.

"We're supposed to be at the cantina just after dawn," Lotus said, turning crisply and cuffing the both of us on the shoulder. "C'mon. Let's meet this man Chester's connecting us with. Bring your attitudes, lads. Mercenaries in this part of the world are a rough lot. I don't expect a lot of pleasantries."

❧ ❧

"That isn't a man," I said in a choked-off utterance. "That is a golden god."

We'd all come to a halt at the edge of the tree-line that separated one steppe of the mountain from the next. Down a muddy lane and an uneven set of chiseled stairs, carved right into one of the rockier areas of the land, was the open-air cantina Chester had told us to meet him at. And even calling it a 'cantina' was being kind. It was more of a pagoda with a few cooking pits and a cart laden with promising-looking barrels. I could smell the rum from here.

This looked to be the watering hole for a lot of the area's farmers, though, so it was busy. Mostly your standard local fare. Rodents, smaller cats, and various shades of tan foxes. The cantina was run by a family of jackals, bustling about pouring tea and booze and delivering banana-leaf-wrapped food parcels of some sort. They smelled spicy and sour, offending my nose but also making my mouth water. Probably rice balls wrapped around something pickled.

There was your odd dog or other obviously non-farmer dressed like they were here from the city, but the main attraction, the fellow who truly stood out, had to be our mercenary. He was sitting beside the weasel as well, so that just about confirmed it.

He was a leopard and one of the largest I'd ever seen at that. They were a striking people as it were, but he looked like he must've had some northern ancestry in him owing to his somewhat thicker fur and bushier tail, as well as the sunset hues of orange, gold, and white his pelt bled into along his chest.

Which he was certainly most prominently displaying, favoring absolutely nothing on his upper body save a sparkling bandolier of gold chain necklaces and a pair of form-fitting leather breeches below. And that was it. It looked like he kept his fur shaved down in places, a common practice for northern folk in this climate, but I could understand wanting to wear as little clothing as possible when you had a pelt like that.

He was all roiling muscle, powerful and sleek. Granted I'm not the best judge, but in my humble estimation he was a particularly fine specimen of a man, and he seemed to know it. I glanced sidelong at Luther, wondering if I was the only one who'd taken note of that particular fact.

I was not.

"Mate," I smirked, "you're staring."

"It's clear he wants to be stared at," he replied without breaking stride.

Lotus for some reason seemed more nonplussed, replying to my earlier comment with, "Oh. Yes, that's probably him. I've seen him around this port a lot; it's got to be one of his haunts. A local, then. Good, he'll know the lay of the land."

We approached along the walking trail, passing several farmers on their way out to work the fields. I didn't miss that over half of them wore collars. But at least they were able to purchase booze... I mean, it was something.

As we grew nearer, both the leopard and the weasel turned their eyes on us, the leopard first. He was leaning his lithe bulk back on a rickety-looking bamboo chair, pulled up near an old crate table that Chester had

clearly already ordered us food at. And a clay decanter that more specifically drew my eye.

Closer now, I noted two more things of interest. For one, the leopard's
weapon was… distinctive would be putting it mildly. I was hardly an expert
on arms, but it was some kind of poleaxe, slung by a shoulder-strap over
the back of his chair and tipped awkwardly, not suited to the seating area
that was already designed for people smaller than him, let alone a 6-foot
weapon. He at least had it blade down.

For two, I was not expecting the blindingly bright smile that lit over
his features as we neared them. A predator of a man with that kind of
presence, you just… you expected a cold, dangerous, calculating stare. An
insidious grin, or smirk, like the kind Denholme often wore. Something
along those lines.

But he smiled at us so cheerily his cheek ruff worked up and his eyes
briefly slipped close. And we hadn't even said anything yet.

"Chester, friend," he slapped a palm against the slim weasel's shoulders,
briefly making him choke on what he was hunched over eating. "You did
not tell me my clients were to be such a handsome group! Why, I was
expecting more elderly dog lords from the north. So rigid! So formal! Not
at all like these fine young fellows." He looked up at us and winked. "And a
beautiful lady, too."

Chester coughed once more, glancing aside at him long-sufferingly. "I didn't think their appearance or age was necessary information for the job, and, you'll forgive me, but you are free with your compliments with most people."

"I hold fast that you should spring for tailored vests," the leopard tutted at him, his body coiling as he shifted to stand to greet us. "With your waistline? You have a fetching figure beneath all that bulky clothing. You should ahhhh," he paused, then smiled again, "show off, yes? Bless my eyes, if we are to keep meeting like this. I take you on the town next time."

I blinked. Was he... flirting with the sales weasel? It was so hard to tell.

Chester certainly seemed to think so if the way he choked again on his food was any indication. He gathered his composure quickly enough after that though, rolling his eyes and brushing rice off his vest. He didn't bother to stand. "Ignore him," he muttered to us. "He's always like this."

"Oh, please do not ignore me," the leopard said, finally standing to his full height, which was as impressive as I'd thought it might be when he was sitting down. He had a few inches on me even, and I was a tall man. He was slimmer when he stood, but still built like a pugilist. I would not want to go a round in the ring with him.

"That would be rather difficult, I'd wager," I said, because Luther's eyes were saying it, Lotus's eyes were saying it, and dammit, someone needed to say it.

He must've latched onto the fact that I was the most talkative of us so far, because that got his attention on me. Gray-green eyes homed in on mine, and soon a hand had clapped forward into my own, seizing it from where it had been at my side—I hadn't even offered it. But I found I didn't mind, as he shook it exuberantly and gave that bright smile again. "Hadeon is my name, boss! Well met."

"Ah," I couldn't help it, his smile was infectious. "Sasha. Well met indeed."

"Shall I say 'Sasha' or 'Alexander', boss?" the leopard asked.

"Oh," I chuckled, "you know that, do you?"

"Poz'mitza vorrossy khoripzatvka," he replied in utterly fluent Kadrush.

Ears perking, I grinned and replied in equally fluent Kadrush, "It's a pleasure to meet a comrade so far from home, as well for me. I've actually never been to my homeland, believe it or not. But I grew up speaking the mother tongue as equally as Amurescan."

"So, formal or informal, boss?" He asked again, switching back to Amurescan. Good thing too, we were getting looks from my two companions. Dubious looks.

I shrugged at them. "Be a little more worldly, you ingrates," I ribbed them, then looked back to Hadeon. "Sasha is fine. Only my father ever called me Alexander and only when he was mad at me. To be fair, he called me Sasha when he was mad at me, too… he was just frequently mad at me."

He gave a booming laugh. "You wouldn't be here meeting with me if you weren't troublemakers, eh? Come, come. Chester continues to glower at me."

"I need to get back to the city," the weasel insisted, sighing. "Let's make short work of this food and get this underway."

We doled out the food and began tucking in. I'd been right, pickled root vegetables wrapped in rice with seaweed and spicy seasonings. No meat, but filling enough, and I was ravenous.

Hadeon poured us each some rum in our rations cups, being as liberal with our servings as he was with his own. While he did, he spoke amicably. "Chester has given me some idea of what it is you need done. But I think you must be as specific as possible, yes? I always prefer clarity."

Luther glanced about at the busy cantina. "Are we safe to speak here?"

"No one will hear you over the wind and their own conversation in a place like this," Chester waved a hand. "That's why I chose it."

"You are…?" Hadeon trailed off, looking pointedly to Luther.

Luther visibly paused a moment. All I could think was 'sloppy, mate'. I'm sure the leopard had caught it, too. Always have your name ready when you're engaged in skullduggery.

"Lucius," he said at length. "And the purse for this particular job, so…"

"Got it, boss," Hadeon said with a flash of smiling fangs. "Lucius it is."

"Mahasha," Lotus said, giving a whiskery smile and a noticeable lowering of her long eyelashes. "Pleasure to meet you, Hadeon."

The leopard gave her a simmering smile back, a curl of his painted jowls that somehow only accentuated his sharp, handsome features. Watching cats flirt with one another should be a spectator sport, I swear. They were both purring, too, and I was seated between them. My whole body was rumbling with it, good God—

"I take it Chester gave you the run-down already," Luther said, his gold gaze flicking back and forth among all of us, looking irritable as ever. "Specifically whose ships we need to infiltrate, because I'm certain that'd be the deal-breaker otherwise."

"I have worked on commission for the Dhole before," Hadeon said easily, sliding back in his chair and loping one muscled arm over the back of it. "Most men of my persuasion in these parts have. And his Captains are hiring on in force right now. I would have considered a job with his fleet regardless, given I am otherwise unoccupied at the moment. But this works too."

He must've caught the mood at the table shifting at that admission, but his only response was to smile again. "Oh, I thought my previous experience with the man was an asset, no? Do we have a problem?"

157

"You know our intentions for him and his fleet are—" I began.

"Unpleasant, I am certain," he said with a quirk of his muzzle, revealing one long fang that overlapped his lower lip. It was just slightly off-kilter, so it was always somewhat visible. Probably a broken jaw at some point in the past. But like everything else, he made it work. "That is no deterrent to me. Provided you have a good plan. They are to go to sea immediately, I hear. To his island. Something is... afoot. This is not usual for him this time of year. You have me wondering."

"We'll tell you everything," I promised him. "But just to be clear, because I feel it needs saying: I'm personally planning to kill the man. That's the goal. There's something I need to pilfer, as well. But I'm not leaving that ship until he's dead."

"The same goes for me," Luther joined in. He looked my way. "We kill the Dhole, we get what Sasha is after, and then we bail. All together." He was still looking at me when he said, "No men left behind."

I wasn't sure if that was a promise meant to comfort me or a threat laid at my feet. Either way, I clapped a hand over my heart, acting as though he'd said something endearing.

"You have exit plan, then?" Hadeon asked, his voice gone more serious. He looked more calculated than congenial now, not upset by any measure, but like he was deep in thought.

"The exit plan is where I come in," Lotus said. "I can't go in with you all, so I'll be coordinating our allies at sea. I wish I could help you infiltrate, but... I'm known to this man and a woman besides. I hear he has a few scattered on his crew, but far too much of a minority for me to blend in. And I can't pass for a man, not with my body-type."

"Mmhh, very much not," Hadeon agreed with a smirk.

"That's my foot," I gasped out, as I felt the curl of a warm-furred tail over my toes. I chuckled nervously. "Not hers."

"I am aware," he purred. "You must forgive me. It has... mind of its own."

"Right, sure," I cleared my throat.

It was on my thigh now. And Lotus was already touching my other thigh, she'd had a hand there since we'd sat down. I was hedged in by big gorgeous cats on all sides. What the fuck was going on today?

"You have big," the leopard clutched at the air, making a gesture, "big balls, saying you will kill this man? This dhole. You must know who he is. What he commands. The many, many vicious men that sail under his flag."

"We are well aware," Luther confirmed grimly. "We have our own men and firepower at our disposal, but this plan requires men on the inside."

"And you are those men," the leopard said, sounding suitably impressed as he stared at us all from his relaxed recline. "But you say... your men.

Your firepower. You are the boss of those men too, yes? These ships. These reinforcements. They are loyal to you. They will come for you. You are certain."

"Certain," I said at the same time as Luther said 'absolutely certain'.

The leopard seemed to consider for only another few moments, before he nodded, brushing back his whiskers. "I would wish for you to lay out the entire plan for me in time. But for now, I say… yes. You speak with conviction." He leaned forward, bracing his elbows on the table. "And I like you. I believe that you believe you can see this thing done."

I looked to Luther and Lotus, who both seemed a little surprised, but were tempering their expressions. Luther spoke first. "You haven't even named a price yet, and you're accepting?"

"You know what you ask," the leopard waved a paw. "You will pay exorbitantly, and I am certain you will be good for it. You are more important… more rich than you want me to know. Than you want anyone to know. You will not short me when the time comes."

"I appreciate your trust," Luther said.

"You are hiring a professional killer, boss," the leopard said, not bothering to lower his voice. Chester was right, though. No one would hear our conversation in this place. Hadeon smiled again, his eyes crinkling around the spotted edges as he did. "I am certain you will pay and pay well. No one but a fool shorts a man in my profession. Theft of services would end unpleasantly for us all."

I huffed out a laugh. "I… don't think I've ever been so charmed while simultaneously having my life threatened."

"I'm insulted—" Lotus jabbed her elbow into my side.

"You can smuggle us aboard his Capital ship?" Luther pressed. "I'm not discounting your skill with that bardiche, only time will tell on that. Not the most ideal weapon in close quarters, but I'm assuming you have a short blade as backup."

"I do," he confirmed.

"I'll bet it clears a deck well enough," I muttered, glancing at the long poleaxe again. Bardiche, eh? I needed to brush up on my rare armaments.

"It does in fact," Hadeon smiled, showing off that long fang again. "And… yes. I can get you aboard the dhole's ship. I can merely enlist to get aboard, I will not be turned down, but I am assuming that is not an option for you."

"We might get past his quartermaster and some of his men at the docks," I said, "but the less time we spend mixing with them, the less chance we're recognized."

"Mmhh, you have been enemies in the past, I'd wager," Hadeon nodded. "I have a plan, yes. I thought on it last night, and I know a means to get you below-decks in the hold. I can make my way to you once we are at sea, and from there… is on you. I hope you have a good plan of your own. Because while the idea of killing the Skull King on his own ship does… excite me," he admitted, "I do also enjoy being alive. Tell me. How do we do this and get away with it?"

To his credit, he sounded excited.

"Alright," Luther said, leaning his own elbows on the table, taking a swig of his rum, and beginning. "Here's how it is…"

That night, in a decrepit old grain storehouse, in a small town at the base of the farming steppes, with the rain beating down on the tiled roof… we went over the plan. In excruciating detail.

Or at least it certainly felt that way to me. I wasn't always the most 'plan ahead' sort of man. I preferred to fly by the seat of my britches and steer into the wind as much as possible. A lifestyle like mine didn't exactly lend itself to ease and comfort, but not fretting the details or living in a constant state of anxiety over every little thing that could go wrong in my future was essential to survival when you were a wanted man with no home port left in the world.

The bottle didn't hurt, either.

But Luther was meticulous. And apparently, so was our new friend. Hadeon, as it turned out, was in fact a consummate professional. Or at least, that's how it felt to me when he began embarrassing me with his knowledge of Roccosal's fleet, catching us up on our mistaken understandings of how we'd all thought this might go down at the tiger estate and not being shy about speaking over us or correcting us.

I guess I'd expected he'd just nod and go along with the plan we'd already hashed-out, but in retrospect, I'm not sure why I'd ever thought that. It's not like I was an authoritarian with my own fleet; I had a lot of trusted men I brought to the table whenever we were plotting a job, and they all got a vote. My crew was a meritocracy, and I'd had no issue being told I was wrong by some of my far smarter—and frequently more worldly—men in the past.

But Hadeon was a temporary hire, a mercenary, and for some reason I guess I hadn't lumped him into that category. I found myself bristling at first, especially when he flat-out said our plan to disguise our way in was foolish and wouldn't work. And he used a Kadrush word that I happened to know was closer to 'stupid'.

Which stuck in my craw a little. Especially since his scheme to get us aboard, which he seemed to have ready-made (suggesting he'd tried something similar in the past, which was mildly horrifying considering what it was) seemed far riskier to me.

But then he'd explained Roccosal's first mate was a mink with an unnerv-ingly-good memory for their crew and, moreover, for crew management. Hadeon believed he did it by scent. Minks could have an incredible mental inventory for how people smelled. He recalled an instance where the man had caught and later disciplined a crew member for using the Crimson Divine, a powerful drug made from poppies in Mataa. It wasn't explicitly banned for use in Roccosal's fleet, but that particular strain was, since it was carried and sold almost exclusively by a rival Cartel.

And yeah, that was a scary instance to take note of. I'm pretty sure—and I'd confirmed this with Luther—that there had been a mink on Dokuro. Somewhere in that camp where they'd held Kafele. Which means the guy might very well have us in that fucking mental inventory of his. We had to be careful.

So, there you see it. We had our plan called into question by this man we'd only just taken on, vehemently and with, as it turns out, good reason. And then a moment later he'd used his knowledge and experience to confirm why he was in the right, and I felt like a fool for questioning him. Humbling. Especially with someone we'd only just met.

No one likes feeling like they're in the wrong, especially on something so important. But as I'd learned time and time again it was exactly those times when you most needed to be course-corrected.

Adding to my humiliation, Luther Denholme, a man from a race of people known for their arrogance and self-righteousness, who had done little in the time I'd known him to prove he was any different... was a god-damn patient saint through the whole thing. He was unerringly polite, cutting himself off and going silent to listen whenever Hadeon or Lotus spoke up, questioning their or my assertions only when his basis for doing so was sound, and never once betraying frustration or hurt pride when we went back and forth over conflicting plans. He was so...

Fucking. Mature. It pissed me off.

I knew the man well enough by now, or at least I thought I did, to have seen his impatience, his bluster, his temper. He was hardly a perfect specimen. I'm sure he was proud, arrogant even, when he was in his element. I'd seen little of that in his time with me, since he was largely in my territory and thus had to be deferential to his surroundings and the will of Lotus and me. I'd certainly watched him be stubborn to his own detriment on more than one occasion.

But when it came to plotting a course of action that required varied knowledge, strategy, and experience, he seemed to know when to shut up. And unlike me, he wasn't making it personal.

It made me take stock of my own immaturity... which just further pissed me off. Which made me feel immature. Which—

I was a mess by the end of the night. I felt outclassed. Not by Hadeon; he was in a position to have more on-the-ground experience with this fleet and that wasn't something Luther or I could have had for obvious reasons. His assertive personality saw to it that he corrected our misconceptions, but that was a good thing.

But Luther and I had the same goddamn job, essentially. Opposite sides of the law, but we were in direct competition. That's what this whole fucking thing had been about. He was already arguably a better Captain than I was. Did he have to be more humble, too? Fuck's sake.

"I can only follow you lot as far as the plantation," Lotus said, dragging a thick paw-pad and claw along the weathered map we were using. It covered roughly the lower third of the island, which was almost entirely dominated by the Rohkash family estate: the tiger lords here. They had Divine fields, workhouses where they produced goods for the local port and processed their drug, and a substantial number of buildings surrounding the compounds where they kept all of their indentured labor and the people who lived alongside the tiger clan in more... legitimate states of employ. Guards, Priests, Courtesans, the usual entourage for Huudari families of means.

The Rohkash compound was a massive sprawling estate that was built into the less rugged, more pleasant and accessible side of the island, which is why it was also where their allies made port. They had their own private marina, plenty of space for their own trade ships as well as Rocossal's, or any other pirates, privateers, or merchants who they chose to do business with.

"I'd be recognized immediately, not just as a woman but by name, no matter how I disguised myself," Lotus said with a grimace. "I'm too well-known in these waters, especially by other tigers. The Rohkash don't have it out for me specifically and would be hesitant to allow Roccosal's boys to cause trouble with me while the two of us happen to be sharing the same land mass, but I'm not sure if they'd stop him from killing me if push came to shove. Also, my presence alone would give us up. Plenty of Roccosal's men saw us together on Dokuro; they'll put two and two together. I don't know if they're actively looking for you any more Reed, but they'd certainly want to 'chat' with me about how to find you."

Luther waved a hand, "It almost doesn't bear speaking on. You've been an enormous help, Lady. But I think this must be where we part ways. And you have your own task to fulfill, equally important in measure."

"Right," she said, blowing out a breath. I didn't miss the way her ears tipped back, though. "You can count on me, provided your wolfhound and your Captains are willing to hear me out."

"The letter I'm sending ought to suffice for that," he assured her. "In case you have any... trouble."

"Oh, you mean convincing a bunch of Amurescan Lords to listen to someone of the fairer sex?" I snorted.

"Let alone a feline," Hadeon cut in, brushing his whiskers back.

"Worked with a lot of Amurescans, I see," I glanced his way.

"You do not need to know many of them personally to know they prefer only to listen to their own kind," he said with a grim smile.

"To their detriment," Luther said, eyes still riveted on the map, his pupils sharp and framed by gold. They flicked back and forth in concentration as he presumably took in the lay of the land.

"Yes boss, but you seem less afflicted by this bias," Hadeon complimented, his dark jowls turning up in one of his—honestly pretty frequent—genuine smiles. "You do not strike me as rich man. Common stock, more willing to reach across with a paw to any soul there, canine or no. And yet your Captains—you call them 'your'—these men, they will listen to you? Curious. Not very... how is it you say... 'Pedigree.'"

"I wasn't born a rich man," Luther confirmed, not looking up.

Hadeon chuckled, long and deep, his voice a rich timbre at most times, but especially so when he was laughing. All of us turned to regard him though. Something was off about his reaction.

When he found our eyes on him, his laughter fell off, and his whole aura shifted. That tone dropped to an even deeper baritone with the rumbling edge only big cats ever truly managed. "Who are you?" he asked Luther, and it was clear it was a question, but not an optional one. "Really. Reed, I know. Lady Lotus, as you say, you are known here. I... am not certain why you bother with false name, at all."

"Fuck!" I snarled, irritated. I scrubbed at the back of my head where my mane had been cut. "I thought at least without this... how did you know?"

"Your pistol," he replied simply, gesturing at the one on my right hip. "It isn't your fault, you betray little. I have a mind for remembering weapons is all, and I know the man who owned that before you. It is well known how he lost it, and to whom."

I bit the edge of my muzzle at that, trying to ignore the quizzical and somewhat suspicious look I got from Luther. Lotus must have already known, or she didn't care, because she was raptly focused on Hadeon now. "Why does this matter to you, suddenly?" she demanded. "Just earlier today you didn't care. You bought the cattle dog's weak bluff or at least pretended to. Why?"

"Something occurred to me," the leopard said, scratching a claw lightly over his chin. "Something I'd only just remembered, in the last hour. Something I heard in port. Idle gossip. But I wonder..."

Luther's ears shot up, and I saw the fur on the back of his neck rise. His hand was far too close to his waist, where his blade was sheathed. We'd all agreed we'd keep our weapons on us, but stowed… and he had. But I knew from experience how fast a draw he was, and how quickly a dispute with him could turn south. For someone seemingly so calm on the surface, so 'mature' in other aspects, he had a hair-trigger temper. And I suspected he drew steel first, questioned his decisions, if ever, afterwards. I didn't have to have known him long to deduce that. He'd pulled his blade on me likely while being fully aware I had a cantina full of backup around me, heedless of the danger to himself, all because I'd insulted him.

"Mate," I warned him with a growl.

He gave me an irritated flick of a glance, but I held firm and stared him down. Here's where my maturity came into play. You wanna be reckless with your own life? Fine. But we were in this together at this point and even a tussle could result in us losing our guide. If not worse.

"Out with it," Luther said to Hadeon, who had clearly noticed the cattle dog's battle readiness and seemed to find it more amusing than anything else. He was still reclining in his comfortable sprawl, his pose relaxed as it had been, even if his mirth was tempered with a more intimidating air now.

"A fishing ship off the Shanivaar east hook caught sight of what they swore was an infamous vessel, drifting on the eastern current," he said, his dark tongue licking his teeth, "kul afeh nokshanna tel'nirym, is what they said."

"'The tail that wags the three-headed dog?'" I parroted back, uncertain what the significance of that might be.

Luther caught it right away though, visibly gritting his teeth and looking… annoyed? I'd expected anger, given the conversation. But honestly, he more seemed humiliated.

Trust me, I know what humiliation looks like on a man.

"Oh, you incompetent curs!" Lotus flopped her arms down at her side. "And you were worried Reed was going to be the one to blow this for us?"

"I'm still in the dark here," I admitted, raising a hand.

"Addison," Luther closed his eyes a moment, pinching his brow. "Sloppy. Shite. This rumor's going around port?" he asked Hadeon, suddenly seeming less angry at the man and more worried. "For how long? Are a lot of people believing it in your estimation?"

The leopard's jaw fell open, revealing his killer fangs and most of the rest of his teeth, but not in anger or rage. He looked jubilant, in fact. "It's true, then! HA!"

"Still lost!" I said, annoyed.

"It's his gods-be-damned scouting vessel," Lotus said, staring daggers at Luther, whose expression said it all. Whatever the both of them suspected, his entire posture was confirming it. "The one you send ahead of the rest of the Cerberus Fleet. They're already here. How could they be that stupid?!

To be seen by locals, when we're trying to intercept Roccosal in a pincer? You'd better fucking hope this rumor doesn't make it to him."

"He has," Luther put his hands out in a calming gesture, "no reason whatsoever to suspect I'm involved with you two, remember? Let alone guess what it is we're trying to do. Even if he finds out—"

"Oh lad," I chuckled, shaking my head. "This must be embarrassing for you."

I swear his ears flushed pink. "I am not with them at the moment," he said between his teeth. "Do you not realize that, somehow? My Captains are acting on their own right now, and someone," he paused at that, a fierce bolt of distaste crossing his features, "someone… must have overruled Johannes and made the decision to move in closer and run reconnaissance."

"This 'Addison'?" I guessed.

"No," he muttered. "He's just following orders. And he's generally good at his job. It's just borderline impossible to avoid the eyelines of so many small ships this close to an island chain. Arrogant to assume you could, and several of my Captains are arrogant. What's more, the fisherman must have had experience on merchant vessels or privateering to recognize that ship; it isn't marked. She doesn't fly our crest or any flags of origin." He let out a sigh. "We got unlucky."

"Whoever the fuck made this call must not care a whole lot for your wellbeing," I said pointedly. "Even my crew, motley though it is, wouldn't risk my life like that, knowing where I am and what I'm doing right now."

"Maybe they just trust their Admiral's… skills and knack for survival," he said unconvincingly.

I tried not to make a face. "Sure, mate. If that helps you sleep better."

"The Cerberus Admiral," Hadeon reminded us all of his presence, still unmoved from his comfortable lazing position sitting astride one barrel, and leaning back against a stack of crates. This storehouse as a hidden place of respite was once again thanks to Lotus. The hidey-hole at least was entirely empty, probably still part of her network and certainly less comfortable than the Inn, but unoccupied save for us. Rather important when you're hatching infiltration plans.

Somewhat lacking in furniture, alas.

"Well, there isn't much point in my denying it at this point, is there?" Luther groused, lifting his chin in the direction of Hadeon as though the reveal of who he truly was had given him reason to start acting the part. Head held high and all that. Defiant, challenging, inviting the leopard to stare him down if he dared.

For his part, Hadeon just looked tickled. "Incredible!" he crowed. "The legend in the flesh. I expected you'd be taller, boss. But I can see it, yes." He shifted his bulk forward, sprawling his arms over his knees, craning his long neck in Luther's direction. When he spoke again his voice was a sultry purr. "Yes. In the eyes. There you are. A murderer, through and through."

Luther said nothing. Which was… chilling, if you ask me. Most men would have a retort, a defense of themselves to an accusation like that. Even if they were a murderer, they'd either mask it with denial or boast it with intimidation and threats. Something like 'damn straight, so watch your tongue'. That's what leapt to mind for me, anyway. What I'd probably say to shut down someone coming at me like that.

I don't know what silence meant. But it wasn't… good. It probably wasn't good.

But then I came from the world of outlaws. You didn't just tacitly accept anything you were accused of in my circles. You denied, denied, denied, until they had you at the gallows, and then maybe if you were a religious man, you begged forgiveness. Maybe. They say you never knew a man until you saw how he acted with a noose around his neck. Did he crumble? Did he fall to piteous begging? Did he curse the law to the very end? Did he seek salvation? Or did he stare down death with weary resignation and silence? That seemed the way to go to me. Leave 'em all guessing. I'd not yet been tested, obviously, but I hoped if the day came that's how I'd handle it.

Luther was, at least right now (although I had doubts about the lawfulness of his entire history, the man struck me as someone who'd crossed that line more than once before) on the side of Imperialists and capital, and thus on the side of the law. He didn't have to defend his actions, his nation did that for him. So maybe that's why he didn't seem to care.

Maybe.

"I think," Lotus said with an uncertain edge to her voice, perhaps sensing the tension in the room, "that… although this complicates things… Denholme," she used his real name notably, probably shifting now to using it as a cudgel, "is right about this being perhaps not entirely catastrophic. It wouldn't be unusual for his fleet to be in these waters regardless. This is one of your primary hunting grounds, yes?"

Luther gave her a sidelong look, before moving his intense gaze back to the leopard, the still unknown quantity in the room. We all obviously had known who we each were going into this. How Hadeon felt about our true identities was still up in the air, and he wasn't betraying much so far other than excitement. Which could mean so many different things.

"Yes," the cattle dog said. "You'd know, after all."

"Right. Because they're my hunting grounds, as well," Lotus said, again airing out who we all were very intentionally, directed at the leopard. 'You know who we are and what we can bring to bear', essentially. "So, I think the question now… is that going to be a problem for you, Hadeon?"

"Not in the least," the mercenary said, showing off his skewed fang. And as if just now picking up on the tension in the air, his eyes crinkled up into a more jovial smile—which I'd begun to doubt the sincerity of at this point—and he put his palms out, the dark paw-pads offered up. "Oh! I'm so sorry! Please do not mistake my curiosity, boss. I do not care whom I work for. Truly. It is of no matter, so long as their coin spends, and the task is laid out before me with no deception that may... complicate things."

"You didn't need to know our identities to help us with this job," I pointed out. "So why the interrogation? If it 'doesn't matter' to you?"

"Whether or not you can bring back-up to bear is important," he replied evenly. "I may be... a man of many talents, but making it from deep ocean to a friendly port without a vessel is beyond most, I'd wager. If your plan goes south—"

"You'll have a hell of a time escaping alive," I muttered. "Yeah, we were sort of counting on that. Good reason not to betray us while we're out there."

"Now, come boss," he tutted. "Why would I do that?"

"To save your skin, like you said," Lotus rolled her eyes. "And trust me, I understand. This is just a job to you. But we do have reinforcement, it's close-by."

"Enough," Luther snapped at her quietly. "He knows too much already."

"I am appeased," the leopard assured us. "Although given the coin you paid, I knew you were men and women of means. But it is good to know you are competent, as well. And, sir," that was directed to Luther, who seemed put off by the formal address, "in your case, it is an honor."

"Why?" I found myself asking aloud, trying and failing to keep the envy out of my tone. I suddenly found all eyes on me, and scoffed, gesturing at Luther with a hand. "Look, I could give a rat's ass what a mercenary I just met thinks of me, but that's odd. Lotus, you and I are far more well known in this part of the world; we actually do business here, we have friends, contacts. Fellows. H-he's just... a...."

"Monster," Hadeon filled in for me, using the Amurescan word and following it up with two similar translations in Hudaari, then Kadrush. "Everyone is afraid of him. He has... big reputation. Intimidating. I do not spend all of my time at sea, but he is like... leviathan. You hear of the Cerberus Fleet, but most never see it. And when they do..."

"You're honored to meet him because so many people are afraid of him," I unpacked that verbally, because I was still trying to make sense of it.

"Yes," Hadeon explained simply. "In my line of work, reputation is as important as competence. From what I hear, boss man here has both." He gave me a simpering smile. "But don't worry. You are all... big fish. All three of you."

"Apparently one of us more than the others," Lotus said, not sounding like she actually cared at all.

"Ah," Hadeon said suddenly, his eyes homing in on me. "I have insulted! I'm sorry, boss. Your fleet is, of course, quite infamous as well. This humble one is honored to know you all."

"Don't placate me," I muttered, crossing my arms over my chest.

Luther made a noise that was as dismissive and fed-up as any I'd ever heard. "I don't give a damn what any of you think of me," he said, leaning over and snapping up the map, rolling it up. "We have a truly revolting, uncomfortable task ahead of us tomorrow if we want to pull this off, and I'd rather rest now while I can. Reed. Stop being a petulant child and do the same. Don't spend all night fucking the felines. I have to smell you all day tomorrow, and we don't exactly have time to bathe."

"I'm not sure if I should be insulted by that remark," Lotus said snidely.

Hadeon gestured between us, either feigning confusion or earnestly being so. "I assumed you were all fucking one another already."

Lotus actually laughed aloud. "Wh… alright. I must know. Why would you assume that?"

"It's half true," I said, shrugging.

"Why else would an Amurescan Admiral, a Privateer, and a Pirate Hunter be working together?" The leopard grinned. "Sex is the only reason that makes any sense to me."

"Good night," Luther said disgustedly, as he stormed off to the farthest corner of the warehouse he could find, presumably.

Lotus grabbed me by one of my bandoliers and dragged me off to the opposite corner, behind stacks of bunched alfalfa so dense and pungent I was certain I'd be smelling it in my fur for weeks.

"He's oddly correct," I said, allowing myself to be dragged. "It was sex that brought us all together. Just not… with one another. Not right away, anyway."

Lotus clapped her palms on either side of my face, forcing me to look at her. "Grayson. Say that a little louder, with more detail, I don't think the leopard knows all the gory details just yet. Another five minutes with you and he will." She sighed, squishing my cheek ruff and shaking my head about fondly. "Denholme is being a salty shit, but he's right. This man does not need to know our life stories."

"Right," I said, tucking my ears back and dropping my eyes. "Sorry."

"Just because your life's an open book." She rolled her eyes. "Not everyone's comfortable exposing themselves thusly."

I shut my jaw briefly, before opening it again to say, "My life is not an open book. I keep things close to the chest, too. Some things."

"Oh really?" she sniffed dryly, dubiously.

"Yes," I said firmly.

She gave a playful smirk, releasing the hold she had on my bandolier and trailing a clawed finger up beneath my chin, playing with my jaw whiskers. "You mean like how you're obsessed with Denholme?"

"What?!" I stammered. Damn it all, why did my speech impediments betray me before my words did? But still, what was she—

"Oh please," she snorted, leaning back onto a half-unfurled roll of alfalfa, wiggling back and forth slowly as she made a divot for herself, getting comfortable. Like a barn cat. "You couldn't be more nakedly obvious if you tried. This whole thing, all of this, is happening because you forced yourself into his life. You're no better than Hadeon, idolizing a myth." She sneered. "Honestly, I don't understand you boys. He's an arrogant, bitter little cock of a man. Maybe if all you knew was his reputation, but we've had to put up with the genuine article for a few weeks now, haven't you had enough already? I don't get the appeal."

"You're way off," I insisted tiredly. "I don't—I'm not—the leopard's hero worship is… seems to be born of bloodlust, if anything. He's 'idolizing' him because of how many lives he's taken, how many ships he's sunk. I go out of my way not to sink ships; I don't respect or admire the violence and death he's inflicted. I'm not like that."

"I know," she said a little more quietly. Kindly. "I know that. But, you're envious of him. Please don't deny it."

"That doesn't mean I'm 'obsessed' with him," I persisted.

"You did all of this to facilitate meeting him. In person. To get his attention."

"Because he's a threat!" I said, louder than I'd intended to.

I knew immediately, I'd fallen right into her trap. She said nothing in response to my outburst, only inclined her head slightly and stared right into my eyes.

I let my gaze drop again. "… that's your point, isn't it? It's always been your point. You said as much before."

"Mmhh," she agreed, tossing her tail over her own lap. "I just don't want you to forget it. Especially going forward, since the two of you will be doing the rest of this together… and I can't look after you anymore."

"I'm a grown man, Lotus," I reminded her. "I can manage my own relationships."

"You know what I think?"

"I'm certain you're going to tell me," I sighed.

"You're not aspiring to be him," she said. "That much is plain to see… you don't want that man's life. If you wanted to be a rich bastard wearing the regalia of tyranny, walking the halls of power, you could have had that. You gave that up a long time ago, and I don't think you want it back."

"Well," I muttered, "I would have had a fleet only in name, if I'd stayed with the Reed Cartel. I couldn't be a part of it, save behind a desk."

"Oh, please," she said. "Whatever you did to be disinherited, you could have strong-armed your family into changing their minds. Or waited for your parents to die. Your brother wouldn't have stopped you from Captaining your own ship, if that's what you wanted to do. He's a little busy being the sort of man you loathe, running the kind of trade Empire you violently dismantle whenever you can."

"You know a decent amount about my family," I groused.

"Most people do." She shrugged. "Like I said. You're an open book. The fallen scion of the Reed Cartel. Everyone knows who you are, the infamous tale of the Manoratha heist, and what sort of world you came from." She reached up, again stroking my lower jaw. And eventually she gently lifted it, so she could make eye contact with me. "And that's won you respect, Reed. Real respect. With the people on the seas that matter. Not bullshit aggrandizing infamy, based on how many people you've murdered. Hell, if you think that's something to be envious of, you should be looking up to a man like Roccosal. Or the King of Amuresca."

I frowned. "I see your point, but—"

"Reputation's important." She shook her head. "I know. I'm not saying it isn't. But I think you've let all the shanties and stories go to your head where he's concerned. You think it's entertaining to barb him? Fine. I'm not gonna tell you you're wrong there. But that isn't a man," she lowered her voice, "to aspire to. That is a broken, lost soul, doing the bidding of an Empire that denies his right to live—over something as paltry as who he beds—because it's the only thing he's good at, and he needs that validation or he'll have literally nothing else."

"Fuck," I choked. "Lotus, that's, come on."

"Tell me I'm wrong."

"That's harsh, even for you," I whispered fiercely. "You traveled with the man, for fuck's sake. You worked with him."

"How do you think I know all of this?" she said. "I've been trying to tell you this whole time. You just won't listen. He isn't someone to befriend, Grayson. He is a brief alliance; I worked with him knowing I had to keep a healthy distance. You're letting him get under your skin, pluck at your heart-strings, feel things. I've seen it. It disturbs me how close you've been getting."

"He treats me exactly the same as he did when we first met," I pointed out.

"It's a one-way street with people like him," she said. "He's manipulative, and you're an easy target. He knows he can toy with you."

"All I get from him is vinegar," I huffed. "I don't know what it is you think you're seeing."

"Then you're blind," she stated flatly.

"You're acting like I'm enamored of him," I said. "Like some... jealous paramour."

"We're friends, Grayson," she said softly. "Don't get it twisted. I don't now, nor will I ever, care whom you bed. This isn't about that. Although for the record, I think if you wanted to start mixing in men, you could do better."

"Beg to differ," I grumbled.

"I wish it was that simple," she sighed. "But... I think... what you envy in him is his... certainty."

I had no immediate response to that. But something rang inside me like a church bell. Something that shook and resounded, and made me want to curse her out loud.

"Explain," I said after swallowing back the lump in my throat.

"Exactly what I said." She tugged at my right hand with her left, urging me to sit down beside her. I eventually did, settling on the floor rather than the alfalfa bale, so I was staring up at her. I felt very tired all of a sudden.

She reached to the back of my head and untied the binding holding back the stubs of my mane, threading her claws through it with some difficulty and piecing out each of the branches of where my dreads had been. Her claws felt good on my scalp.

"He doesn't question his decisions, or at least not externally," she continued. "He's decisive. Confident. It gives the appearance of authority. Whereas you... question. Constantly. I think more than I'm even aware of."

"He let the leopard correct him and talk over him all night," I pointed out.

"Because Hadeon had better information," she said. "It isn't just about being stubborn or being right all the time. The man's purpose-driven, he does what he has to at any given time to accomplish his goals. And he doesn't seem to care what it is he has to do. I mean, the leopard's plan is... well, I don't envy you. But he didn't balk, even at that. He was willing to work with me. He came to meet you on Dokuro in person and essentially alone with no guarantee you wouldn't kill him."

"He probably figured he didn't have a choice."

"Would you have taken that kind of risk? Alone?"

"If you're trying to say he's got bigger balls than I do, you're not really helping my confidence," I pointed out wryly.

"It isn't nerve, Grayson," she said, frustrated. "It isn't even confidence in his abilities. I don't care how deft you are with a sword; it won't help you if someone shoots you in the fucking gut. Don't you get it? He doesn't care. That's why these risks don't matter to him. It isn't bravery or resolve. It's masochism."

I thought about what she was saying, for a while. Some of it did make sense.

"You're a better man than him," she said, her claws trailing paths down from the crown of my head to the nape of my neck. "And it's good that you question. It's good that you care. If you go stagnant in your heart like that, there are very few forces in this world that can reignite that fire. It's harder. It's harder to give a shit, to constantly worry if you're doing something worthwhile, if you're in the right. But it's... Gods, it has to be worth it. It just has to."

"You're right on one thing. I don't know what I'm doing with my life half the bloody time," I admitted softly, closing my eyes and letting my head drift to settle my muzzle on one of her thighs.

"Most people don't, even if it seems like they do," she assured me, her paw rubbing circles into my neck now.

"A decade ago," I mumbled, "I was a bright-eyed lad looking forward to my college years. Blades and pistols were for sport, and... economics was a book on my bedside table, not a reason for revolution. I'd never even met a criminal, at least not a convicted one. I'd pass the gallows in the city in a carriage, never thinking there'd be hundreds, thousands of people who'd want me up there, some day."

Lotus traced the outline of my ear with a claw. "I'd never have met that man, though. Let alone sailed with him, drank bad local liquor with him, hunted a Pirate King with him...."

"I suppose a part of me keeps thinking I'm an imposter," I murmured. "That this is some false skin I'm going to shed. It feels ill-fitting sometimes. I'm surrounded by all of these blood-soaked men, this sea of... predators... who can flay flesh from bone and send their enemies to the bottom and sometimes I look around and realize..."

Lotus said nothing. She gave me time to find my words.

"... I'm... one of them now," I finally uttered. "Have been since that alleyway. But some part of me hasn't come to grips with it yet, so I just keep being... horrified at myself. Wondering how the fuck I got here. How the hell I'm in this deep. And then I remember, right. It was all my doing. I plunged myself into this, and I keep going deeper, and the only way it all ends is... one day, one of the people I've wronged will get the better of me." I closed my eyes, huffing out into her fur. "That or I'll drink myself to death."

"I'd give that option a fifty-fifty chance," she clucked her tongue.

"You know, I used to be a Tea-totaler," I muttered.

I couldn't see her, but I heard the aghast noise she made. "Yet another reason to be glad I met you now," she said. "Why on earth? Some kind of religious conviction? Father who overdid it?"

"My father drank in moderation," I assured her. "Alcohol wasn't his vice; work was. And no one in the family could decide on which religion to practice, let alone practice it seriously. It wasn't much of a leap to atheism for me. Benefits of multiculturalism: all the old ways start looking and sounding like rubbish when you realize how many people think their god or gods are the only ones, and their ridiculous fairy-tales are the only factual basis for how the whole world should live their lives."

"Hey now," she yawned. "I still pray."

"To whom?" I asked, earnestly curious. The Huudari had a whole pantheon of gods and goddesses.

Her answer was less than enlightening. She merely shrugged. "Whoever's listening."

"If it's just out of habit or... desperation for an afterlife, I guess I just don't really see the purpose," I grumbled. "I mean do you really believe in anything tangible at that point?"

"I'm just not ready to accept there's nothing after this life," she said. "I've lost too many people I cared about to accept they're all just... gone, and I'll never see them again."

I understood that yearning, but I also thought she was wrong to cling to it. All the same, I kept my mouth shut. It wasn't my place to dash her hopes, and what purpose would it serve?

"So why, then?" she asked.

I blinked, looking up. And then I remembered what we'd originally been talking about. "Why..." I began, "—Oh! Oh. Why didn't I... drink."

She stared owlishly down at me, waiting for an answer. I was hung up, though. Did I tell her the truth? She knew so much about my past already, obviously. And I trusted her, didn't I?

Something made me stop short. The same barricades went up, the same jolt of fear coursed through me as had ever, when I'd considered exposing this inescapable part of who I was. I can't say if it was fear of exposing my vulner-ability; it would be a difficult one to exploit, so that surely wasn't it. It really only endangered me insofar as it could harm my reputation. If the world knew the man at the helm of the Manoratha was... compromised. Cursed.

Sickly.

Some people thought it meant I was insane or simple. A seizing illness often accompanied various other weaknesses of constitution. A man so unwell could not be of sound mind.

The jury was out on that one regardless, I'd say.

Others thought it was the inevitable product of inbreeding. And that one stung most especially, because while my family were certainly no Pedigrees, marrying cousins was a usual practice in wealthy circles. Which made me fear there was a grain of truth to it.

The worst possible outcome, though, was also the most likely... pity. And fuck, was I tired of that. Even now, years after I'd left my family, the mere thought of being treated like I had been back then—like a stiff wind could break me, like a fragile oddity to be gawked at and whispered about—made my stomach curdle. I'd been ashamed of this weakness my entire life, despite it being one of the few flaws I had that wasn't self-inflicted. It wasn't my fault, and I knew logically that it was pointless to be ashamed of something so far beyond my control.

But I was. So, I lied.

"My... brother drank," I said clumsily. It wasn't entirely untrue. He drank about as much as my father did, anyway. "I guess it was just... to set myself apart from him in some way. We looked similar, we were close in age, we were always competing, you know? He always caught the girls' eyes first, though. Smooth talker. So, I thought I could at least appear more responsible. Women like that."

"Boring women, maybe," she said with a lopsided grin. Good, she'd bought it. It hadn't been all that convincing, so she must've just been tired.

I grinned weakly up at her. "Yeah," I agreed.

She leaned down and kissed me. It was in earnest, it felt meant and affectionate, and I saw no reason to let my mood or the day—the week, really—spoil the moment. Regardless of how we'd come together or any of my misgivings about her, what we had in this short space in time was mutual, enjoyable, and uncomplicated. I didn't know how long it would last and I didn't really care, I just wanted to be with someone, feel someone, have someone to talk to and be heard. And she'd been all of those things for me over the span of time we'd spent together. A man like me wasn't likely to find deeper bonds than this; why ruin it with overthinking?

The poets had it right. If you couldn't love yourself first, it was probably folly to think anyone else could. But most people didn't find that deep, everlasting bullshit. Most people got married to someone they barely knew, because it was convenient or for survival, or because they got pregnant, or because their family told them to, and that was it. Maybe you had a mistress or something.

So, I told myself, it was alright that I wasn't being entirely honest with her. It's not like she'd been entirely honest with me. And it's not like we were unlocking our hearts for one another. I could ration how much I allowed someone in. I was good at it, even.

It was better this way.

"Have I mentioned I'm worried about leaving you tomorrow?" she asked softly, shifting her body down to settle partially over mine on the alfalfa-strewn floor. She straddled my lap, stroking her big paws over my cheeks and smoothing down the ruff along the edges of my ears. "I really wish I could help you two with the next part."

"If not for your luscious curves," I said wickedly, sinking my fingers into the ample expanse of her backside.

She gave me a roguish smile, her muzzle descending on mine, tongue pressing past my teeth and toying with my own. It slid against mine, rougher than a canine's. Some canine men said they found it disconcerting, but I loved it. I'd never been one for a light touch.

My hands kneaded their way down from her shoulders to her lower back, and up again, feeling the thrum of her purring through her chest as well as her mouth. We opened our muzzles further, teeth interlocking, plundering one another for all we were worth. I could be a sweet kisser if I wanted to, but Lotus always went for more, and I was happy to give it to her. Her hand was already undoing my belt deftly, paw-pads sliding down my tuft of pubic fur and into my britches. A pop of a few buttons and she had my sheath out. I'd been half-hard since we'd started kissing; it didn't take much for me, and it was honestly a little too illuminating how much faster my body responded when I hadn't had much to drink all day. I'd... try very hard not to think about that later.

If I could commend myself for anything, I think I was a pretty good drunk fuck. As in, I could get the job done three sheets to the wind, and if you were going to sleep with me it was probable you were drunk, too.

But tonight, we were both tired, not inebriated, and that wasn't nearly as fun to draw out. So, I got my paw down her britches in a hurry as well and found my fingers good and wet before long. Once I brought the pad of my thumb into the mix, I had her moaning.

What followed wasn't deft or tidy and didn't take particularly long on either end. The both of us knew how to please the opposite sex with very low effort at this point, and we were each equally eager for some kind of release from the day and the tension it had brought. Given we were sharing the warehouse with two other men with... relatively decent hearing... we tried to keep things down and kept our clothes on. For the most part.

I thought, when all was said and done, we'd been pretty discreet. And as send-offs went, it wasn't bad. Considering our circumstances.

"Take care of yourself," Lotus mewled softly at me later, lying in the wreckage of an alfalfa bale that had come unspun at some point while we'd been fucking around. It made for a better mattress that way, so I was all for it. I'd be picking the grass out of my fur for weeks, but... eh.

"You, too," I said, my eyes already closed. I could feel my muscles uncoiling, the tendrils of sleep reaching out for me. Sex always helped my frequent bouts with insomnia.

"I have a much less dangerous task," she sighed. "Glorified messenger."

"You have to deal with that bloody wolfhound," I muttered. "I'll take infiltrating a Pirate King's ship any day to one more conversation with that sanctimonious prick."

Lotus was silent, save her soft breathing. For a bit there, I thought she'd drifted off to sleep. But then she spoke again.

"His name is Johannes Cuthbert." And there I heard her swallow, which made me open my eyes. "He's my contact in Amuresca."

My eyes opened fully, and I lifted myself up on my elbow. "Your—"

176

She nodded. "My intel... for the emancipation network. Yes. Even safe harbor, and... sometimes gunpowder. Other supplies. It all comes from him."

"But you..." I stammered, remembering at least to keep my voice to the quietest whisper I could manage. "I mean... and him, you hardly spoke, you visibly loathed him, I mean... you kept flashing him so he'd leave—"

"It's an act," she said, her eyes moving to mine with a hint of something akin to shame in them. She felt bad for keeping up the ruse around me, I realized. That's what that was. "I can't risk anyone suspecting my source, and... what he's doing, it's not Church-sanctioned, so he can't either. It's literally just him and a few others from that... order of theirs."

"Templar," I said softly. "And they aren't committed to emancipation, by the way. That isn't what they do. They're more like... church-sanctioned spies, assassins... they do the Faith's dirty work, and they keep an eye on Pedigree families. Make sure they toe the line." I bit my lip, irritated the man was more than he'd seemed to be. He was easier to write off before. "Fuck," I sighed. "True believers. You hear about them, but—"

"He's how I met Denholme," she explained. "We've inevitably crossed paths a few times. They're always together at sea."

"Does Luther know?" I had no right to ask her further questions, but I had to know.

"No," she breathed out. "Not that I can tell. It isn't as though Johannes is part of the network, he just... gives us information. I think he sees it as penance to hear him talk about it. It isn't a crusade for him, it's just a good thing he can do, because he's in a position to have the information we need. And every slaver we take down is one less pirate, so..."

This begged the question, though.

"Why would you tell me all of this?"

She only took a moment to find her answer. "Because I trust you," she said. "And I don't want you to worry about me. The wolfhound and I have enough dirt on one another that we're not going to cross each other. And he's a better man than you think he is. I'll be fine." She stroked her palm over my chest. "I'm far more worried about you. I don't trust either of the men you're going to be relying—Grayson. Are you alright?"

I wasn't. My guts had fallen through to the floor, or at least that's what it felt like. My ribs ached with pressure, and it felt like something solid was lodged in my windpipe.

Guilt. That's what this was. And lord was I suffering a bad case of it suddenly.

I'd spent a whole day before this internally chastising her for not trusting me enough, and then when I'd actually gotten up the nerve to ask, she'd... opened up. Done so. And she was sharing more and more since then.

And I was still tight as a clam. For whatever reason, I could not seem to expose my inner thoughts, or the actual secrets that laid me vulnerable, to anyone. Not even just her. Anyone. I had this bombastic, shameless reputation, everyone thought I was an open book, and I guess that gave me cover. It made it too easy to hide the things that ate at me, the things I actually really wanted to talk to someone about. I hadn't been like this when I was young... why couldn't I trust people any more? Lotus was part of an underground resistance movement, and she was able to share herself, to talk to me about the things that hurt, or scared her. To open wounds in a way I was apparently too much of a coward to.

"Hey." She snapped her fingers in front of my face. "Look at me, alright? It's going to be fine."

"...what?" I asked dizzily.

"This isn't some final confession because I'm about to walk into the lion's den and I want you to know who betrayed me or anything like that, alright?" She looked me intently in the eyes. "I won't be risking myself by going anywhere alone aboard their vessels. I'll have my ships and my crew with me by then. And Lunden besides. I know you don't trust Amurescans or their holy men, and with good reason, but I've been working with them a long time now. I know how to protect myself. Got it?"

"Yeah," I said roughly. "I've got it."

"Good," she purred, pressing against me again and getting comfortable. "You get this far-off look sometimes when we're talking. I don't know where your mind's at, and it makes me worry you're deeper than you appear."

I guffawed half-heartedly. "Heaven forbid."

"Just... hold me," she said sleepily, wrapping one arm over my side.

I did the same, pulling her in tightly. "Goodnight, Lotus," I said against the crown of her head.

"Goodnight Grayson," she said with a smile. I could feel it where her cheek was pressed against my chest.

It took me hours after that to fall asleep, and when I did, I drifted in and out of a mire of my own thoughts. I felt like shit, and I knew I deserved it.

❧ ❧

The Rohkash were on the western half of the—admittedly fairly small, barely ten mile wide—island, but it was still a bit of a trek on foot, so we set out early in the morning. The rain had abated just enough that it felt safe to traverse the mountain trails, but was still coming down intermittently enough to be miserable. Monsoon weather was insane; we'd get bursts of blazing sunlight in between sun showers and full-on thunderstorms with pelting rain. It felt like the skies couldn't make up their damn mind.

The Huudari had a God of the rains who was known for being wild and tempestuous, and I understood why. It says something when I'd rather be navigating bad weather on my ship than on foot. At least on my ship, I could batten down the hatch-tarpaulins. Here, we were fully at the mercy of the elements, especially on literally the highest point of the island, the rocky mountain path that connected both ends. The road was well-traveled and clear, at least, built for trade and travel. Worse for the wear after days of storms, though, and muddy.

We were almost getting accustomed to it at this point. My spats were all-weather, unlike Denholme's cloth ones, but I was still planning on burning them after this trip, potentially my whole outfit depending on what condition the rest of my gear was in. Anything caked in the island's black mud was a lost cause. I was further convinced I'd never get the stubborn substance out from between my paw-pads or under my claws for the rest of my life. Ten years from now, I'd still be smelling this place, sunken into my body like a scar.

Given all of that, it was hard to believe Luther could in fact smell what Lotus and I had done last night, but I still suspected he could, based on his sour mood. Then again, he was frequently in a shit mood. So who knew.

He and Hadeon had said little to either of us in the morning, a sure sign your travel mates had either overheard or otherwise knew you were messing about if ever there was one. I didn't particularly care, especially in the case of the leopard, but as Lotus had reminded me many, many times the night before, I was about to throw my lot in with Denholme, and only him, for a spell. If he was sore at me, that'd get awkward and unpleasant real fast.

Hadeon would be signing on as a regular hire with Roccosal's crew, and, given our plan, we were hopefully going to reconvene with him by tonight. At most I had one long, very uncomfortable day ahead of me with the cattle dog.

My mood was dull as we trudged up that mountain, and everyone else (even the leopard, who'd been in high spirits for our whole acquaintance basically) was equally low energy. None of us had slept particularly well, I'd wager. I hardly slept at all.

But when we crested the mountain top, it was almost worth it. The mountains here were volcanic, like many island chains in this area of the world, so the younger ones tended to be like this—craggy and wild, with bald black tops and glassy, jagged peaks that reflected the sunlight, dotted with little explosions of wild flora wherever it could take hold. The volcanic earth was hell when it rained, but some of the most fertile soil in the world. And when you had the highest seat on the island and the sun broke through the clouds to spatter down across the freshly rain-washed surface, it was a sight to behold.

Even Lotus, who knew this island well already and hailed from these lands, gave a little sigh and stopped alongside Luther and me as we looked down over the terraced mountainside. From here we could see the finger-lakes of rice patties and little farms carved into the terrain, the fields of red and green that stretched beyond—poppies, all of them—until they abutted against the glittering shoreline and red-roofed manor homes of the Rohkash clan. And further still, moored in the marina, the behemoth galleons we'd come here to find. As well as many, many other beautiful ships, large and small.

I glanced briefly at my canine companion to see, just as I'd expected, that same look of awestruck, boyish wonder I'd seen on his face when we'd set out to sea from Dokuro. It was the only moment you ever caught him looking... innocent. Younger. Overwhelmed in the best sort of way.

I'd imagine it's exactly how I looked, every time I stared out to sea. Or beheld a new shoreline, a new corner of the world I'd never seen before. I knew that look. It was what you'd get if you cracked open any true sailor's chest and distilled their heart.

He caught me looking at him, and instead of awkwardly glancing away or glaring at me he just... smiled. Something moved between us. An understanding.

I couldn't help but smile back.

"I've been here three or four times," Lotus sighed from beside me, leaning against me gingerly. "But you never get over this place... or the other Shanivaar islands. These are some of the most beautiful and forgotten parts of the world." I felt her paw clutch around my waist in my jacket. "Hard to believe there's so much suffering here."

"It's the fact that they're missing on so many maps," I murmured. "'Forgotten', or just never considered. Depravity lurks in the spots in-between, in the grooves you miss with a broom. But... being essentially lawless is why they haven't been touched by Imperialism or overrun by modernity yet."

"They aren't lawless," Lotus said bitterly. "The clans have a stranglehold on them. Whether it's hyenas or tigers, lions... it doesn't matter. They run them like Syndicates, like Roccosal runs his island. There is no difference."

"The difference is that they're part of the Huudari Collective and have political protection because of it," Luther finally spoke up. "Roccosal... does not. By his own choice. But his arrogant insistence on independence is going to be what dooms him. I have been waiting..." here his brows lowered, muzzle lifted just enough to show his canines, "for years for that man to slip up and make himself vulnerable. And he's finally done just that. We can't throw away this chance."

I nodded, and Lotus gave a quiet, "Agreed," and that seemed to end the conversation. Whatever our differences, we'd come into our odd relationship all in agreement on the subject of the Dhole. He was a black stain on all of our maps, a disease that needed expunging.

With renewed purpose, we began making our way down the mountain side. Lotus pulled back the hood on her parka and suddenly bounded away from me while we walked, going only as far as the roadside, where she began plucking some kind of lilies that were growing wild.

I chuckled to myself as I watched her. "Get one for me?" I called over.

"That was the plan," she insisted. "They're tiger lilies!"

"Oh-ho," I laughed. "That so? Fitting."

"For you to remember me by while you're out there," she said cheekily in an overly, ridiculously flirtatious manner. I found her feminine side just as charming as her fierce, stomp-you-into-the-ground side though, so it was all good.

"As though I could possibly forget you, lady," I flirted openly in return.

I felt the cattle dog's presence beside me as we continued to walk. With Lotus falling behind us by a leg, I thought he might choose now to confront me about going strictly against his wishes last night. What with the tomfoolery I'd engaged in with the tigress. But he surprised me, as he so often did.

"Are you prepared for this?" he asked quietly. The leopard was also a bit behind us, so I think his intention was to leave both of the cats out of the conversation, for whatever reason.

"Yes, I'm…" I sighed, "well, as prepared as one can be, I suppose. Why do you ask? Little late to turn back. Having second thoughts about putting yourself in my care?" I joked.

Predictably, he scoffed, but it sounded good-natured. Which was at odds with his mood all morning, so I found his overall countenance confusing. "No, I…" he stumbled over his words for a bit. "I just…"

I had only been vaguely side-eyeing him as we walked, but now I turned to regard him fully, ears, eyes and all. "Spit it out," I pressed. "It's not like you to be at a loss for words. You're worryin' me."

"You…" he was still hesitating and talking with his hands, which he rarely did. I was a lot more expressive with my body, generally. He had that Amurescan decorum thing going for him. Dignity and consideration for personal space, all that worthless tripe.

He finally just gritted his teeth a moment, then let his breath out in a whuff. "Alright." He mustered. "You… know of my predilection. For… partners. Obviously. It's how we met. So, I just… want no misunderstandings, given what we're… about to do. And… how close we'll need to be… to do it."

I finally understood what had his knickers in a twist, and I couldn't help but laugh out loud. The outburst seemed to shock him, but I couldn't hold it in. Before long, I was laughing so hard my eyes were tearing up. We were catching the attention of Hadeon by now I'm sure, if not Lotus, and I saw him glancing back a few times worriedly. "Could you?" He made a gesture with his palms to keep it down.

I snorted through another laugh. "I'm sorry, mate. I really am. I can't help it. Y-you…" I wiped my nose, laughing into a closed fist. "You're so serious about it is all."

"Are you kidding me?" he snarled, ears back. "This is as serious as it gets for me. I've been worried about it all night. I couldn't sleep—"

"Oh, you and me both."

That set him into a defensive posture, or rather more of one than he was already betraying. "So," he licked his teeth, pointedly looking away, "you are concerned about it. About being pressed into a… tight space with… with me."

"No!" I cough-laughed into my palm, trying to muffle my merriment and only half succeeding. "No, you sad lad, I'm not—not scared of being…" I snorted again, I couldn't help it, "…pressed like a grilled sandwich against another… fellow. The thought hadn't even occurred to me until you mentioned it just now. Good lord. You think I haven't been in compromising positions with other men before? I'm a bloody sailor! And…" I gestured at

182

myself, "…well have you met me? I know we're a new acquaintance and all, but you've seen me compromised in every sort of way one can over the last week or so. How do you think I've fared over the course of the rest of my life? Not with any amount of propriety, I'll say that much."

"Fine," he snapped in a whisper, still clearly worried the cats were overhearing this. "But then, why… did you say—"

"Because we're stowing aboard potentially the most fearsome pirate's nest in the known seas?" I choked out, still muffling little hiccups of laughter that threatened to burst out of me. "And planning to sabotage his ship and… engage a nearly eight-foot-tall beast of a man in physical combat?"

"Right," he agreed with a mutter. "That."

"Yes THAT!" I put my hands on my lower back, trying to crack it with a sigh. "Just that little thing. Fuck, that barn was not kind to my hind quarters."

"You're not…" He ran a hand over the scruff at the back of his neck, scratching at it, something I'd noticed he'd do sometimes that might be considered a 'nervous habit', if the man's nerves ever failed him at all. "Just," he kept re-choosing his words, "I guess what I'm asking is—it doesn't bother you, then? That… aspect of the plan?"

"It's going to be bloody uncomfortable," I muttered. "But I'm not claustrophobic, and I'm assuming you aren't either or you wouldn't have agreed to it."

"Not that I'm aware of," he said.

"No, Luther," I chose to use his name this time, since I think he needed to hear me spelling this out directly for him. "I don't bloody care that you fancy," I lowered my voice to a near imperceptible whisper, "men. I'm not… intimidated by that." I made a mock menacing gesture with my clawed hands, swiping them at the collar of his shirt. "Or whatever else it was you were afraid of—"

"I wasn't afraid of you," he snapped, batting my paws away.

"Do you gentile lads across the pond really get twisted up over the thought a man might pop wood on yer thigh?" I asked with a chuckle. "Not always something a bloke can control, you know."

"I know it better than most," he muttered. "Alright, fine. It's not a problem. Can we drop it?"

"In a moment," I cleared my throat, slapping a hand on his shoulder and giving it a squeeze. "First. I just want you to know. Man to man."

He waited, and for once didn't shove my hand off right away. "Yes?" he finally pressed impatiently.

I smirked at him. "Just that I'd be honored, is all. S'flattering, really."

Now he shoved my hand off his shoulder and increased his pace to move ahead of me. "I told you once already. You're not my type," was the last growl of words I got from him.

I stopped in my tracks and fished my canteen from my belt, drinking some of the well water we'd grabbed in town before we'd left. I was immediately reminded it wasn't alcohol, of course, and I was soaked through with water, so it was a real let-down.

"Liar. I'm everyone's type," I grumbled, before jogging to catch up with him.

∾ ∽

"Well, this is... unexpected," Hadeon murmured. The leopard was crouched beside me, tail flicking back and forth measuredly as he surveyed the scene before us.

"That's putting it mildly," Luther groused from my right. "This is a god-damn disaster, and we haven't even gotten aboard yet."

Skirting the majority of the Rohkash compound had been fairly easy, if time-consuming. But it was necessary for Luther and I to stow aboard Roccosal's capital ship in the manner we had planned. We couldn't exactly risk entering the clan grounds like Hadeon could; there was too much of a chance we'd be spotted or scented by that mink or someone else who'd been on Dokuro. We didn't need to get onto the grounds to know they were crawling with Roccosal's men. Both of his ships, one of the Man of Wars and a smaller galleon, were in their marina, distinctive even from a distance. While myself and many other death-dealers on the high seas may have favored a jolly roger on our flags, Roccosal took it to another level, adorning his ships with actual skulls, stripped of flesh by the creatures of the tides and bleached white by the sun. Even from a distance you could see the macabre ring of white, like enormous barnacles, lashed to the bulwarks.

Rumor had it he had several Man-of-War, at least two that were in service, but only his flagship, the Blood Dawn was here. She was more obvious when at sea, distinguished by her red sails. I couldn't imagine the cost that must have incurred to keep up, but I respected it. Roccosal understood better than most that half of what we did was about style. Reputation. Intimidation factor.

Unfortunately for him, he'd suffer the same inconveniences I was frequently a victim of with the Manoratha. And it's the only reason we had a real shot at him here.

To put it bluntly, Man-of-Wars were huge, heavy, and couldn't maneuver worth a damn. I loved my lady more than life itself, but she handled like the leviathan she was named after. There's a reason I didn't want to get into a scrap with Denholme and his far more maneuverable, smaller ships. I think the smallest, the one hardly anyone ever saw (save apparently some fishermen on this island) was actually a brigantine and had been added to the fleet after the fact specifically so that they'd have a vessel that could nose into the wind better to run reconnaissance and messages back and forth. I had one just like it as of a few years ago. It was essential.

Honestly, it was clever that they'd kept the 'Cerberus' fleet name. Hardly anyone I spoke to about Denholme's ships even knew there was a fourth one.

Roccosal had no such subtlety. He may have started off smart and fast, I couldn't say. He mostly stuck to this side of the world, and I'd mostly stuck to the West when I was first beginning my career. I'd only begun to push this way of late, and I didn't know his history. But these days, he was all about balls, brass, and guns. Lots of fucking guns. He didn't hide his presence wherever he went; he pissed a circle in bottlenecks and took everything that was unfortunate enough to fall into his hands. Overwhelming force and a knowledge of the local waters worked for him, and that was all fine and dandy. Except right now, he was falling into our trap. And he didn't even know it.

And if there's one thing I knew first-hand, knew very well, it's that Man of Wars couldn't flee for shit. If Luther hadn't let me go on the unfortunate occasions we'd crossed paths, I wouldn't be around to bitch about it. He'd accomplished what he'd planned to each time: scaring me off.

So, we had to kneecap this ship, somewhere en route between the two islands, but we didn't have to waylay it for long. We had a pretty solid plan for doing so, but we had to get aboard first. And not get caught.

Hadeon had gone in first, while Lotus, Luther and I stuck to the blade grass hills ringing the bluffs that encircled the marina. It's called 'blade grass' for a reason, by the way. So yes, I was now covered in little cuts and irritable about it, thanks for asking. To make matters worse there were paths cut through the grasses that the servants who worked the fields nearby used, but any time we tried for a reprieve on said paths, we found ourselves dashing back off into the grass soon enough when the collared workers or guards walked by. Which was often. These grounds were busy.

There were also men that, despite their current lack of bootblack eye shadow, were most definitely men working for Roccosal. They seemed to be out and about a lot too, lugging supplies from who knows where to the marina. Without the theatrical makeup and a sobbing fennec at their feet, it was easy to imagine they were just… my men. Or anyone's crew, really. They were all just people, going about their work. Loading their ships up, getting ready to shove off.

If our plan was successful, most of them would die. And those that didn't, those that were taken alive, would be tried. And likely put to death in Amuresca.

I'd be lying if I said it didn't get to me. I understood logically that these men were slavers. They were an essential part of one of the most lethal fleets to ever sail. They weren't the same, and yet…

But for a small twist of fate, any one of them could have been one of my men. And at the end of the day, save for a slip of paper signed by a government official, we were in the same business. If this were my operation, I'd press gang them, and sort them out later. Ditch the really awful scoundrels somewhere they'd have trouble crawling out of. I'd sure as hell not turn them in to the authorities.

But Denholme's Captains wouldn't stand by and let that happen. And if I wanted to get out of this with my own tail intact, I couldn't try to stand in their way.

It would be easier to think, blast it all, it's better this way. We were taking down a man who made piracy and privateering look bad, and anyone who sailed with him probably deserved what was coming anyway. Not to mention, he was competition.

That would be easier. Pity my mind didn't work that way.

This is what Lotus had meant when she'd said I envied Denholme's certainty. And she wasn't wrong. Damn it all.

Which brought us back to the present. Hadeon had spent several hours on the grounds as the day waned on, and it grew hotter and muggier, the rains coming and going. It had been a bit nerve-wracking waiting for him, but eventually he'd met us at the rendezvous point, just as he'd said he would. Confident, with fresh information… and his eyes painted black. He was in.

We'd been right about one crucial fact that could have changed or delayed our plans: Roccosal was leaving today. They were just waiting for a break in the weather, but according to what Hadeon had been told, they were intent on leaving port regardless, even if the wind didn't favor them. Which meant one of two things—either he'd heard the rumor about Luther's fleet being nearby or he was hurrying for another reason. He was still suffering a wound as well, had to be, regardless how grazing a hit it had been. So, if he was moving now, it was out of desperation. He only had two of his ships here, and even if one of them was his Capital ship, that only made him more of a ripe prize. He had to know that.

Sitting put on the island wouldn't avail him forever. He must've thought he could sneak off, slip out before anyone would notice. And if not for the fact that we were here already, he'd be right.

Luther's brigantine was far faster than the rest of his fleet and my Manoratha was days behind even his galleons. If we couldn't slow Roccosal down, we would lose him.

Hadeon had gotten the lay of the land so he could cut a path along the bluffs, past some of the tiger clan's nondescript storehouses and down to the coastline to the edge of the docks in the marina. He'd taken us along that very route, skirting most of the gated areas and guard posts the tigers used to defend their manor home from any scavenging locals. It was a massive plantation, though, you could only guard so much of it. We slipped between the cracks, making it as far as the dock warehouses. And that's where we'd run into trouble.

The particular warehouse we were trying to gain entry to shouldn't have been guarded or even occupied. It contained some of the least 'valuable', least likely to be stolen crates they'd be loading up onto the ships last. We were lucky the weather had held out actually, or they may have already loaded them. But we hadn't expected all this rain or for Luther's ship to be spotted, so we'd thought we had more time.

As it is, we'd seen a lot of his men carrying cargo to the ship, so they could be coming for these boxes any second. We needed to gain entry. Now.

The problem is, there was a small mob of sailors gathered outside the isolated dock house, playing dice. Likely here because it was somewhere they wouldn't be found out. There were four of them, two jackals by the look of it, a squat fellow who might have been a badger of some sort, and a large, barrel-chested man that had to be a baboon, although I couldn't see his face at present. They looked and sounded riled-up; they were all armed, and they sure as hell weren't going anywhere until they were ousted from their spot, likely when it was time to leave. It seemed like they were into their cups, too. They'd probably been spending half the day loading cargo in the rain, as miserable as we were, so I didn't blame them.

"Yeah, this is a fine how-do-you-do," I muttered, tapping my claws on my knees. "You said it was unguarded when you came out this way?"

"Yes," Hadeon insisted. "They must have moved this way after I passed. Sorry, boss." He shivered his whiskers a moment, staring across the muddy clearing towards them. They were under an overhang for shade; the rain had once again briefly danced off, which meant now we were treated to the full effect of the glaring midday sun, lighting up every little puddle and glistening off our damp leather.

"I can handle four," he assured us. "If we can lure them this way, where they will not be heard."

"We can't just off them!" I whisper-snapped.

"Why not?" he asked, brows furrowed.

"Because they're just playing fucking dice? They aren't even technically guarding the damn place."

"And?" The leopard arched an eyebrow at me, continuing to look perplexed.

"And—" I began.

"He's right, if for the wrong reason," Luther cut in. "We can't kill them. They'll be missed. They might even find their bodies; it's not like we have a lot of time to stash them. And we can't... disable them somewhere and hope they won't be found to report what happened to them. No. We need a distraction, but one they can brush off. Something temporary."

"Let me," Lotus sighed, beginning to undo her bandolier.

"What? No," I said immediately. "You said yourself, a thousand times, you'll be recognized—"

"By the mink, or one of the Rohkash tigers, or anyone who was on Dokuro," she assured me. "Possibly a local of this island. I'm fairly certain I've never met any of those men before, and I know none of them were on Dokuro. I can't enlist, but I think I can fool a few drunkards. Besides," she undid her belt then, shimmying it off and putting it in a pile beside Hadeon, then she unshouldered her pack and began rummaging around in it, "I have a secret weapon for times like this."

All of us men leaned in curiously. What she produced... wasn't at all what I was expecting. In retrospect I don't know what I'd expected, her rucksack wasn't very big. But it was large enough for the dull metal collar she pulled free from it.

It was probably no more than an inch and a half wide, and had a zig-zag seam on two opposite sides, as well as a small metal plate fastened to the front. A tag with a weathered clan symbol on it. It was so distressed it was not really legible.

I'd seen them before, of course. The infamous mark of indentured Huudari citizens. But you always saw them... on someone.

"Those can't be—" I began, and then she pulled a pin from her mane, and inserted it underneath one of the zigzag seams, pushing a second pin with a stopper on it up and out. And then she opened it like a hinged cuff.

"—opened," I finished, not bothering to mask my shock.

"I've never seen one like that," Hadeon marveled, his tone getting excited.

"Wearing one of these makes you practically invisible," she said, affixing it across her neck fur, and carefully re-inserting the pin, hiding the other back in her mane. "Certainly beneath notice."

"Fine, but remember that you're trying to distract them," Luther reminded her, as if she needed that reminder.

A bolt of irritation crossed her features, and she cocked an eyebrow at him as she began taking off her parka and other outer garments. "Thank you for explaining that to me. My feeble female mind had briefly forgotten why I was doing this in the first place."

The cattle dog's ears settled back, and he mumbled a quiet, "I'm... sorry. You obviously have a plan."

"Yes, but I don't have time to clear it with the committee," she said, stripping to only her loose bloomers and saree top. "Can you menfolk just trust me to handle this? You'll only have a small window."

"Understood," Luther nodded. "We'll take whatever time you can give us. Shouldn't take long."

"Lotus, I..." I stared forlornly at her, not wanting to question her abilities. She gave me a stern stare in return, as if challenging me.

But that wasn't even it. Whatever magic she was planning on spinning on these men, I had no doubt it would work. I'd be the last person to question her cleverness, given how we'd... met.

It was just happening so fast. She'd followed this far to see us off, and because she'd wanted to stay with us to the last possible moment, but now we were here, we were parting ways, it was time and I just... I didn't have enough time... I hadn't said enough to her last night. I hadn't been as honest with her as I should have....

She cupped one of my ears, leaned down and nuzzled her muzzle into mine. I felt something prick briefly near the back of my scalp, and realized from the scent that she'd inserted one of those tiger lilies into my mane, where it was bunched and tied up in the back. She smiled down at me and gave me one last peck.

"I'd wish you luck wolf, but you have that in spades." he tapped my cheek. "After all, you met me."

"Better than some other pirate hunter working with Denholme to take me down, I'll give you that," I said ruefully.

She smiled once more, then looked at Luther briefly. "Take care of him," she said in a tone that was near-threatening. And then to Hadeon, "And take care of my gear, leopard. I'll be back for it."

I noted when I looked at her pile of leathers, belts, and weapons that one of her pistols was missing. She wasn't going in completely unarmed. I had no idea where she'd stashed it, but... that was the point, I'd wager.

We all stayed crouched in the weeds and watched as she moved along in the direction of the men, the bushel of tiger lilies in her arms. She was slick; she didn't make right for the men. A lone woman? That would've been suspicious. She walked around in circles for a few moments near the edge of the blade grass, glancing down several of the pathways that spilled out here, like she was looking for someone. Until the men noticed her.

One of them, the baboon, muttered something quietly to the other men before he stood and walked in her direction. They had a brief conversation, Lotus pushing her small mane of fur back behind her ears and doing a damn good job of acting demure and intimidated. Not easy for a tigress of her size. But the baboon seemed to buy it, and whatever she said to him, it got his attention.

Before long, he'd called the other three men over to him, and she was pointing out in the direction of the fields and the trails into the blade grass beyond. I don't know what she was telling them, my ears couldn't compete with the wind this close to the beach, but whatever it was, it worked. She headed off down one of the trails, and the four men followed her.

I had to hope she knew what she was doing.

"Women are terrifying sometimes," Hadeon shook his head. "How they bewitch us so easily."

"Not all of us," Luther said, standing and glancing left and right down the sandy, muddy stretch that abutted the dock houses. "Come on. Quickly now."

He grabbed me by my coat and hauled me to my feet. My legs wobbled but followed. I found myself stumbling as we ran across the clearing towards the rickety warehouse, staring off in the direction of the fields.

But she was gone.

The smell of death knocked me back a step when Luther unlatched and threw open the door. I'd known, I'd expected, but still...

Luther similarly blinked rapidly and snuffed out through his nose, as Hadeon curled a lip and gave an understanding nod. "Aye, I would not want a nose like a hound now, boss. You have my sympathies."

I went to tug my shirt up over my muzzle, but Luther reached out an arm and tugged it back down, stopping me. "No," he said. "We need to get used to it. Best not to drag it out. You'll become nose-blind to it eventually."

The inside of this particular dock house was decrepit and steeped in old dust and piled sand, cobwebs, and patches of dripping mold. There were fungi growing up through the rotting floor-boards and piles of broken-down barrels and shipping crates, ones that had been discarded long ago and were being stored here for firewood. Or forgotten. It was clear this place was hardly ever used.

Which is why they'd stored the coffins here.

"We're lucky Roccosal's a sick bastard," Luther murmured as we approached the seven... eight? Pine boxes. They weren't crudely-constructed; they were sizable—not like the cheap box you'd see them use in a potter's field—fresh lumber unlike everything else here, and I could smell the wood shavings inside, underneath the miasma of death and... something else. Brine and alcohol? It stung my nose and somehow made the smell of rotting corpses even worse.

"His predilection for keeping and dissecting his dead is a thing of legend," the cattle dog continued, prodding one of the boxes with his foot. "Part of the contract you agree to when you sign on with him, I hear."

"Is true," Hadeon nodded. And he'd know, given he'd just signed on with the man, apparently not for the first time. That confirmed that.

"Yeah, lucky us," I muttered, standing in the middle of the space the coffins were occupying, wondering which one of these I was about to crawl into.

"Alright, let's do this swiftly," Luther said, taking off his belt, his holstered pistol and sword, and setting them aside. He glanced about for a moment, then pointed out one of the boxes. "There, that one will do. Whoever put the lid on it did a slip-shod job. Should be easier, faster to pry open."

"These coffins were made big, probably for larger species," Hadeon said, un-shouldering his bardiche and jabbing the pointed spear end of it down beneath the lid of the coffin Luther had chosen. "One size, ah… fits all, as they say. I think you will both fit. Will be tight."

"I can't believe I'm saying this," I sighed, "but remind me again why we can't both have our own coffin?"

"Twice the chance of being found," Luther said. "Twice as much work to get them back open, too. Time we can't spare. Put those nails back in loose if you can, Hadeon. But not too loose, alright? We don't want the lid coming off while they move us." He looked at me. "And if we get found, better we both be able to mount a defense. I can't imagine a more nightmare scenario than you being pulled out of this thing alone while I'm still nailed in mine, unable to help you."

"Oh, I'm sure I could come up with worse if pressed," I said, staring down at the coffin lid as Hadeon pried it free with a resounding squeal of wood. "Ah, fuck!" I bit out, staggering back.

Luther peered down at the corpse, tilting his head curiously. I could barely look.

It wasn't that it was a dead man. I'd seen plenty of those in my time. It wasn't that he was fresher than we would've wagered for men we'd assumed would be long dead. It wasn't even that his eyes had been carved out, and were already full of maggots.

It was the damn stoat. Of course it was.

I didn't need to see his bad eye to know it was him. The patterns of stab marks, now just red gashes in his tattered shirt, were all the same. The dried blood was still in his mouth, staining his teeth tea-colored. With the boot black still around his eye sockets, he had begun to resemble the skull he'd soon be donating to Roccosal's empire.

My vision blurred, then snapped back into focus with each blink. The light coming through the rotting slats of the flimsy wooden walls to this warehouse got fuzzy around the edges, crossing and re-coalescing in lines across my vision. Luther was talking, I think. But I wasn't there. For a moment, I wasn't there.

My hands felt numb. I got a sinking sensation in my guts, and I wasn't sure if I was going to be sick or worse.

But then I realized Hadeon was speaking to me. At me. He was looming in my vision, all of a sudden. And for whatever reason, reality re-asserted itself.

"Boss?" He blinked his big, gray-green eyes at me. "You alright?"

"Yeah," I said around a dry, clumsy tongue. "I'm... yeah."

He seemed concerned, but said no more.

"They must've packed him up just yesterday. Explains why this lid was put on slapdash," Luther said, hauling the man out and rolling him onto his side. His limbs were out of rigor, so he was like a rag doll. But dead weight. Even the cattle dog seemed to struggle with him. He gestured to Hadeon. "Can you manage hiding him? You can probably stash him under the floorboards here, even. No one's going to find him until it's too late."

"Yes, boss," the leopard confirmed. "Leave it to me. I'll take care of it while you get settled."

Luther stood over the coffin, looking at me. "Good news is, he didn't get around to soaking that one in... whatever that is he uses to preserve them. Smells like brine and grain alcohol. I mean, it won't exactly smell good in there, but it's better than it could be."

I swallowed. I hadn't even finished processing what had just happened, if it had even been anything. It was so hard to tell sometimes. I was pretty fucked up right now for a number of reasons. Everything—exhaustion, guilt, revulsion, self-loathing, anxiety, fear—was just coalescing inside me, and when I was this distraught, it could be hard to tell if I was...

There was nothing to be done. All I could do at this point was press forward.

I found myself talking, somehow. "I'll... take the bottom," I said quietly. "I'm bigger, heavier than you. Best you be on top."

"I guess resting on our sides would eventually get painfully uncom-fortable on the one side," he agreed. "Alright. I'll top."

I nodded, removing my belt methodically, as well as anything else hard or metal on my person that could press into our bodies. As I did so, Luther shook his head. "No comment, eh? I thought that one was low-hanging fruit."

"What?" I blinked.

"Never mind," he cleared his throat. "Get comfortable. I'll put the weapons and bits and bobs at our feet before I climb in."

I don't have to tell you it was eerie as hell climbing down into that box. I settled down into the pine shavings, some of them still caked with blood from the man we'd killed, adjusting and readjusting my body within the confines of the pine box, trying to find a position of 'comfort'. We'd be in this thing for the better part of the rest of the day. I'd relieved myself in the blade grass earlier, right before we'd come upon this place. And we'd all stopped drinking alcohol last night and limiting our water intake, so that hopefully wouldn't become a pressing issue. But it was still... insane. This thing we were doing. Like a self-fulfilling prophecy. We were going on to this boat in a coffin. Fuck knew how we'd be leaving it.

I couldn't say I was entirely numb to the idea of death at this point in my life, but... closer than most, I guess. It was a threat I lived with every day, due to my condition. Most people knew of the dangers of the world, but very few lived with the knowledge that death lurked in your own body. In your own skull. That it could come and take you at any time, unprovoked and without warning. I carried my death sentence around with me; it was a weight on my shoulders I could never truly shed. So, without puffing myself up any, I could safely say I was more accustomed to the idea than most men could boast.

But this was something else. For a moment as Luther settled our things down between my ankles, resting in the space between where our feet would be, my entire vision was taken up by a sight few living men ever witnessed. The view a corpse had before it was laid to rest. Walls of pine around me, encasing my eyeline into a window of sorts. The ceiling above, light filtering down through the cracks. Thunder rumbled in the distance. The storm was coming back in. And then, the cattle dog, his silhouette briefly black as my eyes adjusted. He could have been any canine, laying their friend to rest for the last time.

But then my pupils dilated, and I could make out his features. And he looked concerned. Not grief-stricken, not sad or conflicted, not the face you'd see on someone looking down on a dead man. And I remembered, right. I'm still alive.

"Doing alright in there?" he asked, seeming to know somehow.

"Yeah," I lied. I moved my shoulders about a bit. "Your face to my chest, right? Not lying stacked chest to back?"

"Yes," he agreed. "I can put a little weight on my arms that way. Spare you some of the burden, at least."

"If you just want a hug, mate..."

He rolled his eyes. "Alright, you are in there after all. Brace yourself."

He clambered in carefully, being acutely careful that his knees didn't strike my delicate areas. He was shorter than I was by half a head at least, so we weren't face to face, but the feeling of his body settling over mine, his heat bleeding into mine all but immediately.... Maybe especially because we were all so damp, I'd begun to develop a bit of a chill despite the foggy heat in the air. So it felt oddly good.

I spread my arms a bit farther apart so he could settle his forearms under my biceps and not have them awkwardly splayed at his sides, and also so he could do as he'd wanted and be elbows-down to put a little weight on them. Additionally, I widened my legs so he'd fit a bit more snugly between them. We gradually found a position that worked, that wouldn't be completely intolerable to live with for a few hours. At least I hoped not. Once we were nailed in here, there would be very little room to re-position.

His head settled on my chest, ear flicking, muzzle twitching. I fidgeted with my arms a bit, not sure what to do with my hands. One of them I eventually left resting near his side, the other partially over his lower back, doing my best not to make it feel like an intentional touch. Amurescans got real finicky about being physical with other people, especially men with other men. So we had to somehow be this close without it feeling like it was... 'intimate'. I couldn't help but think this whole thing would've been a lot more comfortable if it were Lotus in here with me....

But she was physically larger and heavier than I was, so fit-wise it wouldn't have worked. And also, once we'd broken out aboard the ship, we had to move through the crew at least long enough to make it to the lower capstan. We could duck the mink for a while hopefully and blend in with the other canines, so long as we steered clear of the upper decks where Roccosal and his closest men were likely to be, but we'd never be able to do that with a woman as distinctive as Lotus.

And, I reminded myself, this train of thought was exactly what Denholme had been worried about. I was lying here, thinking how much more pleasant this would be if he were a woman. It wasn't exactly what he was worried about—I mean, I still didn't care that he fancied men or what that might mean for our current position—but it was up the same alley. No. I wouldn't act any differently with him than I would with Lotus. I set my mind to that.

I eventually just settled my hand on his lower back and gave him a light tug down. I felt him resist, his body tensing. "Relax," I murmured. "You're gonna cramp if you try to hold yourself up the whole time. I'm fine. You're fine. We're fine. Okay?"

I was getting my feet back under me from all that bothersome mental turmoil a few moments ago. Good. I hated that shit.

He slowly settled, not entirely uncoiling but resting more of his weight on me. I saw that ear twitch again as his head rested once more on my chest.

"Something wrong? My stomach rumbling?" I guessed.

"No, I..." he paused. "I can hear your heart, is all. You're not as calm as you're pretending to be."

"Oh," I chuckled. "Busted. Well... trust me. It's not you. It's the pine box and the smell of death."

"I haven't even put the lid on," Hadeon said from above us, peering down. "Are you ready? Will be loud."

"We may not have much time," Luther said. "Do it."

The leopard nodded, and the cover began sliding over us, cutting off the light. "See you on the other side," he said in that deep timbre of his.

In retrospect, I don't know what he used to pound the nails back in. But he did, and lord was it loud from inside that box. I think I clutched at Denholme's shirt a few times, gritting my teeth and tucking my ears back as much as I could. It had to be worse for him, being on top and all. But we weathered it.

Hadeon left soon after, I heard the door clattering shut and latching. From that point on, we had to be quiet. At any time, the men from Roccosal's fleet could be here to collect their dead, and we didn't want them hearing voices from inside a warehouse meant to be containing only dead men.

So we just lay there, listening to one another's breathing. It was oddly... soothing? I don't know if that's really the word, but I was glad I wasn't doing this alone. Denholme's weight was reassuring and not wholly uncomfortable. Despite the man not being my first choice to be literally nailed in a pine box with... he wouldn't have been my last choice, either.

For all the misgivings, all the intimidation factor he carried around with him, for all the trouble he could mean to me and my fleet... I wasn't entirely afraid of him. Not like I used to be. It's not that I felt safe from what he represented. Far from it. It's just...

You couldn't go through something like this, this right here, with someone and honestly insist it wouldn't change you. We'd share something when this was over, for better or for worse. It all but had to be for better, right? Unless we died, of course.

Maybe this was all wishful thinking on my part. Maybe Lotus was right. Maybe I was getting attached, but Denholme was as cold as ever.

I went back and forth for minutes on hand, wondering if it was safe for me to say something to him. Whisper, at the very least. I wasn't accustomed to spending this long in someone's, anyone's, presence silent. It'd be safe to whisper, wouldn't it?

But around the third or fourth time I'd opened my mouth considering what I might say, the door opened. I snapped my muzzle shut, felt Denholme tense up atop me, and then everything following was a blur.

Unsurprisingly, the men collecting the coffins didn't take their time in moving them. They went about the task as swiftly and roughly as possible. I could tell from their muffled voices that they were all wearing wraps around their muzzles, but they still limited opening their mouths as much as they presumably could. When it came time for our box to be moved, it was more jarring than I'd expected. I braced inside, closing my arm around Denholme (who had less of a grip on the sides than I did) in a vice, holding him in place. We were tossed back and forth, leaned from side to side, what seemed like a needless amount, until we were settled with a thud onto a solid surface. Then, I heard oxen and wagon wheels, and we were off down a bumpy road towards the docks.

It was considerably louder once we made it to port, a cacophony of voices, the clattering of cargo and the ever-present sound of the sea, of creaking boats, screaming sea birds, and hollow footsteps on dock planks. All sounds that normally heralded my departure from land and brought with it a rallying of excitement and eagerness.

But today, only dread.

Our bodies jostled back and forth against one another, banging knees, jaws clacking shut too hard, Luther's braced arms beginning to shudder with the strain. I held him fast against me, but his elbows and knees were really the only purchase he had for stability inside the coffin, so it wasn't about propriety or anything like that at this point. He was just trying not to bang around too much inside, lest we alert the gents carrying us that there were two of us in here.

At long, long last, our journey was at an end. With one final heave and a shudder violent enough to make Luther's back strike the top of the coffin lid, coming back down atop me despite his most valiant efforts like a sack of bricks, I just barely muffled the heavy whuff of breath that left my lungs. We both went rigid and still, his claws digging into the pine planks beneath us, my foot paws braced against the back corner, the both of us holding our breath.

And then with a few muffled mutters and some heavy footsteps, they left us there. Somewhere dark, that smelled of tar and brine. They took what little light had been coming through the planks with them. And then it was sheer blackness.

I knew a hold when I smelled one. This one smelled... fresher and less wet than mine, I'd give it that much. But it was clear they'd stashed us in the back-most corner of the hold, far from the entrance to the Orlop deck where the purser might have to smell us. I know my purser would've had my hide if he was forced to smell death permeating up into his quarters.

We heard them loading for another hour or so, aways from us in the spacious hold. My ship was similar enough to this one that I could all but picture where they were at. Finally, I broke our silence when I thought it was completely safe to.

"He has a safe," I said in a barely audible whisper. "That's the creak of a metal door. Only reason you'd hear something like that down here. Probably means they're loading coin or bars from the Rohkash... they did business while they were here. More than the purser could fit in his quarters... but must be near the stairs to the Orlop deck. They'd load that last, so they're nearly done."

"God, this beast's a prize," Luther breathed. "If we can do this... what a take. Legendary. That man's head, his best ship, with a full belly of gold?"

I felt my muzzle twitch up into a smile. "Listen to you," I patted his lower back lightly. "A Crown Admiral doesn't talk like that. There's a Privateer in there after all."

"I have to finance my fleet somehow," he murmured, shifting a bit against me. "Or I'm at the beck and call of the King. Independence is expensive."

"Mmhh, don't I know it," I said ruefully. "How're you holding up?"

"I'm fine," he said stubbornly. But I didn't detect much pain or discomfort, so he was probably being mostly honest. "You?"

"My hands and feet are a little... tingly," I admitted, shaking my wrist out and flexing my toes. "Not exactly good for the circulation."

"My apologies for whatever part I'm playing in that."

"Did you really," I tried to look down at him, but mostly saw the top of his head and his ears right now, "think you were gonna pop wood somehow bein' crushed up against me like this? Really? It smells like a bloody tomb in here and nothing about this's really setting the mood."

"I..." he made a frustrated noise. "No. Not exactly."

"Then why—"

"Because I thought..." I caught the slightest shine of his eyes in the dark from what little light was somehow making it into this box, "...I thought you would assume anything... any untoward touch or... just being in close proximity with me would mean I was... well, you know. People think it's like a curse. A disease. Something I can pass on, or they can be damned by just by being... in my presence."

"Alright first off," I sighed, "I'm an atheist. I don't believe in god."

"I know what an atheist is, I've read up on fringe theological beliefs."

"It's the absence of theological beliefs. But fine," I rolled my eyes. "But that means I also don't believe in being 'damned' or that hell is anything outside of a metaphor. And I sure as fuck don't think it's a 'disease.'"

"Some men, when they know," he chose his words carefully, "they just don't treat me the same any more. They seem worried I'll... want them. Like that. They think I must want all men, all the time. Just because I've taken a fancy to some of them. It... it doesn't work like that. If I had to lust after every man I surround myself with, do you think I'd be a navy man? That would be hell."

"Or heaven," I snarked. He banged his knee into mine, and I laughed quietly with a soft, "Ow. Alright, alright... sorry."

"It's awkward to explain unless you know what it feels like," he muttered.

I wanted to tell him that I did know. I did know what it felt like to have an affliction no one understood, that was demonized, feared, seen as a sign of possession by dark spirits or a mark of something sinful. But honestly, I didn't consider what he had to be a 'disease', and I didn't want to start comparing. I mean what harm did it do, besides offending priests? And people of faith were so easily offended as it stood; it's not like that was hard.

My disease would likely kill me one day if my lifestyle didn't do so first. Every day I was just running out the clock on it. I could make the most of my time until then, but there was no denying the harm it'd done and would continue to do to me. The fear I lived with. The way I had once allowed that fear to limit me.

The cattle dog's predilection would only kill him because other people didn't like the thought of him being alive. To be honest I'm not sure which was worse, but… any way you looked at it, that wasn't the same thing.

"Not until you've lived the way I have," Luther continued, "with this curse hanging over your head."

Alright, so that rung true.

"I've known since I was fourteen," he murmured. "I don't hate who I am, and I have to believe God made me as he did, because I wouldn't have chosen this. But most men seem to loathe men like me, that's for damn sure. Or deny we exist. Or… ignore us. At best."

"I don't think I fit the bill, mate," I said softly. "I don't loathe you, least of all for that. I obviously think you exist, and I'd be hard-pressed to ignore you. Even aside all of this, you're… fascinating. I'm sure once this is over, you'll not want anything further to do with me, but I'll be thinking of you."

"Well," he said carefully, "there is a fourth category of men that are more kindly-disposed."

I chuckled breathily. "Pretty sure I'd know by now if I bent that way. It ain't like I hold off from exploring my vices."

"Then I don't know," he sighed. "You're an anomaly."

"The Huudari don't hang same-sex partners," I pointed out. "They've got boy whores and everything."

"Yes, well they also don't endorse them," he grumbled. "If you're anyone of means, you're expected to have a wife. It's mostly seen as a fetish, as the proclivity of, as you said, prostitutes, soldiers, and sailors with few other options. Men don't fall in love. They can fuck as long as it's behind closed doors and you have a wife at home waiting for you."

"You have a wife at home waiting for you," I said, exasperated. "And, I don't know for sure, but it doesn't sound like you're on poor terms with her. Does she know?"

A brief span of silence. I wasn't actually sure he'd answer me on this. No. Probably not. It was too much information.

"Yes," he said. "She knows. She… accepts me as I am."

"So?" I pressed. "Mate, whatever came before this, you've had a run of fortune. You have wealth now, a helm at your command, a wife who'll back you in your societal demands… go fall in love. I know it can't be easy finding men like yourself. But they're out there. Trust me. I have a few in my crew. They aren't a golden egg. You'll find one in time."

"I have," he said bitterly. "They've all left me or died."

I bit my tongue. "That's rough, but my crew's full of men who fancy women who could tell the same tale. Half the shanties are about lost love for a reason. You'll find another. Hell, the fennec—"

"The fennec wanted me to leave my family," he uttered in one long breath. "He's terrified of Amurescan society. And the sea, on top of that. I don't blame him for either, but—"

"Shite, yeah, now that you mention it," I murmured, "he didn't do so well on my ship. I thought he'd get used to it eventually, but he just never got his legs under him. That's a deal-breaker alright."

"It never would have worked," he said, his whispers puffing out across my chest. "He had his own family to care for, besides. We're from two different worlds."

"So, you keep trying. If finding love was easy, there'd be a lot fewer poets."

"I wish I didn't want this," he said hoarsely. "I wish I could just be content with what I have. With… dalliances and easy living. Like you."

The realization of what he was admitting hit me slowly, sinking into my mind just as I'd begun to open my mouth to say something else useless. To be fair, my thoughts were a mess just then, confused with the resting anxiety of our situation, the ever-present physical discomfort, the incessant numbness in my limbs.

I flexed my paws—all of them—trying to return sensation to them. "Are you… saying you envy me?" I asked uncertainly.

"Isn't that obvious?" he gritted out. "For so many reasons. Men like you have a freedom I'll never have. To be yourself."

I chuckled, and I hardly knew why. "The grass is always greener, huh?"

"I suppose so," he agreed, closing his eyes. And I only knew that because they were the only sight I could really make out in the dark, save vague shadows. In the blackness, my eyes had begun to invent colors and shapes, but I knew none of them were really there. It was easy to feel like it was just the two of us here now, despite knowing I was in the belly of a beast. In this moment in time at least, it felt like it was just Luther and me talking. Things would get rough later. But no one was coming back here to this section of the hold unless they absolutely had to, and we'd hear them far in advance. The creaking of the ship and the distant sound of the water were lulling. I was overtired... I could probably drift off to sleep if I wanted to.

But Luther spoke again.

"Do you love the tigress?"

It was an innocent-enough question... and yet not. What I'd asked about his wife was technically more invasive. It was personal, yeah, but I couldn't think of a way he'd use it against me. He didn't strike me as the type to target your loved ones to get to you. And if he did, Lotus was more than capable of defending herself. Probably more so than I was.

"I don't know," I admitted. "You at least seem to know you've been in love in the past. I... can't say if I have. I'm not certain when you cross that line. I've felt affection and love for my family. My comrades. My men. My ship. But romantic love is supposed to feel different, I hear."

"Different," he agreed with a quiet hum. "But not necessarily less powerful. I love my wife and children. I can't say I love them less than I loved K— than I've loved the men I was romantically entangled with. It was just, as you said... different."

"I don't know if it's a clear-cut line," I said. "Whether you want to roll around in bed with someone or someone you just want with you. Forever. Whether you fuck them or not doesn't seem all that important save, you know, between the two of you. It's a distinction that matters, sure. But if you look at the love you can have for your comrades, the fellows you go to sea with, as being just as important as romantic love, then a whole lot more men in the world are like you than not, Luther. The difference is just in the nitty gritty details. And that's no one's business but yours."

"I wish the Faith saw it the way you do."

"Love for god's a whole 'nother category I'm not gonna begin to touch," I snuffed. "Fuck." I shifted about beneath him, trying to stretch my numbing legs. "I just...wish I could..."

I felt him lift some of his weight up off of me. "I'm sorry, it's... my midsection's putting a lot of weight on your thighs."

"It's not that," I insisted. "Just not used to lying still this long. I move around a lot even in my sleep."

"Might be a mild case of claustrophobia," he said. "Try getting a little more air in your lungs, I can hold myself up for a bit."

"It's not that," I insisted again. Although the anxiety was starting to come back a bit or... something like it. My chest and guts felt sucked in, like I was at pressure, diving for clams under forty feet of water. Was it getting harder to breathe?

200

"There's no shame in admitting it," he said. "This is an unusual situation we find ourselves in."

"It's not that," I said and only realized a moment or so after I'd said it that I'd repeated myself. Multiple times now. "It's not…" I blinked rapidly, shaking out my right hand again. I found I was clutching at his shirt, but I couldn't remember deciding to do that.

"Reed." His voice was a point of clarity, and I wasn't sure if he'd called it once or twice. I tried to look up, finding his muzzle inches from mine. There were his eyes, shining in the dark—or was I imagining that? The yellow was bleeding around the edges into a halo of red, and I thought I could see the slats in the pine lid past the silhouette of his dark face. Lines of sickly-yellowish light. Lantern light.

There were no lanterns back here.

Lines. Shit, I was seeing lines.

My hand spasmed again, clutching at his shirt. I felt the thin fabric tear. I tried to open my muzzle to say something. I think I managed, "Luther, I… should have—"

And then everything went black.

❧ ❧

I never know if I'm going to come back. And every time, every time so far… I have. But in the moment, there's little room for fear. Little room for anything, really, save a brief bolt of panic as I realize it's happening. It's happening again. And I'm helpless to stop it.

Sometimes I'm alone. This time, I wasn't.

I came back to myself all at once. Sometimes it's gradual. This time, it was like someone had opened a shade and let the light in, all in one fall-back-to-earth moment. I gasped, trying desperately to fill my lungs even though I hadn't stopped breathing and felt that I could, so I greedily sucked in as much air as possible, filling them again and again and flinging my arms as far to the side as I could, banging them into a barrier that wouldn't give. My feet found similar purchase below, paw pads scrabbling at… wood? It sounded like wood.

There were those first few seconds of panic, as my primal self forgot who he was, forgot what had happened, only knew I was awake, I was alive, and some invisible force was finally releasing its hold on me… allowing me to feel again. To exist again. And then it all came rushing back as my mind caught up.

Pine box. Coffin. I was in a coffin. There was a weight, just barely pressing down on me now, hovering above me. A pair of wide, frightened eyes, staring down at me, his body crushed against the top of the small space we were occupying. Blood.

There was blood. Not the ever-present reek of death, but fresh, coppery blood. Distilled in the air and…

… in my mouth. Between my teeth. On my tongue.

I gagged, and spat, and realized what I'd bitten was still in my mouth. Warm fur. Flesh. Little give… corded muscle. His arm, part of his wrist. Luther.

Luther Denholme. The man I was sharing the coffin with. The man now atop me, staring down at me with an understandably horrid mix of emotions on his face.

"Reed…" he breathed out, and I could hear the pain as he hissed between his teeth. "Are you there? Come… come back to me. Please."

I tried to focus my eyes in the dark, to look at him, to let him know I'd returned. I couldn't speak. Not yet. In time, he seemed to realize it though. He slowly, carefully extricated the gag—his arm, his own bloody arm—and reached his other uninjured hand up to brush under my jaw, patting my cheek lightly. "Alright," he said with a shuddering breath. "Alright. You with me?"

"Yes," I managed to choke out, unable not to swallow some of his blood. I felt sick, and my eyes were stinging. Damn it. Damn it all.

"It's alright, we're…" he glanced past me to the seam of the coffin lid. "We're alright. I don't think anyone heard that."

"I'm so sorry," I said, hating how hoarse and pained my voice sounded. He's the one who'd been hurt. Because of me.

Because of my fucking condition. Because I hadn't warned him of my fucking condition. Because I shouldn't even be here, doing something like this, knowing what could happen at any given time—

He sounded forcibly calm. "You… I think you tried to warn me," he said softly, dropping his voice to a whisper again. "Before it… so, this isn't new? This has happened before?"

"Yes," I answered, swallowing. There was no point in being anything but honest right now.

"Alright," he said, breathing out slowly. "Well, that's… good, at least."

I couldn't help it, I gave a dry, mirthless laugh. "How is it good? Please. Explain that to me. I have gotten every possible reaction to this bloody affliction over the course of my life, but no one has ever called it 'good.'"

"I'm sorry," he said, shocking me with an apology I knew I didn't deserve right now. "I meant it's good it isn't new. That's all I meant." He flexed his wrist, glancing at it briefly with a frown. "I've had men seize from head injuries, or drink, or food poisoning, or… many things. If you know you're prone to these, we can rule those out, at least."

I couldn't think what else to say to respond to such a level-headed assessment of what had just happened, so I went with, "I'm sorry I hurt you."

"It's the same arm the stoat tore up," he muttered. "And others before. I'll live. I'm ambidextrous for exactly this reason. I was worried you'd bite your tongue."

"That's a bit of an old wives' tale," I said, groaning as feeling slowly began to return to my limbs. Shit, I should have caught that. It was one of the signs; it's just… so many things could be a sign. That odd episode I'd had earlier, too… my body had warned me. I just wasn't listening.

"Well, it kept you quiet, too," he reasoned. "Wasn't sure what else to do, I just acted on impulse."

"I'm sorry," I repeated again miserably.

"You've some kind of falling sickness, then? Why didn't you tell me?" he asked the obvious question, finally. Before I could answer, while I struggled to find the words, he said, "Because you don't trust me enough to know."

"…yes," I admitted.

"Because I'm a 'threat.'"

"Yes," I again admitted.

"I heard you last night," he said, voice still a soft whisper. He didn't sound angry, though. There was an emotion there I couldn't place. I didn't dare hope it was genuine sadness, but it might have been something close. Something more guarded, but in the same sphere of emotions.

"I'm sorry," I said again, for the fifth or sixth time. All I could do at this point was apologize. "I…"

"No," he murmured. "You have every right to see me that way. I haven't exactly tried to soften our working relationship, and… I can be… rough around the edges. I know."

"You've been genuinely decent to me, despite our adversarial," I sighed. "Well, everything."

"Let me say this much." He took in a long breath, then let it out. "This here? What we're doing? This mad plan? I would not do this with someone I do not trust... to a certain extent. I would not put my lot in with you if you were someone I still wished to kill. I didn't even want to kill you before all of this. Why do you think I let you run both times we met at sea?"

I swallowed. "Appreciated."

"And now we both know one another's secrets, so," he looked me in the eyes. "can we just agree not to be afraid of each other from here on out? At least enough to tell each other things that will... help us get through this together? If I'd been prepared for this, I... I may have known what to do. To help you."

"You... you want to know how to help me through a seizure?"

"Yes," he said, as though it was obvious. "Please."

I swallowed again, and I knew my eyes were watery, and for once I was glad it was so fucking dark in here.

"Alright," I said. "We've got time, so I'll tell you what I can."

∽ ∾

The third time we heard footsteps descending the distant staircase into the hold, they didn't stop short of the shallowest storage, where the last two men had. Likely sailors down for a drink from their private stash or a whispered liaison of some sort. No, this third man—heavy, by the creak of his footsteps—made his way fully across the hold, crossing the boundary of the 'dead deck' at the furthest bowels of the ship where the coffins were stashed.

Right up to our resting place.

I couldn't be sure how long it had been, but if my straining bladder was any indication, we were close to the tail end of how long Hadeon said he would wait to make contact with us. I could tell by the smell in the air... oil lanterns and cool, briny mist... that it was night. There was no light down here, so it was all I had to rely upon. But it was enough. We'd been cocooned with the dead nearly a full day.

I felt as well as heard Luther hold his breath, and I'm certain I did too. There was a sharp crunch from directly overhead us, the metal teeth of a prying bar embedded themselves in the lid above my head, and then it began to dislodge with a dry snap and the splinter of straining wood.

A thin strip of dim light washed over us, immediately catching shine in the eyes of the feline predator staring down at us through the crack. Hadeon was honestly as good as a stranger to me, if we were talking trust levels, but I was incredibly glad to see him nonetheless. The alternatives were all worse, given where we were.

"The skull-faced Dhole is on the warpath," the leopard said around the edge of a long fang, gritting his teeth as he worked at prying the lid off, visibly straining to do so. He sounded worried, which made me worried. He hadn't sounded worried since we'd met him. "I am guessing that there is more to this than you tell me. Something recent? He looked angry and unwell when briefly I see him."

"Bloody hell," Luther grunted, shoving himself up on his palms and pressing his back to the top of the coffin lid. He planked himself up against it and then pushed, and the straining boards splintered and gave way. He shook off the debris and straightened up, then blinked down at me in the dark.

I shuddered, grimacing at the display. "God damn," I shook my head, wincing as I much-less impressively pushed myself up into a sitting position and only just barely. "Do you have to make me feel like less of a man once a day? Is it like a quota?"

"Your time to shine's coming up," he reminded me, extending a hand to help me up. I took it without complaint. "Your knowledge of nautical engineering puts mine to shame, and that's just based on the few conversations we've had on the subject already. Were you studying to be a shipwright or something in that vein?" he furrowed his brow.

"Oh, I was obsessed with the ins and outs of everything maritime," I said, groaning a bit as I unashamedly palmed my sheath when I stood. "I think it was sort of that 'if you can't do, teach' mentality, but really I just put off leaving the Academy as long as I could, lest I have to take up a real job. Fuck, I have to piss…"

We found a corner that smelled like a tannery already, likely owing to whatever foul merchandise had been stored there last, and once we took care of business, Luther got back to the matter at hand. Specifically what Hadeon had been going on about when he'd broken us out.

"Roccosal's alive," he surmised. "And on guard, you said?"

"Yes," the leopard confirmed. "He seems to know something is afoot, although it is probably the sighting of the fleet you mentioned that has him so spooked. I doubt he realizes we, specifically, are aboard. Or he'd be having the ship searched, which he is not. He is secure on his vessel of death, just… keeping all eyes to the horizon."

"He's scared of you," I said, ruefully impressed, in Luther's direction. "That give you a bit of a chub, cattle dog?"

"It surely does," he confirmed. "And he ought to be."

"He should be turning-in to his quarters once the second night shift begins," Hadeon continued. "If chatter among the crew is to be trusted. He keeps a routine at sea. Honestly, this ship is very well-run, compared to others I have crewed up with. It is almost a pity what we plan to do to it."

"Shite, is it too much to ask the bastard succumb to an infection or bleed out internally?" I groused. "I don't ask much from the world, but that would've made all of this a hell of a lot easier."

"You want him to die before we can get to him?" Luther asked, seemingly genuinely perplexed. "That'd deny you the pleasure of repaying him for what he did to you. And me, but... he didn't know who I was or who Kafele was. In your case it was personal. I would think you'd want to sink the blade in yourself, given what he took from you."

"You'd think that," I sighed as I buttoned up my britches, "because you're a sadistic lunatic. Not everyone needs to taste blood for the wrongs done to them."

"Isn't that what this is about?" he snorted. "I'm the pirate hunter, remember? This is literally just business as usual for me. I'm just generally," he shook, and buttoned his own trousers, "aboard my own ship when I do it."

"The dhole made it very clear to me when we spoke," I said darkly, "that he sees me as a sort of hypocrite or imposter to the kind of people he thinks he's sat at the throne of."

"Pirates?" Hadeon asked, clearly intrigued by our conversation. "He resents you because you Privateer?"

"No, he works with Privateers and Huudari Clans, even Amurescan and Carvecian merchants sometimes," I shook my head. "This isn't because I take contracts. The way he spoke, it cuts deeper to the bone than that. This isn't about our trade or lifestyle. It's about the Empire he wants to build." I turned to move my gaze across the packed hold, what little of it I could see by the dim lantern light from the staircase, anyway. Cargo, cargo everywhere. A good haul by anyone's standards. Who knew what all of it was... whale oil, spice and salt, rum, gunpowder... but whatever it was he carried right now, it wasn't his main trade. It wasn't how he made his riches.

No, his most valuable commodity, he'd offloaded already at the island we'd left. The empty rings and chains along the walls, threaded through stained, narrow benches and bunks, were testament enough to his true calling.

It always came back to the flesh market somehow, didn't it? Slavery was like a bile on the back of your tongue whenever you trafficked in my circles. You could never entirely ignore it, even if you chose not to partake in the sickness. You couldn't even fully resist profiting off of it if you bought, stole, or traded... anything. That kind of labor was involved in some link in the chain. Always. It underwrote every fucking industry.

Maybe Lotus was on to something.

"He hates me because I'm an Anarchist," I said with certainty, looking back at the two of them. "He hates me because I won't come to heel. Because I won't trade on his island, sail with his boys, and ply my trade the way he thinks is best for all of us. He thinks he can save us all. Lead men like us to a freer, more prosperous future of our own making with our own Empire, out from under the heavy clawed foot of Empires like yours. Or the Huudari," I said, looking between the two of them. "He wants to establish an independent port where we can live as we choose, do business as we choose, and swear fealty to no one except ourselves."

Luther gave me a long, hard look. "You'll forgive me for saying so," he murmured, "but that does sound like something a man like you would pledge themselves to."

"You don't know me as well as you think you do," I said coldly. "He made me—all of us, every Captain with a reputable ship to his name—an offer, years ago. More of an ultimatum. Most of them answered the call."

"But you didn't," he guessed.

"No, I damn sure didn't," I said stoically. "I've never set foot on that island. And I won't lie, if I see his skull anywhere, I'm more likely to hunt the fools flying it. Contract or no. I doubt he can prove I've poached him before, but... he has ample reason to humiliate me, whether he knows that or not. It's as good as calling open season on the Manoratha. All we have amongst our peers is our reputation. If I'm on the outs, if the other Captains see me as weak..."

"Blood in the water," Luther nodded. "Ripe to be culled. So, this is about survival for you, then?"

"Yeah, but it's more than that," I said.

"I would hope so," Hadeon spoke up, calling both of our attention to him. He lifted his chin boldly. "I have no dog in this fight, as you Amurescans might say," he glanced briefly to Luther, then to me, "but what you say about Roccosal's island is right. It is a free port. No Amur Governor. No Huudari Clan Hold. No flag except the black coat of arms. No mandatory religion or Monarch—"

"He calls himself a Pirate King," I interjected. "And he certainly rules as one."

"But Roccosal is a man more like yourself than most rulers," Luther said. "It's a fledgling nation of your own... kin, as it were. I see what Hadeon is saying."

"You are working with an Imperialist Captain to bring all of that down," Hadeon said pointedly. "I do not pledge myself to this dhole or his cause. I do not care if he lives or dies. I make my own way in the world. But you must know killing him will threaten the dissolution of this free port. So, it must be personal. A grudge. Ya?"

I felt my jaw tighten, my teeth slotting together firmly. I wished Lotus were here, so I could tell her I was sorry. As so often happened in my life, when I began to realize how wrong I was about something, the person I needed to apologize most to was gone.

I was beginning to understand the frustration she faced. The inability to explain something that should have been so simply understood.

I was silent for too long. Luther tilted his head curiously. Perhaps suspiciously. I stared into his eyes, remembered staring into them in the dark as the seizure took me and wanted so desperately for him to trust me. And at once, finally, the words came to me. I could only hope they'd make as much sense to them as they made to me.

"No port is free until it's free for all," I said simply. "The truth I've… tried… not always successfully, but I've tried… to live my life by… is not his truth. He's a despot garbed in a more familiar mantle, that's all. And I won't kneel at his throne any more than I would another's. His 'Empire' stands on the shoulders of the people he trades like commodities." I looked down, shaking my head slowly. It felt light. I ached for what I'd lost.

My gaze fell on Luther again. "I don't think your fealty to your King is any better. But it's also no worse. The world seems to endlessly repeat these same patterns of cruelty," I counted off on my fingers, "consumption, and oppression, and I don't know why. I wish I understood it, but better men than me have tried and failed, and many more have died trying to end it. I used to study them academically—Philosophers, Revolutionaries, people history remembers as criminals. Now, I guess, I'm one of them."

Luther gave me a hard look. His eyes said he didn't disagree. But I pressed on, regardless.

"Contrary to popular belief," I scrubbed a hand over my face, "Anarchy isn't about pointless chaos. It means bucking and fighting that kind of power, the hierarchies that crush us all beneath them to your dying breath, while knowing it's probably a futile effort. It might sound pointless to you, I get it, especially when you're, say, killing and stealing for an outcome you admit yourself is probably impossible," I said, my breath failing me on the last word. "But I want no part of what exists now. Because it's obviously not fucking working. Roccosal tried to remake a little slice of the world for people like us, and look," I gestured around the room angrily. "Right back to operating a bloody slave galleon. If you play their game their way, this is what you get."

The silence following that was deafening. I hated silence. I always felt the need to fill it, lightly and, if possible, with a joke. But right now, my tongue felt too thick in my mouth. Some part of me had finally learned to shut the hell up when the time called for it.

"Alright," Luther said, at long last. "I can respect that, even if I disagree with some of it."

"Yes," Hadeon agreed.

I let out a breath. "Just like that, huh?"

"It tracks," Luther nodded. "We've spent weeks together, you really think I don't have a feel for you, yet? I could've called you were an abolitionist day one."

"Wh—I'm not—" I stammered. Wait. Was I?

He arched his eyebrow. "There's only one of two positions on the matter. Are you honestly going to tell me you're the latter?"

"No," I said quickly. "People aren't property. Not for labor, not for marriage, not for procreation, not even for imprisonment. It's abhorrent anyone thinks otherwise."

"You're quoting someone," he squinted.

"Guilty as charged," I said with a lopsided smile. "Lyefield. A… lot of that was pulled right out of books written by smarter people than me, if I'm being honest. I'm not nearly so well-spoken at a moment's turn. But all the same, you… you think there's only two positions on the matter, so. Are you—"

"Of course," he said offensively, snuffing. "The hell kind of man do you think I am? I may not be particularly devout, but I'm Amur after all. We fought a whole damn war over this." He paused, then carried on. "And moreover, I did time in a work camp. I would've thought given all your extensive digging into me," he said that part with particular bile, "you'd know that."

"I… did," I said, embarrassment creeping into my voice. No wonder he was upset I'd assume otherwise. "But it isn't as though you or I directly take on the institution," I said insistently. "That's all I meant."

"Speak for yourself," he muttered. "What do you think half the vessels I hunt carry as cargo?"

"You sink half of them," I pointed out.

"Closer to a third," he reasoned. "Cost of the trade. I can't force every Pirate I encounter to surrender without a fight. But that's the point of all of this. The more scared these men are, the less they'll traffic in illicit trades, including slavery. And if we can take out the dhole, the worst of them all, that'll put the fear of God in most men who'd consider it."

It was humbling, hearing it all put so bluntly, and my own inaction thrown in my face for the second time this trip. But also, as most conversations went with him, cold and dispassionate. Which set him apart from Lotus. They might have ultimately had the same ends, but he was more chilled about it. Means to an end, grist for the mill… I'm not sure I could look at it so plainly. It would be more complicated for me. Sinking a ship with a few hundred souls aboard, two-thirds of which were innocents? Just to make a point, towards some ultimate goal of making the industry less profitable? Even if it worked, I'm not certain I could stomach the process. As it was, I killed for my 'principles' more than I liked.

"If I'm to call myself an abolitionist," I said, my words measured, "I ought to be doing something more towards that end, shouldn't I?"

"Well," Luther reached down into the coffin we'd been sharing and pulled back the cloth covering our weapons. He lifted my sheathed saber by its bindings, looking it over in his hand for a moment before offering it to me. "You can start tonight."

"Aye," I agreed, taking it from him.

"You wanted to know the last fathom reading taken?" Hadeon asked, producing his own polearm from the coffin and flexing it over his shoulders, using it to stretch his sinewy, speckled figure. Damn thing had been poking me in the neck all day, even covered in cloth. It had only barely fit in the coffin.

"I've a vague idea where we are," I said. "But yes."

"Better once we can get outside," Luther added in. "Although with the rain… is it still cloudy?"

"Unfortunately, yes," the leopard confirmed.

"Shit," Luther growled. "Well, I'm of no use. I've a good star map in my head, I can usually discern relative position if I've got a sky to go by."

"We're nowhere near the Shaking Trench," I assured him. "Which means we're probably still shallow, thirty… forty fathoms at most."

"That's too wide a margin," Luther shook his head. "I doubt he has forty fathoms of chain. What's your maximum depth?"

"Thirty-two," I said. "I understand your concern. But, even if we can't drop anchor on the bottom, we can still drag it through the depths, which will make positioning, let alone fleeing, nigh on impossible for him. All is not lost."

"Nothing we can do about the other vessels," Luther said as he tightened his scabbard belt. "But I'm confident if he can't outrun us and our whole force comes to bear as planned—"

"We are counting on your fellows quite a lot, then," Hadeon said with a toothy grin. "Yet, you do not seem worried."

"We don't start the ruckus until we see the flare." I reminded him.

"What if we don't?"

"See the flare?" I bit at my lower jaw. "Well, then… you blend back into the crew… and Luther and I figure out our next moves. Whether that's retreat or…"

"If there's some kind of delay, we can try waiting it out," Luther said. "But not for long. Once he gets closer to his island, other ships will join him. At that point it might just be worth it to try to take him out, alone."

"Whoa there," I cautioned, chuckling nervously. "We'll... talk about suicidal death charges if it gets to that, alright?"

"Right," he nodded.

I shook my head. "Bloody. Lunatic."

"You knew this was going to be dangerous," he countered, checking the laces on his spats. "Are you really not prepared to die?"

"Not that prepared. Fucking hell," I growled. "I like being alive, thank you."

His expression got wistful for some reason, and I was left to wonder if it was envy. Which would've been... awful. I made a mental note to get him utterly shitfaced when this was all over. I was incredibly curious what a man like that would be like drunk. And it seemed like he could use it.

"The fathom reading, Hadeon?" I reminded him.

"Thirty, thereabouts," he said. "But that was hours ago."

"So, we're likely right on the edge of the shelf," I sighed. "But, of course."

"We'll find out soon enough," Luther's palm struck me on the back. "Come on."

"Wait," I scanned the dark space until I caught the vague, cast-iron outline of what I was looking for. I bent over and picked up the crate pry bar. "I was going to use a tent spike I picked up in the city, but if we can manage it, this will work better."

"It is awful," Hadeon said disgustedly. "But it was all I could find without bothering anyone for tools. It is bent, look. There is hardly any hook left. That is why it was so hard to get the lid up."

"I know," I grinned. "That's the point."

～ ⌒

On a ship as large as this, making our way from the hold to any patch of sky meant navigating our way up through the Orlop deck, dispatching the guards there somehow without waking the Purser so we could get as far as the lower gun deck, where some of the crew were likely to be in their hammocks, then the middle deck where the bulk of the crew were sleeping, until finally ascending to the upper gun deck, the first open-air space we'd have access to. And then we'd somehow have to make our way towards the stern, to the quarter deck, where the Admiral was likely to be sleeping in his cabin during the night shift. If he was, for some reason, in his day cabin? Then this whole plan had to change.

I had never appreciated how large and impenetrable a maze a Man-of-War might be until now, and I spent most of my life on one. It just wasn't as obvious when you had free reign of the ship versus infiltrating one, you know?

"Needless," Luther muttered when I tried again to explain the route we'd be likely to take as we ascended the steps quietly. "Unwieldy, opulent, expensive."

"I'm sorry our class of ships aren't convenient for sabotage," I rolled my eyes. "Complain a little louder, why don't you? We're almost at the Purser's cabin."

"He had but one guard, and I dealt with him already," Hadeon assured us quietly, slinking up at the rear as we walked. "Just shut your mouths when we pass his door. The guard will not be missed until his shift changes, but I do not know when that will be."

"Aye, we can't be sure how much time we have until the alarm's rung," I nodded. "We may need to kill or dispatch another man or two. Although we should avoid it as long as possible."

"There was no way to explain my trip to the hold or how I would return with two other men," Hadeon said.

"Shh-t-!" Luther held up a hand, hissing sharply. We all stopped, and I nearly bumped into him. The hallway ahead wasn't well lit by any means, but one lone lantern shined somewhere down the way, enough that I caught the wet glint of streak marks on the floor, dark and shiny against the wooden planks. The door beside them was labeled in Huudari. I wasn't as good at reading the language, but it was clearly a name.

"Purser Jeseric," Hadeon filled in softly. "The guard's body is in a storage room nearby."

"Good thinking," Luther nodded. "Avoid the blood, the smell might give us away."

We moved carefully down the hallway, stepping around the blood and passing a few rooms that were unfamiliar to me; it was natural to assume some things would be different about the construction of this vessel to my own. Even if they were built in the same style, they were hardly sister ships. And the Orlop deck was a functionally versatile space regardless, sometimes a secondary hold, more often storage for sensitive goods or whatever the carpenter might need. If you were lucky enough to have a carpenter, that is, and not just a badger who claimed he was 'a good hand at carpentry if pressed'. Like some less... responsible... Admirals might get by with...

Regardless, we found little to get in our way there. But once we got to the lower and middle gun decks, it was another matter entirely. I could tell just from the ambient sounds when we reached the staircase that the night shift was awake, and others besides. There were voices, grunts and groans, footsteps heavy and light, even distant singing. It sounded like what I'd hear on my own crew decks. I had to keep reminding myself this was enemy territory.

We'd already used boot black and chalk on our faces, both because that was standard fare here, but also to disguise ourselves. I'd have to do up the disguise later when I had access to a mirror, Hadeon had complimented me on how well I wore the paint. It was a given with my black fur that I'd nail it, though.

The chalk stuck and clumped poorly in Luther's wire fur, and made him look nearly ghoulish or diseased. The yellow eyes didn't help. It would take hours to get it out of his fur, too. But if it helped us fit in, it was a small price to pay.

The sweet, intoxicating aromas of both good and bad pipe weed, stale rum, and salted, preserved foods were strong even here, and there was little chance they took their meals on the lower gun deck, so that meant the staircase to the middle deck wasn't far. The small portion of the crew that kept their hammocks here were on duty specifically to man the fourteen—no, looked like fifteen—32-pounder cannons lining each side of the deck. The base of his defense and offense. And damn if they weren't ship-shape. Even by the low light I could tell the deck was kept cleaner, more free of debris, and more orderly than my own. And we only had twenty-four total that worked. I'd hazard a guess all thirty of theirs were operational.

Other than the occasional lifted head or trailing set of eyes in the dim light, the crew here paid us very little mind. Plenty of souls came and went from the hold… likely few this late in the evening, but still… and there was a guard below for the Purser (or at least there had been), so it isn't as though they had reason to wonder. I did notice a troubling trend as we passed the mostly sleeping gun crew, though. One I would have confirmed when we ascended the stairs to the middle deck.

The lanterns were less sporadically lit there, centralized more in the mess area, which was precisely where the steps emptied out. The mess was always busy, regardless of the time of day, even on my ship, so I don't know why I'd thought it would be different here. 'Busy' didn't mean 'lively', though. While most of the tables were occupied, the air hazy with smoke, dust, fur, and body odor, the mood was subdued. There was an edge to it, an underlying anxiety that might have had something to do with the Admiral's poor spirits and suspicion of an attack, or it might be your usual amount of restlessness that lingered with the crew after a recent stay in port. Still, there were far more eyes landing on us as we emerged onto this deck; more than I'd like.

And most of their faces were unpainted.

I say most, but it was more like half. The ones who still wore chalk or boot black had clearly applied theirs long ago by the look of it. I hadn't thought to ask Hadeon how many of the crew re-applied their masks while underway, let alone in the middle of the night, and that had been an oversight on my part. While I knew it was tradition amongst his crew, it was probably done more for show when they went into port, before they hunted, or—for any reason—met with their Admiral. It made sense they'd neglect it when on their own time or resting.

It made us look like amateurs. Like we were newcomers here. And while I'm certain there were quite a few other men in that position right now, given he'd just hired on, it made us targets.

Someone deliberately dashed into my shoulder as they walked past towards the cookpot. It was a hard enough blow that I knew it wasn't an accident. I dipped my head and gave no response, even when I felt the lion's eyes on my back.

I heard mutterings in Huudari that, alarmingly, called Luther out as an Amur. It was an easy guess, with a dog you usually had about a 50/50 shot, and we were closer to Amuresca than Carvecia. But another hushed whisper as we made our way through the alley between the tables cautioned someone about 'making a go at the leopard's fellows', and I was intensely grateful in that moment that we'd found a mercenary with an intimidating reputation. The last thing we needed now was an avoidable altercation while we were trying to keep a low profile.

"Word of advice?" a voice deliberately caught our attention as we passed a low-slung hammock near the cook's area. It might have even been the cook. The man weighing it down was a hefty babirusa boar with tusks protruding through the top of his snout and curling back around nearly to his eyes and a second only slightly smaller set curling up out of his lower jaw.

We stopped, but he kept speaking before any of us had the nerve to answer him. "You jus' crewed up, yeah?" he asked, his voice strangely affected and lisping, likely because of whatever was going on with his tusks. "Don't paint your face a'night," he continued. "Th'only folk who bother on th'night shift are the boys wot sideline as mollies. Al'dough they usually rouge 'der ears. Sho, you're shafe. Shtill. Might make folk wonder," he tapped his skull, grinning around his big teeth.

"Thank you," I said quietly. "We were just trying to uphold the Admiral's rules."

"Is'sha good ship, if'n you can eshtablish yerselves," the babirusa said. "Ain't no one shinkin' 'er. Good takes too, once we get back t'huntin.'"

"Thank you," Luther said as well, nodding to him. We moved on before the conversation could drag out any longer. And as soon as we were far enough from the mess and into the darker crew quarters, I reached up and dragged my paw over my face, smearing and patting away some of the chalk and boot black. Luther saw me and soon followed suit. It wasn't exactly the same as those who'd let it fade and flake off in the sun over time, but it would do in the dark.

214

"Why didn't you tell us that?" Luther asked Hadeon, irritated.

"I've never worn it before when I crewed with them," he admitted. "This was the first time I bothered. I am a mercenary. I have my own pelt; I prefer not to wear another man's colors. If it has been problem, none have dared tell me so."

"You seem respected here," I agreed.

"Feared," he corrected. "I have less use for respect."

"Whatever," I sighed. "Alright, we're nearly up. Let's try to avoid any more long conversations and hope that boar was right about this lady being hard to sink. I have a feeling she'll fight like hell, and I don't want to be aboard if that happens."

The scent of the sea was unmistakable, and given the literal death cocoon we'd been wedged into all day, about the most welcoming it had ever been. Purplish-gray clouds blotted the stars from sight, but the halo of the moon behind them still kept the utter dark at bay. The winds were powerful, the mainsail and the main topsail puffed proudly, a welcome sight were it any other time. But right now, today, it meant this ship was gaining ground faster than we wanted it to.

Of course the same could be said for our own allies, wherever they were. So, hopefully, all things being equal, they were hot on our heels.

The upper gun deck was much the same as the middle, but even less crewed. I could see the distant shadows of men walking the far railing, laughing about something amongst themselves, their lit pipes glowing in the dark. Something bulbous on the topsail yard… probably a nocturnal fellow who liked his space, so feline would be my guess. There'd be eyes overhead us, of course, but even those that could see well in the dark could make out little from up there. We had no lantern intentionally: It made picking our way past the small boats lashed in their cradles a bit difficult, but it's not as though there weren't lanterns lit here.

"Men on guard," Luther pointed out. "Marines… or whatever the hell his equivalent is."

I tried to glance casually in the direction he was indicating and saw what he meant. Two very large, very obviously well-armed men, a jackal and a tiger, stood at ease but with their blades prominently on their hips, and pistols besides.

"They're protecting his day cabin," I said softly.

"Any chance he's in there now?" Luther asked.

"Would you be?" I asked back.

"I'm not spoiled by two cabins," he said snidely. "I don't know the protocol here."

"Not if he's ready for a fight," I murmured. "He'll be closer to the stern on the forecastle. Better line of sight, closer to his best men. Safer."

"The man is seven foot tall and built like a bear," Luther muttered. "Even injured, he doesn't strike me as a coward."

"It's also a nicer cabin," I said ruefully, missing my own. "Larger, likely where he takes his meals… more spacious bed if he's got someone keeping him warm."

"He is not in his day cabin, I can confirm," Hadeon said as we found ourselves a place to casually recline near the railings on the farthest side of the deck away from the other men. "I saw him and his cadre making their way stern after his last address. He keeps a larger guard than two men. And attendants."

"Attendants?" Luther queried curiously.

"Owned folk or courtesans… something like it," the leopard waved a hand. "They wore very little, save jewelry. Some men keep parrots—"

"Pets," I surmised. "Pleasure slaves or, like Hadeon said, courtesans of some sort. Hangers-on. Take care, though, and don't discount them. If he's letting them sleep in his bed, he trusts them to a certain extent. They might even be dangerous to us. Less obvious bodyguards."

"Large?" Luther asked.

Hadeon shook his head. "Half his size. Raccoon and rodent."

"Still," I cautioned. "Means he's not alone in there when we get to him. Worth keeping in mind."

"Let us first confirm help is underway," Hadeon said, looking out to sea.

"Alright," I snuffed, unbuttoning my jacket and reaching to one of the inner pockets to pull out the odd object we'd had to search half the city to find, when we'd been gathering supplies for this caper. They would have been easy enough to find if we'd been in a larger port, and most ships kept something similar on hand… but earnestly, we'd been lucky to find anyone dealing in gunpowder sky flares on such a small island. The locals used them for celebrations sometimes, apparently.

"Once we light this, Luther and I need to be gone," I said to Hadeon. "You're certain you want to be the one to stay up-top?"

"I am a known past associate," he said, "and few want trouble with me. I will be certain I am far from where you launch it when you do, so there is no indication I was involved."

"You know how to make it to the lower capstan?" Luther checked.

"It isn't far from here," I assured him.

"I saw it earlier," he nodded.

"It's the last place they'll be concerned with at full sail," I blew out a long breath. "Hopefully unguarded. Alright. Go. And keep your eyes on the sky."

"Once you light that thing?" he chuckled. "Everyone will be. It will not be hard to explain why."

"We need to move as one when the time comes," Luther said.

"I know, boss," the leopard winked. "I will see you soon. Hopefully with good news."

"Yeah, let's all hope so," I said.

We parted ways, moving to opposite ends of the deck. Luther and I wedged ourselves between the cradles of his crew boats, which were tall enough to obscure us quite well at a crouch. I fumbled briefly, then eventually found the sulfur-head matches in my pocket, craned up to press one of them to the hot metal of the underside of a lantern, and waited for ignition.

It went up, thankfully. Which was no small miracle given what I'd put the contents of my pockets through lately. It fizzled and sparked though, which meant I didn't have long, so I brought it to the flare wick quickly, then planted the stake as well as I could in a knot hole in the deck boards, and threw myself to the planks, shielding my eyes. I assume Luther did the same based on the thump beside me, but there was no time to check.

I felt the heat and saw the flash through my eyelids as the gunpowder ignited, and the flare sung off into the sky with a shrieking, ear-piercing whistle. Before I could even begin to recover, a hand fisted in my collar and yanked me sideways.

I fumbled for my blade for just a moment before realizing, obviously, it was the cattle dog. We took off through the rows of boats, running at a crouch, diving between the small barnacled hulls. My thighs blazed from the strain, the wood and sharp edges of the barnacles grabbed and tore at my coat, but we got clear before the first shouts of the alarmed men honed in on the location the flare had erupted from.

And there it was in the sky. Flaming out slowly, dancing down through the purple moonlight like a falling star. It wouldn't fully extinguish until it hit the water, and there was nothing all the men on deck doubtless watching it now could do to put it out. It was a beacon in the dark… announcing Roccosal's presence to all with eyes to see.

We couldn't wait around to see an answering flare. That was Hadeon's job. All we could do was hope. I pounded Luther's shoulder with a palm, grinning. He shot me a smirk right back, but that was all we had time for. We had places to be.

❧

The capstan for a ship this size was enormous; it actually connected to a second drum on the deck below, which is where we'd be doing our dirty work. We could close ourselves in better there, since the deck was partitioned. The hawser cables used to weigh anchor were readied in loops nearly thrice the length of the anchor chain all along this deck, too, which might provide cover if things got desperate and we needed it. But a real tripping hazard, if you ask me. You'd usually keep them stowed in the hold, but it spoke to me of his preparedness. Roccosal was acting paranoid, alright. The hawser hole wasn't even plugged at the moment, he must've considered these seas gentle enough to keep the cable threaded through. I plugged every available hole on my ship, she leaked enough as it was. Regardless, it worked fine for us. We didn't want to cut the cables, after all. That'd make it all the easier for them to abandon the anchor rather than go through the time and effort of hauling it back in, and time was what we were looking to cost them.

I'm not sure if there'd been men near the doorway before. It was unlikely he kept it guarded, but who knew. The flare we'd launched not only served to signal our allies, it also worked as one hell of a distraction for every man above-decks and several who'd been down here, too. I heard doors opening, stirrings from below, footsteps on stairs… we'd be dealing with far more men on the upper decks soon. It was a risk as well as a help. But it couldn't be avoided. Nothing about this plan was safe.

Honestly, this was probably the stupidest, most foolhardy thing I had ever done in my life, and that was saying something. The fact that I was undertaking it with an Amurescan Admiral was the truly strange part, though. I had to keep reminding myself this wasn't some disgruntled Amur criminal.

I mean… he was. But not just that.

We, both of us, had fleets at our command. We could be going about this behind the helms of said ships with someone else fulfilling the role of saboteur if we even chose to go about it that way. We could be standing beside hundreds of our men right now, atop a fortress of timber and cannons.

It was mad. Utterly mad. And I might have seen something like this for myself, alone, but the fact that I wasn't was…

What the hell was this feeling? Some kind of fucked-up camaraderie, I guess. A shared illness, more like.

"Oh, hell," Luther muttered when he got sight of the lower capstan's enormous drum. "How many men does it take to weigh anchor on a beast like this?"

"Aye, she's a big lady," I said. "All her parts are sizable. And to answer your question, depends on the type of men he employs. Dozens, usually."

"I'd say you fellows are compensating," he muttered, "but unfortunately, I now know otherwise."

I laughed as I tugged the pry bar out from where it was shoved into my belt. "Did you just," I snerked, "compliment my—"

"Information I really shouldn't have, by the way," he interjected.

"Well, whose fault is that?!" I guffawed. "You hatched the plan to have me seduced in order to have your way with me—"

"Shite, please don't phrase it that way," he groused, sidling up alongside one of the small windows in the room. "And I didn't, by the way. Seduction was the tigress's plan. I thought it would work just as well if we got you hammered."

"I mean, it did—both of those ideas, actually." I chuckled as I bent down to eye the spokes meant for the trundle head. "So, thank you for the good time, I guess. I'll need to get you piss drunk in return one of these days."

"I'm not a happy drunk," he murmured, then went rigid. I didn't miss the way his body froze and went bolt upright.

"Wh—" I began.

He was smiling, thankfully. Staring out the window. "The flare," he said. "I can see it."

"Still?" I blinked. It should've gone out by now.

"No," he moved back over towards me, crouching beside me. He was still grinning. "Ours. Hard to say how far out... but close. They're here."

"OH!" I felt excitement bubble up in my chest. "Oh, hell, that's good news! But I had no doubt," I lied, "Lotus would pull through for us."

"Let's hope she's rallied all of our forces," he said, reaching out to touch the drum. "Good Lord," he grunted. "Is it even necessary we jam it? It's going to be hard enough for him to get the ship under control anchored on one side. Spin her right 'round in circles. Let alone turn this?"

"The more time we can buy, the better," I reasoned. "But this is going to be... obvious... so I'd rather we be together when—"

As if on cue, we heard a fiercely-whispered, familiar voice through the locked door.

"Boss! Flare's gone up."

"We saw!" Luther sprung to his feet and hurried over to the door, glancing out the cloudy glass exactly once before unlatching and quickly opening and shutting the door enough for the leopard to slide inside. He looked unharmed and definitely alone.

"I keep waiting for the other paw to drop," I muttered, shaking my head. "This is going well."

"Yes and no," Hadeon said, resting his polearm against the door. "Many have seen the flares, it is only a matter of time before—"

The alarm bell began to ring, first on our deck, then in answer on others, all down the length of the ship.

"We knew that was inevitable," I said quickly, ushering the two of them forward. "C'mon. No chance they don't notice this, but let's do it while it's noisy out there all the same."

"This is going to wreak havoc on the ship as a whole when it hits bottom," Luther said, dusting his paws with some of the chalk from his face.

"Oh, before then," I snickered. "The drag alone…. Whatever amount of havoc we can cause, I say, the better."

"Amen," Luther nodded. "Just makes me wince thinking about it."

"Stand clear of the drum, mates," I said as I headed out. It had been quite some time since I'd released an anchor with my own hands, but thankfully, one of the things I'd been certain to do when I first crewed up on the Manoratha was get hands-on experience with each and every job on the ship. It was, in many ways, the realization of a dream. To do the things I'd previously only read about. No matter how simple, how droll they'd seemed at the time, I wanted to know her inside and out. To actually live this life, rather than live vicariously through the stories of others.

Thankfully I didn't need to worry over the anchor's weight. I just needed to….

For some reason, I heard my father's voice from when I was a child. That rough baritone, which my own voice even into my adult years always felt a pale impression of.

Unfasten the lashings, so the anchor swung down vertically on its stopper from the cathead. Skip the buoy… it's not as though we were in port. Detach and unfasten the stopper, and…

The anchor plunged down into the roiling waters beneath, the chain growling out behind it, and I hurried back to my fellows, fur and leathers freshly wet with spray and cold from the light chill in the night air. My heart pounded in my chest, blood stinging through my extremities. No going back now.

"Bar the door!" I heard Luther bark out as I stomped down the staircase inside, clearing the last two steps, my claws stabilizing me despite the slick on my paws as I raced towards the drum. I heard the cattle dog and the leopard latching it behind me, then dragging crates in front of the door. I bent down and scooped up the pry bar as I came to a stop beside the drum, catching my breath as my eyes followed the dense chain uncoiling, faster than I was comfortable with.

I waited for my opening, readying the bent bar in my palms. This was going to be a tense finish; the anchor still hadn't struck bottom. But the ship was moving, dragging the length of it diagonally through the water, so that didn't necessarily mean we didn't have enough chain. I waited until there was very little leeway left. When one link in the chain looked particularly exposed, I followed its short path unwinding for the second or so I had, then carefully… like threading a needle that could jam up and break my arm… stabbed the pry bar through the small gap, and let go.

The drag through fathoms and fathoms of water, the weight of the anchor, and the momentum it had built up were powerful. And just as I'd hoped, far more powerful than an old, rusted, and previously bent pry bar. The chain drug it along at a whipping pace until it hit the hawser hole, and then it banged to a stop for a moment, before groaning and giving way, buckling into the hole in a V. For a moment I was honestly afraid the force of the chain was going to snap it fully in two, but that would have been a tall order even for that much weight. What it did instead was… somehow, exactly what I'd hoped.

It jammed inside, with nearly every fathom of available chain and one distant, dragging anchor pulling it taut.

"Holy hell," Luther gawked to the left of me. He and Hadeon had blocked the nearest doorway fairly well by the look of it. Certainly enough shit in the way that it'd take anyone a while to get through it. Which was good, because—

Pounding, and not the kind I liked. Muffled voices and shouts, and then, most shockingly, a pistol shot right on the other side of the door. Smoke burst in through the gap. Someone had shot the lock off on their side.

"You do know your engineering," the cattle dog complimented with a chalky clap on my shoulder. "Can't believe that worked."

"One part knowledge, the rest's luck," I laughed, relieved. "But I figured if prying off a coffin lid could bend the damn thing, the force of an anchor certainly would."

"There are other ways onto this deck, boss!" Hadeon reminded me with a snarl as he grabbed up his polearm. "We move now, ya?!"

"Hold the line!" I said, stumbling back over towards the drum and tugging loose one of the spokes, then beginning on a second. "You, too, cattle dog, unless you want to help me here."

"What are you— OH." He realized suddenly. "Right, that'll sure as hell make it hard on them." He pulled his blade and marched over towards one of the battened hatches, lifting the latches and throwing it open before securing it for me. I could tell from the moment the spray kicked up into the opening that we were wheeling, now… and listing, besides. The ship was in a spiral 'round the anchor we'd lowered. Hadn't taken long, which means we were still at speed. I could hear the masts groaning.

"Go!" I shouted as I hefted two of the spokes, my limit, apparently. I drug them over to the hatch and fed them out, not bothering to wait for the splash as they hit the water before starting on gathering the others.

I wasn't done dumping four of the beams before I heard the thudding cavalcade of paws traversing the gundeck towards our partition. I chanced a glance once at where Luther and Hadeon were on either side of the open

221

entryway, just in time to see the leopard jab his polearm forward, fast as a lightning strike, cutting the two canines trying to barge through off at the shins. One pitched forward, the other sideways into Luther's waiting long knife. The cattle dog had his saber held in his off-hand, or... was it his main one? Hard to tell, now that I thought on it. I think I'd seen him switch back and forth in the short time I'd known him. It was bad enough if he was a southpaw, but ambidextrous swordsmen were pure demons.

Hadeon wheeled back a thick, spotted thigh and brought the weight of half of his body down on the felled man's head with a crushing blow from his hind paw. The man had been trying to look up, unfortunately, which meant his skull rattled back down on the planks with a cracking noise that made even me wince. Luther pulled his long knife from the second canine's guts, then shoved him with a shoulder in time to bring his saber up to parry the third man coming in behind them—a sloth bear with a heavy cleaving blade of some kind. He twisted his saber and locked the man's weapon on his hilt, then spun it sideways until the bear's wrist gave way and his weapon clattered to the ground.

Yes, very, VERY glad I'd never crossed swords with that man.

The continuing fight between the cattle dog and the sloth bear effectively blocked the doorway, but not so much that Hadeon couldn't, after a measured pause, jab the pointed spear-tip end of his weapon through an opening and puncture... someone. Impossible for me to see, all I heard was the shout.

I tossed another two spokes out into the briny depths and decided that would have to be enough. They had a good bottleneck going over there, but they'd be overwhelmed soon enough. And even if Roccosal's crew could somehow operate the capstan with something improvised or with half the spokes left, they'd still have to fix the jam. We'd bought the time we'd need.

I hoped.

I stowed my pistol, knowing I'd have no chance to reload it. That was for saving your life or the life of one of your mates. Not clearing a doorway.

I strode forward towards the melee, feeling the very same seizing in my guts, the same flutter of my heart, the mortal fear when I got my first whiff of blood... but I was no soft academic any more. I was a bloody Privateer, damnit. Grayson Reed, Admiral of the Manoratha. The gilded black wolf, tempest of chaos, the unwanted castoff of a Cartel Magnate, gone rogue.

And more importantly, I wasn't about to be a whimpering bitch in front of my greatest rival.

When real nerve won't avail you, pride often will. I joined the fray with a fair amount of confidence for me, pulling my long knife and waiting until the bear muscled his way through the archway and turned in his clutch with Denholme, so I could flank him. I may not have been fancy enough to fight with a long blade and parrying off-hand at the same time, but I was good enough with either and preferred my long knife in close quarters. It did the trick when you didn't care about keeping someone at a range.

The sloth bear didn't need his blade to be a threat; his claws were small knives in their own right, and he was swinging them faster than you might think a man his size was capable of. Luther was avoiding him handily up until now, but I saw him lock eyes with me for a moment as he half-stepped aside from another one, and jerked his head to the right. I took the cue, waiting for my opening... then he feinted a thrust with his long blade, sending the bear juking wildly to the right to avoid it... and I had my opening.

I plunged my blade into the bear's kidney; he bellowed out and yanked away, and then Luther mercifully drove his short blade through his open mouth. I say 'mercifully' because that kidney wound would have seen him in agony for hours until he died.

I spun just in time to see Hadeon employing his polearm somehow in the limited space to alarmingly-accurate effect, an arcing swing driving the axe directly into the collarbone of the last man bold enough to make a try into our space. It sunk in several inches, and the fellow gargled out a cry of alarm before jerking back away with a crunching of bone I'm certain he probably... needed.

No one was fool enough to get in our way after that or were too busy readying the cannons. We sprinted down the deck past looks of shock and alarm, Hadeon leading the charge. Vaguely behind us, I heard those crates giving way. The men who knew what we were up to were about to discover the whole of it. The clock had begun ticking. If they could somehow weigh anchor in time to run, this had all been for naught.

We had to get to his cabin. As soon as possible. If we could, before—

Thunder crackled out in a concussive line, somewhere distant but still far too close to have come from the sky. It perforated the air, echoing in that rolling, directionless way gunfire sounded when you fired out over the water.

Every man on the deck went still, ourselves included. Hadeon skidded to a stop before the staircase to the upper decks, Luther and I thudding into one another.

"That's—" I began.

An answering barrage, smaller, lesser... but closer.

"They've begun assaulting his escort vessels," Luther said with a toothy grin.

"That'll be one of yours, then," I grunted, shoving him up the stairs. "Lotus's little gals don't have that many guns, and my girl will be lumbering behind."

"Long guns," he said, his ears twitching. "It's Fenrir."

"You preferred to run up my tail before firing in all our encounters," I groused.

"Aye, well, the flares didn't give us much choice." He shook his head, turning to begin taking the steps two at a time. "This one'll be fought at a distance for a while yet. The two hunters will take the fore, Reynolds and Shaw, and they'll sink his escorts if they have a chance at it, no quarter. Clear the way for the ships he doesn't know are coming."

"While we are stuck in a death spiral," Hadeon clucked his tongue. "Most vicious, boss."

"Lotus likes to board," I said. "She might be the first alongside."

"Your tigress has nerve," Luther laughed.

"She's not 'mine'," I stowed my short blade and pulled my saber as we made it above-decks, "but aye."

Hadeon put out an arm as we made it up the staircase, cautioning us. "Blades out, yes. But do not engage unless we must… they still do not all know we are the interlopers."

"Blend in if we can," I agreed.

As it turned out, that wouldn't be a problem. The upper gun deck was sheer chaos: controlled chaos, mind you. The kind of chaos you get with sailors going into unforeseen combat, who are nonetheless doing their jobs. Mostly, at the moment, trying to bring in the sails. I could feel as well as see the ship listing, the chain pulled taut somewhere under water, the vessel as good as caught in a whirlpool. They'd have no choice until they got their speed down, and it looked like their plan was to plant in place broadside and eschew any chance at maneuvering. They still had guns… a lot of them, and if they could get the ship under control, plenty of time so their ass wasn't exposed. The two escort vessels would keep Denholme's fleet at bay long enough for that, and it's not as though they were helpless, even stuck playing defense. His 'hunters' would have a hard time cracking that nut. Then by the time they got to the Man-of-War, they'd be worn down. And you didn't want to be worn down while trying to take on one of the most formidable floating platforms on the seas. That had to be Roccosal's best course, here. It would've been mine, too.

Of course, he didn't know what we knew.

Somewhere out there was Lotus with her quick, deadly little fleet. Like magpies circling an eagle. With his wings clipped, she'd be able to skirt his firing range as he clumsily maneuvered what little he could and pick apart his sails with chain shot. Once he was well and truly stationary, my lumbering lady would come in from the south and clear his decks with smaller shot from afar. Nothing that would crack the mast… and hopefully with enough warning that we could take cover.

Then Lotus would come alongside and help us seize control of this beast.

That was the plan. That's what we'd all come up with, putting our heads together on that beach. And even up until now, we'd not been able to invent anything better. It was foolhardy as hell, rife with chances for failure, and much of it hinged on three disparate groups somehow working together. But…

It had to work. Because it just had to.

One way to stack the deck would be to kill him… to kill Roccosal… or otherwise keep him busy, before he could think his way out of the trap and command his ship. But getting to him in the midst of all of this had always been up in the air…

"He has to be on deck by now," Luther reasoned, keeping his voice down as we moved—rushed, in fact, because that made us seem like we knew what our tasks were better than if we were just meandering—across the ship.

"He's injured," I reminded him. "And nowhere near as stupid as you—"

He glared.

"—or me," I continued. "We don't even know how mobile he is right now."

"He is still inside," Hadeon said suddenly.

We all looked to him, then followed his arm as he pointed towards the distant lantern lights that adorned the quarter deck. From here, you could see the cross-hatched, intricate windows that must have encased his cabin, lit with a warm glow that glowed through the… skull motifs….

Fuck. The man had style, I couldn't deny that.

More importantly, the cabin was still ringed with guards, those men adorned almost like marines. Four of them, near the door. Looked like a waiting procession.

"He won't be for much longer," I said. "You ready, mates?"

Roccosal's night cabin was slightly raised, so that the only way in or out was up a short flight of stairs, which is, of course where, his guards were stationed. His men buzzed about, most stationed on this high of a deck shouting orders to the lads desperately trying to control the straining sails. Their attention was, understandably, focused right now on getting the ship under control. Which meant we'd get no better opportunity than this.

The quarter deck was also home to his 12-pounders, a dozen of the cannons ringing either side, and the few men here who weren't shouting orders were readying those for fire. The only fellows standing between us and Roccosal were his four guards. All of them armed to the teeth and large, of course. The man didn't skimp on his personal entourage.

One of the higher-ups who apparently wasn't so distracted that he hadn't noticed our approach (and more importantly that we probably shouldn't fucking be here) shouted at us from where he stood at the mizzen mast. But Hadeon had leapt to a full-on charge by then, wheeling his polearm in a figure eight that was more an impressive show of force and skill than anything else. I'll say this much though, it had its desired effect. The few men on this deck and not up in the rigging who could have done anything to stop us gave us a wide berth.

We began to sprint as we neared the stairs. There was really no choice here except a frontal assault; we'd done everything possible to give ourselves an advantage, but we were at the zenith now. I only wished I was as seemingly fearless as my companions.

The decks behind us began to erupt with cannon fire of their own, as well as the whizzing, shrieking of lead through air, and explosions of wood and debris that signaled Roccosal's Man-of-War was within firing range of… who knew. My ship, Luther's, even Lotus's. They were clearing the deck. We probably should have been taking cover, but we were so close.

The forward guards were two enormous tigers, one's fur nearly brick red, the other lighter, but thicker and more accented with white, likely from the Kadrush. He had a rifle he was bringing up to aim down the deck at us, which was… worrying. Firing anywhere near so much gunpowder being loaded was a risk we had to hope he wouldn't take, though. It might've been for intimidation factor alone.

One of the others further up the stairs, a hefty mixed dog with the skull painted over a thick white coat of fur, had a crossbow. And that was the first weapon discharged at us, staggering Hadeon's charge as the bolt clipped his thigh and sent a spatter of blood back on Luther behind him. He didn't pause for long, giving a cackling feline roar as he crashed into the man, using his polearm to ram into and wrench the crossbow out of the canine's hands. It looked like he'd given up on it already though, easily dropping the weapon when pressed and going for the blade on his hip.

It was in that moment that I saw Roccosal for the first time. The stairs were short, and we were close enough that I could see through the windows. The distinctive red mane, the rust-colored eyes, the gold adornments and the shine in his teeth… but moreover, what caught my attention was the flare of a match or something like it. He had a cigarette in his mouth, being lit for him by someone. A woman, and as Hadeon had said, distinctly a rodent. She was thicker of face than most mice or rats I'd ever seen, curvaceous and sturdy of body, and nude from the waist up. I only had a brief glimpse in there, but it looked as though someone else— his other servant, most likely— was helping him dress or at least put on his coat over a bare chest. A bare… wrapped chest.

The man may still have been injured, but he was readying himself, he wasn't alone. And the four guards besides...

The deck near enough to us was being peppered with small shot, the men loading the cannons taking cover in between firing. The tigers were descending the steps...

Shit, shit, shit. Could we do this?! Could we, really?

It's self-defeating insanity how your thoughts and anxieties can wander, even when you're in a life-or-death fight. I circled into a clutch with the redder-furred, slender tiger, simultaneously falling back on my tournament training and, at this point, years of actual experience... but thinking too much was giving me flashes of the last tournament fight I lost for some reason. A dalmatian, a spotless ring, my body younger and slighter, my brother watching disinterestedly from the sidelines....

Distracting! No, enough thinking!

The tiger snarled at me in Huudari, hunching his hip up, and instinct kicked in. He was going to knee at me and go in for a grapple, and that's all it would take for him to bite me with that falchion. I thrust my own knee up in time, counting on the slight advantage I had in bulk. The fact that he was one step above me on the stairs was a factor I didn't calculate for, though, and I didn't end up overpowering him as I'd planned. Instead, I tipped off-balance, saw him bringing that falchion in towards my opposite hip, and let myself go dead weight instead, falling down onto the decking on my back.

My body bounced—a good sign, I'd realized by now. A decade or more of literally falling-down-drunk living had taught me to fall as harmlessly as possible. It still hurt and knocked the wind out of me for a moment, but the tiger hadn't seemed to expect it.

I caught sight of Luther while I was on my back staring up at the melee, giving me a worried and perplexed look from where he was tangling with the fourth man, a sea lion. Despite the fact that the massive, leathery skinned pirate must have outweighed him twice over, he seemed frustrated

227

and overwhelmed by the cattle dog's vicious, ceaseless, biting strikes at him. He was already sliced and bleeding in several places, the big ax he carried coming nowhere close to the swerving canine in any of its wide, sweeping slashes. But Luther was in no place to turn his back on the man to help me, so I tried my best to give him a confident nod as I attempted to get my feet underneath me again.

The tiger wasn't about to give me that much time, though. Before I could get up from being prone, he was on me. He leapt the last step to stand overtop me, double-handed his falchion, and tried to chop it down at my neck. I gave up on trying to right myself and brought my blade up instead, the man's dramatic leap giving me more than enough warning of what was to come. But then we were locked, and he was straddling me, bearing down on me, gaining in inches…

Well, it's not as though I wasn't used to this.

I did what had become second nature to me by now when I was being overcome: I gave in. I glanced down our bodies for a fraction of a moment to be sure he didn't have me caged in with his legs yet, then gave way with my blade at the same time as I forced my body down the slick planks, my arms up, and suddenly my nose was in his stomach and his sword was locked with mine over my head.

My arms were indisposed, but my teeth weren't. I lunged forward and bit at whatever flesh I could get in my mouth—which turned out to be a portion of his bare abdomen and hip. My teeth sunk in an inch or so, blood pooled on my tongue, making the bile rise in my throat. But I didn't let go.

He roared and jerked away from me, bits of his fur and small shreds of flesh coming away as he twisted and rolled to the side. His falchion fell away, and I willed myself to hold on to my own saber despite the pain in my wrist.

As I stood, I saw Hadeon keeping the big white dog at bay, standing over the fallen body of the thick-furred tiger. The canine was faltering mentally by the look of it, eyes darting about as if he were looking for an escape. Hadeon's whole right thigh was covered in blood, but he barely seemed to notice, his long ivory fangs sparkling with saliva in the lantern light, his eyes wide and feral as he snarled through another bout of mad laughter. The man was a terror, and I'm sure some of that was bravado, but it was still disturbing to behold in all its fury.

The slender, darker-furred tiger was more measured than his counterpart had been, clutching a palm at where I'd bitten and assessing me warily, his falchion still held at the ready. We circled one another after I'd taken a moment to collect myself and get to my feet. He seemed unwilling to pounce on me again.

"What is this?" he demanded in Huudari. "Who are you?!"

For once, I was in no mood to blather my way through an encounter. I owed the man no explanation, and I was acutely aware he was trying to buy time for the dhole to arrive. Which would be any time—

The doors to the cabin banged open, heavy footsteps thudding out onto the balcony above. I growled and went in hard, pressing the attack with a series of three strikes, overhand to force him to my left, underhand as I came up from the twist of the arc, and then a quick, measured thrust to get in under his guard.

I had long since forgotten the name of this technique, but the comfortable, sterile foundation of sword-form I'd used in my youth had little bearing on the life I lived now anyway. It was woven into a greater tapestry, the specifics lost to time and addled by drink and hard living. All I know is, this time, it worked.

My thrust caught him in the shoulder, near his clavicle. It wasn't his sword arm, but it didn't matter. He gave up the fight at that point, falling back away from me and tumbling down to the decking, cursing and clapping a paw over the injury. I couldn't say for sure if the wound was mortal, likely not, but he was giving every indication of falling back either way, and I knew the dhole had arrived. I didn't have time to finish him off.

Cannon fire was breaking out on the seas all around us, the mist of gunpowder smoke filling the air and gusting on the torrents of wind that had thus far been carrying this ship so swiftly. What little I could make out from over the railing was a constantly-changing battlefield. Distant masts and the dark shapes of vessels lining up on the horizon, facing off against one another. Most of the men here and on our ships could see somewhat well at night, but I still hated fighting in the dark. The rain may have cleared up but the skies were still murky and cloud-covered, not enough moonlight to see by. I briefly made out the masts far off in the distance that could only belong to my ship... the only other vessel here as large as this one. She was closing in on one of Roccosal's escort vessels, a galleon utterly cloaked in smoke and the flashes of cannon fire by now, circling with one of Denholme's larger hunters. Some of the shot on our decks might have been from her, she was certainly close enough.

"MAN OF WAR!" a voice cried from the rigging above, about the same time I'd seen her. And then I heard Roccosal for the first time.

"Kalic varr," he swore out, "you must be joking. How... who?!"

It was at that moment that he finally seemed to notice me. The dhole's eyes bore down into mine from where he stood on the walkway in front of his cabin, mane flaring out in the wind around him like a lion's, the tattooing on his face throwing those sickly gore-red eyes into stark relief, like gems in a skull's sockets. He was clad only in a pair of leather britches, his towering form stooped slightly at the shoulders, bandages wrapped cleanly around his shoulder and the top half of his chest. His gaze flashed with recognition, at long last.

And then he laughed. Opened his big, toothy maw wide, the gold fangs catching the lantern light, and bellowed.

"You stupid, traitorous mongrel!" Despite the words, he seemed genuinely, darkly amused. "What have you gone and allied yourself with out there? Sold your soul to those rotting, inbred Imperialists, did you? For what?" He clucked his tongue at me, putting out a hand, as one of his servants settled an elegant golden-inlaid falchion into his grip. "This can't all be for some knotted fur, now can it?"

"My dislike for you began far before that," I assured him, flexing my paw around the hilt of my own blade. I did not want to fight him on those steps; I'd much rather he come down to me.

"This is a bit much for 'dislike', wouldn't you say?" he sneered as he took the steps slowly. I watched his body language, hoping to see signs of his injury weighing on him, and I wasn't entirely disappointed. He seemed sluggish, lazy… like maybe he was drugged with something. The injury was on his off-hand shoulder, of course. Because I had no luck whatsoever, and also because the wolfhound had been aiming for his heart. But if he was taking something for the pain, that would work, too.

"Men like us weren't meant to be ruled," I snapped out. "You had to know your downfall was only a matter of time."

"I would have fought you honorably if you took so much issue with me, you cur," he snarled. "Can you not even muster that much respect for your brethren?"

"Duels are for Pedigrees," I snorted, glancing left and right to see where my companions were at. Luther was still in a desperate fight with the sea lion. The man may not have been accurate or able to gain ground against his more maneuverable opponent, but he wasn't going down easy, either. He was cut in half a dozen places, including the dome of his head and was still somehow roaring and swinging that ax around. The seafaring folk were a durable lot.

Hadeon seemed to be chasing the white canine down where he'd retreated to the mizzen mast and had gotten embroiled in a fight with the man who'd shouted at us earlier. He was keeping the both of them at bay with his long weapon, but he was surrounded now.

Where was Lotus? How long had it been since I'd last had that thought? We'd hoped to have Roccosal dead by now, and locked ourselves in his cabin, waiting for her and her men to board before we fought our way out.

He was feet away from me now. Taller, broader, more intimidating than I remembered. And looking at me like I was worthless. Like I was dirt. Like nothing about this whole scenario we'd engineered scared or even concerned him. The man had always acted like he was untouchable. If you go that long cloaked in the kind of power he could bring to bear, I suppose any man would.

"Seems like you've got the fight you wanted, regardless," he said, licking his teeth. "Or you can just stand down like the bitch you are, while I kill your boys. Easier. Painless. I might even keep you. That mane of yours is a trophy, but I'd much prefer the whole..." he punched the words out slowly, "...man. Body... and soul."

"I wasn't about to be your vassal when you offered it with spoils and false promises," I swung my blade out, readying myself. "What makes you think I'd do so now?"

His eyes flicked back up the stairs to where his two servants stood. In addition to the woman I'd seen before was a raccoon with a grim expression on his face, unbefitting the sparse harem outfit he wore. The both of them were armed, but standing back, allowing the dhole to approach me on his own. I wondered in that moment what sorts of lives those two had led, before they swore themselves to him... or became his property. It was impossible to say, but they seemed loyal. For all his barbarity, Fathom had followers. People who believed in him. I could understand why, to a certain extent... but I'd never be one of them.

"You can fall at my feet willingly," he said, his voice hissing between golden fangs, "or bathed in your own blood. I'm giving you a choice."

"You're scared," I realized aloud, suddenly. I laughed despite myself. "You can't throw your men at me or you lose face, but you don't actually want to fight me alone."

"This time I take your tongue!" he snapped.

"You're not exactly a man known for your mercy," I continued, trying not to let my gaze wander. I'd noticed something he had yet to. "You're hurt, high, and you know you might lose."

He howled out an enraged shout and leapt towards me, faster than I'd hoped, but his golden blade was easy to follow, so I sidestepped the first swing. I brought my saber up to guard against the next, and it came cutting across my left side this time, where my guard was weaker. I still tipped him, but it was like trying to stop a falling mast. Our blades clattered, and he overwhelmed me, his sword edge shrieking down mine to my guard and forcing my blade down to point at the decking with little effort on his part. I had next to no warning as he balled his off-hand fist, driving it into the side of my muzzle.

If the injured shoulder was affecting him, it sure as fuck didn't feel like it had tempered his strength. My teeth rattled in my mouth, my vision blacked in and out between blinks, dizziness overtaking me as I stumbled aside, very nearly going down. It was only through sheer force of will that I stayed upright, knowing if I fell prone now, he'd have me.

He spun his blade into an overhand position and brought it down and across in a wide swing that I knew I could, at most, tip again, which might not be enough, if the last time had been any indication. But before he could do so, his jaws jerked open, spittle spraying out as he gave an alarmed cry of pain.

Luther was at his back, and the tip of his saber was plunged out the edge of the dhole's ribcage. He'd probably been trying to jam it between his ribs from behind, but Roccosal had been in the midst of moving and had barely averted it. The cattle dog twisted and pulled his blade out the side, flaying a long strip of flesh off the lower right of his chest. It was a flesh wound, but it'd bleed… a lot. And it had to hurt like hell.

"COWARDS!" the dhole screamed in anger, whirling and dashing the pommel of his blade into Denholme's wrist. I heard how hard he'd been hit, saw him wince, but couldn't discern how bad it had been. I pressed the attack with a quick thrust of my saber at the massive man's exposed back, trying for a kidney. The thrust was too shallow though, Roccosal had already pressed Denholme's back to the nearest rail, which brought him out of my reach. Out of the corner of my eye, I saw one of his servants climbing up on the balcony railing. I had a second to warn the cattle dog, and I got nothing intelligible out. Just a shout of, "Look!"

The raccoon dropped down beside Luther light as a sparrow and jabbed with a two-fisted hold, some kind of small blade, aimed for his chest. Roccosal got in the way before I could see how that panned out, turning on me with utter ferocity and malice in his eyes.

"Luther!" I cried out, without thinking about it.

Roccosal looked taken-aback, actually stopping mid-swing for a moment to voice his confusion aloud. "What-who? The Cerberus mongrel? Are you fucking serious?!"

Gods, he was three feet behind him, and he still didn't recognize him.

The whole deck shuddered, suddenly. All of us were nearly pitched off our feet, Roccosal included, swaying into the nearest shrouds to steady himself. I saw the raccoon thrown to the decking, rolling down into the railings and realized with a bolt of relief that Luther must have held him at bay. Then, my heart soared further when another sound met my ears… the distinctive clang of boarding hooks. I looked to my left, then my right, and there were the masts. Smaller—you could have lost them in the forest through all of the Man-of-war's rigging—but emblazoned brilliant red with the unique outline of a lotus pod. I could almost imagine amidst the din of shouting and cannon fire that I heard her voice, calling out a battle cry.

And farther out, but close enough that I knew we'd be boarded on both sides before long… a sight that would have sent me swearing and shaking, but a month ago. The Fenrir herself, flashes of Amur red all over the deck as his men prepared to come aboard. Luther saw it too, his jaw open as he panted, the start of a grin carving its way into his jowls.

And that brief distraction was all it took for the whole endeavor to go sideways.

Roccosal was not nearly so interested in the ships around us as we were. It was hard to say what the man cared about at all any more, save killing us. He seized on our moment of hope, palming something from his belt, and taking the one wide step necessary to jam it into Luther's abdomen. It brought me back to that stoat in the alley, cold, efficient, no wasted momentum or effort. The kind of practiced kill I'd never yet managed. Except Luther was the one on the receiving end this time.

All of that tumultuous fear, loathing, respect, and growing admiration I'd held for Luther Denholme fell away in that moment, replaced by a profound feeling of emptiness and immediate loss, as I watched the dhole pull the knife from his guts. I hadn't even lost the fight myself yet, but… it felt like I had. Every racing thought, every pounding of my heart, told me as much.

Roccosal turned on me, wild savagery in his every feature. He still held his sword, but dropped the knife from his weaker, now blood-slicked hand. He brought his palm up to his muzzle and licked it clean. Like a dyre animal.

My heart thudded, my mind issuing one clear thought in that moment. One painfully-obvious realization.

He wasn't worth this.

He… hadn't ever been. Roccosal didn't matter. None of this had ever really mattered to me. I'd re-grow what he'd taken, I'd always have my memories of my family and my heritage, my anger at him wasn't even at him, it was at the lie he sold to men of my ilk as freedom. But if he was dead, another would take his place. There'd always be a Roccosal. There's always be a man calling himself 'King'. Someone willing to finance his world and way of life on the backs of others.

What I'd never be able to replace… was the comrade bleeding out on the deck. A friend… as unique, as fascinating, as maddening as he was. And that's what I'd really wanted, this whole time. Wasn't it? It had taken talking to him in a bloody coffin, hunting the most dangerous pirate alive, and watching him run through in front of me… to realize it.

But he wasn't dead yet.

Roccosal was bleeding too and had grown even more sluggish. But his attacks were no less ferocious and were ceaseless, now. I parried one, felt my shoulder jerk painfully with the blow, ducked aside another, and dove around him to stumble towards Luther. He was down, but I could hear his heart beating, could see his chest rising and falling. His eyes were open, he was even flexing his fingers against the deck, trying to push himself up.

Lotus's men had a long climb, but the first of them were pulling themselves over the rails, now. And there she was... leaping the last length of the rope, landing with her paws splayed, one hand catching herself on a loose, frayed piece of rigging. She had her saber in a deck hand before she had even caught her balance, yelling out towards me. But she felt worlds away....

The ship shuddered again, groaning as it was pulled taut between the two enemy vessels. A brief glance confirmed it—Fenrir was alongside. The ship was taller, Luther's men more able to board quickly. The two-pronged attack would subdue the deck in a short time, but I wasn't sure the cattle dog had that long. Not with Roccosal and—

The second of his servants, the rodent woman with the thick face, luscious curves, and a teased-out mop of unruly black mane was above us still on the railing. I barely caught her pulling back an arm and hitched my breath, grabbing at Denholme's downed figure and rolling us both aside as a dagger stuck in the decking where we'd once been. Roccosal fell over the two of us a moment later, bringing his falchion down inches from my face, where it stuck. He growled irritably and strained to pull his blade from the wood, but I couldn't get my sword out from underneath me to any effect against him.

To hell with it. He wasn't worth it.

I hauled the cattle dog into my arms and with a straining groan, forced him up over my shoulder, the heat of his blood seeping into my chest as I did so. I knew I was stressing the wound, but it couldn't be helped. I could possibly do one of two things here: take the time to kill Roccosal and still be stranded in the midst of his crew and his armed bodyguards with my own allies tied up all around me but unable to get to me... or I could run. The dhole was hurt, and, even carrying someone, I was probably faster.

I wanted to live. And I wanted Luther to live, too.

I pulled my flintlock from my belt with my free hand, my left and hardly stable besides, and aimed it as well as I could at Roccosal amidst the smoke, flying debris, and a tilting deck, and fired.

The chances I hit him anywhere vital were slim to none, and I knew it. But the concussive crack of the pistol firing and the smoke of the gunpowder igniting were enough to stun him into stumbling back away from us, long enough for me to turn tail and run.

I was closer to the Fenrir than Lotus. I saw the flash of a blue coat when I stood. That had to be one of his Captains, which meant I could get him to his people, to help, hopefully to a waiting physician on his ship. There was no guarantee Lotus would have that… but a Navy ship definitely would.

I thought I had more time to get clear of the dhole. But carrying another man's weight while standing had taken more out of me than I'd thought, and my legs wouldn't carry me fast enough, my knees buckling repeatedly as I started to run. I heard rather than saw Roccosal swear his outrage, then a searing pain assaulted my back, nearly causing me to pitch over. I barely had time to register what had happened—the falchion, probably—slicing a line across my shoulder blades as I fled from him. But then I was gaining ground…

…another dagger struck the deck just inches from my feet…

…I was gaining ground…

I saw Hadeon, twirling like a pinwheel, the flash of his beautiful blade painting a stripe of gold across the field of battle like a smear across a mural.

… Roccosal's roars faded into the din behind me….

Ahead were men in tans, whites, tied at the waist with red, clashing into battle with the remaining skull-faced pirates trying in vain to continue operating the 12-pounder cannons. I think I heard Lotus screaming my name from across the deck, yelling at me to stop, for some reason…

I didn't even slow down. I hit the railing and leapt, falling nearly a deck's-worth down and tucking my body as I crashed into the planks of the Fenrir beneath. I don't know if I hit my head… I don't think I did… but everything just went out like a snuffed lantern for…

…I blinked, awake again. My body ached, my shoulder felt dislocated, everything was spinning around the axis of where I was laying, clutched at…

He looked battered and crusted in blood, boot black and chalk, one ear tattered, dark, almost black blood dripping out his nose onto my palm where his head was cradled. I'd landed partially on my back, partially on my side, and even through the dizziness and the haze of gunpowder smoke, I could tell we were on unfamiliar decking. Clean. Lighter wood than my own. Paws pounded around us, voices blurred in and out in Amurescan.

I rolled onto my back fully, immediately regretting it when the wound I'd sustained throbbed. I felt eyes on me, everywhere. The shadow of a large figure, brown, huge paws at my side… then one settling on my chest, flexing its claws.

Luther was unconscious. But I could hear him breathing. Could see his chest rising and falling.

Distantly… very distantly… I thought I could hear Lotus. And then, momentarily, I thought I could see her. On the quarter deck of the Man of War, above us. Staring down at me from the railing. Fear etched into her every feature.

235

I wasn't sure what that expression meant. Was she worried for Luther? Was I hurt worse than I thought?

"Grayson Reed," a deep, heavily-accented Amur voice growled at me from above. I thought I could vaguely make out a mastiff, wearing a blue coat.

"…present…" I said weakly around a cough. My lungs felt about ready to dislodge from my chest, after that fall.

"It's him," the same man said. "Get the irons."

"Luther…" I groaned, rolling my head to the side, looking again at the crumpled cattle dog. "Mate…"

Several men were gathering around him, readying what looked like a litter for carrying him off. One of them was pressing something to his wound.

"Grayson Reed," that same voice repeated for some reason. That was getting annoying.

"I already said—"

"You are hereby under arrest, by the decree of His Majesty the King of Amuresca's Royal Authority, enacted on this day by a servant of the Board of Admiralty for crimes against God, the people of Amuresca, and the Pedigree Counsel of Lords. You have no rights save those of life and appealing your crimes in a Royal Court of Law, when your sentence is determined by said Court of Law—"

"Wait," I coughed again, nearly choking, "wh—you must be fucking with me!"

Before I could say any more, my vision went black. Not because I'd lost consciousness, but because someone had wrestled a blinding muzzle over my head and mouth. They tightened the straps behind my ears before I could say another word, and then began manacling my wrists.

Three Months Later

I was losing weight. Not because I was being underfed, but because I couldn't fucking tolerate the food here.

Being sick for weeks aboard the Fenrir hadn't helped, either. I hadn't gotten seasick in my life, not even when I'd first taken to being on a ship. My father had always said sea legs were in our blood. But going off alcohol, combined with a host of debilitating injuries and the treatment for said injuries, had secured my utter misery for the entirety of the trip. If I wasn't sleeping off the nausea or chills from the previous day, I was entering into a new round of them. They had me bled and force-fed teas that were supposed to help, poultices that smelled like shit and the permeating stench ensured I retched up whatever I'd eaten that day whether I was feeling ill before then or not.

To their credit, the Physician earnestly seemed to be trying to keep me alive. He was a soft-spoken, small man, canine of course… and he seemed to mean well. I tried to do what he told me.

The navy men who handled me whenever I needed to be moved, have water tossed over me to rinse off the filth, or to come in and out to get my bucket were less kind. They held off on outright beating me, but addressed me with every manner of slur and often pinned me to the far wall with an oar when they wanted me out of the way. The few times an officer had come to talk to me to explain what I was being accused of… the specifics of which were no surprise to me… they were no more kind. Slightly less swearing, but no less bile and contempt. The big mastiff in particular seemed to despise me, and, given the coat he wore, he was the Captain of this vessel and a Pedigree. So, I could take a guess why.

The worst part of all of it, though… the worst part by far… was that Fathom Roccosal was in the cell opposite mine.

I don't know when they'd captured him, and I didn't care. At some point after I'd leapt onto the Fenrir, I suppose. He'd been hot on my heels running into a wave of Amurescan navy men, after all. The only frustration was that my allies hadn't killed him to spare me the humiliation of sharing my current situation with him.

Lotus was alive, that much the Captain here had assured me of. They were less inclined to arrest her, despite her dubious legal status, because she had no specific warrant out on her head for crimes committed against Amuresca. It made sense. Luther had been working with her, and apparently so had the wolfhound. She hunted pirates and privateers; so did the Cerberus fleet. They may not have been friendly, but they had every reason to leave her independent.

The Manoratha had been forced to retreat following the assault on Roccosal's ships. Which… was bullshit, but I was glad at least to hear that my men had gotten away, even if they hadn't gotten any spoils out of it. They'd never had to board, at least. Or even get close enough to suffer much in the way of cannon fire. So, I'd probably lost few, if any, men. The Amur seemed content enough just to have me in custody; they'd either not wanted the bloodshed and the risk of trying to take down my ship or they had only really wanted to punish me.

A fact which I accepted, given what I was being arrested for. It stung just a little, knowing my men hadn't pushed the offensive. But they would have lost, and they had standing orders for any situation like this. No one life was worth the lives of the entire crew. Not even mine.

If Lotus was fighting for my fate with the Amur, I had no idea. And Luther….

I'd heard nothing from him. The Captain here didn't want to speak to me about him; he seemed particularly cagey on the subject for some reason. I think if he were dead, he'd have told me and probably blamed it on me somehow. So, I had to hope he'd survived his injuries.

But if he had he wasn't trying to help me. And that hurt, somehow worse than imagining he was dead. Which was selfish, I know. But it's how I felt.

Roccosal was… oddly calm, accepting of his fate and his treatment. And he was enduring it better than I was, at least mentally. Just stung all the more, really. We didn't talk much, especially in that first week. I was too sick to do much of anything besides lie curled up in my own squalor and pass out intermittently.

I seized. More than once. Honestly it was hard to tell in between the bouts of sickness. The one silver lining to all of that was that the guards attested it to my current condition, rather than a born weakness. And none of them seemed to give a shit. I seized, and suffered… and the only one who noticed was the dhole.

After the first week, we talked. Because what the fuck else were we going to do? It started off about how you'd imagine… with him taunting me for falling prey to my own traitorous inclinations, a prisoner to the very bedfellows I'd signed my soul away to… etcetera. That led to my pointing out to him how much of a hypocrite he was, for conducting his 'empire' the same way as the Amur and the Huudari he claimed to so despise. And that's when he surprised me.

"I never wanted it," he drawled, his voice permanently a rasp now, from some kind of infection he had in his chest. The Physician said it was a common affliction for people who'd suffered as many injuries in such rapid succession as he had. I knew the affliction myself, having seen it happen to men in my crew. Water in the lungs. It would probably kill him.

And I couldn't help but feel that, even for him, it was a terrible death for a sailor. To drown while dry.

"Wanted what?" I muttered, not bothering to rise from where I was slumped.

"The flesh peddling," he muttered. "I know that's what you'n the others who refused the pirate alliance took issue with."

"You decorate your ships with the skulls of your enemies," I said, aghast. "Pickle your own dead men so you can harvest them for their bones… it isn't just the slaving."

"It's a rite for the dead," he explained, oddly sedate and peaceful in tone, considering what he was discussing. "It's how my people honor our fallen and carry their spirits with us into battle. My ships are my fortresses, every day aboard them is a battle, and those men died under my command. The rite is for the most loyal, it's a sign of my respect for them." He rolled his head to the side to address me directly for the last part. "You cock. You're a bloody tribesperson, you didn't bother thinking we Dholes might have our own ways? How… Colonial… of you."

I bit back the burning embarrassment at having my disconnection from my tribal lineage thrown in my face, but reminded myself what really mattered here. "But… you said you knew the slaving was losing you allies. If you knew that," I said, frustrated, "and you didn't want to do it… then why? I mean, fuck. It isn't even like you put restrictions… made it hard on'm… taxed the shit out of it. It was your bloody mainstay."

"D'you know how many previously collared folk I have on my rosters?" he chuckled dryly. "We have a Liberator, for fuck's sake. It's how I bolstered recruiting when I was building my fleet. We even hired on women."

"I'd heard that," I said, confused. "It never squared with what your island became, eventually. Never made sense to me."

"So… many… hauls… were just that," he said, flexing his claws and staring up dully at the ceiling. "Just… people. My Captains wouldn't have it. They wouldn't abide by every other take being worthless. You can only kill so many'f 'em to send a message before you've got outright rebellion. Something had to give. It's just…" He tongued at his maw, where he was missing several teeth. All of his fangs. The Amur had taken them.

For the gold.

"It's just a part of the world," he said, at last. His voice had that gargle in it. It got like that sometimes when he was about to have a bout of coughing. "Not natural, just… a part of man's world. And it always will be." He turned to regard me. "There is no such thing as freedom, no such thing as a free world, so long as men draw breath."

"That's not true," I said, my jowls twitching. "You've just given up."

"If you try to maintain that righteous lie," he chuckled dryly, "that you can fight them on even footing, without somehow using the same methods they all do? You lose. Every time. If there were a better way, someone'd be using it to rule the world right now. All you can do is ensure you're the one at the top of the pile. "His chest shuddered, a racking cough working its way wetly up out of his mouth. "And do right by your own."

"Fuck you," I growled, pressing my nose against my knees. "I found my own way. I don't need yours or theirs."

"Yeah?" he chuckled around another painful-sounding cough. "How's that working out for you?"

That was the last 'conversation', if you can call it that, that we ever had. Anything past that was murmured, short sentences in the dark, as his condition worsened, and mine improved. And then, we were in Amuresca.

Everything about being hauled off that boat, drug down the dock through a procession of leering navy men, busy dockworkers, and gawking onlookers was a blur. I wasn't even sure what city we were in until much later. Leifolk, apparently. It hardly mattered.

The one bright spot had been the moment when I'd been turned on the docks to be led down a straightaway, and I'd seen the Cerberus. She was docked in the bay close to the Fenrir, the two ships had probably been sailing side by side the whole while; I just hadn't been able to see her from the hold. I had no particular affection for the ship, but there was no mistaking the silhouette standing near her figurehead, watching us. The triangular ears, the bushy tail, even the way he stood, I could pick out by now.

He was wearing his red coat, but his arms weren't through the sleeves. It looked like the wolfhound was standing at his side, supporting him. Or perhaps I was just imagining that. Because hoping, even briefly, that the reason he hadn't helped me yet was because he'd been bedridden with injuries, was soothing the ache inside me.

I was processed at some kind of government navy office. I hardly paid attention to the specifics. Everything on my warrant was precisely what I'd thought it would be. Some trumped-up charges, but mostly accurate. One in particular that would seal my fate. I stood through it all, side by side with Roccosal. His list of crimes was longer... but only just barely.

I waited for the cattle dog to arrive, to explain our agreement, to pardon me, but he never came. And that's when the real, mortal fear set in.

My court date was a month after that. The sentence was death by hanging. I couldn't very well plead for any kind of leniency. In addition to the years of Privateering that were literally on record, many of which had been for rival nations, they had evidence of more specific crimes.

I should have left that bloody pistol on the deck.

But I hadn't. I'd carried it on me for years. And maybe this was ultimately why. I had to entertain the possibility that I'd wanted to be punished at this point. It's the only explanation that made any sense.

I wasn't given a sentence date right away. For some reason, they brought me to an island prison. A dismal, dreary place where I spent the next... two... months. I was apparently a high-value prisoner, enough that I got my own cell. Somewhere no one could harm me.

Or talk to me.

The guards didn't even see me most of the time. They took the bucket through a latched opening in the underside of the door— the same spot my food was pushed through. Grits with what could charitably called 'meat' of some kind, ground and dried, tasting of copper. Organ meat, probably. Dried, salted fish sometimes. Lemon juice in my water, so the poor fare didn't kill me.

In the beginning I tried to keep my strength up, but... the solitude and the creeping hopelessness eventually got the better of me. I waited, and I waited... and help didn't come. And the worst part was? Some part of me felt I deserved it.

Underneath the years of Privateering and the blithe, reckless, jovial mask I wore, the truth of it was I was still sometimes horrified by myself. And by the things I'd done. The things I'd seen. The things I'd seen other men do. The truth of the world, outside the little bubble of comfort I'd been raised in, was so much darker than I'd ever imagined. And I had well and truly become a part of that darkness. I couldn't hide from it when my mind was so cruelly clear.

Here we were again, the same thoughts, except now I was really entertaining them. No one knows what sort of a person they'll be when they stare down the inevitability of death. I'd thought, because of my condition, because I'd spent my whole life poised on the edge of it, never knowing when it could take me but always knowing it was a possibility, that I'd be more prepared. Braver in the face of it. At least resolved, in some way. More than a layperson.

I finally had my answer. And unfortunately, I found I was none of those things. I was no stoic, resolved, hardened man. Weepingly afraid didn't fit, either. I was... adrift. Anxious and uncertain how to feel, unable to moor myself in any kind of peace.

When the Priests came with my sentence date, they tried... repeatedly... to assert the futility of holding onto my 'atheistic beliefs', as they called it. When would holy men stop talking about denial of god as though it were a religion in and of itself?

They gave me the usual pitch. That I had nothing to lose by accepting their truth. That the risk of denying it was worse than any gamble I might be taking believing in their god. What harm could it do, to accept faith near the end? Even if I didn't believe it in my heart, it would be better to swear myself to him, to absolve myself of sin, before I met him. Just in case.

What could it hurt?

Well, I didn't particularly feel like bathing myself in guilt and fear, right before the end. Let alone for the sake of a fairytale concocted thousands of years ago to keep one species of people in power. They didn't have to understand. I wanted no part in their assurances, their lies, even if I could believe in any of it. I didn't want to die in denial.

Mostly, when I contemplated death? I was sad. And I guess that's sort of pathetic, isn't it? Because ultimately, I was sad for myself. But it wasn't as though I didn't understand why this was all happening to me. There was a very clear line from actions to consequences, here I'd been making my own choices since the day I'd left my family.

Moreover though, I was sad because… it seemed like I was going to die alone. And that confirmed some very dark things in the back of my mind that I'd long believed about myself, but rarely entertained.

The execution would be public. They'd make a show of it even, I'm sure. I was infamous here in Carvecia, in Mataa, all over the world. I'd secured a legacy for myself, alright. And they'd celebrate my death in more ports than just this one.

But I'd be alone on that stage. They'd strung Roccosal's corpse out by the pier a month ago. They hadn't even had the chance to execute him… he'd died of his infection. In a twisted way, I'd gotten my wish.

His death made me sad, too. I only knew of it because the Priests had told me of it. In some ill-fated attempt to hold him up, and his refusal until death to atone, as a lesson to learn from. I wasn't sad he was gone; the world was certainly a better place without him. But he should have died in our last fight. Or against anyone else in that melee. He should have died then… not by this drawn-out misery. It's not that he deserved any sympathy whatsoever, I just didn't think anyone should die like that.

The Cerberus fleet wasn't even in port any more. I had one small slit of a window in my cell, and it faced the bay. I stared out of it most days for as long as I could bear. I had to cling to some of the flagstones to get high enough to see out of it. The day I'd seen his ships missing…

… that had been a dark day.

Somehow, time had passed faster after that. I stopped eating for the most part. When the pain in my stomach was too much, I forced a meal down. I waited.

And I thought about my family. A lot.

I wished, again and again, that I'd had the nerve to contact my father over these many years. Force him to meet with me somehow. I'd kept up tabs on the Reeds as well as I could since I'd left, and, last I knew, he was still alive. Ailing, old, and unable to travel much anymore. But alive. If I'd wanted it enough, I could have gone to him. My brother was the Magnate now, traveling between Amuresca and Carvecia. There were many times we'd been close, many times I'd known we were close, and still....

My thoughts fell into this repeating spiral, every day. When you were alone this long, it's like your body and your mind desperately clung to any bearings they could find. In my case, it was the passing of the shadows in the room, the visual representation of each day coming and going. My thoughts inevitably walked the same paths, the same times of day. Brief horror upon waking and discovering it was all real, anew. Self-pity, then sadness. Then guilt, as I reminded myself I'd made my own bed. Then... loneliness. Wishing for anyone, anyone to relieve me of it. Someone to get angry with, like the Priests. Someone to lash out at, like the gaurds. Someone to cling to and plead with.

Someone to hate, other than myself.

When the door—the whole entire door—opened that day, I wasn't prepared for it. By my count, I was still two days away from my execution date. I was almost looking forward to it at this point.

My whole body shook as I twisted over onto my side in my bunk, blinking blearily at the yawning doorway. It was early morning, the sun through the one small window was directly on my bunk, the only time of day I could enjoy it with any level of comfort, and it blinded me to the darkness in the hallway beyond. It took until the door had shut and the man had stepped cautiously inside for my eyes to finally adjust.

"Good God," he breathed out. "You were supposed to be kept healthy. What have they been feeding you? Are you still ill?"

I lunged off my bunk, claws scrabbling at the stone floor, flinging myself halfway across the room with a ferocity I never knew myself capable of before, let alone now. And he let me. He let me pin him to the wall, my fist bunched in his overcoat, my body pressing his back flat.

His gold eyes were wide, his teeth obviously clenched in his muzzle, and he was staring up at me with alarm. But he held off from doing any more than that. Just stood there and waited. Like he expected to be struck and would do nothing to stop me.

"How..." I barely found my voice, "...fucking... dare you! Come to me now?!"

Luther swallowed, dropping his eyes for just a moment. Just a moment, but it was a concession I'd never expected from him. Which left me even more unprepared for the next.

"I'm sorry," he said, his voice laced with genuine regret. "Let me explain..."

243

I released him, stumbling back away from the wall and collapsing in the middle of the room. He followed me, seeming concerned and looking as though he were going to offer a hand.

"Don't," I snapped.

That was all I had in me. All this time, I'd been waiting for someone to talk to. And now, the man I... probably most wanted to talk to... was here. And I had nothing to say to him. No words that would come readily.

"Alright..." he said carefully, observing me from where he was. He looked concerned, but measured. As ever. Not overly emotional.

And there was certainly no pity there.

"Just," I stammered for a moment, then pressed on, "just talk to me."

He gave me a pause, as if waiting for more. Then he simply nodded. "Alright," he repeated. "I'll do just that."

I stayed where I was, moored to the cold stone floor. And he began to speak.

"I was injured, after... after everything," he said, slowly lowering himself into a sitting position across from me, legs folded neatly in front of him. "I'd lost a lot of blood, and they kept me heavily sedated for a time so I didn't strain the muscles in my abdomen. It was a near miss... nothing vital. But they were concerned it would get worse, and... it could have... if you hadn't...."

I stared at him, accepting the unspoken thanks. But I said nothing.

"And then there was the risk of infection," he continued. "But I had the best care, so... here I sit." He didn't sound profoundly happy about the fact, but he also didn't sound aggrieved. Neutral.

"I'm sorry my fleet didn't honor the agreement with yours, but I had no ability to assert my authority. All the same. You know the moment you set foot on that ship, I couldn't have helped you regardless, right?" He pointed out. "The Fenrir is Amurescan soil. And you have several outstanding warrants. Some of which I've only recently learned of." He paused. "I'd like to talk about one in particular."

"You never came to visit me in that cell," I said venomously. "Nor here. Not for months. What are you even doing here, now? I die in two days. Need to assuage your conscience? Is that it?"

"I have been appealing your case," he said, annunciating each word. "And I couldn't see you when we were at sea, because you were on the Fenrir. And I was moved to the Cerberus. I was barely conscious for most of that trip, anyway."

"Lucky you," I growled. I hated how much sense his argument made, but it was doing little to diffuse my anger.

"Yes, the Physician kept me apprised of your troubles," he said quietly. "Apparently quite a lot of it was due to Shaw's insistence on keeping a dry ship."

"A what?" I said, wincing as the transition to speaking again made my head throb. Or maybe it was the hunger.

"The man prefers diligent sobriety," he explained. "They don't even keep watered beer for rations on that vessel. The barest amount necessary for keeping the water potable, that's it. And I doubt that would have been enough for you. When's the last time you were sober before all of that?"

"Shaw," I ignored his question. "The mastiff? One of your Captains?"

He nodded. "Be glad you weren't aboard Singh's vessel, that's all I'll say. Shaw is a hard-ass, but he's by the book. Singh would have subjected you to cruelties beyond what regulations allow."

"Good people you have at your side," I muttered derisively, then let my paw fall to my knee with a slap. "Get to the point of why you're here. If you'd gotten me pardoned, you'd have led with that. And we'd be having this conversation outside."

"Aye," he agreed ruefully. "I went up through the High Court in Treneval, even. Exposed more of my dealings with you than I probably should have for my own sake. But I failed. You're right about that."

My heart sunk, and it was a real disappointment, because I'd thought I had no further to sink. But apparently, I'd been holding onto one last thread of hope, somewhere. And now, it was gone. Denholme was the very last person out there who could have helped me.

I was going to die.

"I bought you time," he said quietly. "A stay of execution, at least until you're well. Johannes helped me, believe it or not. Unearthed this ancient doctrine that states you have to have sustained no undue damage in the custody of a holy man before you can be legally executed. Even if your soul isn't, your body must be absolved of mortal sin before you meet your maker. That includes cruelty and injuries subjected upon your person by anyone under the banner of God."

"I wasn't harmed by any priest I can recall," I muttered.

"Shaw was responsible for your care aboard the Fenrir," he said. "He ministers to his local congregation. You're fortunate one of my Captains happens to be pious. We were able to argue the illness and general degradation and worsening of your condition aboard his vessel were his liability, and, thus, you had to be healed and recover before he could atone."

"You may as well have just let me die sooner," I said, refusing to look at him. "You've only lengthened my suffering."

"Oh, stop being so dramatic," he said. The light tone, and the lack of care with which he said the outrageously cold statement, caught me so off-guard I was mute in the wake of it. "I also used the time to arrange a few things on your behalf." He continued. "But first, I need you to talk to me."

"What more could you possibly want me to say at this point?" I asked disbelievingly.

"Benjamin Hornfell," he said, the name leaving his mouth like a pronouncement of guilt, already.

It was the same name I'd heard shouted, read off legal papers and whispered about in my presence for months now. And it's exactly what I most feared he'd ask about. He'd started asking about it at the start, and I'd deflected. Hoping I could avoid this. Because I had no excuse that would suit. No means of defending myself. Not against this.

He waited a time. Quite a while. Eventually, finally, he spoke softly, "So, it's true."

"I had his pistol on me when I was arrested," I said dully. "What do you think?"

"Why on earth would you do that?" he asked, confused. "Carry the evidence of such a crime on your person? Do you have a death wish? Were you proud of what you did, for some reason—"

"No!" I said quickly, vehemently. Then I backed off my anger, my voice falling more desperate. "I don't know," I said, threadbare. "I don't know why I kept it. I don't know why I kept it with me. I... I wish I could tell you."

"You don't strike me as the type for trophies," he said, measuredly. "Not like the dhole. Oddities. Trinkets, maybe. But Ben's pistol was distinctive. The rubies inlaid in the grip... I can't believe I didn't remember it. It's infamous for all the wrong reasons, now. The antiquities dealers have been looking for it for years. Since the slaughter—"

"Eighteen men," I bit out. "There were... eighteen. Counting him. We kill dozens, hundreds every time we sink a ship."

"Fine," he said, his voice still hard. "But most men can't boast they've killed eighteen unarmed, bound, and gagged prisoners." He narrowed his eyes at me. "Not even me. And the number I've heard was higher, and... not all men."

"You don't understand," I said, barely above a whisper.

"Then please, enlighten me," he said openly. "Because while I'm not always the best judge of a man's character, I consider myself analytical-ly-skilled, at least, at knowing the capabilities of the men I take up arms with. And this..." his words bled off for a moment as he slowly shook his head. "This doesn't track. Not with the man I thought I was coming to know."

I looked at the door. "Are we alone?" I asked, voice low. "Well and truly?"

"It took hell to arrange it, but my plans necessitated it... so no hall guard today." He nodded. "The nearest guard is two floors down. Please, explain what happened." His eyes softened for just a moment. "How does a man like yourself, who flinches from blood and drinks to forget killing even his worst enemies… how is it you of all people orchestrated the taking of a tiny personal ship, far beneath anything you should have been hunting, and murdered every soul aboard after they'd surrendered? What could old Ben have possibly done to you to deserve such vengeance?"

"It wasn't him," I closed my eyes. "It was the family aboard. Do you know why Benjamin Hornfell took the Avonwind across the eastern passage in the middle of winter to begin with?"

"Some sort of family emergency," he said, "I'd been led to believe, in any case."

"I…" my throat closed up. The tears came. It was instant, there was no stopping it. I was too weak to fight it.

To his credit, he said nothing. No assurances, no patronizing words, no admonition. He just watched me crumble in stoic silence. When I was finally able to speak again, my voice was terribly weak. "I had… a cousin…."

His eyes widened, marginally. He was on the verge of realizing. He probably knew vaguely of the tangential connection by now.

"Her name was Mischa," I said, trembling. "I… loved her. I have loved… so few people… in my life… like I loved her. She was smart, independent, witty, funny… every other retort in my vocabulary, every good impulse, I probably learned from her. She never made me feel…" I could barely get the words out, "…lesser. Because of my condition."

"Slow down," he eased, putting a hand out but stopping short of touching me in any way. "Take whatever time you need."

"She was my best friend," I said, the shape of the cattle dog blurring before me as I squeezed my eyes partially closed. "And when I left my family I left… her… angry and disappointed in me and… alone, facing a fate I didn't know the risks of then, but—"

"She was the Lady on that ship," he said, his jaw tensing. "Wasn't she?"

"She was already dead when I caught up to them," I said, reliving every. God-damned. Moment of it. Memory. By memory.

That little sloop, with its sails stowed, signaling immediate surrender. The ghastly looks on the faces of the crew when we boarded, and several of them realized who I was. The old Captain, retired Navy, threads still hung on his coat, his brown fur graying around the muzzle. The pistol with the ruby grip, as he threw it in the pile of armaments.

The small, cramped staircase as I descended into their quarters.

The figure shrouded, wrapped, laid out with care and affection with dried flowers and herbs around her bed.

The smell.

Sometimes I caught the whiff of death, and horrifically... I thought of her. The curse of a canine was to spend your life connecting scents to people, to memories. And for some reason, the smell of her rotting there, in that bed, had erased every good memory of her scent. It was overlaid by this one putrid, horrible moment.

Forever.

Maybe... maybe the gallows wouldn't be so bad. I would never again have to smell death and think of Mischa.

"Come back to me," he said. I blinked up at him, and... it was like we were in the coffin again. The way he'd looked down at me in that moment, begging me back to the world of the living.

I felt the strength to press on. I swallowed it all back, pressed it down, at least long enough to get this out. This one man, at least, would know.

"I thought her husband was just a fool," I said. "I left on the day she married. I wanted her to come with me...."

The cattle dog gave me space to continue. And eventually, I did. "But she didn't," I said, gritting my teeth a moment. "She didn't want to. She was worried the life I was heading towards would get her killed, or worse, and... and she was right. It barely took a few hours. That very night, someone tried to kill me. And she was a woman without the basic privileges and respect I had. More worldly, more wise, braver than me... but she was right to worry about throwing her lot in with the kind of men I did. Let alone with such reckless abandon. I should have kept that in mind when I made my plans. I should have done more to secure her safety... her escape..."

"Escape?" he asked uncertainly. "From?"

"Marriage," I said. And for some reason when I said that, a word, an institution most would consider innocuous, Luther leaned back and looked grim. Like something I'd said had resonated with him. "I didn't understand how much danger she could be in, just being a wife. Her husband was droll, but he seemed harmless to me. I tried to keep in contact with her, through the years. Most of my letters probably never made it. But at length... finally... two of hers reached me."

I sniffed noisily. "She was pregnant. For the second time, and... she'd lost the first. I knew; I'd kept up with my family as much as I could. What I didn't know is how dangerous it had been for her. How it had nearly killed her. She was terrified of it happening again. She told me she'd tried to leave. Tried to run away. Because her husband was intent on having pups, and she didn't want to die. Some women just can't have children easily. It isn't their fault."

"I know," he assured me. "You don't need to convince me. I don't believe in all that horse shit."

248

"She was so scared," I choked. "You didn't know her. She didn't speak frankly about her fears, let alone in writing. She'd sent several letters... two of which I got at the same time. The one, earlier, asking me for help. For a way out. And then the second, telling me she was with child...."

I looked up at him. "She wouldn't have allowed herself to conceive. Not willingly. You tell me how that happened."

He was still holding my gaze, but his eyes were distant. Thoughts briefly somewhere else, maybe.

"Don, her husband," I spat, "weak man... he thought they could make the passage home in enough time... so his child would be born on Carvecian soil. That's what mattered to him. He knew Hornfell because he was a friend of his father's. I don't know how they arranged it, but he offered to take them on his personal ship. I was frantic, trying to track her down. Shot my crew's morale to hell, chasing down that one little ship... paying outrageous sums to find out how and where they were traveling from, what route they were taking..."

I lifted my chin slowly. "But I found them."

"Why kill every soul aboard?" He asked at length. He sounded more understanding now, but still unable to put the pieces together. "Just sheer rage?"

"I didn't kill every soul aboard," I said bitterly. "She died giving birth. Early. Before I found them. She died in agony, bringing his child into the world. Continuing the family line. Little girl... small. So small.... He named her Emma."

"The pup lived?" he asked, shocked.

I nodded. "He at least thought to have a Physician aboard. The Physician was married to a woman who'd served as a midwife, and she was aboard, too. They did their best. I don't blame them for what happened to Mischa." I breathed out, slowly. "That's why I let them live."

"And the others...?"

"I killed Don first," I said coldly. "He made the mistake of opening his goddamned mouth. Said it was his 'right' to have an heir. I shot him between the eyes. It's as close as I've ever come to feeling nothing when I killed someone. The rest," I knitted my fingers over my knees. And here, the guilt settled on me like the weight it truly was. With no alcohol, women, drug, or distraction to stifle it, it was so much heavier. "Emma... was born with my condition."

"...oh," he said quietly.

"Or at least, we thought she might have been," I said. "The Physician said the seizures could have been because of how prematurely she was born. We didn't know at the time. Since then, since she was a babe, they've never recurred. So, maybe she's been spared the curse. Maybe they'll manifest later in her life. I don't know. Regardless of what may have happened, Don was the heir apparent to a massive cotton fortune, a dozen plantations or more, I can't fucking remember. Wealthy. Powerful. Possibly more so than my own family. And Emma would have belonged to them. He was their only son. They would have claimed her."

"You killed everyone aboard that ship so that his family would never know they had an heir?"

"The Physician said," my voice quavered, "Don... discussed the possibility... of drowning the pup. When they realized she might be sick. She was a day old, and he was already talking about discarding her, because she might be useless to him."

He had no response to that. Only dropped his muzzle, his brows creasing.

"I came to the decision quickly," I said. "Maybe it was anger, maybe I had to put the blame for it all on someone. I was in a dark place. And yes... I regret it. But there were masts on the horizon, navy vessels like yours. We had no time to consider our options. And I was terrified for Emma. That no matter how I tried to protect her, even somehow if I kept her, that she'd be pulled back into the clutches of that bloody family eventually. Or the Reeds."

That made his ears perk. "You were that scared of your own family?"

"No," I said. "I've never been frightened of them, as people. But the family is a Cartel, Luther. It's the obligations that trap you, not the people. Mischa... never escaped. She died, bound up in her obligations. Doing what was right for the family. I don't think she even went to my uncle or my father for help, because if she had, they would have murdered Don themselves. She was ashamed, afraid she was failing. She asked me for help because I was outside of all of it."

Flashes assaulted me behind my closed eyelids. A grayish yellow morning, a whimpering, tiny creature clutched in my arm, wrapped in a blanket I could tell Mischa had made herself. At some point in her pregnancy, she had begun to plan for the little pup's arrival, despite knowing it could very well kill her.

And all I could think of was how scared she must have been. Terrified of her own body, unable to prevent what was coming. How she'd had no choice.

If Emma's existence was known, she'd be drawn back into the same world, the same lack of choices, that killed her mother. Inevitably, inexorably... and she'd be as trapped by its deadly laws and expectations as Mischa had been. I wanted to save her, as I'd been unable to save Mischa. I wanted to at least give her a chance.

"I press-ganged the Physician and his wife," I said. "Wasn't a hard sell. Kept them with us on the Manoratha until I was certain they'd never speak of the pup's origin. To anyone. Ever. They're alive, last I knew," I finally opened my eyes again. "Somewhere in Carvecia, inland. Living well. They'll never need to work again."

"And Emma?"

"I knew the only place she'd be safe, ultimately, was in obscurity," I answered. "So, you'll forgive me if I tell you no more. She's very well-cared for, and, when she's old enough, I plan to ensure she has a crack at whatever kind of life she wants." I was silent a beat before continuing with the finale. The part he'd been trying to get out of me this whole time. "I did it. I killed every soul on that ship, save them. Your Captain Ben. His First Mate. All the deckhands. The cook. All of them."

"You did it yourself?"

"What does it matter?" I sighed. "That would have been cruel, killing them one at a time, while they heard their fellows die. No, I ordered them all shot, of course. At once. I pulled the trigger on Hornfell myself. But it doesn't matter whose pistols dropped each individual soul... I gave the order."

"Ben was a retired, well-liked Captain," he said, his expression hard to read. "I met him at a few events. Can't say we were close, but he had a lot of friends. You really stepped in shit, here."

"And?" I asked, waiting for the hammer to fall.

"... and I understand it to a certain extent," he said at length. "But the only one who will ever fully appreciate it is you. This... this is the crime they all want to hang you for."

"I know."

"All the Privateering, even Piracy, is easier to excuse. But this is flat-out murder they can sell to the masses. Make an example of you... hold you up as a villain for the ages. The representation of Privateering gone wrong, defeated and swinging from the pier. Alongside Fathom Roccosal, the infamous Pirate. Two sides of the same coin, is what they'll say."

"I know."

"Then why keep the pistol?" he demanded insistently. "You knew it would literally hang you."

"I don't know!" I repeated my sentiment from earlier, laughing mirthlessly for some reason. "I don't... know. I... wish I had an answer for you. But I don't. I couldn't let go of it. Hornfell wasn't even the man I hated; he was just there. And..." I stumbled over my words, "...maybe that's it, right there. Maybe I wanted to remind myself that I'd killed indiscriminately. Remind myself of what I was. I don't know. If I'd wanted to hide the crime, I would have shelled the ship when we left."

"They'd seen your Manoratha by then," he shook his head, "lurking near the scene of the crime."

"They didn't need to know I'd shot them all while they were bound," I said bitterly.

"Everyone, Johannes and my Captains included," he said carefully, "thinks you were making some kind of statement. For the life of me, that never made sense. It didn't fit. Not with everything else I knew about you."

"Does it fit now?" I asked, unable to mask the shame in my voice.

"... yes," he said softly. "Unfortunately."

He stood then, and I didn't have the energy to follow suit. I just watched him, as he paced his way back over to the door. "What now?" I asked him. "You said you had some kind of 'plan' in the works. I hesitate to get my hopes up where you're concerned, but—"

He knocked on the wooden door for some reason. Then said, "Did you hear? You should come in now."

"You bastard!" I recoiled, falling back on my palms. "You unbelievable, lying—"

The door opened. And my father stepped inside.

I was too stunned to breathe.

He was stooped, graying and white in places he'd never been when last I'd seen him, his body somewhat shrunken down... but not frail. That man could never be frail. Not to me.

His blue eyes, the same as mine, were wet with tears, and his pace was addled by a limp as he crossed the small room towards me. He had a cane, I think, I hardly noticed. He threw something to the ground as he approached me and fell before me, pulling me into his arms.

"I never thought of you as 'lesser'," he choked, that voice—that voice that I'd looked to as a beacon of strength throughout my whole young life—faltering and wavering with a sob. "I just wanted to protect you."

I hardly knew what to say or do, except cling to him. He smelled the same. He smelled the same as I remembered, like cedar cologne and familiar fur. He was real, and here, and—

The door shut, Luther leaving without another word. I think he paused for a moment to look at us, but then he was gone. I didn't even have a chance to thank him, or to say good-bye, but he seemed to know this time between my father and I was not to be intruded upon.

I held fast to my father's mane, familiar relics from my past still threaded through it, same as they'd always been since I was a child being carried around by him. Turquoise, worn coins and beads, the mementos and treasures of dozens of lifetimes, passed down through our tribe. I hadn't gotten to spend as much time with my father growing up as I wanted, but somehow, I was awash with memories of being held by him, just like this. Maybe he'd been with me more than I'd thought....

"Please," he begged, "please don't tell me, all this time, that you thought so ill of me because we fought over that rotting boat."

"She was a burden," I said, my voice crumbling. "Defective. I thought… you'd be better off without the both of us—"

"It is a ship!" He pulled back enough that he could look me in the eyes. "You are my son!"

I felt the first, fragile inclination to smile I'd had in months. It made it, trembling and weak, to my muzzle. It felt raw, almost painful. And a moment later, it fell away, as I remembered why.

"I'm sorry," I said helplessly. "I'm so sorry. Please, please don't stay here. Don't watch. I don't need you here for that."

Every word pained me. Because I did very much want him here when I died. I wanted nothing more.

His expression fell grim, but oddly determined. He reached for my mane, what little of it had grown out, and brushed it aside back into place over my shoulders. "Not my boy," he growled. "They will not hang my boy."

"You know what I did—"

"You said it yourself," he snapped. "I would have killed the man myself if I'd had the chance. I don't… approve… of the life you're leading, but—"

"You don't need to excuse it," I choked, my nose dripping as I let it fall. "I feel the man I am. I don't want this, but maybe… it's right…."

"I don't care what's right!" he roared. His hands tightened on my shoulders. And when he spoke again, his words were measured. Angry, but calm. "I have read… every book you ever touched, since you left. Trying to understand you. Desperately."

"Dad…."

"I can't say I share… whatever views led you to… this," he said, frustrated. "But I've learned more about the kind of man you wanted to be. I think you were naïve to ever believe any of this utopian, anarchist nonsense was possible," and here he sounded briefly angry again. "But. With whatever years I have left, I want to stop reading these bloody books, and… come to know my son, as much as I can. Even if that means arguing with you, worrying myself to death over you, hating the things you do. Grayson."

He leaned in, embracing me again. "Our family hasn't survived as long as we have because of our trade empire. That's just the work of this generation, and it is not a legacy worth losing our bonds over. It is a means to make coin. That's all. Our family has survived as long as we have through bountiful and slim times alike, because we persist in our connections to one another, regardless of adversity. Fortunes come and go. We will be destitute again one day. But, we, as people, form a chain. That's our fortitude, that is how we endure. The trinkets are a reminder of that, but what matters is that we not lose sight of one another. Like linking hands in the snow."

"I got my gift for prose from you clearly," I said with a half-hearted, sniffing chuckle.

"You sure as hell didn't get my sense," he growled.

"I'm sorry I didn't explain… didn't reach out," I said softly. "Tell you what really happened with Mischa."

He clenched his jaw, then nodded, shakily. "The river runs both ways. We were, both of us, stubborn, all this while."

"I hate that it had to be now," I laughed bitterly. "But I guess, better late than never. I'm so sorry, dad."

"I don't know how you did it, but you seem to have won over a sodding Admiral," he said, ruefully impressed. "He's going to get you free of this."

"He already lost the appeals," I said, my shoulders slumping. "I'm sorry if he hadn't told you, yet."

"Oh, lad," my father sighed. "I didn't mean legally."

～ ～

I did my best to clean up in the hours following his visit. I tied my start of a new mane back and secured the turquoise my father had given me into it with knots that would hold until it grew out. Three beads. His own. He'd cut them out, to replace the ones I'd lost. I hadn't been able to help him through the tears.

I used the wash basin I'd had provided in the cell this whole time to finally… wash. At least some. And I ate my meal. There'd be no undoing the weakness of my body with one meal, but that had been due to my own carelessness, and I was resolved to do my part despite it.

I tucked the small slip of paper—one of the things my father had left me with—into the worn, scratchy britches they'd given me to wear here. Scrawled on it was the name and address of the dark market courier in Treneval who would ferry my letters to my father going forward. He would be in the city long enough to know if I escaped successfully, but he wanted to hear from me often from now on.

I hoped, rather than believed, we would be able to meet in person. At least sometimes. It would be highly difficult, the both of us being known figures in most modern circles. But Cullen Reed was a tenacious man, when he was determined to get his way on something. So, who knew.

I was relieved to discover he'd never truly thought I was responsible for Mischa's death. That had been my greatest fear all these years and a big part of why I hadn't dared make contact with him. But my cowardice had cost him the full story, the truth of it, and the not knowing had taken its toll. I wasn't certain that was a wound that could ever be truly mended.

But at least now, we could try.

I'd never forgive myself for what I'd done. He'd said nothing of forgiving me for that, either. It was probably a question I didn't want answered. But, maybe…

… maybe you weren't supposed to forgive yourself in a situation like this. Maybe living with it forever gnawing at your insides was penance. Not the kind Priests sell to you, but the real kind. Like grief. Never truly gone, always there beneath the surface, like the jagged edge of a reef. Waiting to cut you open whenever you got too close to it.

It was a hard, unsatisfying resolution. But the world was hard and unsatisfying sometimes.

Because nothing was normal about this day, my dinner was chicken and buttered bread—real chicken. I was almost afraid my body would reject real food after this long, but I'd always had a strong stomach.

And I got to eat it with Luther.

He'd rejoined me shortly after my father had left. My dad had departed promising he'd see me again soon on a small island in neutral waters, a few days' sail from here. He'd come across the whole bloody ocean to see me, in failing health, and neither of us were about to let that go to waste. He and Luther were both sparse with me on details as to how I'd be transported once the 'escape' was sprung, but the assurance that I'd see him again, soon, was going a long way towards lifting my spirits.

Given the events that had all led up to this, the horror of my still very real death sentence hanging over me, and the many gut-wrenching revelations of the day, you'd think it would have been an awkward, uncomfortable dinner. But honestly, the air between us was so oddly… peaceful. Comfortable.

Friendly, even.

I don't think either of us were ready to say it aloud, but that's what this was. A friendship. At least, the start of one. It felt more like the resolution of a swordfight. Parrying back and forth, going even on blows, drawing blood, then easing off. But there was no denying we'd both been enjoying it, at times.

What can I say? Masochists, both of us. Too alike in some ways, very different in others. I think this kindling spark of connection, this incessant magnetic force to be near someone, even when everything imaginable stood in your way, was what some might call 'finding your soulmate'. I, idiotically, had always thought that was reserved for romantic relationships. Which was especially blind given how many sworn brotherhoods and comrades in arms there were amongst sailors. Even on my own crew. Perhaps especially in my crew, since I'd brought so many disparate people looking for family under my wing.

He gave me a fucking flower. Insisted up and down it wasn't from him, but from someone else who wanted to help me, and was part of his apparently very intricate plan. I don't know why, but at the time, I thought it was that old 'I have a friend who—' excuse, and treated it as such. As an eye-roll-worthy joke. My head was muddy after so much time behind bars, I guess. I'd remember later.

I wanted to hug him, I really did. But even a brotherly embrace was pushing it with an Amurescan man. I accepted the dinner, some conversation, and the first chance I'd had to laugh in months, instead. It felt like it opened up my lungs. It felt like breathing after having my head held underwater right up to the point of death.

When he finally left, I watched him go with a smile. But unlike with my father, it was a sad smile... because those barricades were still up. The line of communication with my family may have reopened, but Luther was still an Amurescan Admiral, with no plans to leave the Navy anytime soon. I had gotten what I wanted at the start of all of this... a ceasefire, and a promise from him that he would not hunt me once I was back out on the water.

Insanely... I sort of wanted him to.

I had to hope fate would bring us back together, in time. I wasn't sure how that would be possible... it would behoove me at this point to stay as far from Amuresca, and Amurescan waters, as I possibly could. But....

I wasn't good at letting go of things I wanted. Even when it was very, very stupid to pursue them.

I fell asleep almost as soon as the sun set, and dreamt of Mischa. Of my home growing up. The first time I'd seen my ship. It was a tangle, much of it nonsensical, a mix of memories and things that never happened. But for once, it didn't end in nightmares.

I woke in the dimmest of morning light with a start to pounding at my door. This wasn't like when Luther had arrived. It was loud, insistent. I obviously couldn't open the door in my cell, so I wasn't certain what purpose it served. Were they waiting for me to be decent?

"Come in?" I called out, confused.

The door unlocked, and the man who stepped inside was—

"Shite," I sighed. "I don't know why I didn't realize it would be you. I should've figured."

The wolfhound's eyes were daggers, dispassionately pinning me down across the room. "Wrists, behind you," he growled out.

I rolled up into a sitting position and obediently put my arms behind my back, rolling my eyes as he approached me. "Ending as we started, huh?"

"I don't know what that means, and I don't care to," he said stiffly, as he clapped the irons over my wrists and tightened the bolt, enough that it hurt. I didn't bother complaining.

"Your name is Johannes, right?" I asked, while he finished affixing them.

"My name is not your concern," he answered.

"We ought to be on a first-name basis after all of this, I feel like," I insisted.

He jerked me to my feet at that, twisting my arms in the process to the point where my biceps burned, my wrists strained, and his grip on my forearm was punishing... bruising. He looked down on me like all those men on the Fenris had, but with more evident emotion.

Shit. I knew hurt when I saw it.

"I knew Ben," he said, his anger evident in every word. "He was old guard, one of Lucius Denholme's personal friends. He served with courage in the Kadrush and later on the Dark Continent. He has five children. He'd only been retired a year before you killed him."

I took it all in silence, tipping my ears back and wilting under his gaze. I deserved it. Every word.

I knew things about Benjamin Hornfell that the wolfhound wasn't mentioning. How he'd fired on a settlement in the Kadrush that was feeding and sheltering raiders in their bay. How he'd been an integral part to the 'civilizing' of the Dark Continent, which saw the destruction of countless native settlements to clear way for the Amurescan Colonists. All things that he'd be lauded for by his fellows. 'Accomplishments'.

Were they worthy of what I'd done to him? Who could say. But one thing was more probable: that the other men on that ship hadn't deserved it. We killed all the time, living this life. Sometimes indiscriminately. If a ship wouldn't surrender, if we accidentally shelled her instead of debilitating her, or sometimes just for the utility of it. You didn't bother taking a sloop when the prize was the larger ship she was escorting.

We all killed. And we'd all killed innocents.

But I wasn't about to dismiss this man's pain over his lost friend. I wasn't even going to make excuses to him. I could never be that heartless. At least, I hoped so.

"I am honoring Luther's arrangement because of my sworn oath to him and because you may have saved his life," he said. "I do not, nor will I ever, forgive you."

I swallowed, dryly, ensuring he was done. At length, I said, "That's fair. And for what it's worth... I'm sorry. I can never bring your friend back, and I know this must sound hollow and worthless now. But, I'm truly, deeply sorry."

He said nothing. Only stared into my eyes until I could bear it no longer, and had to look away. That's when he pressed on and spoke again.

257

"Know that this next part, I do not do to punish you," he said, pushing me forward towards the door. "That, I leave to God."

He led me down three flights of stairs, past several tiers of guards, then stopped at the main gate, where he had a brief, clipped conversation with the men there. "Confession," he said, keeping his explanation brief, "must be made in the Light of God."

The guard on duty looked us both over, then glanced down the length of my body. "This one's a fighter. Really ought to put irons on his legs, too."

"I can handle him," the wolfhound assured him, but there was an edge of irritation to his voice. Resentment.

Walking out into the cold, humid air, bathed in sunlight and really smelling the sea again... it knocked me back a pace. I stood there, enraptured, until the wolfhound yanked me forward again. The bay stretched out before us, the beautiful billowing clouds of sails, amidst a forest of masts, just about the best sight I had ever seen. I could smell the brine, the sea birds, the shellfish living and dying on the rocks all around this little speck of an island. The city stretched out distantly through the haze of morning mist, the spires of churches and fortifications piercing the fog.

I couldn't see the pier where Roccosal's corpse was still strung up, not through the fog. The pier I was supposed to be displayed at alongside him after I was hanged. And that was fine. I never wanted to see it again.

"So, what's our play, here?" I asked as he released me near the rocky beach. I walked out onto the nearest flat, moderately dry rock I could find, so I could stare down at the crashing surf. I missed the water. Fuck.

"Our 'play' is that I humiliate myself," he groused.

"That's usually my role," I said with a hoarse laugh.

"Luther explained to you about the Edicts for the Condemned Sinner?"

"Yeah, and my father told me you'd have to hurt me, in order to make this work," I assured him. I heard him shuffling something behind me, but wasn't sure I wanted to look. "I mean, that someone would have to hurt me. A holy man. So... you, I'm guessing."

When I did finally turn, I saw to my alarm that he had pulled his hand crossbow from his back and was adjusting it. It already seemed to have a bolt loaded.

"Whoa, hang on!" I tried in vain to put a hand out, but of course they were bound. I nearly lost my footing on the rocks, wobbling where I stood. "I thought... you were going to knock me around a little, s'all—"

"I brought a bolt specifically for you that isn't barbed," he said, eyeing the sight for a moment. "I can't just hit you, however satisfying that would be. Even a broken nose could be treated here. It needs to be serious enough that you're transferred off the island for treatment."

"What the hell's your excuse going to be for shooting a bound man?!" I insisted.

"That you escaped my grasp and were going for the row boats," he said, pulling the crossbow up. "Thus, humiliating myself. Now hold still... but turn around."

"Can you just..." I stammered, "... graze me or...?"

"Turn around or this won't look right," he said, gesturing with the tip of his crossbow. "In fact, if you want to start running for the shore, I might actually enjoy that. And it'll sell this better."

"You could've gone about this another way!" I snarled fearfully, before taking off clumsily down the rocky path. "You can't fool me! You fucking sadist!"

Despite my wobbly retreat, the bolt caught me—likely—exactly where he intended. Right through my fucking thigh in the meat of it. Clear of my artery, clear of my knee joint, but through my entire god-damned leg. He could have chosen a less painful place and certainly a less serious injury. I spent the next several hours spitting and cursing a blue streak while I was forcibly detained by the guards on the island once more, man-handled and muzzled again. The pain was indescribable. And they gave me nothing for it, only padded the injury to staunch the bleeding until they could get me to a surgeon.

I was ferried off the island by some of the men working there, as well as Johannes himself, who saw me as far as the surgeon. I didn't know what the plan was from that point on. I had to trust in the people who'd put all this together. I wasn't even certain how I was going to get out of the surgeon's place, let alone Leifolk. I was weak, in horrible pain now, and... following the surgery... on a mixture of drug and drink that was just about the most welcome concoction a man in my predicament could ask for.

The surgeon's recovery ward was a small room with three beds, none of which were occupied save mine. I knew, even fuzzy as my senses were, that there were two guards outside. Just bored men with sabers and flintlocks, but still. More than I could hope to take on in my current state.

I don't know how much time passed. It was hard to tell, as blissed-out on the pain tonic as I was. I was still in irons, shackled to the bed itself. I had never been so tired or worn-down in my life.

I slept, wondering if I was supposed to be doing more. And if so, how.

I woke to the startled shout of a man outside. I blinked blearily, just in time to see the shifting shadows of scuffling feet outside and hear the successive thuds of someone's body striking the door. Once, twice... then the soft scrape as they slid down to the ground. I watched, confused... waiting. More rustling. The clink of keys.

After a considerable amount of time spent trying one key after another, a disgruntled noise. Feminine. Familiar. One key fit, turned in the lock, and the door yawned open.

She was swathed in a cold-weather cloak, lined with rabbit fur and wrapped in a scarf bundled up around her muzzle. But there was no mistaking those eyes. Those cinnamon stripes, painted around her deceptively soft features. Those green eyes. The tiger lily tucked behind one ear....

Oh, shit. The flower.

I gaped at her, and even with the scarf on, I could see her smile in the ruff of fur around her muzzle.

She hurried across the room to me, yanking her scarf down and throwing her arms around me, hunkering down at my bedside. I gasped out into her too-tight hold, enveloped by her thick arms, smelling the patchouli in her fur, and was certain this couldn't be real.

"Gods, you look like hell!" she said, rocking me, then curling back her nose with a laugh. "And you smell even worse than you look, somehow."

"This is even," I huffed out, "after I cleaned up."

She shook her head, leaning back, but moving a thigh to half-sit on the bed beside me. I tried to warn her, "There were two guards..."

"I got the first one when he went to take a piss," she assured me. "They aren't dead. But this could get messy if anyone finds them, so we need to get you out of here now, while we have a chance. I have a carriage waiting a few blocks over."

I smiled sleepily. "You're a goddamn queen, you know that?"

"Oh, you just wait until I get you back to your ship," she snorted. "Then you can sing my praises to the heavens, kiss my feet, worship me, all that."

"My ship," I mumbled. "Do they even—"

"The way I understand it, your crew all but unanimously agreed to forestall voting on another Captain until they were certain you were dead," she said, slipping an arm around me and helping me sit up. Then she began sorting through the key ring she'd pilfered, presumably looking for the right one to undo my irons. "They're in neutral waters, not far from here. Enjoying their spoils on some... whore island somewhere, I'm sure."

"Those are the best kinds of islands," I muttered. "But... what... spoils?"

"Denholme's people left the contents of Roccosal's hold to me," she explained. "They took the ship. Worth a hell of a lot more than all its cargo, but I wasn't about to argue. I thought it only fair we split it. Once the navy dogs had shoved off, anyway."

"That's mighty fine of you," I said, blinking rapidly, trying to wake up.

"Yes, well," she sniffed, "I'm a woman of my word who honors my alliances, whether they be of convenience or no. By the way. I won't be so petty as to say 'I told you so', but—"

"You'll infer it," I grimaced as I accidentally moved my leg. "Shit. I don't think I can walk."

"Luckily, I could have carried you before, let alone now," she teased gently. "Skinny. We need to get some beer into you."

"Hell. Yes," I agreed vehemently.

"Denholme was supposed to be taking care of you while you were in lockup," she growled. "He promised me. But then again, we know how good his promises are, now don't we?"

"It wasn't his fault," I insisted weakly.

"When you make a deal with one Amur, you're making a deal with all of them." She turned the key in the lock on my irons, extracting them carefully, since one was around the ankle on my bad leg. Intentionally, I'm sure. "But I'll begrudgingly admit I was... at least somewhat wrong... about him. At least insofar as you're concerned. He may have passed out on us when we needed him most, but he's stepped up since then. He did a lot to help arrange this. But what the fuck were you thinking, huh?!" She slapped my arm. "You don't go aboard an Amurescan ship... alone! Not when you have a warrant out for you! Harrosha's balls, you should know better!"

"He was dying," I said. "I couldn't get to you, and you couldn't have helped him the way his own people could."

"You don't know he was dying," she said, sounding tired. "He might've been able to wait... less than a minute, until we could get him over there without you having to swan dive into the arms of the enemy."

"Think of the story I'll have to tell, though..." I mumbled.

She sighed. "Alright, you're drugged. We need to get you out of here. Give me your arm."

She guided it up over her shoulder, then slid off the bed, adjusting me for a moment before standing gingerly with me in her arms. I rested my head against her chest, smiling as my eyes slipped closed. "My hero," I crooned.

"I have the... trophy... Roccosal took from you," she told me, as she walked us down the hallway, stepping casually over the unconscious body of the guard, towards a bright, sunlit doorway into the back alley. "The start of this whole mess. It's one of the many things we seized on his ship, but... I have to warn you, he'd done a number on it. Sick bastard attached it to a skull with some kind of adhesive tar—"

I shook my head. "They'll grow back. Thank you, though."

"His body's still hanging off the pier," she said. "What he deserves."

A bolt of cold, dreary sadness moved through me like passing under a shadow. It would be impossible to ever explain it to her, so I didn't bother.

"I got your beads and trinkets out of the mane, at least," she said gently. "Cut them out carefully. I thought you might want them right away, so they're in my pocket. Do you want to hold them in the carriage?"

"… Yeah," I said after a while. I had my father's now, but there was no reason to feel bad for wanting that kind of additional comfort. No shame in that.

"Hadeon insisted on coming with me, despite endlessly bitching about the weather here," she said long-sufferingly. "He's on my ship."

"He lived," I let out a breath. Wasn't sure why, but I'd grown attached to the man for some reason. "And he stayed on with you?"

"We've had plunder aplenty since that take," she snorted. "I think that's more why he's stuck around. But for what it's worth, he kept asking after you once we hatched the plan to get you out. You make friends easily."

"Is that what we are, now?" I asked her, weakly stroking my fingertips over one of the arms she was carrying me with.

"Of course," she said with a smile that touched all the way up to her eyes. And as we reached the doorway outside, she leaned down and nuzzled me with her nose. "Friends. Comrades. Lovers, whenever we get a chance at it. Just don't get all infatuated with me, now. You know how it is."

"I know how it is," I chuckled. "The sea is a jealous spouse. Barely tolerates paramours, as it is."

"As long as you sail under a banner of freedom," she said more seriously, looking down at me as the sun lit up the beautiful patterns of her fur, "you'll be my friend, Grayson."

I smiled. Despite the ache, the weariness, the loss and the hard recovery ahead of me, I felt luckier than I'd ever been.

I had good friends.

I had family, even if there were barriers between us.

And they didn't think I was worthless. They didn't think I was defective. They saw a future for me. Enough that they did all of this….

Maybe in time, I'd feel that way about myself. Every day, I got a little closer.

FIVE YEARS LATER

The Manoratha Fleet, docked for a brief time in Treneval, is celebrating after their highly lucrative take-down and subsequent liquidation of the Lancaster Cartel. While living the high life at a rented-out Social Club in the Pier District, Grayson Reed's festivities are disrupted by the appearance of an old 'friend' and very much uninvited guest—Admiral Luther Denholme. The only thing stranger than the Admiral's sudden arrival to a building full of men who very much would prefer him dead, is the fact that he came alone, unarmed... and shitfaced. It isn't often someone catches Grayson Reed on the back foot, but this night promises to be one he will not soon forget, and sets a chain of events in motion that will shape both men's lives, and affect the lives of thousands more.

Lifeline

The staircase clattered noisily beneath the heavy, rushed footsteps of my boys and I, our overgrown claws clicking on the hardwood. I'm pretty sure I found every single poorly-nailed-down board on my swift descent, of which there were many. Normally, I might have watched my footing more carefully, especially when I had reason to expect there might be trouble—or a troublesome person—ahead. Not that I'm not a fan of making loud noises mind you, I just tend to prefer the element of surprise when I might be walking into a fight.

But see here's the thing. This aging, enormous, port-side Social Club was our penthouse, our place of respite for the next week at least, and I should have had no cause to sneak around in it. We'd rented the whole of it out, legal-like and all. Fully paid up-front, and I'd made sure the owners got coverage for damages in advance, since I knew my men, and there were very likely to be damages, when all was said and done. For the time being, this place was our fortress, not some public rooming house.

Was nothing sacred? For once, I wasn't even looking for trouble. Couldn't I just bloody relax every now and then?

This was the third day we'd spent here, and I'd only just woken an hour ago, so I was annoyingly sober. The fact that this was happening during the scant few hours a day I tended to be sober was absurdly unlucky. I wouldn't have taken odds on that.

To be honest with you, I had no idea what time of day or night it actually was; this was Treneval after all, the weather just about any time of year could be summarized with the word 'grey'. For color, temperature, light, and overall 'mood'. Why the Amurescans had chosen such a dreary, dismal, frequently storm-wracked port as one of their primary places of commerce and society, I could not make sense of. The simple answer was geographic location. Just like them to prioritize practicality over pleasure.

But whatever time of day it was, I'd only just rolled out of bed (and the arms of a mink who'd gotten too drunk the day prior to do her job), and I hadn't had a chance to chase last night's drink with anything other than a pounding headache. It took a lot to get me in what you might call a 'foul mood', but I was rounding that corner.

"How did he even get in here?" I demanded of the boar on my right, who only shook his oversized head.

"Still haven't figured that out."

"Our best guess is through the kitchen," the rat ahead of us—I think his name was Jeffrey—said as he fished a key ring off his belt and thrust one of them into the locked door at the bottom of the staircase. The jangling made me wince and tip my ears back.

Really needed a drink.

"That's where he came strolling out from, anyway," Jeffrey continued, glancing back at us. "And a few of the boys said they propped the door out to th'back open last night, let out some of the heat after dinner."

"I take it no one thought to shut it afterwards, let alone lock it," I grumbled.

"Well," Jeffrey paused, "what with all the women came by last night…"

"Yeah, yeah," I moved in beside him, grabbing around him for the door handle. "Out of the way. I'll handle this."

"You sure, Adm'ral?"

I let out a ragged sigh. "I've handled him before. You're absolutely certain it's him? There are a few thousand cattle dogs in Amuresca, I'd wager. If I dragged my ass out of bed for some bum who crept in off the street to filch food—"

"It's him," a man from further up the staircase whom I couldn't see insisted, raising his voice so he'd be heard. There was quite a crowd gathered on the landing above by now. I'd had to push my way through them on the way down here.

For some reason—through what I'm sure had been an epic scuffle I'm only sad I'd missed—they'd managed to corner the intruder in the cellar. Which was, if bleary memory served, a large, dirt-floored basement primarily used for storing old furniture, vegetables and casks. We weren't supposed to break into any of the booze down there, but the fact that my men had forced our party-crasher inside and then locked him in with keys they somehow had access to… well, it suggested I'd be paying even more damages down the line. May as well have bought the place outright.

"I remember him from Dokuro," the sailor affirmed. "Hard to forget those eyes. Goddamn… demon, that one."

"I'm sure he gave you hell," I muttered, pausing near the door and steeling myself. "Where'd his boys get to? They bail?"

I felt, rather than saw the uneasy looks that passed between my men after that question. When I turned to regard them again, the same man spoke up, "He came alone."

"Bullshit," I said defiantly, "we're in his territory. Why would he've—" I stopped myself short at that.

This was Luther Denholme we were talking about. It was actually entirely possible he'd come alone, for some purpose that would make terrifying sense once he explained his reasoning to me. Some gambit I didn't know of, some master-stroke he'd lay out before me as my world unraveled and I scrambled to catch up.

I was not prepared to deal with this shit right now. I just wanted to go back to bed.

I didn't bother asking if he was armed. I just braced my shoulder against the door, gripped the handle, and called back to my men, "Stay outta this. Last thing I need is one of you all getting trigger happy and murdering a fucking Crown Admiral in an Amurescan port."

"We know," Jeffrey insisted. "That's why we locked'im up. We didn't know what else to do. None of us want to fight our way out of these waters, Admiral."

"Good, because we wouldn't make it past the bay. I'm betting he counted on that, too," I realized aloud. Might explain why he wasn't worried about coming alone. I twisted the nob, shouting once more, "If I start hollering, just send a few of the biggest lads in. No killin'!"

A chorus of 'yessirs', and then I stepped inside, shutting the door firmly behind me with a backwards kick. Resting my hands on my hips, I didn't immediately bother with the hilt of my saber, even though I had come armed. This was Luther. And despite what the public perception of us was, even amongst my own men… he was not in fact some sworn blood enemy of mine.

I hardly knew what the cattle dog was to me, really. A friend? I hope he saw me that way. I think he did. I think I did.

But given the nature of our interactions over the years, given our diametrically opposed careers, we'd been both predator and prey and everything in between to one another. The sands our relationship stood on were constantly shifting, and I actually hadn't seen him in over a year now. A lot could change in a year. It had for me. I'd nearly lost my flagship to the Black Flag fleet this past season, and the Black Flag Admiral—one Heinrich Richard Cross—was pretty tight with the Denholmes, or at least he had been with Luther's stepfather. I knew Luther worked alongside Cross from time to time, but as to whether or not they were friends… let alone friends who might swing one another's favor for or against someone like me…

Impossible to say. In all our encounters, I'd never thought to ask Luther about the nature of his relationship with Cross, the old Shepherd. And maybe I should have. He was definitely our enemy—the last battle between my Manoratha and the Black Flag fleet had been bloody on both sides. I think we'd given as well as we'd got and there was no telling what condition his ships had been in afterwards, but he'd nearly sunk my girl to the bottom, and all souls aboard with her. We'd barely limped out of that one.

I needed to know these things, is the point. It was part of my job—no, part of my obligation—to my men. I couldn't afford to be as reckless with their lives as I was with my own.

Shit, maybe we shouldn't have been here at all? While my ships were technically on a legal contract right now, we had enemies a-plenty here, some of them like Cross, incredibly dangerous.

My spirits lifted as I began to walk down the central line of shelves, peering down each row looking for the cattle dog. Maybe that's why he was here. Maybe this was just a friendly warning. That'd be damn decent of him. And you know what? I'd listen. To hell with our plans in Treneval, if Denholme was being courteous enough to look out for me, give me a head start away from trouble, I wasn't about to spit in his face. It would explain why he was here alone, why he'd come himself, why he'd felt the need to slip in unseen—

There were a few lanterns hung from the ceiling down here, but not enough to fully illuminate the place, in my opinion. Not for an underground space. Were I outside, or were there any windows or doors letting in natural light, it'd be enough for me to see by, regardless of the weather or time of day. But in between the rings of flickering orange were dead zones, usually in the corners near the end of each rows of shelves, where even a wolf's eyes couldn't see through the empty pitch. It was in one of these that I found him, and if not for his legs lying slumped partially in the light, I might have missed him. His eyes flashed once when I grabbed for the lantern above, tipping it towards him. Gold pin-pricks in the dark. A demon indeed.

"Bloody hell," I took a step back, my nose just now catching the sharp scent of iron in the air, in addition to the stale, lingering smell of most cellars- old wood, tar from the barrels, mold. And... whiskey. Definitely whiskey. Well, at least I now knew what they'd broken into down here.

The iron though, that was blood. Unmistakably. Fresh blood, too. Not very much, but...

"The great Luther Denholme," I said with as much bravado as I could, putting up an air of strength. Whatever his game here, I didn't need him seeing how tired I was. "How in the hell did you let a couple groggy lads get the better of you?"

I hooked a finger around the top ring of the lantern overhead, easy enough in a cellar meant for shorter species, and held it out in his direction. The man was a sight. I felt the air leave my lungs in a punched-out huff.

He looked like he'd aged ten years since the last time I saw him, thinner and gaunter all around, but most noticeable in his cheeks and the deep pits in the hollows of his eyes. His nose was bloody and had stained the simple white cotton shirt he wore, beneath a frayed brown coat. He had none of his finery on, no blood red coat, no cravat, not even a sword that I could see. In fact, if he was armed at all, I couldn't tell. A knife, perhaps, hidden somewhere on his person. Maybe tucked into the side of his leather spats, or beneath the coat somewhere. I couldn't imagine he went anywhere completely unarmed.

But there was nothing in the cattle dog's slumped, lifeless posture, or in the air surrounding him, that read as intimidating or dangerous. And for a man that exuded intimidation as easily as most men breathed, that was saying something. He looked ragged, hazy-eyed... almost sickly.

In short, he looked like I felt. In fact, if I didn't know any better, I'd say he was hungov—

Wait.

He tipped his head up slowly towards me, pupils sharpening marginally at the sound of my voice, but they were blown-wide in the dark, lacking the predatory edge they generally had. Luther had this intense way of looking at you, as if he was analyzing you, sizing you up, all the time. In all the years I'd known him, I'd seen him exhibit a range of emotions, but his gaze had never lost that focus.

Without a further word, I crossed the space between us and knelt down in front of him. He sniffed noisily, sucking blood back up into his nose- the work of one of my boys, no doubt. And he opened his muzzle as if to say something, but I gave him the chance and the words just... never came. Just a slow, labored exhale. Which confirmed what I'd suspected, once I breathed it in.

"LADS!" I raised my voice, as loud as I could with my throat still thick with sleep as it was. I turned my gaze back down towards the cattle dog as the door was thrust open noisily somewhere back the way I'd come, and asked far more quietly of him, "Can you walk?"

He pushed himself up, palm grabbing unsteadily for one of the wooden shelves nearby and clamping around the edge of it for purchase. I had about a split second to warn him of what he should've noticed already— that there wasn't much other than gravity holding it in place—but mostly what I got out was, "Don't—", and then the plank gave way and flipped up, on one side. I don't think it'd ever been nailed down, it was just a flat piece of wood resting on slats.

But it had been the only point of support he had, so with a clattering crash that I'm absolutely certain half the house must have heard, I had the extraordinarily rare privilege of watching one Luther Denholme laid low by sub-par shelving. Several glass jars of preserves rolled off and littered down around him, thankfully without breaking (glass jars and bottles are tough let me tell you, did you know you could beat someone to death with one?), and he slumped back down against the wall, nearly to the ground. But by that point I'd caught his shoulder and leaned over him both to steady him, and block him from the prying eyes of the men I'd called in.

"Pull it together," I whispered fiercely, a few inches away from one of his ears. "C'mon, up..." I moved a paw beneath his shoulder, beginning to heft him. Thankfully, he was a smaller man than I was, and lighter now than I remembered.

What the hell, what the hell…

"Can you walk if I drag you along?" I asked him, still lowly. He blinked back a wince against the encroaching glow of the lantern, but nodded.

"Admiral," I felt a paw settle on my shoulder, heavy and with retractable claws. I recognized the spots immediately. "Seems like you handled him," the leopard said, sounding only marginally concerned once he took in the sight of him same as I had.

"Taarush," I sighed. One of my trusted men… good. But there were a few others with him, Jeffrey included, and he was a new-ish hire. I didn't know him all that well, yet. "Yeah," I confirmed, "knocked him stupid. You lads must've softened him up for me, eh?" I raised my voice at that so the others heard me clearly.

There were a few nervous chuckles of assent, followed by one bold man raising his voice and asking, "So why's the Cerberus bastard here?"

I cleared my throat, thinking quickly. "Didn't really get to that," I said, sounding as forcibly bored as I could manage. "Wanted to set the record straight about walking in on our territory this way, bold as brass. I don't care who the fuck you think you are, cur." I directed that at Luther, who still hadn't spoken, but at least seemed to be listening to me now. He was leaning on me heavily for support, but I had my paw clamped up beneath one of his arms in a way that at least looked like he was being man-handled. "We're here legal-like," I continued, then louder, "ain't that right boys?!"

A bevy of confirming shouts went up, a bit of bluster and profanity, about what I'd expected. Taarush was looking at Luther oddly, though. He'd probably smelled it by now, just as I had when I'd finally gotten in close enough. It was downright embarrassing that the men who'd forced him down here hadn't realized what was actually going on. But then, they were all as brutally hungover as I was, if not worse.

Luther was incredibly lucky he'd come here when he had. Last night, he'd've been torn apart.

"But the Admiral and I need to speak now," I continued, "so here's what I need from you lot. Clear the hall up there. And one of the sitting rooms… get me somethin' to drink while you're at it. Us. Get us something to drink," I corrected quickly, even though that was clearly the last thing Luther needed right now.

"Y'want us to clear out the boys upstairs in the main room?" Jeffrey asked, uncertainly.

I knew why the request confused him. It wasn't often I conducted business—of any kind, legit or black market—behind closed doors. I

270

had a policy of allowing my men, regardless of their rank, to weigh in on decisions that affected the fleet, so long as they were present for said negotiations. We were Anarchists, sure… but that didn't mean I didn't believe in the power of a public forum. Also, having an ever-present flock of my boys around me served as a means of intimidation, protection, and was extremely off-putting to more rigid men—like say, Amurescan Pedigree Lords—who were not accustomed to people they considered low-brow lessers having any say in negotiations. For all these reasons, I rarely met alone with anyone, save the women I took to bed. And… not even then, sometimes.

But this was different. And I couldn't explain to them why. Many of my men would feel understandably betrayed if they knew I was sparing any concern for a pirate hunter, a man who'd frequently made our exploits less profitable, or too risky to even undertake. We'd even traded shots once or twice, although I don't think we'd killed any of each other's men. Yet.

"Just do it," I commanded, stone-faced. I didn't have the energy or the creativity to concoct a lie right now. I'd come up with something later.

I felt the air grow colder, that palpable aura of discomfort settling in more heavily. Thankfully, no one questioned me.

Goddamn this man. We'd been having a good month… I didn't need morale issues right now. But I didn't want to run the risk of someone doing something absurdly stupid while they thought they had the chance of it. Denholme had put himself in a hell of a spot, here.

I wasn't used to being the one stuck with cleaning up someone else's bad decisions. This just wasn't me.

Taarush stayed at my side, which I was grateful for because although Luther had lost a bit of weight and wasn't as large a man as either of us, the cattle dog was still… dense, and hardly someone I could princess carry up a narrow, rickety staircase easily. Having two men to help support him seemed to do it, though. We made it into the main hall, which Jeffrey had obediently cleared as asked, and I took him into the nearest sitting room from there. There were quite a few of these rooms meant for smoking, entertaining smaller parties and whatnot. We'd converted most of them into bunks or, as my men so elegantly put it, 'fuckin' rooms'. This looked to be the former, the single table and chairs all pushed closer to the fire, heaped in blankets and discarded clothing where the men taking up residence here had passed out last night.

I settled the cattle dog down in one of the chairs, then went about bundling up the various linens over my arm and tossing them all into a corner, away from the still-smoldering fire. It was low, but still… stupid. Sailors should have been smarter about that.

"Bloody... children," I grumbled, balling up someone's shirt and tossing it off the arm of the couch I chose to drag closer to Luther with a squawk of wood on the floor. "Going to burn the damn place down."

Taarush had paused in the door and was saying something quietly to a man outside, before fetching a pint bottle from whoever'd gotten it and setting it down on the edge of the table for me. "Will that do, sir?"

I uncorked the bottle and sniffed it, confirming it was rum. I didn't really drink much else in the mornings. "It'll do," I said, "but Taarush, get me a Brukicker tonic." I glanced briefly at Luther, "A double. And two cups."

He nodded, shutting the door with a gentle click behind him as he cleared out. It really hadn't been a slam or anything approaching it, but I saw Luther wince and tilt his ears back all the same.

"You look like you skipped 'drunk,'" I informed him curtly, tipping the bottle back and swallowing, embracing the burn with a relieved sigh, "went straight to the hangover part."

"Feels... that way," he confirmed, voice rough and disused.

"How long?" I asked, drinking again.

He moved his head slightly at that, eyes slim slits when they finally settled on me. "I don't..." he mumbled, "...unh? What?"

"How long've you been on a bender?" I asked more descriptively. "You look like shit."

"Oh," he seemed to understand, finally. "I... no. Just... the night."

I gave him a wry smile. "How long's that 'night' lasted, bud? Or've you lost track?"

"I've been sick," he said, eyes slipping closed for a few moments.

"Look, if you're gonna be sick, just try to be quiet about it," I sighed. "My boys don't seem to realize you stumbled in here shitfaced like some drunk off the street yet, and it's in your best interest they don't comprehend how vulnerable you are right now. Not all of 'em are as good-natured as I am, and you'd be a hell of a feather in a Privateer's cap—"

"No," he insisted with a little more vehemence. "Not... sick from drink. Sick. Seer's Fever."

That got my attention, real fast. And it explained a lot.

I leaned back against the tattered cushion of the cheap couch. "Oh, hell," I breathed out softly. "Are you... through it?" Come to think of it, everything about his condition could just be the result of the physical effects of the Fever. "Are you even drunk? Wait, no, I definitely smelled whiskey on you—"

"Drunk, too. And not... I don't have it. Inoculated," he pressed his knuckles to his muzzle, clearing his throat and sniffing noisily again, although I think that had more to do with his bleeding nose than any symptoms. Sympathetically (and as one who'd had his fair share of bad punches to the nose) I got up and rummaged about the room for something he could use, settling on a bar rag someone had left on the table.

"How long ago?" I asked, handing it over to him.

He took it slowly, inclining his head in a half-nod of thanks before pressing it to his still bleeding nose. "Finished the course... two weeks ago," he tipped his chin back slowly, his whole posture going lax in the chair. "You don't seem worried," he noted.

"I'm not. I know how inoculations work," I sat back down heavily. "I really ought to get me'n the boys treated. We don't go near the Southwest seas often, but," I paused. "Wait, is the Fever ripping its' way through the Navy, now?"

He shook his head slowly. "It is thankfully rare. For now."

I blinked. "Then, why—isn't it a rough course, to put yourself through just because? It must be. You're..." I gestured at him. "I mean no offense, but holy shit."

"I know," he grunted. "Not a'my best, for sure." His chin tipped further back, eyes fixed on some point on the ceiling. "It's been... a month."

"Yeah, well getting fucked up on whiskey on top of all that couldn't have helped," I pointed out, feeling so unnatural chastising someone else for drinking to excess.

"Wasn't the plan, exactly." He spoke with his eyes closed and his brow pinched as if fighting back dizziness. Or nausea. Hard to say. "Usually know what I can handle."

"You lost weight," I pointed out. "Guessing you were on bedrest for a while—"

"Mnh," he confirmed.

"Not exactly in peak physical condition, mate. What the hell were you thinking?"

"I s'pose I wasn't," he admitted quietly.

"Thinking?" My muzzle twitched, this whole scene setting me ill at ease. I didn't like seeing him like this. "That isn't like you."

He didn't respond. At all. Only stared ahead, into the fire. And sure, he was drunk. Apparently recovering from a rough inoculation process that I'd heard could actually kill you same as the disease it was intended to protect you from, if you weren't tough enough to endure it. He'd gotten his face kicked in by a few of my boys, dragged up and down a flight of stairs I'd gotten winded taking, and I was only a bit hungover.

But this was Luther fucking Denholme.

"What. The hell. Is going on?" I annunciated, reaching out and grabbing him by the lower jaw, to turn him to face me.

"Too much," was his simple answer.

"Why are you here?" I tried to get him to look me in the eyes. "Why are you," I gestured vaguely at his condition, "in this... state? Why are you alone? Where's the wolfhound?" I realized belatedly at that point that he was without his shadow. That man was essentially his minder, or his personal bodyguard, I hardly knew what to call him. But I could count- twice now- that I'd ever seen them apart.

"Johannes is... unwell," he said, barely above a whisper. I hardly knew what that meant, but it sounded bad.

"Inoculation take poorly for him?" I guessed.

He shook his head. "He is grappling with his demons."

"Well that's spooky as fuck, mate," I said, curling a lip. "What does that even mean?"

"I..." he paused like he was trying to form words in his mouth, but it took him considerable time. A quicker wit than this man, generally, you could not find. This couldn't be all the drink. "I cannot burden him now," he finally said. "He is with his family." Then after another consid- erable pause, so quiet I barely heard it, "If I were kinder, I would leave him behind. But I need him..."

I decided to leave that one alone. Sounded like they'd had some kind of falling out or something, but that really wasn't my business. I most certainly did not consider the wolfhound a friend or comrade or whatever (my thigh ached in remembrance of the bolt he'd put through it, the bastard could rot in hell for all I cared), and it really had no bearing on the situation at hand.

"Fine, but you've got other people who ought to have been looking out for you," I reasoned. Not that I'd ever thought the cattle dog couldn't handle his own damn self, he was worldly and clever enough to make his way in just about any port. But life can lay low the strongest of us—as was evidenced here—and if I'd had the month from hell, I know at least two dozen of my men would've intervened to prevent me from doing something as fool-hardy as stumbling off drunk, despondent, ill, and unsupervised into enemy territory. Maybe one or two of those, but all at once?

He was once again staring off into space, like he was very carefully considering what I'd last said to him. "Not... really," he said at length. But I'd forgotten what he was replying to at this point.

"What led you to my doorstep?" I asked. "Is there something, I mean," I bit back the urge to sound snappish. "Is there something I can do for you?" I went with instead.

I couldn't bear to be an asshole to him right now. I didn't even want to risk hurting his feelings, truth be told. Normally I could handle a crying drunk, but the thought of seeing this man in particular weep was... it made my chest hurt just thinking about it. And he looked that bad, like he might very well be on the verge.

An impulse I can't explain led me to cross the few feet between us, grab him by the shoulders and shuffle him bodily to sit on the couch beside me, rather than across from me in that rickety chair. I felt like I'd get more out of him this way. But right off, he mostly seemed bemused, grabbing at one of my sleeves to stabilize himself as he plopped down. Wincing for him, I quickly reached down and tugged his tail to the side; he'd nearly crushed it sitting on it.

"Do you…" I paused, thinking on my own drunken exploits in the past. He seemed to be on the downslide, so he'd probably been worse when he'd first arrived here. And he didn't have a whole lot of answers for me, so…

"Do you even remember why you're here?" I asked him, letting a long breath out slowly.

His eyes moved to mine, almost pleading. "No," he finally confessed.

Blessedly, then came a knock. I didn't bother turning, but called out, "Come in!"

The leopard entered, albeit briefly. Taarush—always professional, only took one glance at the two of us, likely to assure for himself that I was still in no danger. He seemed unworried, and set two tin cups and a taller glass down, filled to the brim with an ochre concoction. The pungent smell was an old friend to me now, and that looked to be a freshly-mixed batch, based on the way the ingredients hadn't begun to separate yet. I'd have to thank the cook later.

"How are the men?" I asked him before he left.

"Curious," he responded simply, "but calm. All's well, sir."

"Thank you, Taarush."

He nodded at me, then took his leave.

"Good man," I muttered as I stood, pouring a bit of the rum into both cups, then splitting the Brukicker tonic between them. I handed it over to Luther, who curled his nose at the scent, but otherwise took it without further question, likely familiar with it, or something like it.

We sat in silence and forced it down, and apparently some of the man's resolve was still there, because he downed his faster than I did mine. I clapped the cup back on the table and waited for it to kick in, the popping of the fire the only sound in the room for a time.

"I'm flattered, by the way," I said after a long while.

"Hnh?" He glanced my way. It might have been a trick of the light, but it seemed like his gaze had sharpened marginally. Or maybe it was just because we'd been staring into a fire.

"That you came to me, of all people, when you were blackout drunk," I filled in. I flashed him a light smile. "I'm hardly a deep man, but that's gotta mean something, right? A drunk mind… something, something… a sober heart? I don't know," I laughed.

"Don't laugh," he said softly.

"And why not?" I snorted. "You have a problem with my laugh?"

"You've a good voice," he said, once again with the enigmatic answers I couldn't make sense of. "And a good laugh. It's not that."

"I'm just glad I've got you talking," I said. "Go on then. Explain it to me. Why can't I laugh?"

"Because it's nothing to laugh off," he answered simply. "It's the truth. In my fugue, I came to you."

"You have to be the only man I know who uses words like 'fugue' when you're hungover," I said dryly.

He glanced down at the empty cup. "This is working."

"You were verbose even before," I waved a hand, "once I got you talking, anyway."

"Was…confused," he confessed, whiskers twitching as he continued to stare down into his cup. "I still am."

"That'll happen," I said ruefully. "You don't drink like this often, do you?"

"I did more when I was young," he murmured.

"It's a wonder you survived your youth, then," I arched an eyebrow.

"I wasn't trying to."

There was that pain in my chest, again. Everything about this was worrying.

"Luther," I leaned in close, forcing him to look in my direction. He seemed momentarily startled by my proximity, but didn't flinch again when I cautiously placed a hand on his shoulder. His expression was… 'fragile' is the best word I can think of, and it's still not quite right. Everything from his stooped posture, his too-narrow shoulders, the light, involuntary shivers of his muzzle and the deep circles beneath his eyes… it felt like he could crumble beneath my paw.

"Grayson," he said, haltingly. The fact that he'd used my name—not my surname—was the first indication I had that this was going to be bad. Very, very bad.

"It's alright," I eased him on with a light squeeze of his shoulder, my blunt claws sinking into the fabric of his jacket. "I'm listening."

"A… man came to see me," he began, with a shuddering breath. "A man from my past. A lover of mine, from a long time ago."

"Alright," I said, simply nodding. I didn't dismiss the gravity of what he'd just put to words; those words could have seen him hanged in the Treneval square, simply because this man from his past and this lover were the same person. Years ago, I'd unearthed this secret of his and tried to use it against him. To my everlasting shame. But we'd gotten past that, and now he was trusting me with this. That was big.

"He's moved on," he said hoarsely. I didn't miss how he gripped his cup a little tighter. "I'm happy for him," he continued, and to his credit, he earnestly sounded it. "But, despite that, he came to me... cared for me, while I recovered."

"Good of him," I said.

"Cruel," he countered softly. "I'd come to believe—to make peace with the fact—that he'd left me behind because there were no mutual feelings between us. But, then, he does this. He comes to me, when I'm at death's door. Cares for me. He cared this much for me, and he still didn't want to be with me. He said he couldn't..." he swallowed; the action so evident beneath the fur of his throat that I could almost feel it in my own. "He didn't want to move on, until he'd made peace with me. He was asking for me to release him from my heart, from any remaining obligation he had to me. So that he could be happy in his new life, with no regrets."

"I'm sorry, mate," I said with utter sincerity. "That's fucking awful."

I wasn't about to chastise him for falling in love in the first place. It wasn't an illness I'd ever been afflicted with (thankfully), and that was by design, but I couldn't fault those who fell victim to it. Luther was a passionate man, I'd only known him a few hours when I'd first learned that, and he was in the unenviable position of having to hide those passions for the sake of himself, his partners, and his family. It was hard enough that his predilection for men limited his opportunities, but based on what little I knew of his personal life, he'd also had lousy luck. Death, fear and misfortune had befallen those few I knew of, so hearing that he was mourning another missed chance at happiness was no surprise.

Coupled with the inoculation, that was a double-blow that'd knock most men on their ass. But at least it was something I could understand. Maybe something we could solve.

"You just need to chase his memory off with someone new," I reasoned, shrugging. "You know I've got a few lads on my crew—"

"Trust me, that's the last thing I need right now," he muttered.

"Oh, come on," I said. "Maybe not now, not in your current condition, and it ain't gonna be some whirlwind romance, but it doesn't always have to be that way, y'know. Sometimes you just need to shake the water off," I straightened up, putting an arm up over the back of the couch and leaning closer to him. "I happen to know a few men'n particular who fancy the same sorts of leisure activities you do, and are all too eager to make poor life decisions."

He let out a 'hah' of breath that might've been a laugh if he were in any condition for one. "I don't have the time, I'm afraid."

"You just need to sober up, get a warm bath, maybe take another week to recover. We'll be in port all month—"

"I sail in three days."

I stalled, opening my mouth to ask the obvious question. But then the pieces started to fit together on their own.

"Oh, fuck," I said aloud.

Seer's Fever was a horrible disease from the Dark Continent. It drove men mad, made them see things, thus the name. As bad as it was though, it could be relatively hard to catch. The only people who tended to get it were sailors who actually went to that accursed southern continent, and the people who had relations with them. Family, whores, whomever. You didn't get this disease casually.

I'd seen a few cases over the years in my fleet, but it was rare. Not one of the ones we worried about, because we didn't traffic much in the southern seas. That was contested territory, and more importantly, an active warzone. The Amur had been fighting a losing battle to maintain control over their flagging Colonies in those unbroken lands for two decades now.

They'd made an ill-fated attempt to colonize the continent the same way they'd tried to do with Carvecia, where they'd met with—and eventually lost to—rebellion. And now they were dealing with a similar situation with the natives of the Dark Continent, except they were being more... proactive about it. They'd never welcomed the Amur incursion, had fought them tooth and nail from the outset, and now the continent and all the waters surrounding it were a whirlpool of death and carnage that few escaped from. Yet in defiance of all logic, the bloody Amurescan King was clinging to the idea that they could prevail and bend the place to their will, if they only threw enough bodies at it.

The inoculation, the old flame coming back into his life to make peace with him, his Second-in-Command abandoning him to spend time with his family...

"I'd heard you were in port," he said, as if just now remembering it. "I don't remember how I found out... exactly where you were," he spoke like a man stumbling through his patchy memory. "I suppose I must have wanted to... talk? To say goodbye, maybe." He flicked his gaze over to mine, eyes wider and clearer than they'd been so far. "You've been a friend, Grayson. Almost unwillingly, at times, but... I don't know what else to call what we have."

I swallowed, heavily. So, there it was. He'd said it. "You can call it that," I said. "I think of you that way."

"Hnh," he hummed, contentedly. It was the first moment of peace I'd seen wash over his features since he'd come here.

A low growl, coming on like the distant rumble of thunder, disturbed the companionable silence that followed. It took me a few moments to realize it was coming from me, unbidden. Luther's brows rose, concerned.

"Fuck you, man," I managed to get out, the growl an undertone to every word. "I knew…" I hissed, clenching a hand over the back of the couch, feeling the cheap fabric against my claws, "…I knew if you were walking into my life right now, it'd be to drop somethin'… shattering, on me. Some uncomfortable truth that'd tip me upside-down and set me reeling. That's what you fucking do."

"I'm… I'm sorry?" He said, sounding like he wanted to mean the apology, but was still confused. He was so lost—had been searching for every word and trying desperately to explain himself since he got here—and it was honestly a wonder he'd followed along with our conversation as much as he had, given his condition.

But I couldn't help it. The anger had come, finally.

"What do you expect me to do with this?!" I asked, staring him in the eyes, our muzzles inches apart so that if he chose to look away from me, he'd have to make a real conscious effort to do so. "Wish you good fucking luck?!"

"I-I don't know," he admitted. He wasn't looking away, at least. He'd never been a coward. Steeling himself visibly, he reminded me, "I don't know why I came here. I really don't. I'm only guessing it was to wish you farewell before I left. I don't remember where my head was at when I was drinking."

"What the hell happened?" I demanded, swiping my free hand through the air, out in the direction of the dark blue windows beyond, and the distant sprigs of masts silhouetted against the early dawn or late dusk, I still wasn't sure. "How—why are you sailing out to war?!"

He set his jaw. "It's my duty," he replied stoically.

"Hang that!" I belted out. "You're a pirate hunter, Denholme! Not some lapdog to your bloody Colonizer King. I feel," I huffed out in sheer audacity, "like the biggest fucking fool… reminding you who you are! It would be better for me and mine if you forgot."

One of his eyebrows raised, and there came an inkling, a hint, of the dry snark I knew him for. "Would it, though?" he asked pointedly.

"I mean, fine," I confirmed, "you do poach my competition more often than you've been a thorn in my side specifically. We've brokered a few good deals over the years, too. But you have to admit, they were far more beneficial to you than me—more bloody protection rackets than anything."

"Well," he closed his eyes for a moment, "you won't need to worry about me for a while."

"If ever again," I said, the growl back in my voice. Despite what some might call my 'explosive personality', I didn't actually like to growl at people. It was too rough for me, too angry. Not my style. I felt like I didn't have any control over it now, though.

He didn't respond to that, but he did finally look away from me. Which I took as a tacit agreement.

"You know damn well," I said, aghast, "that taking your fleet there is suicide. How are you letting them do this to you?! It can't be for the Crown's endorsement—you've been kicking ass these last few years. You're bloody infamous, man… my men call you a 'demon'. Most everyone I know in my trade is terrified of you."

"The flattery's unnecessary," he insisted, with the barest hint of a self-satisfied smirk. The one he usually wore like a second skin.

"I know I'm not the only Privateer you're on the take with," I said, trying not to sound as petulant as I felt about it. I'd been his first, at least. I'd always have that. "Are you hard-up for some reason? Whatever this commission is paying, it can't be worth it. Look, I just got off a job that paid absurdly well. What do you need?"

"It isn't about coin," he assured me, then brought his eyes back to mine, the firelight catching in them. "Although it's… surprisingly good of you to offer."

"Fuck you," I said good-naturedly. "I'm a great guy. And yeah, it's been a bit tumultuous, but I'd call us 'friends'. Comrades, for sure. Right?"

He nodded, silently. I didn't miss the way his shoulders lifted, either. There was a lightness in his eyes, that 'peace' I'd seen earlier, every time we'd confirmed this simple fact. It was stunning, really, how much of an effect it seemed to have on him. Maybe give some credit to the alcohol, but still, heartbreaking to think it might've just been a rarity in his life. In anyone's life.

I had so many people I considered friends, across the world. Dozens of bosom buddies, just in this one building. People I trusted with my life. Knowing I could count the Cerberus Admiral among them was nice, but… hardly as profound as it seemed to be to him. Treneval was his port city, he had a place of residence here, it's where his ships docked most of the time in between hunting seasons. With the wolfhound occupied elsewhere, was I really the only one he could think to come to, at his darkest moment?

"So, if it's not about the commission," I pressed, "then why the hell are you letting them pull you into that maelstrom? You've never concerned yourself with those waters, before."

"It's the legacy I inherited," he said, voice laced with misery. "Lucius Denholme founded that Colony for the Crown. He later regretted it, told me about how he'd gotten pulled into the politics—it hardly matters why, now," he shook his head. "Serwich is Denholme land technically, even though it's no boon to me. I collect nothing from it, with the losses they suffer every year in the ongoing conflict, the place has never been profitable. Although that hasn't stopped the Crown from taxing it."

"Give it up!" I said as though it were the most obvious thing in the world. "Let the Crown inherit the responsibility. Just give up whatever claim your family has left on it. It isn't worth it."

He huffed. "I tried. No one wants the burden of protecting it, the Crown is content to continue collecting their due and leave the management to my house. Which I let my Seneschal handle, and honestly, if that's all there was to it… fine. But it's gotten much, much worse there over the last few years. The natives are growing more and more warlike, some kind of plague is making its way through the populace—"

"Seer's Fever?"

"Not just that," he sighed. "There are so many new diseases there, Grayson. I hired on one of the best Physicians willing to take the trip, I'm hoping we can do something to alleviate people's misery. Anything."

"That place is a hell for canines," I shook my head, the coins and beads in my dreads clicking against one another. "We were never meant for it. It should be left to the natives, it's their land. Even the natural order is rejecting us."

"I don't disagree," he muttered. He leaned, his back sliding down marginally against the mostly-flattened cushion of the old couch. I felt the scruff of his neck brush past my knuckles where they rested, and resisted the urge to reach out. It behooved anyone to remember, Amurescans weren't nearly as open with their affections as those of us in the free world. Especially between men.

Honestly, how they survived on so little physical contact… it boggled the mind. Just the fact that Luther and I were sitting as close as we were now, our knees occasionally knocking together, would've been high scandal amongst his peers.

Just… stunningly stupid.

"So, let it go," I repeated, emphatically. "Send aid, send your Physician, hell send firearms if you think it'll help."

"They need more than that right now," he said, rubbing a hand between his eyes. "I've had agents there for a few years, reporting back to me—those that survive, anyway."

"Fucking hell," I snarled.

"I've even paid off a few men in your profession for intel," he continued. "The waters are ripe for Piracy, given the chaos. There'll always be vultures, opportunists, in situations like that… but for the right price, they tell me

281

what they know. It's worse than the Garrison there thinks it is, or worse than they are choosing to report, anyway."

"I know," I said. "Word gets around. Some people do business with the lizardfolk, you know. Those that don't shoot on sight."

"Oh, I'm well aware," he said. "They have gunpowder now. And did you know that some of their soldiers can fly?"

I took a long breath in and out. "Yes, I've heard. So, that's not just some fanciful story about... war kites, or something?"

He laughed mirthlessly at that. "No. Though I wouldn't put that past them. No, there are creatures there- intelligent or beasts, I'm not sure- who can fly, for limited times of the day. And they've recently been engaging in this tactic of dropping cauldrons of boiling pitch, sometimes with gunpowder charges, on ships' sails."

"Mother of—" I nearly bit my tongue. "What the hell are you thinking, man?!"

He shrugged, helplessly. "The Crown will not send any additional vessels to protect Serwich, or the shipping lanes. They don't have the firepower to defend their supply lines, and I'm talking even just essential voyages. I've shut down most exports, which isn't making the Crown happy, but it's all I could do to stem the bleeding. Grayson, they are trapped," he emphasized. "The people there—most of them are just workers and their families, a lot of them were sent as part of a sentence for minor crimes—"

"They turned Serwich into a bloody Prison Colony?"

"It isn't some posh city," he explained, voice growing more and more strained with a desperate edge. "They built the Fort first off for the Pedigrees, then let the settlement spring up around it, but they've never spent any 'unnecessary' resources to reinforce where most of the populace lives. I have little to no control over how the Colony is run, unless I am there asserting my authority. The Pedigree there do as they please and their primary interest is getting as much lumber out of the rainforest, and as much silver out of the mines as possible. Bringing in new labor is less costly than protecting the workforce they already have. The terrain is impossible to tame, the natives can appear and disappear into it like ghosts, hell, they can fly over barriers."

"I get it," I held up a hand. "You want to whip the place into shape, to protect the people there. But Luther," I leaned in, "can you? I mean no offense to you whatsoever, and I'm sure the fools running things there right now are utter bastards, but are you sure you can do any better than they have? Running a Fleet and running a Colony are two completely different skill sets."

"I know I can't," he said quietly.

"Then... what—" I sputtered.

"Serwich is lost," he said, with dead certainty. "They've just not realized it yet. There's an alliance of tribes, an army massing, amongst the Cathazra—the natives. One of their tribal chieftains, an 'Elekk', they call themselves. A war leader. They're pushing back, into the east coast. Two colonies have fallen to them already. Serwich will be the third."

I was starting to hate the fact that I'd sobered him up. He still looked and sounded like hell, only now he was making sense.

"Even with my fleet there, we… are just so severely disadvantaged," he sighed softly. "My Captains are confident, because we have the Fort, and we still hold the bay. They discount the natural advantage the terrain gives the natives and refuse to realize how entrenched they are, because they don't recognize their forms of architecture and style of war, yet. But they will soon. They believe if worst comes to worst, we'll be able to fall back and rely on our superior firepower."

"And will you?" I asked.

"If we abandon ninety percent of our populace?" He narrowed his eyes. "Sure. We could hole up in the Fort. For a while, anyway. What we need is a larger force. I cannot make the numbers work the way they are. I've been pleading with the Crown for over a year now. If they want me to protect their assets, I need assistance to do so. But every time I've tried, it's the same answer. Nothing additional can be spared."

"They're stretched thin," I said. "Tryin' to hold onto half the world will do that to you." Something occurred to me, then. "What about Cross?" I asked. "Piracy's rampant down there, like you said. And I'd thought your fleets were working together a lot, of late. Couldn't he spend a season down there with you?"

"Well, he might have been able to," he cleared his throat, "if someone hadn't shot his ships full of holes. They're in dry dock, you know. Might not be worth salvaging, at this point. He is livid, by the way."

"Man came after me," I pointed out. "I wasn't about to let him sink me without a fight."

"I don't blame you," he assured me. "Your scuffles with Cross have nothing to do with me, and honestly, I'm not sure he would've helped me, anyway. He hates politics even more than I do, he's no friend of the Crown, and I don't think he would've wanted to put his fleet on the line to protect their assets."

"Wait—is this maybe why you're here?" I asked outright, turning to look down at him. He was normally shorter than me, but slumped as he was now, it was much more pronounced.

He blinked up at me, still sleepy-eyed and ragged. It was so hard not to put a hand between his ears and at least smooth back the fur. "What?" He asked simply.

"You don't think you might've come to me for help?" I said pointedly. "I'm another man you know with a fleet—"

"I don't want anyone else pulled down into this nightmare with me," he insisted, immediately. "I wouldn't ask that of you."

"I don't expect you would," I assured him, "but you've got to put yourself in the mindset of a depressed drunk—"

"I'm not 'depressed,'" he insisted.

"Oh, not in the least," I drawled out, rolling my eyes. "You just got wasted—"

"You do that constantly, regardless of your mood."

"But you don't," I stabbed a finger into his chest. "And you didn't let me finish. You got wasted, stumbled out into the night looking for some kinda lifeline, with your usual stalwart wolfhound gone missin' and all... found your way to my doorstep, broke into my place—"

"My memory's not all there," he coughed, "but I'm pretty sure the door was open."

"You coulda' knocked."

"I... think I was trying to find you, specifically," he said, sounding more certain by the moment. "Bypass your men. I'm a lot stealthier in my mind, when I'm drunk."

"You're lucky you're not dead," I said. "I was on the third floor. You never would've made it all the way to me without running afoul of my boys."

"Mmh," he dragged a breath through his nose. "Not alone, either. You were bedding a... mink, last night?"

"No, actually," I said irritably. "I mean, yes. She was there. But we never really got that far—it doesn't matter. Look. You find your way to me, blackout drunk, you practically cry on my shoulder about a lost love—"

"I did not," he insisted.

"Fine, you were a big damn man about it," I bit back my frustration. Amurescan men. Good fucking God. "You just went through a rough battle with one of the world's worst illnesses. You had to make peace with an old flame, your... Second-in-Command, your fucking shadow, can't support you right now, I'm guessing your family can't be with you either—"

"Delilah is angry with me," he said quietly. "She doesn't want me to go."

"Smart woman," I growled out. "You should listen to your wife, Luther."

"I don't have a choice," he said, voice hoarse. "Someone has to protect those people."

"You are going off to war," I emphasized, "against a group of people you hardly understand—and I know you, man—that has to terrify you. You can't out-maneuver an enemy whose moves you can't predict."

"No," he agreed shakily, "I can't."

"You're depressed," I said. "Scared. It's alright to admit that, no—stop," I reached forward with my free hand and grabbed his opposite shoulder, turning him towards me forcibly before he could look away again. "Stop... with this false bravado bullshit. You think I can't see through it? You think I don't know how it feels to put up a front to my boys, when we're in deep?"

"You don't hide who you are," he said, his words almost a challenge, like he dearly wanted me to confirm for him that he was right. Was he envious of me? "You're the freest man I know," he said, his voice coming from his gut.

Alright, yes. He was.

"You think I don't get barked at and challenged by my boys?" I laughed. "You think I don't have to put up a strong façade, sometimes?"

"No, I..." he trailed off. "You have your own demands with your fleet, I'm sure."

I couldn't help it. The sentiment had always been there I think, it just chose this moment to boil out.

"You could've been one of us," I said.

His eyes widened.

"You should have," I put more force into the words, "been one of us. Luther. You still could. You and I? We'd be fearsome together."

I saw it the moment he tried to shift away from the point, the forced smile, the huff of breath. "As proposals go, you could stand to work on yours—"

"Who you are," I growled out, "everything you are... we would have accepted you. Valued you for the things that matter, for your mind, your skills. Everything else? Everything that's made your life a living hell amongst your countrymen, your... blood, your past, your choice of bed partners... none of that would matter in my fleet. You want to be free?" I dragged my arm from where it was looped over the back of the couch, settling a paw on his back, pulling him in closer. "It is literally yours for the taking. You just have to let go of all this," I gestured out the window.

His gaze hadn't left mine, but his irises were shaking. His whole body was shaking, I realized. It was subtle, barely a shiver. Like someone with a bow drawn taut, straining.

"It pains me to watch you suffer," I stated openly. "Your Crown does not deserve your loyalty. You are too good a man to be thrown onto the pyre of their pointless war. Leave all of this. Get out now while you can, before you die for them."

He opened his mouth, and I cut him off. "Your family will be fine," I insisted. "Hell, we can relocate them if you want. Carvecia. Mataa. Anywhere. They're about to lose you, anyway. And do you really think the men in power won't still hate you, if you give all you have to defend this territory, and fail?"

"It doesn't matter what my countrymen think of me," he said quietly.

"I'm glad you feel that way," I said, not believing him, "because if they knew who you really were? The man you truly are, the man I know, they would loathe you. And you know it. You live in fear of the people you protect, man. People call me insane sometimes, but your life? Your life is the craziest con game I've ever heard of. And for what? How have they earned your fealty? What has your country ever done for you?"

He was silent for a long, long time.

"It doesn't matter," he said at long last, "if my country loves me. I'm accustomed to unrequited love."

My breath stopped. I couldn't find the words to tell him how achingly sad he was making me. No one made me feel things like this. God damn him.

"I'm a protector," he said softly. "It's all I've... ever wanted to be. The only thing that makes me feel whole. I don't need them to recognize it. Or even you. I just want to make the seas safe. Free. It's the only place of respite I've ever found."

"For what it's worth," I choked out the words. "Thank you. I know that matters very little, coming from someone like me—"

"It does matter," he assured me.

"There are some unbelievable monsters out there," I said. "In my trade. Knowing you're out there, it... honestly does comfort me. I understand what you're fighting for."

He nodded, slowly. "I hope you'll forgive me, then," he murmured. "The people in Serwich need help. I'm going to do all I can."

"You're going to die there," I said between my teeth.

"Maybe," he agreed, smiling bitterly. "But I have to try. I have to. No one else is coming to their aid." He lifted his muzzle some, then breathed out a quiet, "Oh."

"What?" I asked, trying to swallow around the pain in my throat.

"Your eyes are blue," he said. "I just noticed."

"Bastard," I breathed out, staccato. "We've known each other how long now?"

"I... try not to linger long when I stare at other men," he admitted. "Especially with those who... know." He glanced aside at that. "I-I don't want to unnerve anyone. Assumptions are easily made, tempers can flare. I have to be careful."

I felt my brows knit, anger rising again. "You can stare at me all you like, mate. I don't fucking care. I can't imagine how exhausting that shit must be. Please, please don't worry about that, with me. I'm fine. Nothing about being around you 'unnerves' me." I lifted my eyebrows, conscious of how angry I might look right now. "I... I want to... damnit," I gave a 'tch' around my back teeth, "I know I said I don't mind you looking at me, but would you just… please stop looking so sad…"

He shut his jaw self-consciously, uncertainty moving over his features. "I-I'm sorry. How am I—"

"Why did you come to me?" I insisted, even while knowing he still had no answers. "You won't let me help you."

"That isn't your responsibility," he assured me.

"It ought to be someone's," I ground out, my paw on his back balling in his jacket, the other gripping his shoulder a little tighter. "I… shit. I just want to…"

He continued to look up at me, lost. I had nothing for him. No answers, nothing I could offer. Except…

A frustrated growl tore its way out of my muzzle, and throwing caution to the wind, I pulled him the few remaining sacred inches we'd kept up this whole while, like a barrier. His head fell in between my shoulder and jaw, our hips pressed together, his side against my side. His whole body went stiff, but before he could push back, I used the arm I'd had behind him to loop around his waist, pulling him more firmly into the embrace. He was weak right now, but he still could have fought back if he'd really wanted to. And for a moment, I thought he would. I felt him poised to push back, to disentangle us—

But then he just… gave way. All at once, he began to uncoil. His shoulders loosened, his body went heavy against mine, his muzzle bent into the crook of my neck, and the finale—he let his breath out in a long, slow sigh. I felt it all the way down my chest.

I moved my arm a bit, slipping it up beneath the hem of his already bunched coat, so my hand was splayed more comfortably around his hip. I could feel the heat of his pelt beneath the thin cotton of his shirt. For some reason, right now, that was immensely reassuring. I'd had more than one of my men bleed out in my arms, like this. A warm body—regardless whether they were a friend, a lover, or something in between—was always a comfort.

"Is this alright?" I asked, most certainly too late.

The only noise I got out of him was a quiet, "Mmhh," that sounded… accepting? My guess was confirmed a moment later when he nodded shallowly, and leaned against me with what must have been his full weight. I shifted a leg and vaguely readjusted my arm to get comfortable, but otherwise made it clear I wasn't going anywhere.

I did my absolute best to just hold him like that for a while without fidgeting, or saying anything. I didn't want to push my luck. But I'm just not good at sitting still, and my hands tend to start moving first, before the rest of me. I settled with gingerly moving my fingers in semi-circular motions against his shoulder at first, then slowly shifting my paw up through the scruff of his neck. I had been fighting the urge to smooth out the unruly, damp fur there since he'd arrived. I set to it slowly, easing into the idea of anything beyond the embrace with careful measure- because even being held seemed to be an adjustment for him.

"Your fur is a nightmare," I muttered, noting how much coarser it was than my own. "I've often thought you must not take good care of it, but… it's just like this, isn't it?"

"Luckily, I'm not so hung up on my vanity as you are," he muttered against my collarbone.

I gave a belly laugh at that. "Bullshit," I countered. "I might preen over my fur, but I've seen you without a shirt on. We just prioritize different things."

"Fair," he agreed, his tone gone tranquil and lethargic. I briefly entertained the possibility that he was coming down from a lot of booze and what must have been a truly exhausting night—he might actually just be falling asleep. I wasn't entirely sure what I'd do if he passed out here, let alone in my arms, but I quickly decided waking him wouldn't be an option. I'd just have to move him elsewhere in the house and keep him from the men until he'd slept it off…

He dragged in a breath through his nose, then let it out slowly. "Your shirt," he murmured.

"Hm?"

"It smells like you," he observed.

"Well it's mine, so it ought to," I huffed.

"You've a tendency to smell like whatever you're drinking," he said, "or smoking. Or that oil you put in your dreads… or whatever woman you're currently seeing. It makes your scent hard to pin down."

"Not intentional," I shrugged, then smiled a bit. "Sounds like it bothers you, though."

"I'm a dog, Grayson," he cracked his eyes open for a half a second, before shutting them again. "You're canine, you should understand. I commit people to memory that way. Some scents you can associate with people, but yours are… hectic. Always changing. It's hard to pin-point your own, beneath it all."

"I understand," I assured him, tapping my own nose. "I guess I'm just not as hung up on it as you are. Also, if I want a whiff of someone, I have no issue just sticking my snout all up in their business. I guess you're rarely this… close with people, huh?"

"Very few," he said quietly. Then, a moment later, his voice tentatively curious, "Is this normal for you?"

"With other men?" I guessed.

"With... people other than those you bed down with," he said carefully.

"You mean friends?" I clarified. "Yeah. I'd say so. I mean, I don't go embracing strangers, unless I'm drunk. And that usually doesn't go well. But with my closest men, this wouldn't be all that unusual. If they needed it. If it felt warranted. Is it helping?"

A beat of silence. Then, a simple, "Yes."

"Good. I'm glad," I said, content to leave it at that. There really wasn't any need to complicate this. Obviously, physical affection between two men could have other context for someone like Luther, but that wasn't... this, and I saw no reason to compare or connect one to the other. I moved the hand on his hip to rub at his lower back, comfortingly. And for the first time, he pressed in closer against me, of his own will.

"If you can't protect these people..." I said, feeling his body stiffen expectantly. But I had to get this out. "Then, you should get them the hell out of there."

Silence. Which meant he'd already considered that.

"I know it's something you've run scenarios for in your head," I said, resting my chin on top of his head, "if even I've landed on it as a possible solution."

"An evacuation," he said quietly. "It would be... unheard of. Moving an entire population at once like that."

"Could you do it?" I asked.

He shifted slightly, breathing in and out deeply, once. I could practically smell him burning lamp oil, running the possibilities over in his mind. "Not as it stands," he finally said. "Even with the vessels they have on hand in the Serwich Bay—and I'm working with out-of-date information here, mind you—we just don't have the capacity. Not if I want the warships to be fully operational. I'd have people crammed to the gills on the gun decks, we'd be running lower in the water, there'd be morale issues, obviously..."

"Unhappy men are better than dead men," I pointed out.

"None of this even addresses how I'd get my Command Staff to agree to an evacuation," he continued, "let alone the Pedigree Landlords of Serwich. That's... a dozen, at least... very 'well-bred' men with a lot of their resources invested in that land. Imagine the conversation where I attempt to explain to them why we have to abandon the Colony. Cede it willingly back to the natives? I'm going to show up on their shores with four brimming warships, and a flock of seasoned Navy men, including five Captains who've been cutting their teeth on Pirates for the last five years. The Lords are going to expect results. My Captains are going to expect results. They refuse to accept how hopeless our situation is, there. If I come to their aid, only to tell them the plan is to surrender their investments and shell the place out—"

"Wait, five?" I was counting on my fingers. I was fairly certain I knew all of his Captains.

"Johannes is technically a Captain," he filled in. "Since the Crown appointed me an Admiral, officially. I was only an acting Admiral, before."

"So, you'll have him on your side, at least," I pointed out. Then paused. "Or will you? What happened between you two?"

He made a quiet noise of discomfort. "It's not... entirely my story to tell," he said weakly, "but he's not... not handling the idea of returning to the Dark Continent as well as—"

"Don't say 'as well as I am,'" I said, horrified at the mere notion.

"Mmhh... well..."

"That man is a rock," I gasped. "At least, the few times I met him he was. I didn't even know he'd been to the Dark Continent. What the hell happened to him there?"

"That's the thing, he doesn't like to talk about it," he said darkly. "I've gotten bits and pieces. It's the only subject I've ever seen shake him so badly. He very nearly begged me not to bring him along. But he's a Templar, and Lucius left him with the care of the Cerberus fleet. He'd be turning his back on every duty he holds sacred if he refuses this mission, and he still considered it. Whatever his experiences there when they founded the Colony, they... damaged him. The Physician calls it 'Soldier's Fatigue.'"

"I've heard of that," I said softly. I felt, rather than saw, the way his ears had begun to quake as we spoke. I moved the paw I'd been uselessly trying smooth back his bristly nape with, and cupped his ear, rubbing it between my thumb and forefinger.

He groaned, almost sounding irritated. "That feels better than it has any right to," he muttered.

"I'm good with my hands," I shrugged.

"How is it you just... do... these things?" He asked almost in wonderment, "So casually?"

I shook my head, chuckling. "What d'you mean?"

"You cross every boundary—I haven't even done things like this with most of my lovers," he protested, while simultaneously tipping his other ear. I didn't miss the gesture.

Smirking, I switched to the other. "It's no skin off my back," I pointed out. "And I know this sort of thing helps me when I'm down."

"Yes, but with women I'd wager," he said, voice slightly muffled by my shirt.

"Mate, sometimes it ain't about feelin' randy," I said. "Sometimes you just want someone to reach out. And you don't need to be fuckin' to reach back."

I saw his eyes open to slim slits, his features slowly going lax, like my words had plummeted him deep into thought. Before he could get lost in it, I said, "I'll help you."

"Hnh?" He rumbled.

I gave a long sigh, closing my eyes and carefully considering my words before finally landing on, "I want to help your people."

He opened his mouth, and I cut him off, "Not your bloody Pedigree curs—your people. The people livin' in that Colony; none of this is their fault. And I know that's why you're risking your ass, too. There's what—a few thousand souls there?"

"Roughly 3,400, last I heard," he said, voice coarse around the edges. "Grayson, I can't ask this of you—"

"You're not gonna ask," I informed him, taking on an authoritative tone, "you're gonna demand. A'least, that's the story I'm telling my men. You pulled my ass out of the fire a few times now, I'd be hanging from a noose on at least one occasion if not for you."

"We had an arrangement then," he insisted.

"Just shut the fuck up, man," I growled again, but there was no malice in it. "Listen. I'm not helping you hold the place. I'm not killing lizardfolk to make your King richer."

"Then what—"

"Evacuate the populace," I said. "You know it's the only option. We've been going back and forth here for too long—I can tell what it is you want to do. I know you well enough by now. It's the only way you stop the bleeding, put this nightmare behind you. Otherwise, you'll be fighting for this hell-hole 'til the day you die, which... could be sooner than we'd both like."

"Every Pedigree Lord will be against me," he said, with certainty.

"That's what you'll need the extra firepower for," I asserted. "Look, you can't always reason your way through things with people—especially if they're arguing in bad faith. That's the point in the conversation when I pull a fucking pistol; sometimes it's just how you have to handle things. The Lords there don't have the might to push back against you, if they did they'd've used it on the lizards by now. I know dealing with your Captains'll be tricky, but you'll have your man Johannes, right?"

He nodded, seeming more and more settled by the moment. "Yes. He'd agree to this. I'm certain of it."

"And you'll have me," I jerked a thumb back towards myself. "Just set the wheels in motion. I'll come calling when you need me, and I can bring supplies... powder, rations. Provide escort. Just won't agree to gettin' sucked into your war. Support only, alright? So, you'll need to have a plan ready."

"That could take time," he said, considering.

"I've got business here to handle, anyway," I assured him. "And if I'm taking the Fleet into an active warzone, I need to get my big girl ready for it. And the men…"

"Shit," he swore, "I'm so sorry. I'm…" he looked torn, "…I really don't want to turn you down. You've no idea what this would mean to me—"

"Trust me, I do," I muttered.

"—but is this going to throw your Fleet into chaos?" He asked. "It's going to be hard enough selling my Captains on the idea of hiring on Privateers, your men would need to behave. If you're going to be making landfall in my Colony, even briefly—"

"Mate," I said, "I guarantee you my men have better morale than most of yours. They can be a bit wild, but a job's a job. Speaking of, I'm tripling my rate for this nonsense. Bloody… flying, flaming oil buckets? Fuck."

"Whatever you need," he said, his voice quiet, but laced with the sincerest gratitude I think I'd ever heard in my life. When I turned to look down at him, I nearly gagged.

"Ugh," I shoved him away at last, playfully. "Stop that."

He smiled slowly. And it was fragile like before, but earnest. "Grayson," he said, my first name still sounding so unnatural coming from this man who'd always been so formal with me, in the past. But I guess now, this was how we were. "Thank you," he said, gripping one of my hands and squeezing it tightly.

Slowly, I let the irritation slip away from my features; to be honest, I'd been faking it. Luther might have been resistant to the sorts of affection I found second nature, things as simple as embracing your fellows when they were torn down, making friends easily, talking about the things ailing you… but I was similarly unused to the gifts that he could bestow so easily. Gratitude. Loyalty. Respect.

I guess we'd both have to expand our horizons a little.

Smiling rakishly, I clapped my other hand on his back. "You're welcome. And you can thank me again in the Southern Seas. Every fucking day, until this is over."

He gave a tired, crooked grin, "I'll do that."

SPECIAL THANKS TO

Bryan Ezawa
Conrock
Trejaan
Lunden
Skunkbomb
Pyraeron
Drew "CopperCheetah" Maxwell
Marcwolf
Spirit
CastJudgment
BlueTippedWolf
Shapes the Fox
R. E. Thorburn
Ruby Akuma
Græ
Jai Mu
Kenti R Bengali
Verager
Trejaan
YFoxy
AiraActual
Cosmo Shepherd
Alex Demers
TJ Hedges
Glassan
Squeaky El Lobo
Ari Yena
Lucian Greywolf
Randall Lupus
Multiroit
Dyxxander
Matthew Hoffman
Adrian Perez

Shiantar
Nameless Imp
Hania The Jaguar
Dunkelpfote
Aelius
CopperCheetah
Shapes the Fox
Kivuli Riler
Tyde Ratmeat
Artiko
R. E. Thorburn
BlueTippedWolf
CastJudgment
Spirit
BlackDawg
Tahlmorra
Walter Wells Jr
Rakceyen
Bruma the Traveler
TaylorAndCo.
Benjamin "Wolfen Lightstone" Pedraza
Hopcyn
Kit Glosson
Netolu Shadowlin
Arron Cass
Nulizz Volkaire
Dave
Aqwah
Samuel Barbosa Fernandez
Chris Haneke
Colin Leighton
Scrye
Akula
FuzzWolf
Jinx
Trenton Wood

www.ingramcontent.com/pod-product-compliance
Lightning Source LLC
Chambersburg PA
CBHW051637050726
47502CB00011B/906